INTO THE NIGHT

A collection of Science Fiction and Paranormal stories

Caroline Giammanco

INTO THE NIGHT

Copyright © 2021 Caroline Giammanco

ISBN: 978-1-312-02012-2⌗

ASIN: ASIN: B09BSKLRBY

Published by Tuscany Bay Books
Star, Idaho
Fruita, Colorado

www.tuscanybaybooks.com
rpaolinelli@tuscanybaybooks.com
jchristina@tuscanybaybooks.com

ACKNOWLEDGEMENTS

Science fiction and paranormal stories were a part of growing up in my household. I have great memories of staying up late to watch Kolchak: The Night Stalker, Twilight Zone, and The Night Gallery. My family pondered the possibility of aliens and ghosts, and I have my mother, Charlotte Hagaman, to thank for my interest in both the seen and unseen. She had an inquisitive mind, and she passed her questioning nature onto us kids.

Some of my stories have more than a sprinkling of truth to them, but I will allow you to decide which ones they are. Special thanks go to my friend Peggy Koppen who provided the inspiration for "The Importance of Good Neighbors." Sometimes a nurse just never knows what will come through the emergency room doors.

"The Cardinal" is a tribute to my brother, Luke Hagaman.

Thank you to the talented Nari Kwak who has brought some of these stories (and others of mine) to life in the Into the Night podcast.

Thank you to my husband, Keith Giammanco, who is my trusted sounding board anytime I write. I love you, and I will never, ever stop.

Thank you to my family, friends, and followers who have joined me on this journey *Into the Night.* You've added more meaning to life, and I appreciate you.

Dedicated to all who believe in more than what we can see.

Caroline Giammanco

TABLE OF CONTENTS

THE IMPORTANCE OF GOOD NEIGHBORS

Alice Cameron lived at the end of a long tree-lined drive. Few would even notice her three-bedroom farmhouse tucked under the shade of the hillside, and she liked it that way.

Neighbors are like fleas," her grandpa used to say. "It doesn't seem like they would bother you, but once you get one, you usually end up with several."

What her grandpa said made sense to Alice. She watched the area where she grew up change from a few scattered farms to subdivisions in a matter of ten years. Once people "discovered" the beautiful countryside, they told others, who told others, and so on, until the influx of people destroyed the beauty.

Grandpa's heart would have broken to see what happened to the place he loved most in the world.

Alice searched carefully for a secluded piece of property where she could build her home. She considered that eighty-acre plot her sanctuary. The surrounding large tracts of land were undeveloped and owned by people who had no desire to live so far out in the sticks. They used the property primarily as a hunting spot a few weeks a year, and the rest of the time Alice was utterly alone on her piece of paradise.

It's not that she didn't like people. She was a nurse and enjoyed her patients and coworkers. People enjoyed her bubbly personality and quick wit. At the end of the day, however, Alice wanted the peace and quiet of her farm. Her dogs, cows, and chickens were the only companionship she craved outside of work.

That's why she was so disappointed when construction crews cleared land a half mile down the road from her farm. Each week "progress" continued on the construction project. Whatever home was being built was down a long driveway and not visible from the dirt road.

Hmm... Maybe someone else wants to be left alone out here too. Still, I'd rather they'd found another place to build.

There wasn't much she could do about it, though. It was, after all, still a free country, and other property owners had the right to build homes there if they wanted to. Alice vowed to keep her distance, however.

I don't need someone coming over to borrow a cup of sugar or wanting to sit on the porch to chitchat.

To Alice's surprise and relief, workers installed an imposing and elaborate gate at the entrance of the new neighbor's drive. Intricate designs decorated the wrought iron bars, and unusual insignias, perhaps Arabic or some other language, were embossed on the concrete pillars holding the gate panels.

Looks like they might be foreigners. At least they don't seem to want company either.

A few months went by, and construction activity ended. Late one night. Alice awoke to lights flashing around the vicinity of the new house.

They sure picked a weird time to move in. I didn't even hear the moving van.

Dead tired from a twelve-hour shift at the hospital, a bleary-eyed Alice crawled back into bed. She wasn't the type to be nosy, and she would afford the new people the same respect she expected in return.

Alice went about her routine as the days passed. With winter approaching, she had plenty to do. She needed to stack hay for the animals, and there was wood to cut for her fireplace. She used propane as her primary heat source, but she found comfort in curling up on the couch with a cozy fire blazing in the fireplace as she watched winter birds eating from the feeders.

Alice had a soft spot for things that flew. Grandpa bought her a bird identification book when she was five, and she loved tracking what species came to her feeders.

She never had the heart to cage a bird that could take flight. To satisfy her love of feathered creatures, she raised chickens. They couldn't fly far on their own, and the flock seemed to appreciate her doting.

As winter's grip found its way into the world, it dawned on Alice that she hadn't seen any activity coming from the neighbor's house. She knew someone lived there. Smoke billowed from the chimney, and on rare occasions, delivery trucks dropped packages off at the ornate gate. She had yet to see anyone who lived there, however.

I sure hope it's not some weird religious cult. I don't need a Waco to happen next door.

Alice imagined police helicopters flying overhead, dramatic footage on news stations, and a sensational inferno ending her solitude. No doubt, the infamy of the cult would lead to onlookers, and onlookers would lead to people thinking how pretty this area was, and she knew what that led to.

No, please don't let them be fanatics or nut jobs.

Shrugging it off, she continued life as it always was. She went to work and spent twelve hours on her feet, changing IV drips and catheters while dealing with sometimes difficult patients—and even more difficult doctors. Her sense of humor carried her through most shifts. Most of the time, the monotony was the worst aspect of working the evening shift. One night, however, an interesting case entered the doors.

A woman in her late sixties with a burning rash on her extremities was wheeled in by ambulance. Usually, the EMTs stayed for a moment, but they must have had another call because they left before anyone could speak to them about the patient.

Alice had never seen anything like the woman's injuries. The attending doctor, however, had seen a lot in his forty years as a physician. He ordered medication and told the nurses assigned to that room to apply the prescription cream and then wrap gauze around the woman's affected areas. She was to be placed under a lamp, much the same as jaundiced babies are put under, for one hour, four times a day. During daylight hours, the shades to her room were to be drawn.

The woman, a Marjorie Henson, according to the papers left with her on the stretcher, was unconscious and immediately admitted to the hospital. The treatment required several days to complete, according to Dr. Steinman. Monitors checked her vitals, and an IV drip was started. Antibiotics began as a precautionary measure.

This almost looks like a burn of some sort, but her skin isn't reacting like a burn patient's skin normally would. What are those blisters? They look green.

While unusual, it wasn't the first odd case Alice had treated, so she shrugged her shoulders and followed the doctor's instructions. Her best friend at work, Janice, was also on duty that night. Together they wound the gauze and placed the woman under the lamp. It took two people to lift her as she was rather large.

Down at the nurses' station, Janice rubbed her aching neck. "We sure see some doozies, don't we, Alice?"

"Yes, we do. I've never seen blisters on someone quite like Mrs. Henson's. I've never heard of this treatment, either, but Dr. Steinman was confident this would do the trick."

Right before visiting hours ended, Mrs. Henson's son arrived.

"Hi, I'm Lenny Henson. I'm hoping to see my mother."

Alice and Janice looked at the clock. It was a quiet night on the floor, and while policy said no visitors were allowed after nine o'clock, exceptions could be made. Neither wanted to make him leave. He looked frazzled and worried.

What could be the harm?

Sure, come this way. As long as you're quiet, you can stay as long as you want to. There's no one in 12-B tonight, so she won't have a roommate to disturb."

"Thank you. You don't know what this means to me."

The two women smiled and escorted him down the hall.

The next night, Lenny arrived at the same time. He held two bouquets for the nurses.

"I know it's an inconvenience to have me show up like this, so I wanted to bring you something special."

"Mr. Henson, you didn't have to do that."

"No, I insist. Call me Lenny. I can't get away from my work at home until after dark. I really can't go anywhere until after dark. I appreciate the good care you are taking of my mother."

"Well, thank you. We'll put these in some water."

"I appreciate it. It takes a while to get into town from McGinty Road."

Alice stopped. "McGinty Road? You live on McGinty Road?"

"Yes, ma'am. We've been there since early last fall."

So, you are my neighbor?"

Lenny cocked his head slightly. "Do you drive a blue Chevy?"

"I do. You have a rather impressive gate at your drive. We haven't had a chance to meet yet."

"That's true. We like to keep to ourselves. We don't mean to be rude."

"No, it's completely okay. I'm the same way you are."

Lenny gave her a look, as though he doubted something she'd said.

"Truly, I'm not much of a socializer," Alice added.

"Oh, yeah. Now I see what you're saying. We prefer to be homebodies. I'm glad you understand."

Once at Mrs. Henson's room, they parted ways. Lenny stayed until nearly two in the morning, and throughout the evening, Alice and Lenny shared several friendly exchanges as she checked his mother's vitals.

"He seems nice enough, but he's a little socially awkward, don't you think?" Janice asked as she returned from the supply cabinet with a new box of gloves.

"Yeah, it's obvious he doesn't get out much. He seems shy and just... different. I hope not everyone who lives on McGinty Road is that eccentric."

"Oh, I don't know. I hear his neighbor is a weird one."

Alice snorted. She always snorted when she laughed hard. "Yeah, that Alice Cameron is a weird one, for sure."

The next night, Lenny arrived at his usual time.

"Is she still unconscious?" Lenny asked as he approached the desk. This time he carried two boxes of chocolates.

Too bad I can't find a boyfriend who's as attentive.

Alice never could turn down chocolate. She gladly took the boxes. "Oh, these are the really good kind. Thank you so much, Lenny. I'll make sure Janice knows they're here when she's done in Room 3."

Throughout the night, the trio became familiar with each other, and conversations lasted longer when other patients had been cared for.

At around midnight, Lenny stood in his mother's room with his forehead pressed against the window overlooking the hospital courtyard. Deep in thought, he sighed occasionally.

"The stars are beautiful tonight." Lenny turned to the nurses. "Do you ever just sit and stare at the stars?"

"I do, sometimes, when I'm sitting on my porch on a warm evening like this. As you know, we're the only ones out there on McGinty Road, so there aren't any lights to dull their sparkle."

"That's true. It's one of the reasons why we chose that spot to build our compound."

"Compound?"

"I mean house. Excuse the slip. I'm a military pilot. I think in military terms."

Janice gave Alice a skeptical glance. Lenny was short--maybe 5'6" with shoes on. He was on the pudgy side and didn't resemble anyone's image of a military man.

To break the awkward silence, Alice thought she'd better say something.

"The military. Well, you must have traveled to some interesting places."

"Oh, I have." Lenny's eyes twinkled, and he stood a bit straighter. "I'm very proud of my service."

Both women nodded in agreement. Lenny turned back to the window as his mother's dressings were changed.

Most men are squeamish. Alice smiled at the thought and gently shook her head.

"Do either of you believe in UFOs?"

Alice and Janice finished the last of the dressing changes, and as they removed their gloves, the women shot each other looks, unsure how to take Lenny's question.

"I'm sorry, Lenny. What did you say?" Janice had a habit of asking people to repeat something she was nervous about.

Turning from the window, he faced them. "It's not a typical question, I'm sure, but I asked if you believe in UFOs. Do you think there are aliens out there?" He pointed toward the window and the sky.

Alice, a lifelong science fiction buff, spoke first. "Actually, I think it's possible. Why should we be the only beings in the universe?"

"What about you, Janice?"

"Oh, my mother and I have talked about it from time to time. She's a big fan of those shows. She even bought herself a telescope thinking she might spy a UFO. All she's ever seen is the occasional shooting star. She's still got the thing set up on our back deck."

"Your mother lives with you?"

"Yes, she has since Dad died two years ago. It's just easier that way."

"I completely understand. My parents live with me for the same reason." Lenny patted his mother's still hand. "I insisted they move in. They needed someone to watch over them, and they're so much help with the lab."

"Lab?" Alice raised her eyebrows. "Is that why you have a gate?"

"Oh, yes. We thought security would be important."

A pause filled the air.

"Would you like to see it? The offer stands for both of you—and your mother, Janice. I have some UFO artifacts you might be interested in."

"Wait--you've seen UFOs?" Alice nearly had to put her jaw back in its socket.

"I've seen them. I've been on them. Would you like to find out more? As I said, you can bring your family, if you would like, to our home. I just ask for discretion. We deal with sensitive government contracts, as you can imagine."

Oh, I can imagine they'd be very sensitive. This sounds fascinating. Alice's mind spun.

"I'm game!" Before this moment, Alice hadn't realized that she sought some excitement in her life--and she wouldn't even have to leave McGinty Road to find it.

"I'm sure Mom would kill me if she ever found out I passed up this opportunity, so count us in too."

"Splendid. When is the next night you have off work?"

"Tomorrow," they said in unison.

"How about you meet me at my house at eight o'clock tomorrow night? Just park at the gate, and I'll let you in." He looked at his mother and the monitor displaying the rhythmic beating of her heart. "I'm sure she will be fine for one evening without a visitor."

The next night, Janice and her mother met Alice at her house. She was the only coworker who had ever been to Alice's hideaway home in the woods, and that spoke volumes about Alice's opinion of Janice.

"Jerry couldn't come with us tonight. He was sent on an emergency call. Electricians kind of have to go when a customer has a serious problem. Mr. Patterson's weatherhead on his house was damaged by this morning's storm, and he needs it working for his wife's oxygen machine, so Jerry left. He told me to tell you he'll miss seeing you, Alice."

"Oh, he's just sorry he isn't here for some of my chocolate chip cookies. Here, grab a few and we'll be on our way."

Alice held the platter out for Janice and her mother, Connie.

"Oh, these are still warm. Thank you, dear." Connie grabbed a third and fourth one for good measure.

They piled into Alice's blue Chevy, and soon the three of them pulled up to the gate. Lenny stood in the dark waiting for them. Alice jumped when he appeared at her driver's side window.

"Excellent. You're right on time. Give me a moment to put my dog up, then I'll open the gate for you. Thank you for coming by. We wouldn't invite just anyone here, but it's so important to have good neighbors."

Lenny smiled, stepped back behind the gate which closed after him, and whistled for his dog.

"That's not any ordinary dog. What is that thing, Alice?"

"I don't think I've ever seen one like that." Alice rolled her window up for added protection.

Connie chimed in. "It sure looks to me like one of those wolves we saw when your father and I went to Yellowstone."

Yes, a wolf. It certainly looks like a wolf. Alice worried. What had she gotten herself into? She thought of her sweet English shepherds and her little shih tzu and wondered why anyone would need a beast the likes of Lenny's "dog."

A few moments later, the metal gates slowly opened. As the car approached the house--a mansion, really--the three women couldn't help but gawk. In addition to the house, three or four other large buildings lined the paved drive.

"When he said 'compound,' he wasn't exaggerating." Alice pointed at a building to her left. "That looks for all the world like a hangar."

"It most definitely does, dear." Connie had already had more excitement than she'd had in a while. Not since she dialed a wrong number and enjoyed an hour-long conversation with some nice man in Brooklyn had she had so much fun. She couldn't contain her glee.

Lenny met them in the circle drive in front of the Spanish-style villa. They introduced him to Connie, and then Lenny walked them inside. While not posh, it was splendid in its own eclectic way. Artwork, including detailed sculptures, decorated each room as Lenny gave them a tour.

Is that an African mask? Native American, perhaps? Lenny did say he had traveled many places. Alice was impressed.

A tall man, exceptionally tall, in fact, entered the living room where Lenny sat with the ladies. He smiled and extended his hand to greet them.

"Good evening. It's nice to meet you. Lenny has told me so much about you. I'm Lenny's father, Melvin."

He doesn't look a thing like Lenny, but then again, family genetics can be weird. I look nothing like my sister. People have asked me for years how on earth Cheryl and I could be related, let alone sisters. She turned her attention back to her hosts.

"It's a pleasure to meet you, Melvin. Your family has a lovely home. Thank you for having us over."

"Alice, right?" He looked to his left. "And you must be Janice. Lenny has described you so perfectly that I feel like I already know you."

His comments raised the hairs on Alice's arms, and his oddly long arms and hands didn't help matters, but it was the photo hanging on the wall that captured everyone's attention.

"That's a nice shot, isn't it?" Melvin beamed.

"Is Lenny standing next to what I think it is? Is that really a UFO?" Alice stared in disbelief.

"That it is. It's been a while since that was taken. Would you like to see some more?" Lenny nodded towards his father who motioned for the women to follow him down a hallway.

"If you need to use the restroom, it's this door to the left, ladies. We're going to the control room at the end of the hallway."

Control room? Alice glanced at her companions. Janice squeezed Alice's hand for support. Connie looked like she was on a grand adventure.

Maybe at her age she's not as worried about death, but I am. Are these people crazy? Are we going to be on the next episode of a missing persons show? This may have been a mistake. A slight shudder rolled over Alice's spine.

Lenny pulled a strange triangular-shaped object from his pants pocket. About three inches in length, it filled his pudgy hand.

"Give me just a moment, ladies. There's a code I must enter as well." He flipped open what could have

25

passed for a wall thermostat and punched numbers on a keypad.

A clunking sound signaled that the door unlocked. Lenny turned the handle and ushered them in. "Control room" aptly described what they saw. Panels and switchboards with flashing lights filled the room. Monitors lined the walls, most flipping from view to view like those behind the scenes at Las Vegas casinos. Alice wasn't sure exactly what was shown on the monitors, but the room was quite busy. Computer screens rolled digital readouts across them, and an occasional buzzer or bell went off. Sitting on one desk was a red phone.

Lenny saw Alice staring at the phone. "That's our direct line. Anytime anyone--anywhere--wants to contact us, they use that red phone. All they have to do is pick up the receiver and dial '1' to be connected."

Connie drew Alice's attention to the walls where more UFO photos hung.

Connie, never one to hold her tongue around strangers, said, "Just what movie studio did you take these pictures at? I don't recognize these from any movies I've seen, and I've seen about all of them. Although, that alien character here with Melvin looks like one of those beings from *War of the Worlds*."

Melvin cleared his throat and shifted from one leg to the next as he stood behind the ladies. "Connie, I can assure you that these are not movie props. They are real aliens and ships."

Connie squinted her eyes as she peered closer at the photograph. "Ya don't say? I've waited my whole life to see a real one. Do you think there's any chance you could introduce me to one?"

Lenny and Melvin stood in awkward silence, then Lenny spoke up. "Miss Connie, we work in very classified conditions. I'm afraid such a meeting is not possible. However, would you like to hear some of the recorded interviews we have with the aliens?"

"Recordings? Ya don't say?"

Connie wasn't the only one interested. Alice and Janice silently nodded their heads up and down.

"Very well. You must understand something first, however. There is a battle going on up there." Melvin pointed his long index finger upwards toward the sky. "There are good aliens, and there are evil ones."

"How come none of this is on the news then?"

Janice nudged Connie with her elbow. "We don't want to be rude, Mother."

No kidding. We don't know what these people might do. Alice patted Connie's shoulder as she smiled apologetically at Melvin.

"It's quite alright, I assure you. She reminds me of my dear Marjorie, always asking questions that make our son, Lenny, uncomfortable."

Right then, Lenny came from a back room with reels of tape and an audio machine. For the next several hours the trio of women and the hosts listened to recordings. Melvin from time to time brought trays of delicious foods and drinks around for his guests.

"I apologize that we didn't plan a formal dinner. Please forgive us."

"Oh, these are wonderful," Janice assured him.

"Yes, these are like nothing we've had before. We're enjoying them very much," Alice added as Connie smiled and took another helping.

Time got away from them, and none of the women knew just how long they had been there. They listened to computerized voices on the recordings, and the three women were mesmerized by what they heard.

"Their languages have been synthesized by our computer program, so they are audible to humans--I mean to us, people." Melvin gave Lenny a stern look.

Aliens from planets far beyond our own solar system shared their messages with Earth. There were the usual promises of peace and goodwill. A few mentioned the galactic warfare Melvin previously talked about.

The longest recording came from an alien named Insinyor, or at least that's what it sounded like. Alice secretly jotted down notes on a pad she kept in her purse while supposedly searching for a piece of gum. She hoped no one noticed.

Insinyor said one day his people would make themselves known to humankind. He told of epic battles to protect this planet. He spoke of faraway planets and gave details that were meaningless to the three captivated women in the room. Melvin and Lenny, however, nodded in agreement from time to time and interjected the occasional "yes" or "absolutely" in support of what the alien said.

Finally, Lenny shut the audio machine off. "There are so many other tapes, however, you have gotten the gist of our research. Now, if you please, I will escort you to your vehicle."

Melvin rose. "Thank you for a lovely evening. We do so enjoy having you as a neighbor." He shook Alice's hand, then those of Janice and her mother.

Lenny walked them to Alice's Chevrolet. "Ladies, it's been a pleasure. Alice, may I speak with you for a moment, privately?"

Glancing towards her two friends, Alice tried to act fearless as she heard the sounds of Janice and Connie slipping into her car while she walked down the darkened path with Lenny.

At first, they walked in silence. He cleared his throat and stopped. "I realize this was a lot to take in. Please understand that we allowed you insight into our lives for two reasons. First, we are forever indebted to you for the marvelous care you have given my mother. She has a rare skin condition. Sunlight causes terrible blisters, far worse than a normal sunburn. We received a call from Dr. Steinman earlier, letting us know she is conscious and ready for release. I can't thank you enough for the care you have given her, and for the kindness you have shown me."

"Lenny, we've been happy to care for your mother. We've devoted our lives to caring for those in need. As far as being kind to you, there's no need to thank us. We like you."

Lenny lifted his face to the sky. For a moment, Alice thought he might cry. He took a deep breath and exhaled slowly.

"What was the other thing?" Alice now looked at the sky too.

"Hmm?"

"You said there were two reasons you had us over tonight. What is the second?"

"You're a good neighbor, Alice. When we moved here, you didn't try to force yourself into our lives. You gave us our... space. That means so much to us."

"I think we both live out here to have our privacy.

"Yes, it's true."

The two stood quietly for a moment. Crickets chirped in the night, and a lonesome whippoorwill called out. No mate answered.

"Listen, Alice. To a certain extent, we are kindred souls. What you learned tonight is true. There is a great battle raging over this planet. The government keeps it secret. No more than twenty people in the world, and now you three ladies, know of this war. Things could become dangerous someday, and if you ever need us, please call us. Our red phone works both directions. We will help wherever we are. Just dial 1. After all, it's important to be a good neighbor."

With that, he walked her back to the car and bid them goodnight.

The three women sat in stunned silence as Alice drove them to the opened gate then to her own home a half mile away. The stars blazed brightly, and a full moon illuminated their faces through the windshield.

Only once they were inside the farmhouse did they let their guard down.

"I've never been so frightened and excited and enthralled at the same time!" Connie grabbed three more cookies off the platter on the countertop as she spoke.

"Mother, I know this was a huge event in your life--in all our lives. I don't think we should ever speak of this to anyone outside the three of us. What do you think, Alice?"

"I agree. It could be dangerous."

The three women swore to carry the secret with them to their graves.

The next night at work, Marjorie Henson was no longer in Room 12-A. The day shift had no record of her being discharged, but she was gone.

Life resumed its normal routine. Alice never again saw Melvin or Lenny, and if she was busy, it was possible for her to forget for a moment or two that the compound existed.

Two months later, sitting on her porch enjoying a late summer evening, Alice witnessed a spectacular meteor shower. *Funny, I hadn't heard on the news that one was expected. They usually make a big hoopla when these things happen.* She watched for an hour or so, then she went to bed.

The next morning on her way to work, something caught her eye. The gate to the compound was flung open.

Maybe I'm crazy, but I feel like I should drive to the house to see if they're okay. Pulling into the circle drive, she saw the doors wide open to the house. The scene looked like the hasty eviction of renters who squatted too long and who now fled into the night. *Whatever happened, Lenny and Melvin left in a hurry.* It left Alice unsettled.

The next night, the meteor shower continued. Two days later, a delivery truck driver knocked on Alice's farmhouse door.

"A package for Alice Cameron."

"That's me."

"Here you are, ma'am." He handed her a nondescript white box. "No need to sign. Have a good day."

Stepping inside the house, she set the box on the kitchen counter and pulled a steak knife from the utensil drawer to slit the packing tape open. Inside, wrapped in tissue, was the one item Alice would never forget from the compound: the triangular key. A note sat at the bottom of the box.

Dear Alice,

Please use the red phone. It's urgent. The war tides have turned. The code is 86392.

Your neighbor,

Lenny

OUT OF NOWHERE

Lincoln Hayes breathed in the smells of the first pleasant spring evening of the year. Relaxed and happy, he reveled in the breeze ruffling his blond hair. The stress of the day melted away, and he slowly swayed on the wooden porch swing.

It's nights like this that I live for.

As he enjoyed the moment, he thought of his family, his friends, and his good fortune. He taught high school science at the same high school he attended, and he was thankful that the hard work he put into college paid off. He was right where he wanted to be.

I have a house close to Mom and Dad. I see my lifelong friends every day. I'm giving back to the school and community that gave me so many good childhood memories. I'm home.

Being near his family brought Lincoln a great deal of satisfaction. The four years he spent at Purdue University provided many great experiences and opportunities, but his heart yearned for the familiarity of his hometown. He'd missed his friends and his favorite places, but more than anything, he'd missed his family.

Maybe some people are happy cutting ties with their roots, but I'm not one of them.

Lincoln's parents, Max and Patricia, were the greatest influence in his life. Their home was just three blocks away, and Lincoln spent at least a few evenings a week having dinner with them and seeking their advice.

Max and Patricia set excellent examples for him. They worked hard providing a comfortable upbringing for their family. They attended every game and school event Lincoln was in, and he could depend on them. Lincoln knew he was lucky to have his parents.

They gave us the best they could, even when that meant sacrificing their own wants. I hope I can be a parent like them someday.

Max and Patricia were proud of Lincoln and his little sister. Italia was their bright star, and she outshined any effort Lincoln ever made, but strangely, he never felt any childish pangs of sibling rivalry towards her.

Have I ever been jealous of her?

The answer was no. Granted, he was much older than she was, but still, he couldn't think of a time when he resented her.

In fact, Lincoln couldn't remember a time before his sister was a central figure in his life. Feelings of protection and pride flooded over him when he thought about Italia, the brown-haired, blue-eyed girl who was the adoration of the entire family. Always a natural beauty, her talents in music, art, and most recently dance, made her the highlight of every family gathering. A few months ago, her acclaim spread to the community as a whole when Parkville High School's performance of *The Nutcracker Suite* showcased both her talent and her beauty.

"That little sister of yours is something else," his colleagues at Parkville High told him.

"Yes, she is. Mom and Dad are very proud of her. I am too," Lincoln had said with a warm smile.

Lincoln's thoughts now turned from his immediate family to the community and how it had changed since he was a child.

Parkville has become quite a magnet for talented children. Prodigies of all types, from piano to mathematics, overflow into the halls at school. Sports are flourishing, and academic awards just keep pouring in.

Life was good in Parkville, but it did make people wonder at the newfound success of the community.

Just last week Gary Lister, the local grocer, expressed his surprise to Lincoln as they visited while Gary rang up his purchases.

"Since when did we become state champs?"

"Certainly not when we were in school," Lincoln replied with a chuckle.

"Well, I don't know what's in the water, but I'm not going to jinx us by talking about it. We've got a shot at another baseball title this spring."

"Let's certainly hope so." Lincoln walked to his car, groceries in arm, thinking about Gary's comment.

I know several students who outdo anything their parents accomplished. No one I graduated with holds a candle to the average student I teach in my classes.

The Carter twins, for example, were star athletes, which surprised many because neither of their parents, Elaine and Dan Carter, were athletic. The Lundquists' daughter scored a perfect 36 on the ACT, but neither of her parents showed exceptional intelligence. Then there was Kyle Larner, the freshman successfully taking college courses ranging from art history to calculus. Kyle explained to one of his classmates just the other day that reading math books was like music playing in his head. Kyle's parents were, on the other hand, past retirement age, and both Lonnie and Sandra were simple people living simple lives.

Lincoln's cart rattled across the parking lot asphalt as he puzzled over the changes in his community. *How did they end up with a son like Kyle? Actually, how did any of these kids come from the people in our town? Out of nowhere, we are winning championships and raising geniuses. I don't remember any of us performing at such a high level. This isn't normal for Parkville.*

He hit the button on his key fob, raising the hatchback of his vehicle. As he placed the groceries down, the teacher in him forced Lincoln to consider the most reasonable explanations.

Maybe the helicopter parents, the ones grooming their children for success straight from the womb, are making a difference. Maybe we've focused on bringing out the best and the brightest in all our children, and now it's working. After all, "No Child Left Behind."

Lincoln didn't spend much time thinking about it, but it did intrigue him.

Parkville was a modest town that most people passed on the highway without giving it a second thought. It was a quiet suburban sanctuary where middle-class families sought a better life than the frenetic pace of the big city. Crime was almost nonexistent in Parkville, and the people there liked living stress-free lives. The town motto emblazoned on the city limit sign read "The World's Best-kept Secret." He drove home and forgot about it for a while.

Tonight, however, Lincoln swung on his porch swing and once again was deep in thought. What had changed in his hometown? This was Lincoln's fifth year of teaching in Parkville, and he was proud of his students' accomplishments. Just this year, three students qualified for national competitions in physics. Two more won awards for their research project on cells and their regenerative properties in some amphibians, such as the frogs singing a lullaby on this spring evening in a nearby pond.

Tomorrow was a big day for Lincoln. He'd been nominated for Teacher of the Year. His students' excellent scores on state tests and their success in high profile competitions put a spotlight on Lincoln and the science program he developed at Parkville.

I'd like to think I'm the reason for their success, but I'm not so sure I am.

A nagging doubt plagued Lincoln. A suspicion had slowly crept into his mind that he didn't have anything to do with the abilities of his students.

This evening, however, Lincoln sat on his porch, enjoying the warm breeze and the smell of the earth awakening after a long winter's rest. The aforementioned frogs created a pleasant din of noise in the background, and Lincoln's thoughts shifted from the unsettled thoughts that had preoccupied him. He wallowed in the memories of magical nights like this he enjoyed in his childhood.

As a boy, he'd beg his parents to let him play one more inning of baseball with his friends or to let him make one more cast into the creek before he came in to go to bed. Visions of warm days, picnics, and leisure that can't be found in the icy haze of winter swam in Lincoln's head.

Recollections of growing up, some vivid and some a little fuzzier, passed through his mind. The fact that some were indistinct bothered Lincoln, once again bringing the unwelcome sense of dread to the otherwise pleasant evening.

Why can't I remember the day Italia was born? I can't remember life without her, but oddly, at this moment, I can't remember her coming home from the hospital--or Mom even being pregnant with her.

That thought, along with a slightly out of place sound making its way through the chorus of frogs, caused Lincoln to pause for a moment as he rose to go in for the evening.

It's probably just a night creature. I'm turning in for the evening. Deserved or not, tomorrow could be a big day.

Tomorrow was a big day.

***

In a grove of trees less than a hundred yards from Lincoln Hayes's porch, a group gathered. Italia, the Carter twins, and roughly one hundred and fifty other teenagers sat in a circle, deep in conversation.

"I think we can safely say that our five-year pilot program has been a success." An athletic, brown-haired Chet Carter stood before his comrades. "It's time we broaden our scope. Our people depend on us, and time is running out."

Nods of agreement swept through the crowd.

"When we began this expedition, we weren't sure if we would survive. Much like the early Pilgrims we learned about here on Earth, we faced uncertainties. We now know we can survive, and it's time for us to begin full-fledged colonization of this planet." Chet scanned the crowd for questions.

"Do you think we can be successful in other parts of the world? We've masqueraded as children here in Parkville, but once we begin to outnumber the residents on Earth, can we continue without war?" Kyle Larner, skeptical by nature, was known for his lack of adventurous spirit. Back on their home planet, many had worried about including Kyle on this mission. A few people shot annoyed looks at Kyle.

"I think we've proven that mind control works well on these weaklings." Chris Carter stood next to his brother Chet. "In no time, we were able to manipulate the people of Parkville into believing we were their children and brothers. If we can do it here, we can do it anywhere on Earth. As Chet said, time is running out. We need to move quickly, and tomorrow was our target date from the start."

Italia raised her hand. "Some are less likely to be manipulated. You read the thoughts of Lincoln Hayes just like I did earlier this evening. He is catching on. He is questioning why he doesn't remember. Others will be difficult to control, too. What will become of the Lincolns?"

"Our leaders have considered this. Starting tomorrow, we will deal with Lincoln Hayes."

***

The warm breeze blew, and the chorus of frogs sang out into the darkness.

CELL TIME

The dripping water from the cracked ceiling in Cell 234 created a rhythmic monotony that could either lull someone to sleep or cause him to go insane. Arthur Cranston had too much rage within him to do either.

Ten years into his sentence, Arthur thought he'd seen it all. His transfer to the Carmichael Correctional Center lowered the bar. He'd been here three months, and the conditions were worse than anywhere he'd been held captive before. All inmates tend to complain about bad food and uncaring or cruel staff, but there was something more to this place.

I can't put my finger on it, but there's something ... unnatural ... about Carmichael.

The physical conditions of the rundown facility were remarkable on their own. Lead-based paint peeled off walls, and cracks large enough for rats to crawl through, which they did, were everywhere. The cold dampness, an oppressive clammy shadow, that permeated the structure created a chill that settled into Arthur's soul. That was only partially responsible for his rage today, however.

Never before had Arthur encountered a staff, from entry-level corrections officers to warden, that seemed to bask in the inhumanity of his conditions like the ones at Carmichael. It wasn't just Arthur, either. He'd seen glee in the eyes of staff members who beat inmates mercilessly or who mocked, baited, and framed inmates only to throw them into the hole.

Back at the Armstrong Correctional Center, in his younger days, Art Cranston spent a few stints in the hole. It happened, and Art knew he'd deserved it. The fights he'd gotten into back then were worth it, though. He was young, just barely twenty at the time, and fighting was the only way to keep from becoming someone else's sexual property. Going to the hole in Armstrong had definitely been worth it. Still, Armstrong was bad, but it wasn't like this place.

No, Carmichael was an entirely different beast. The level of savagery—the unadulterated evil—he witnessed daily troubled him. In one week, Art saw more violence toward inmates than he'd seen in years at Armstrong. But whom could he tell? No one cared about inmates, and the system did everything it could to break inmate ties with anyone on the outside. Art knew that whatever happened inside Carmichael would not be stopped. That hopelessness fueled his rage too.

However, it was the rape and beating of poor old man Murphy this morning that accentuated Art's rage today. In front of everyone, almost as sport, three guards beat and assaulted a man who was too old to defend himself against one, let alone three. The other inmates, caged in their cells, were helpless to stop the attack. Art's anger reached the boiling point today. It festered since the first day he stepped foot in Carmichael, but what happened to Murphy brought the anger inside him to the surface.

These guards are monsters. Art clenched his fists as he paced the confines of his cell.

Officer Dick Martin led the brutality Cranston and every other inmate in Cell Block C witnessed that morning. A stocky man with black eyes and a blacker heart, Martin was an ever-present force in the housing unit.

Martin seems to always be on duty. As Art Cranston's mind churned over Martin's viciousness, his pacing quickened.

I haven't met a good one here yet, but Martin is the ringleader. Whatever he does, the other guards fall in line with him. I've even overheard him telling the warden what to do.

It was true. Martin rejoiced in making life hell for those on the other side of the bars. Society expected a certain level of revenge to be meted out on those convicted, but even the most hardened career employees at Armstrong would have been shocked by Martin's ruthlessness. He loved inflicting agony, and then, when he'd had his fill of fun with whichever unlucky man he targeted, he'd laugh and say, "You need some cell time."

"Cell time" meant a trip to the hole, known as solitary confinement to those unfamiliar with prison. Art hadn't been to the hole at Carmichael, yet. It was located in the dark basement area of the complex that other inmates referred to as "The Dungeon."

Art was new to the prison camp, but he'd heard stories from men who'd lived at Carmichael for years. Their stories often centered around why Carmichael was so draconian. Mankind throughout the millennia has struggled to make sense of his surroundings, and inmates were no exception. The men at Carmichael grasped for explanations. They craved some way to understand the inhumanity of their condition. Why was life so hellish there? How could the staff be so cruel? What was it about this dilapidated stone building, oozing water from its pores day and night, that brought out the worst in humanity? Left with nothing but time to consider the answers, inmates came up with their own theories.

One day, not long after Art's arrival at the camp, Art walked laps around the recreation track with one of those long-term Carmichael residents, Asher Adams. The men exchanged small talk, then Asher glanced over his shoulder at Art and spoke in a whisper. "Man, I've heard it's haunted down there."

"Where?"

"Down in The Dungeon."

Art chuckled. "I don't believe in ghosts, Asher. Try that story on some young kid. I'm not buying it."

"It ain't a joke. I hope neither one of us finds out for sure. Those ghosts torment the men down there. You just watch. No one comes out of the hole the same. Look at Proctor's eyes, man. The dude's not right now. And that asshole Martin just laughs when he sends people to The Dungeon. He loves telling guys they need "some cell time.""

Martin did love using his favorite catchphrase every chance he got. He became antsy if he couldn't send a man to The Dungeon at least a few times a week. His eyes snapped with anticipation when he narrowed in on his next victim. Men avoided him as much as possible, but it was impossible to escape him once he set his sights on someone.

What kind of a sick man is he? Art winced whenever he thought of Martin

Ty Williams, a man Art worked with at the chow hall, warned him of the same fears Asher Adams shared. "If you listen late at night, you can hear things moving in the walls."

"Those are rats, Ty. You've seen them, and I've seen them."

"No. Not rats. Whatever it is scares the hell out of the rats. They quit their squeaking and scurrying when those other noises start."

Art paused. The ferocious sincerity in Ty's face couldn't be denied.

"You just listen some night, Art. Late at night when nothing should be stirring, you'll hear what I'm talking about."

Ty was a formidable man. He stood a foot taller than Art and weighed no less than 280 pounds. Whatever it was he heard had this mountain of a man spooked.

Art did listen, and he did hear. At first, it sounded like the soft rustling of papers in a breeze. Then an almost imperceptible sound--a voice of sorts--could be heard humming through the walls and floors. The more intently he listened, the more it grew into a whistling howl, causing a hardened man like himself to shiver. Goosebumps covered his arms, and he pulled his one blanket up under his chin, tightly closing his eyes to try to block out the sound—and the sensation that ghosts filled the midnight air.

He first noticed the sounds a month ago. Since then, Art began meticulously observing every move made by those around him, staff and inmates alike. Asher Adams was correct. Men returned from the hole changed. Once talkative men became quiet and sullen. Those who previously seethed with anger now sat in their cells in silent submission. Their eyes were vacant, and even in the few weeks since Art took notice, those men wasted away. He barely recognized some who'd been strapping young men when he'd arrived at Carmichael.

The stress of this prison took a toll on Art Cranston. Today's rage was a conflagration of emotions: disgust over the inhumanity of his captors and the growing fear that welled up inside him.

I don't believe in ghosts or demon possession, but what in the hell is going on here? I'm about to blow, and I know that won't help me. I need to keep my head together, but my nerves are shot. I can't take one more episode like what happened to Murphy. No man should go through what those bastards did to him in the middle of the bay. Try as he may, he couldn't shake the memories of what he saw earlier that day.

Art's blood boiled, and the sounds of Murphy's screams pierced his mind. He held his head in his hands, rocking himself on his bunk, begging for the visions to go away.

Then he heard it. Not the rustling of papers in the wind nor the dripping of water from a clammy ceiling. He heard Martin's laugh.

"Adams, you and me are going to have a little discussion."

Art stepped out of his cell onto the walk to watch Asher Adams nervously step to the door of his cell. Martin motioned for him to come closer as he leaned against the railing. Art knew the fear on Asher's face wasn't simply because of Martin. No, Asher was compulsively afraid of heights, and he was terrified of approaching the railing as much as he was the sneering guard.

Why would they force a man so deathly afraid of heights to live on the top walk? Why, he hugs the wall every time he comes up here. Martin knows he'd never go near that railing unless he had to.

Art had wondered a thousand times why the prison forced Adams to live on the top tier. Now his heart rate quickened as he watched Asher slowly emerge onto the walk and edge toward the railing. Martin smiled so sweetly that a casual observer might think Martin was offering Asher a cigarette or piece of chocolate. Art Cranston knew better.

He wanted to scream, "No!" Before the word could escape him, however, it was done. In a viciously smooth movement, Martin threw Asher Adams over the railing. The sickening sound of his skull cracking on the cement floor below brought the entire housing unit to a standstill.

The rage could be contained no more. Art rushed toward Martin, screaming in a fury. Just as he reached for Martin's throat, four guards appeared out of nowhere and took him to the ground, beating him with their blackjacks and billy clubs.

"Get him to his feet!" Martin ordered.

A bleeding and battered Art was lifted to his feet, but the bloodletting hadn't eased his temper.

"You son of a bitch! You just killed that man! You killed him for no reason. You're going to rot in hell!"

Martin flashed his standard grin and said, "Looks like you need some cell time. I'll take you down myself."

The other guards chuckled and tightly shackled Art Cranston. His arms were handcuffed behind his back, and his feet could only inch along in a shuffle. Martin grasped his left arm as two guards grabbed him at the handcuffs.

I don't care what they do to me down there. They won't break me.

Progress was slow. The Dungeon was far below the regular prison complex, and it lived up to its name. Water trickled down the walls of stone as Art clumsily took the endless rock stairs leading forever downward. The light was poor, and the guards turned on headlamps, much like those used by underground miners. Art blinked to see while blood from a gash on his scalp trickled down into his eyes.

As the light hit the darkness down below, Art realized The Dungeon was part of a cave. As a boy, he'd spelunked with his uncle in the caves of Kentucky, so he knew what he was looking at. A small stream trickled down the manmade hallway leading to what looked like catacombs lining its sides. The smell was dank, and moisture clouded the air.

This must be what death smells like.

Art's shoes and socks became drenched as he sloshed through the water. A pair of rats chattered, almost mocking him, as his slow march to a dark cell continued. Finally, he reached his destination.

"I'll take it from here, boys," Martin barked.

The two guards dropped their hold on Art and quietly retreated down the darkened corridor.

Martin shoved a door open with his foot, unlocked the handcuffs and shackles, and tossed Art through the doorway. In the dark, he stumbled on something in the cell that clanged. It was a metal bucket that served as a toilet.

"How can you get away with treating people this way?"

"You know why. You've been down long enough to figure out that no one cares."

The truth in Martin's statement couldn't be argued. Art stood silently in the darkness. Martin pushed him toward one side of the cell.

"Have a seat on your bunk. I'd like to have a little talk with you."

"Like the one you just had with Adams?"

Art braced for the blows he expected to follow. Instead, Martin sat next to him on the bunk.

Doesn't he know I'd like to kill him with my bare hands? Why is he sitting next to me?"

"I'm thinking you're smart enough to figure out a lot of things, Cranston, so I want to have a little talk to fill in some of the blanks for you. I've seen you watching what goes on here. I'm going to tell you a few secrets."

Art sat silently.

"Tell me what stories you've been told about The Dungeon."

"Some of the guys say it's haunted."

Martin let out a low chuckle. "No, it's not haunted. At least not in the way you people think. It's more complicated than that, yet oh, so simple really."

"I don't follow you. If you're done, just leave me here. You've had your fun for today."

"Yes, today has been quite eventful. It's almost night time. You know what that means."

A slight breeze blew into the cell, and Art heard the rustling of papers. Subconsciously, goosebumps rose on his forearm. He could swear he heard a low whistle leave Martin's lips. Cranston pressed himself against the wall to put distance between himself and Martin.

"We've lived here for centuries, you know. At first, my people were angry that your kind built this prison on top of our lair. Then we saw the great benefits."

Martin uttered the low whistling howl again, which was answered by excited howls outside the cell.

"Man, if you're trying to screw with my head, it's not going to work. You've had your fun, now go."

Martin leaned into him. "Oh, this part of the plan has nothing to do with fun. Eating is serious business."

A chill ran down Cranston's spines.

"You see, my people are an ancient society. Few of you know about us, but we've been called 'shapeshifters' and other names throughout the years. We've lived here longer than you have."

For a moment, it seemed that Martin's body wavered. It was more than the trickery of darkness. Something had changed about Martin, and Art Cranston pushed himself further against the damp wall. Fear replaced rage.

"I love a good turn of phrase, don't you, Cranston? When you hear the word 'cell,' you think of your cage. When we think of a cell, we think of nourishment."

Cold dread consumed Art Cranston.

"My people need you and your ilk. You're an intelligent, observant man. I've watched you. You've seen

50

the demise of men who return from The Dungeon--how they wither before your eyes."

Cranston nodded. He could think of nothing else to do. There was nowhere to run as the howls increased outside the door.

My people are hungry. We feed on your cells. They give us the energy we crave. You've noticed we staff work as a team. We masquerade as humans, but our job is to provide the meals our people need. Your 'justice system' provides us a steady supply. Unlike you humans, we value our people. No one goes uncared for in our society."

Leaping to his feet, Art tried to flee. In a split second, Martin had him pinned against the wall. His feet dangled in the air. A low hum reverberated from Martin's being.

"It will be uncomfortable for you at first. My loved one will enter your body and begin to feed. We prefer the brain first. All the electrical synapses are like carbohydrates to you. We leave it operational for basic functions, but your ability to be cognizant will fade rapidly."

A wind gushed into the door. Martin forced Art Cranston's mouth open. A moan escaped him, and he fought a valiant fight, but it was no use. It was "cell time."

A MARVELOUS SUNRISE

The pastel palette of the morning sky was soothing to the eyes. A few clouds drifted above the horizon, outlined in dazzling silver as the rays of a new day began to creep above the placid waters of the cove. This was Sutton Kincaide's favorite place on earth. Ever since their first vacation as newlyweds to the quiet coastal community of Serenity Beach, Sutton and Maralee Kincaide fell in love with the sights, sounds, and smells of their version of heaven on earth. The waves lapped a lullaby that was as comforting as the morning vista.

Sipping on his second cup of Kona coffee, Sutton reflected on the happy times he and Maralee had spent in Serenity, first as vacationers, and then as permanent residents as his salary and career ambitions peaked. Yes, working for the Department of Defense and later for NASA had provided them an incredible life full of travel, interesting coworkers and friends, and a more than comfortable lifestyle, including this spacious beach house.

It's too bad Maralee isn't here to see this. We had so many sunrises together. She'd have wanted to be here with me today. Then again, she would have been philosophical about how all things must come to an end.

Maralee's death less than a year ago changed many of their plans. No European ski trips. No Costa Rican getaways. No more dinner parties for their friends and visiting dignitaries. No growing old together sitting on their balcony watching sunrises like the one today. Those days were gone.

Those days were gone...

Sutton rose from his chair long enough to pour himself another cup, then settled back down in his favorite spot to witness the glory unfolding before him. His thoughts began to drift in peaceful contemplation. In his youth, Sutton was known for letting stress get to him. Maralee always said he was "high-strung," but Sutton knew he'd more than once let his worry spill out in the form of dictatorial behavior. Sometimes at work, and sadly, sometimes to his beloved Maralee. Sutton had learned, though. Life lessons and irrefutable truths tempered his urges to control, and now he sat in careful thought, resigned to life as it was--and wasn't.

Memories of times spent with Maralee flooded over him. She was the epitome of a gracious hostess. Entertaining guests, making others feel at ease, and knowing how to create just the right mix of people at a gathering were some of her many strengths. Sutton jokingly referred to Maralee as his "secret weapon." She had it all, and her social skills had helped his career on more than one occasion.

A particular dinner party changed Sutton's life. Shortly after he began at NASA, he had the pleasure of meeting Gene Shoemaker and his wife Carolyn at a conference. As luck had it, the renowned astrogeologist would be speaking at the University of Florida, not far from lovely Serenity Beach. Shoemaker was already famous for his discovery of the Shoemaker-Levy 9 Comet, and Sutton had long admired the Shoemakers and their work on Near-

Earth Objects. Sutton jumped at the opportunity to speak at length with Gene and Carolyn.

"Would you like to have dinner with my wife and me some evening while you are in the area?" Sutton proposed.

A smile had spread across his idol's face. "Sutton, I'd be honored. Here's my card with my personal phone number on it. Call, and we'll make arrangements. Carolyn will be thrilled."

That chance conversation turned the course of Sutton Kincaide's life. The lovely dinner Maralee made was the backdrop to an hours-long discussion of what dangers lurked beyond our atmosphere. Craters around the world proved that impacts had happened before, and here he was, Sutton Kincaide, sitting with the man who discovered countless cosmic objects. Gene Shoemaker's life revolved around the search for threats, most completely unknown to us even today, that would result in a cataclysm rivaling the extinction of the dinosaurs.

Under Gene's supervision, Sutton began working alongside him in earnest. Finding a way to protect Earth was as worthy a cause as he could imagine, and the NASA project they led produced groundbreaking (*No pun intended*, Sutton chuckled) discoveries regarding potential celestial bodies that could impact our world.

Gene's death years earlier in an automobile accident in Australia was a blow in Sutton's life that came second only to Maralee's death last year. His mentor, his friend, the father he'd never had, was gone.

Our best chance of detecting a cosmic killer died with you, my friend.

When Gene died all those years ago, Maralee had rallied to Sutton's side and given him strength. "Sutton, I know you are crushed, but you must continue this work. Gene would have wanted you to."

She was right.

Over the next several years, Sutton and the team scanned the universe for signs of trouble. Universities, scientific associations, and public and private entities sought his wisdom on the topic. Sutton traveled the world, giving lectures and advising governments on ways to combat the threat.

But it was to no avail.

As Sutton Kincaide sat on his balcony, savoring the aroma and taste of the fine Kona coffee he had special ordered from Heavenly Hawaiian Farms, he was captivated by the glow of the sky. Breaking through the pastel hues, the golden rays of light became blinding.

This, however, was no ordinary daybreak. Asteroid N26549, completely unnoticed by scientists until it was too late, hurtled through the atmosphere.

Sutton, at peace with this irrefutable truth, took a final sip.

This has been a marvelous sunrise.

ARE YOU THINKING
WHAT I'M THINKING?

Heavy snow wasn't uncommon in the high country. Ally Carpenter watched through her bedroom window as the snow glistening in the moonlight continued to fall. As a girl, she dreamed of living in a cabin in the woods, having herself cut off from the world in the way she was tonight. An unexpected inheritance from her great-uncle and a few wise investments allowed her to fulfill her dream.

Her mother chided her for her plans to live in the woods, and her friends back in Sacramento asked her time after time, "Why would you want to live in the middle of nowhere? Won't you be afraid?"

They will never understand that it's people I fear, not nature.

Ally stretched, rose from bed, and put water on to boil. A soothing cup of hot tea would heighten her sense as she enjoyed the beauty unfolding outside. She pulled a large mug from the cupboard and found the teabags in the pantry. A specialty blend of black tea infused with cinnamon was exactly what she was in the mood for tonight.

The fire crackled in the potbelly stove, and Ally checked the flue to make sure the air flow was just right to keep the oak logs burning. Her cousin from Missouri drove a trailer full of split wood to her cabin the summer before.

The one thing she didn't want out here in the middle of winter was a chimney fire, and that was a threat if she used too much pine wood. It was readily available in the area, but oak burned hot without depositing creosote. She wondered how many of her friends would even think of such things back home. Living alone required thinking ahead, but Ally was good at doing that.

The teapot whistled, and she poured hot water into her cup and rejoiced in the smell wafting from her steaming tea. She pulled blankets over her lap as she sat on the edge of her bed to watch the snow falling. The flakes were large, and they already weighed down the branches of the fir trees in the yard.

Such a peaceful scene.

Ally's thoughts returned to her cousin's visit the summer before. Firewood wasn't the only reason she wanted to see her cousin Andy. He was one of the few people she missed from her previous life--the one she had before she pulled up stakes to live in her mountain hideaway.

She'd grown up in California, but her parents took her on frequent trips to visit Aunt Lela and Uncle Waylon in her father's home state of Missouri. Andy and his four brothers were Ally's favorite playmates growing up. City life never appealed to Ally, and those trips to the family farm had only fueled her desire to live in the countryside.

Andy was her best friend in the world, and it did her heart good to see him, for her sake and for his. Andy's year was difficult with the loss of his mother in February. Then Uncle Waylon's health also failed, and only the determination of the boys kept the farm running. Andy's wood delivery meant a quick trip across the country to visit Ally and gave them the opportunity to give each other much-needed encouragement. The two cousins spent the time visiting, sharing heartaches, and hoping for brighter days ahead.

The family worried about her living alone in the isolation of the mountains. Ally suspected that her mother was at least partially behind Andy's enthusiasm to bring her firewood. Andy understood her and was most likely the one Ally would open up to if there was reason for concern.

Andy needed consolation for his losses, and Ally had endured plenty of tragedy herself. A year after the car accident, Ally told her family she saw no reason to remain in Sacramento. They understood, or tried to. The loss of her fiancé, Curt, in the wreck pushed Ally to seek refuge in the mountains. Her family knew she needed a timeout, an escape from the pain and constant reminders, so they supported her decision as best they could, but they still worried.

Ally's parents hoped she would heal from her injuries, both emotional and physical. She'd spent months in the hospital coming out of a coma and weeks of what the doctors described as a "touch-and-go" condition. After this much time, Ally still reeled from the ramifications of her injuries.

Tonight Ally watched the snow fall and thought about everything she'd faced in the past few years. *Ramifications. Yeah, I'll say. That's putting it lightly.* She rose from her place on the bed to bring in a few more pieces of wood from the back porch. A little more wood on the fire wouldn't hurt. Ally's aches and pains while lifting the wood reminded her that she may never be free from the accident. Her back ached in ways it never had before. Her left knee throbbed every time she climbed steps.

What will I be like when I'm eighty?

The psychological changes worried her the most, however.

It's the voices that frighten me.

Her grandmother, Emma Sims, used to tell her, "Ally, don't always believe who people seem to be. We don't know what happens behind closed doors, and we don't know what people are really thinking."

But that's where you're wrong, Grandma. I do know what they're thinking.

It began when she was in the coma. Ally remembered it vividly, perhaps because all her other senses were muted at the time, so what she heard was amplified in her mind. She was in her hospital bed with the ever-present hum and beeping of machinery. While monotonous, that noise was comforting compared to the other sounds she heard.

She first noticed it one day when a dayshift nurse loudly complained to herself, while checking her vitals. "I wish that Mr. Hampton would just hurry up and die. I'm tired of dealing with him and his family."

What's wrong with her? Saying something like that out loud could get her fired. Does she think that because I can't speak or move it's okay to talk like that around me?

Nurse Davis wasn't the only one who made inappropriate comments within Ally's earshot. Dr. Stevenson, in front of the nurses, talked about the sexual fantasies he had about them. "My wife doesn't have a clue," he'd say. Strangely, the nurses acted as if he hadn't said anything or that they didn't care.

Are they just used to him being a creep? In this day and age, you'd think he'd have a dozen lawsuits filed against him by now.

Then, one day, she heard voices in the hallway. Philip, the son of a patient down the hall, spoke to a nurse and doctor outside Ally's room about his mother's prognosis. It wasn't good, but there was a chance for her to improve according to Dr. Kaiser. Ally heard the doctor and nurse's footsteps as they headed toward the nurse's station. Philip remained outside her door.

In a loud, clear voice, Philip said, "Why doesn't that old bitch just die? I need the insurance money and my inheritance. She doesn't need all that money. She never goes anywhere. I could travel the world. It sure would be a shame if something 'happened' to her if she ever comes home. Maybe I could help her 'fall' down the stairs? That would solve a lot of my problems."

Horrified, Ally struggled to call for help, but her body remained unresponsive. She fought to yell a warning, to alert someone, anyone, of Philip's plan, but her body wouldn't allow her to move a muscle or utter a word. Surely, someone else had heard him?

Over the course of days and weeks, her body awakened. First, her eyes fluttered. A day or two later, they opened. She couldn't respond to anyone, and even though doctors pricked the bottom of her foot with a pin, neither her toes nor her legs moved.

The conversations she overheard continued, but strangely, as she looked around the room at the people speaking, none of their mouths moved.

How can this be? I hear them talking.
Then it dawned on Ally. She heard their thoughts. They weren't speaking at all.

That's why they're so careless with what they say in my room. I'm the only one who can hear them. I know what they are thinking. But why? How?

When she came out of her coma, Ally tried to talk to her parents about her newfound ability, but they didn't believe her. Worse yet, while they told her she'd just been dreaming or imagining it, she heard their thoughts as well.

"She's gone crazy. The brain damage must be worse than the doctors thought. This nonsense she's going on about has to stop. What will the neighbors think if she says this kind of thing to them? I love her, but we can't have her going around babbling like an idiot."

Gee, thanks, Mom.

Time passed, and eventually Ally was released from the hospital, first to rehab and then to home. Rebuilding her life took hard work, and her heart struggled with the loss of Curt. The wreck happened three months before their wedding date, and Ally was emotionally devastated. Depression hit her hard. She withdrew from the world and spent most of her time in her room. Her mother's efforts to drag her to social events failed, and that only increased the tensions between the two of them.

Ally's father tried to be less intrusive. He suggested she take walks in the city park to ease her mind and strengthen her body. Ally considered it. The weather warmed and the peacefulness of spring settled across the city. Walks in the park were a refreshing idea after her confinement.

Ally stirred her tea as she came back to the present. The clock chimed one o'clock.

Too bad those walks in the park became a nightmare.

Ally's ability to read minds only intensified. During her walks in the park, passing strangers' thoughts revealed themselves to her. Some were happy and heartwarming. The gentle and romantic thoughts of young couples were bittersweet, however. They reminded her of what she lost when Curt died. Still, Ally was a fan of love, and the adoration she vicariously shared with these couples made her smile.

Others were not so sweet and sentimental. She learned of hatred, jealousy, and careless indifference. Ally was not used to these emotions. Her parents never fought, and even after thirty years of marriage, their devotion was true. She knew this for a fact because she could read their thoughts, too, and there was no doubt their love was genuine. However, many people who passed her on the park paths or as she sat on the benches carried resentment and hard feelings toward others. Ally's heart ached over the ugliness of the world.

Some people's thoughts terrified her. Acts of violence stabbed their way into Ally's consciousness. Crimes of every sort, even murders, were planned by some passersby. Visions of killings, rapes, drug use, and beatings burned into her psyche. To the average onlooker, the perpetrators were regular citizens: fathers, sisters, and even church leaders. People from every walk of life unknowingly revealed their hardened hearts and darkest secrets to Ally. Over time, she saw images of events yet to happen. The premonitions kept her up at night. But what could Ally do?

The answer was nothing.

If I go to the police, they won't believe me. Who would believe that the nice businessman in a three-piece suit is going to kill his mistress and dump her in the woods? I have no proof. They'll think I'm crazy and will lock me away in a psychiatric hospital. My mother already thinks that's where I belong.

Then one day, as the Japanese crabapples bloomed in all their glory, she read the thoughts of a man who hadn't killed just once. He was a psychopath with a penchant for blondes, and he sat next to her on the park bench. Ally rubbed her temples to try to drown out the visions flooding into her mind.

The handsome man in the designer shirt stared at her and smiled. "Hello. I was wondering when I would find another one like you. You are a true catch."

Ally's blood ran cold.

Randall Trivett. That's his name.

"I'm sorry, what do you mean?"

He looked at her with piercing green eyes. "What pretty blonde hair you have. But you already know I like blondes, so let's *cut to the chase*. Oh, what a funny turn of phrase."

Ally winced. She knew Randall's method of killing, and somehow he knew her secret.

"How about we become friends? I could use someone with your abilities."

"I don't understand. How do you know about my abilities?"

"I can read minds too, Ally. You're not alone. There are others of us out here. Car accidents, blows to the head from an assault, brain tumors. There are lots of reasons for our ability to read the minds of those less gifted."

"I need to go."

Randall Trivett grabbed her by the arm. "Not so fast. Some people waste their gift. I prefer to use mine to satisfy my rather unusual tastes."

Ally yanked her arm from his grasp. "Leave me alone! You're sick!" She leapt from the bench and ran.

"Don't worry. I can find you. It's a pity you can't tell anyone about our conversation or they will claim you're crazy. As for me, if the police come knocking on my door, I've covered my tracks well. My alibis are airtight. I'll tell them you're just an angry one-night stand who couldn't accept that I'm not interested in her." His voice invaded her mind.

Weeks passed, and he reappeared time and again. Sometimes he was in the park, but more frequently he walked down her street. He'd stand on the sidewalk across from her house smoking a cigarette. A Cheshire cat grin spread across his face as he sent his thoughts her direction.

"Just wanted you to know that I'm here and I'm thinking of you."

Finally, Ally could take no more and confided in her parents the nightmare she was living. Afterwards, she overheard her mother on the phone making arrangements for a psych eval for her.

Thankfully, fate stepped in before she was sent to a hospital. Her great-uncle in San Antonio passed away, leaving her enough money to make her move to the mountains. Ally jumped at the chance to distance herself from the outside world. With her inheritance, she could finally fulfill her childhood dream of living in the country, and she immediately searched for her hideaway. A week later, she found the most remote property she could locate using an online real estate site, and she bought it sight unseen.

I need to escape from people. I'll be safe in the woods.

Ally's thoughts came back to the present, and she shifted her position on the bed. The moon had risen high into the night sky, and the blue-tinged wonderland outside her window looked like a Christmas card scene. Drinking the last of her tea with a final swig, she placed the empty mug on her nightstand.

I'll take care of that in the morning. It's time for some shut-eye.

Ally wriggled under the covers. Sleep was almost upon her when a noise broke the silence of the night. Faint at first, the unmistakable sound of a snowmobile made its way closer and closer to her cabin.

"Hello, Ally. Your mother is so sweet and gullible. We happened to meet when I was walking down your street. I asked about you, and she was happy to tell me where to find you."

The distinct baritone of Randall Trivett's voice resonated in Ally's head. "I have you at last. Oh, what a team we will be."

MIRROR, MIRROR ON THE WALL

Milwaukee, Wisconsin languished under a brutal cold snap, not uncommon for the Midwest in wintertime. Icicles hung from rooftops, and mounds of gray snow piled on the sides of streets. Busy commuters ignored the cold and wound their way through the city and onto the freeways. Shoppers braved the brutal sub-zero weather to buy necessities. Children huddled against each other at bus stops since school districts in Wisconsin seldom believed in canceling school.

Towering above the downtown area were numerous skyscrapers filled with financial planners, architects, corporate executives, city government offices, and more than one news outlet. The movers and shakers of the Milwaukee economy had made their way to their offices and were already at work building dreams and orchestrating hostile takeovers. In other words, it was an average Tuesday. A haze of pollution hung in the air, and no refreshing breezes blew on this frigid morning to offer relief. The day was surrounded by a drab aura, and it wouldn't be farfetched to say a cloak hung over the city.

In one of those massive skyscrapers, the ticking of the clock on the wall next to him numbed Jason Phelps into a near hypnotic state. Stacks of papers covered his cluttered newsroom desk, and nothing but caffeine, adrenaline, and frankly, fear, kept him awake. How many days had he gone without sleep? He'd forgotten.

His muddled mind tried to make sense of what he'd uncovered in recent weeks. Just where had it begun?

It began in my bathroom mirror.

What a crazy thought that was. Jason focused on the ticking clock as he tried desperately to drown out the sounds ringing through his skull.

Jason was right, in a sense. It began for him in his bathroom mirror. One morning as he shaved, a dizzying rush took over his body. He fought it, but in that moment, he *knew*. He knew as certainly as if he'd watched it on his television station's nightly news or if he had been an eyewitness to some spectacular event of history. A world had opened up to him that others were blind to, and more than anything he wished he could put the proverbial genie back into its bottle.

It's my job to tell the world about "Breaking News." What an overused term these days. We've beaten that one into the ground. I'd be hounded out of my career if I reported something like this. There's never been a bigger story than this one, but no one would believe me.

His concerns weren't unfounded. He'd tried to talk to his mother about this, but her suggestion was that he see a psychiatrist.

Yes, a psychiatrist will make this all better.

For the first time in days, Jason Phelps let out a chuckle.

Blaring sirens broke Jason from his trance. Two fire trucks sped past on the street below, forcing their way to an inferno. Somewhere the bitter cold was at war with searing heat as a structure burned in a fury.

What was that he had read in Dante's *Inferno* years before as a college sophomore? According to Dante, hell was a frozen wasteland, not the burning pit of damnation we envision it to be. With no offense meant to the Italian great, Jason Phelps had to agree with popular opinion. Those flames burning in the distance were real representations of the hell he learned about as a young boy in his Baptist grandfather's church so many years ago. Remembering those sermons, he could smell the brimstone. No, the arctic chill that assaulted every Milwaukee resident this morning was a stark contrast to hell.

Suddenly, the clamor around him brought Jason to his senses. Just like every other morning at Channel 10 News, the newsroom was abuzz with activity. Phones rang and people shouted information to each other. For the first time that morning, Jason was aware of his surroundings in a real way.

"Hey, dreamer! I said, 'Do you have the name of the victim in the shooting?' Or do I need to call Channel 3 for that information?" Ed Tinsley stood impatiently over Jason. Not a small man by any means, Ed was a formidable figure.

"Uh, yeah. Just a sec." Jason flipped through his notebook.

"You know, you haven't been yourself lately. Normally, you'd know it off the top of your head. Are you having relationship problems or something? You better come alive soon, Jase. The bosses won't like you daydreaming like that."

Jason shook his head. "No, they won't like a lot of things. Here it is. His name was Michael D'Angelo. He'd just moved to the city a month ago. No suspects have been caught. No leads on the killing either."

"Thanks, Bub." Ed slapped him on the shoulder with the papers he held in his hand before racing across the newsroom to talk with Claire Baker, the morning anchor. Her auburn hair was perfectly coiffed, and she wore one of those dresses that fit just right.

If I was going to have any relationship issues, I wish it was with her. So much for that now.

It took only a moment for Jason to be pulled back into his own thoughts, blocking out the bustle of the newsroom.

My bathroom mirror. Did it really have something to do with this? Or was I just the unlucky son-of-a-bitch who would have seen this anyway?

Jason's mind wandered back to the morning he first saw it in the mirror. The spinning, the flames, the faces. The faces scared him the most. Even though his grandfather preached a thousand sermons about the threat of hell, part of Jason always thought it might be some sort of fairy tale. Heaven and hell were stories parents told their children to make them behave.

"Don't fight with your sister, or Santa won't bring you any presents."

"Don't fight with your sister, or God will send you to hell."

Jason, however, now knew it was no fairy tale. His mirror didn't lie. The first time he saw the visions in it, he thought he was hallucinating. Maybe the pharmacist had mixed up his blood pressure medicine with some sort of psychotropic drug. However, it wasn't his imagination.

72

When he stared into his mirror he not only saw glimpses into hell, but he smelled the brimstone and heard the voices.

"We're coming, Jason Phelps. You can see us, but you are powerless to stop us. Your mirror is our portal, and there is nothing you can do now." The demon's eyes glowed red, and the hatred exhaled in his putrid breath singed the hair of Jason's beard.

In subsequent days, he'd watched, helplessly, as demons flowed out of hell through his mirror and into the world around him. Knowing his impotence against them, the demons laughed as they shared visions with Jason of the impending end to Earth.

Jason knew that today was the day. He *knew*. They'd told him.

Quietly, without drawing the attention of his coworkers, Jason stepped into his boss's office. He'd always been jealous of Ted Reagan's office space. A sliding glass door opened to a small balcony that looked out across the city. What Jason would have given to have a view like that. For a few moments, he had it all to himself.

His breathing slowed as he calmed himself. He placed his jacket onto the back of Ted's chair and loosened his tie. He slipped his patent leather shoes off, leaving them just inside the glass door as he stepped onto the balcony. It was cold, yes, but strangely peaceful outside. He could smell the smoke. It wasn't the fire from earlier. This smoke came from much farther away, and the sulfuric taste of brimstone filled his nostrils and mouth.

It has begun.

Knowing that neither good nor bad mattered now, Jason stepped to the edge of the balcony. He marveled at the gray haze that enveloped his city. It wasn't typical pollution. It escaped from the pits of hell itself. Jason now considered himself lucky because he could end his misery before the coming onslaught. Taking one last breath, he held it as he plummeted to the pavement below.

A deep rumble followed by a howling scream escaped from the cracked sidewalk where he made impact. A demon hovered for a moment above Jason's body, then it flew to the balcony and enjoyed the view. His work had just begun.

THE DESERT DRIFTER

A hot wind blew across the desert landscape. July was always hot in southern Arizona, but this one seemed unusually torturous. Clouds to the west teased an expectation of rain as they cast darkening shadows on the Tucson Mountains. How many days had it been since the last time there'd been more than just enough to settle the dust? Weeks? Months? Velma Atchison had lost count.

Still, this land rooted her in place. It was harsh. It was uncompromising. Hell, at times it was downright dangerous. Some of the people were too.

The wind picked up, and the ocotillos danced. Maybe the rain would happen. Maybe it wouldn't. At this point in her life, Velma had stopped counting on much. Too many hard lessons and unanswered questions left her devoid of hope. That didn't stop her from watching the horizon morning and night, hoping to see the familiar silhouette of Chance Bostick.

A flicker of anticipation flashed through her eyes. Foolish as it seemed, the only hope she clung to rested on seeing Chance again. He'd come home. He'd promised to.

The distinct smell of creosote wafted on the wind rushing from the storm's outflow as the grey haze of rain pelted the mountainside in the distance. Velma could taste the creosote, so strong was the odor that filled the air. Nothing smelled like the scent of this desert plant when it rained. She felt weary, but the smell was invigorating. For far too long, Velma had tasted salty tears more often than she had the cleansing rains the summer storms produced.

She waited. Sometimes patiently and sometimes angrily, but she waited. The weeks she spent with Chance were too real--too incredibly heartfelt--to not keep the faith that he would return.

She'd first seen Chance when she and her father were in town to buy supplies. They'd stopped at the mercantile to pick up enough of the basics to get them by.

And there he'd stood. Six feet five inches of rugged man. She hadn't meant to stare, but she did.

"Ma'am?" He'd leaned over the counter to get the clerk's attention.

"Yes, can I help you?"

"I'd like twenty-five cents worth of gumdrops, please."

Velma gasped as she watched the clerk fill a bag with the candy treats. She'd never seen a man waste so much money on something so trivial. Maybe he had children--a lot of children. That meant he was married, and she needed to stop staring at him right now. But no. The man walked around the store, looking at tack and farm supplies, eating one gumdrop after another. Velma couldn't stop watching him.

She told herself she should be horrified at the wonton avarice of a man eating that much candy with no care for anyone but himself. Instead, an overwhelming sense of relief and excitement swept over her as she told herself he must be single.

Just as Velma considered how to approach this stroke of luck, her thoughts were interrupted.

"Howdy, ma'am."

The two locked eyes. For a moment, he even stopped chewing his sticky treat.

"Hello." Velma felt her knees wobble.

"Would ya care for one of these? I'm afraid I've about made myself sick with them."

She couldn't turn down any reason to continue talking to this man. He was more appealing than any sugary morsel.

"Why, yes, thank you."

He tipped the bag to its side so she could peer into it. Velma, at five feet eight inches in height had never considered herself short, but his size caused her to feel downright dainty in his presence. Going onto her tiptoes, she took a look at the candies.

"Go ahead. Take a handful. I guess my eyes were bigger than my stomach. I've got a terrible sweet tooth, and the whole time I've been on the cattle drive I couldn't think of anything else than eating a bag of these. Now I realize I may have been too greedy. Please, do me a favor and take a handful."

So she did. Velma had a weakness for sweets herself. Her frugal nature, however, kept her from spending money on such things.

"Thank you for being so kind. I haven't had one of these in ages."

"I'll be disappointed if you don't take a bunch of them off my hands."

Velma giggled. It wasn't something she did often. Suddenly her father, distressed by the unusual sound of her glee, appeared at her side.

"Just what's going on here?"

"Father--"

Jeb Atchison glared at his daughter, cutting her off. He then stared intently at the dusty man holding a bag of candy.

Unshaken, the newcomer extended his hand. "Sir, I'm Chance Bostick. I just arrived in town on my way back from a cattle drive in Texas. We took a bunch of 'em up to a railhead in Kansas. I'm from Yuma, and it's nice to be back in familiar desert. It's a pleasure to meet you."

Surprised by Chance's friendly nature, Jeb slowly reached out to shake the young man's hand. "I'm Jeb Atchison. I see you've met my daughter." Jeb's eyes narrowed.

"Yes, I have, but I haven't had the pleasure of learning her name yet."

"Velma. It's Velma Atchison." Jeb's tone of voice sounded more threatening than cordial.

"Miss Velma, it's nice to meet you. I'm Chance. I decided to go on the cattle drive to see some sights. It looks like I have."

Velma's face reddened. So did Jeb's, but his was out of anger, not embarrassment. "Sir, you need to watch your smart mouth."

"I apologize, Mr. Atchison. I've just never met a girl as beautiful as Velma, and I've never been one to not speak my mind. I'm sorry if I was too forward." His eyes met Velma's again. A blush spread across her cheeks.

"Kindly tell me why you're talking with my daughter. I heard her laughter all the way across the store, and it wasn't fitting. Velma isn't the laughing type."

"Sir, if you'd give me permission, I'd like to court your daughter."

Shocked, Velma and Jeb were speechless. Velma didn't have any callers, and Jeb had begun to think he was raising a spinster. She was, after all, nineteen. If they'd been the religious type, he might have sent her off to a convent like his cousin Mary Catherine had done with her daughter. Jeb Atchison wasn't exactly a pew on Sunday morning kind of man, however. He was too practical for that. He had a ranch to run and a daughter ro raise by himself.

"Sir, is that a yes?

Chance's deep voice brought Jeb out of his trance.

"Yes, I suppose."

That began their courtship. Chance proved Jeb Atchison wrong. Velma was the laughing type. She couldn't resist his quick wit. He brought out a part of her she hadn't even known she had. In the middle of an arid desert, love bloomed.

They were happy, and happiness wasn't something either of them was accustomed to. Chance had been on his own for quite a while. His mother died in childbirth when he was seven, and his father took off on a business trip and never returned when Chance was fifteen. For the first time, they both sensed they'd found something permanent.

"Velma, you know I've got that cattle drive coming up next week. I hate leaving you, but I need the money. I promised old Buck Thomas that I'd be back to help him. I don't want to leave him shorthanded."

"I wish you wouldn't leave, but I know you have to do this." A tear trickled down her cheek. Chance softly wiped it away.

"I'll be back. I promise. Will you promise me something?"

"What's that?"

"I know I don't have a lot to offer you, but will you marry me when I get back? I'll ask your pa's permission. I just want to hear it from you."

"Yes! Yes, I will marry you, Chance Bostick!"

Chance lived up to his word and asked her father for her hand. Jeb hesitated and grumbled, but he finally agreed. He didn't want to deny Velma what could be her only chance at marriage. She couldn't live with him on the ranch forever.

The next week, both Velma and Chance had tears in their eyes as he rode off to join one last cattle drive before settling down. Chance's mind was made up to use some of the money to buy Velma a ring. His ma had never had one, and that pained her. Her sadness over it was one of his clearest memories of her. He was going to make sure Velma never felt that disappointment. In another four weeks, he'd return, and they could make their love official.

Velma occupied herself during the next month by planning a wedding and making arrangements to set up her own household. She'd dreamed of this her entire life. She nearly floated on air as she went about her days.

Jeb Atchison wasn't nearly as jubilant. He still had doubts about that no-account cowhand who came to town making his daughter all kinds of promises.

When four weeks dragged into five, Velma's joy was replaced by fear. As five weeks dragged into six, seven, and eight, fear became terror. Why wasn't Chance returning?

Jeb had the answer. "He's not coming back, Velma. He was nothing but a drifter. I knew he was no good the first time I saw him. Thinking he was so funny and making a fool of you at the mercantile."

His words stabbed her as much as the heartbreak of Chance's absence.

So she waited. And waited. Jeb continued to tell her how Chance was nothing but a drifter who'd never meant any of the things he'd said to her.

"I just hope you're still a reputable woman."

How could he say such a thing to his daughter?

To Jeb's dismay, Velma never courted another man. His fears of her living with him on the ranch forever came true.

Velma's thoughts returned to the present. The strong smell of wet creosote and the sound of pounding rain called her back to the scene playing out before her. There was no silhouette of Chance Bostick on the horizon. There hadn't been, and there wouldn't be. Three bad men and a ten-inch blade made certain he wouldn't return to Velma.

In her heart, she believed he'd loved her. She knew she loved him. A hundred years hadn't changed that. Eternity wouldn't change that.

Velma passed back through the closed doorway. She would walk amongst the desert landscape she loved once the rain stopped. Her earthly ties no longer bound her as she floated through her father's ranch house that had long ago been abandoned. Velma embraced her existence as an eternal desert drifter.

THE BEAST

The water gently laps at the dock jutting crudely from my front steps. Night will fall shortly and, for some reason, I become more reminiscent at this time of day. To some, this bayou evokes fear as the alligators bellow to one another while the shadows grow long. This place holds no fear for me, however. Just a melancholy sadness that ebbs and flows like water in a dark eddy within the confines of this bayou. It's the only place I've ever known.

I remember brighter days. Memories of happy times give me a fleeting respite from the loneliness. I can picture childhood as clearly as I can the events of yesterday. My friends and I spent hours exploring every nook and cranny of our neighborhood. As my mind harkens back through the years, I can hear my mother's sweet soprano lifting above the voices of the other mothers beckoning their children in for the evening.

"Lennox, dinner's ready!"

"Mama, can't I play just a little longer?"

"No, son. Even the gators are going to bed. It's time for you to join us."

I seldom disobeyed my mother, but if I tarried too long chasing bullfrogs or tossing rocks across the placid water with my friends, I was rewarded with the less-than-comforting calls from my father.

His deep baritone drowned out the more pleasant sounds of the impending evening. His booming voice growled, "Lennox, get in here this minute or I'm going to tan your hide!"

My father was an imposing figure. Not only was he taller than average, but he had the strength of ten men, it seemed. My brothers, sister, and I seldom received physical punishment from him, but that's not to say he was above applying a swift and forceful blow to our backsides when he deemed it appropriate. Needless to say, that added to our willingness to respect our mother's sweet soprano calls the first time.

Oh, how I wish I could hear her voice again. It's been far too long since she's been gone, but she is not the only one I've lost throughout this life of mine.

Which, of course, brings my lovely Adeline to mind. She was the prettiest girl I'd ever seen. And cook? She could make a meal worth dropping anything for. It was her kind and loving heart, the softness of her brown eyes, and the serene touch of her hand that left the most significant marks on my heart, however. In my younger days, I'd been a ruffian, and I played the field a good deal with the other beauties who lived nearby. Once I locked eyes with my dear Adeline, though, I was a reformed man.

My brothers, all fine fellows in their own rights, followed suit and married, as did my sister Cici. Happiness was short for that girl, however, as she died in childbirth not long after she and Enos moved to the other side of the bayou. Her death was a dark spot in our hearts for many years. Our mother couldn't bear to hear her daughter's name without tears trickling down her cheeks.

Years went by, and my friends, brothers, and I raised our families. We worked hard, provided for our wives and children, and cared for our parents as they aged. It was a sad day when our once-robust fathers had to set aside their tools and admit that they now needed to be cared for by us. Our mothers may have fought the inevitable even harder when the day came for us to dote on them. That is the way of life, I suppose.

Then life changed. It started with whispers that there were newcomers to our bayou. I had my doubts about their existence, but the rumors continued. According to the stories, at first they simply passed through. Some were stricken with malaria. Others succumbed to the alligators and other bayou predators. Steadily, they continued to come. As I said, I heard the rumors, but I had my doubts.

In fact, I didn't believe my youngest brother, Merle, when he told me he'd seen them with his own eyes.

"Surely, you're pulling my leg." What he was telling me was not possible. I believed the intruders were simply myths that fueled stories around our campfires at night.

"I swear it, Len. I hid behind a cypress and watched as five of them crept through on a boat. I don't think they saw me, but when I gasped at what I saw, they stopped and listened for a long time. They are real."

In the quiet of the evening, after our children were put to bed, I shared what Merle told me with Adeline.

"Lennox, you know that Merle has always had an imagination."

"That he does, Adie, but there was a fear in his eyes that I've never seen before. I know my brother, and he didn't look like he was telling a tale."

"Please be careful tomorrow when you're out fishing. I don't like the sounds of this if it's true."

The next morning as I checked my trotlines for catfish, I heard unfamiliar voices speaking in a language I'd never heard before. I knelt behind a tree and held my breath as a canoe passed carrying four figures. Suddenly they raised a long stick and pointed it at a rising heron that took flight as they approached.

Boom!

The noise deafened me and I fell backward. I'd have been noticed, no doubt, if they hadn't been so preoccupied with their joy. The heron fell dead on the shore, and the intruders laughed and shouted triumphantly. Then they did the unthinkable. They drifted away without taking their kill. They left it there to rot. They didn't even eat the magnificent bird they just killed. The thought of their senseless slaughter sickened me. I checked my remaining lines and returned home shaken by what transpired.

That evening I called a meeting of my neighbors. Some didn't want to believe what I witnessed, but I didn't have a foolhardy reputation, so most took me seriously. We tossed around ideas of how to handle this new menace, but since we were by-and-large peaceful people we were at a loss.

"I fear what that weapon of theirs can do, Lennox," my brown-eyed Adeline said to me as she snuggled next to me that night.

"I'll watch over you, dear. No one will harm you." I held her until her breathing became deep and regular, and I knew she was resting soundly.

If only my promise to protect her had been the truth. Within a year, our community and our family were on the run. The intruders brought dogs with them and hounded us until we found refuge in the remotest corner of the bayou. Food was scarce, our wives and children looked pale. We feared the booming sounds of their weapons and the baying howls of their dogs. Little did we know booming sticks and relentless hounds would not decimate us, but something else would.

My Adeline was one of the first to become sick. The fever hit quickly, and then the scabbing blisters covered her whole body. Nothing I gave her soothed her pain or lowered her fever which seared so hot that she became delusional. For hours she writhed on our pallet, pounding her fist against the wall, muttering unintelligible words. She died within three days. Then our children, all six of them, did the same.

I was distraught and nearly went out of my mind. One by one, my brothers and their families perished. My family's destruction was repeated throughout our community. Finally, only I was left. I don't know why I was spared. I would've rather died alongside my family and friends, but it was not to be. This disease, known as "the pox," wiped out everyone I knew or ever cared about. For centuries we had lived in peace in this bayou, and then we were gone.

Today I live a quiet life, still afraid to venture far from my own front steps. Sometimes on the occasions when I stray too far from home I've had close calls with these men who maraud our homeland.

One day I barely dodged sure death as two of them fired their weapons at me. These careless hunters called "humans" yelled, "Look, it's a beast! A swamp monster! Get 'em!" Bullets sprayed around me as I quickly made my way into the shadows.

I'm left to wonder who the beast really is.

As I rock in my favorite chair this evening, I watch the heavy shadows fall around me and listen to the crying sounds of a night bird. Such is the end of another lonely day.

THE FATE OF SARAH WASHINGTON CRANE

Sarah Washington Crane sat in my office. As a psychiatrist, I'd heard a lot of strange things during my twenty years of practice, but I'd never heard anything quite like this. Dr. Hallford, her primary care physician, was a college roommate of mine, and he asked me to begin treating her as a personal favor to him. He'd been her family's physician for years, and he'd been a family friend of her parents, Katherine and Garret Washington, for nearly as long.

After meeting with her once, I initially assumed she suffered from the confusion brought about by early-onset dementia or possibly a brain tumor. Cliff Hallford assured me her situation wasn't as simple as that and asked me to do my best to get her to discuss the trauma she suffered in hopes that she could rebound to some degree. He hinted that I might need to meticulously record every detail for future court proceedings. I agreed to help in any way that I could.

"Can you tell me about yourself?"

"Who?"

"You, Sarah."

"I don't know her."

"Have you ever heard of anyone named Sarah Washington?"

"It was Sarah Washington Crane."

"Can you tell me about her?"

"I don't think you'll want to know."

"Could you do your best to tell me what you know?"

She sat, nearly catatonic, staring at a chipped piece of drywall in the corner of my office. Slowly, her words came. As though she told a scary story around a campfire or was telling a friend a blow-by-blow account of a movie she had watched, she recited this tale. The more she spoke, the more animated she became.

Cliff Hallford confirmed that what she relayed in my office was correct. While mentally I tell myself it can't be, my heart can't help but believe her.

"I'll start at the beginning," she said. "There's no sense starting anywhere else."

"Take your time. I'm here to listen."

She took a deep breath and began. Almost as if she'd rehearsed the storyline in her mind a thousand times, the details poured out. I have to add that her complete emotional removal from this chilled me to the bone. The following is as accurate of an account as I can put together, combining what details Dr. Hallford gave me of her background and the transcripts of my sessions with Sarah.

***

It all began in the house. Once located in a grove of trees outside of town, the old house now found itself in the middle of one of Arrington's modern residential areas. While functional, the ranch-style houses lacked the charm and elegance of the Antebellum homes they replaced. Now only the Washington home remained of the stately residences from days gone by. It was a beauty.

Sarah Washington Crane grew up in the much larger city of Glenwood, an hour west of Arrington, but cousins and extended family lived throughout a four-county area. The homebase for the abundant kinship was Arrington, however. Family lore held that three brothers settled the area, fathering twelve, fourteen, and seventeen children respectively. Washington was a common last name, and nearly everyone was connected through blood or marriage in this pocket of Missouri.

Sarah's father, Garret Washington, grew up in Arrington. However, thanks to a family rift that surfaced when he was still a child, his branch left the familiar territory of Arrington and moved to the "big city" of Glenwood, population 75,000 when he went to college. The Washingtons of Glenwood had little to do with their kinfolk, most of whom were regarded as country bumpkins, especially by Sarah's mother, Katherine Hensley Washington.

Garret attended law school then built a thriving practice in Glenwood. Katherine was a socialite, at least to the extent that a socialite could be found in southwest Missouri. Garden clubs and charitable events filled Katherine's calendar. A respectable amount of time after their marriage, they produced one child, an auburn-haired beauty christened Sarah Elizabeth.

Kept busy with ballet lessons, piano recitals, and an active social group, Sarah was oblivious to the loss of any family ties. Her parents supplied her with a perfect childhood. They showered their little girl with as many opportunities as they could provide, and with her father's courtroom successes, they could provide many.

After graduating high school, Sarah first earned a bachelor's degree and then a master's degree in psychology at Ohio State. In June, after finishing graduate school, she married an up-and-coming engineer. It was love at first sight for Sarah and Elliott Crane. Life was perfect for the two lovebirds, and they were thrilled to add three beautiful children to their young family. Evan arrived first, followed quickly by Elaina and Alissa.

Having more than one child was important to Sarah, and they tossed around the idea of having one or two more children once Alissa began kindergarten. Being an only child had its perks for Sarah, but loneliness also shadowed her youth. She gladly set aside her career plans to stay home with her young children, and the sound of giggles and pattering feet gave Sarah a satisfaction she'd never known before. Elliott made good money working for a nuclear plant, and time with her son and daughters was worth the temporary sacrifice of career goals. Neither Sarah nor Elliott foresaw the tragedy on the horizon.

Driving in her car one summer day, Sarah questioned the universe.

Who dies of a heart attack at thirty-two?

Elliott Crane did.

Insurance money softened the financial blow, but Elliott's death left Sarah with an identity crisis.

Life isn't supposed to be like this. We had plans. We knew what our future looked like. Now I don't know who I am, what I am doing, or which way to turn next.

Nine months passed after Elliott's death, and knocking around their 3,000-square-foot home in suburban Ohio wore on Sarah's spirit. Even the children didn't need her in the same way they once had. This year, Evan started third grade, Elaina first grade, and Alissa kindergarten. A sharp pang hit Sarah knowing Alissa's venture into kindergarten no longer meant the possibility of another child or two. With no more babies to care for and no husband to grow old with, Sarah wondered what her purpose in life was.

A few weeks later, a phone call brought an unexpected prospect.

"Hey, Dad, why are you calling at this time of morning?"

"Well, I may have found an opportunity for you. A fresh start. Five years ago, I'd have never mentioned it. A year ago I wouldn't have. But I may have found something you've been looking for back here in Missouri."

"In Glenwood?"

"No, but only an hour away. It's in Arrington, where I grew up. Mr. Perkins, the superintendent of the school, called. The district needs a counselor, and he thought you might be interested."

"Dad, I don't even know what I'm looking for. I haven't worked in the field in years. I set all that aside when Evan was born. I'm not even sure what kind of certificate I'd need to work in a school."

"I know, but this may be your chance to get back into the world. You and the kids are living over eight hours from us, and I know your mother would enjoy having you and her grandchildren close by. At least give it some thought."

Sarah did think about it. A lot. Two days later, she gave Rod Perkins a call. A phone interview was scheduled for Tuesday, and by Wednesday, the job offer was there for the taking.

"We can get you a waiver until you take the state test and pick up any hours you may still need to practice here in Missouri," her new boss explained.

Sarah had a sneaking suspicion the job was hers before she even called the Arrington Central Office the week before.

While Dad doesn't talk much about growing up in Arrington, the one name I did hear a lot of was Rod Perkins. He and Dad were best friends all through school, and they've kept up through occasional calls and golf games over the years.

Garret Washington had, in fact, asked his old friend for a favor. He knew Sarah felt lost and needed a boost to her confidence. His motivation was also, in part, self-serving. He and Katherine weren't getting any younger, and they realized the importance of getting to know their grandchildren.

Everything moved quickly for Sarah. It had to. It was already the middle of July, and school began in Arrington on August 12. There was no time to waste.

Well, it looks like it's settled. I'm selling this place and moving back home with the kids. We don't even have a house in Arrington yet, and there are so many details left to take care of. How am I going to swing this?

Those concerns were short-lived. Garret and Katherine arranged for a moving company while Sarah drove to Arrington to look at houses. Evan, Elaina, and Alissa spent the day with Grandma Katherine while Sarah met the realtor on the town square. Driving through the comfortable small-town neighborhoods, Sarah was on edge about finding the right place for her and her family.

This move has to be done right. The kids and I have already been through too much. Life needs to come together for us finally. This past year has been hell.

Once she spotted the three-story home with the expansive wrap-around porch, complete with a five-acre lot that gave the children enough room to even have a pony or two, Sarah knew where home was. She signed the contract, and by the following week, the house was hers. Granted, the old place needed some work, but the price was remarkably low, and Sarah had always loved a challenge. The realtor explained that a series of short-term owners had left the property in disrepair. A failed attempt at using it as an apartment building created most of the need for renovations to return it to its original beauty.

Within a few weeks, Sarah and the kids were moved into their home on East Willow. Sarah relaxed for the first time since Elliott's death. No longer haunted at every turn by the life she'd lost, she had a chance at a familiar, yet clean, slate. Days were spent catching up with high school friends in Glenwood, shopping for items needed for the renovations, and simply allowing herself to breathe for the first time in what seemed like ages.

Katherine's wholehearted embrace of grandmotherhood took Sarah by surprise. The kids quickly attached themselves to her parents, and she had to admit that she was astonished by how much she enjoyed spending time with her mother now. During her teenage years, heated battles raged between them, but now they could spend hours visiting and laughing together.

As she settled into Arrington, Sarah enjoyed meeting her coworkers and acquainting herself with the school and her new position. Jumping back into the field of psychology was terrifying and exhilarating at the same time. Rod Perkins paved the way for her, and it took a weight off Sarah's previously overburdened shoulders.

I have the chance to help others with their problems now instead of fixating on my own.

The house on Willow Street also excited her. It had so many areas to explore. Besides the three stories, complete with five bedrooms, the house had an unfinished basement and an attic. The house held so much potential, and Sarah found herself browsing interior design magazines and watching home improvement shows on television.

I can almost feel the presence of history in this place. I want to keep the romance of this place as I renovate it.

Early one early morning, as the kids fished with her father and Rod Perkins at Table Rock Lake, Sarah made her way up the narrow staircase to the dusty attic.

From the looks of things, no one has touched this room for years.

With her electric lantern in hand, Sarah squeezed through the doorway and began searching through stacks of boxes. Most were filled with miscellaneous junk: Christmas decorations, assorted clothing, and an old box of porcelain dolls.

When I was a little girl, I had a porcelain doll my grandmother gave me. It had been my great-grandmother

Washington's. I wonder what happened to that old thing? I think Mom packed it away years ago.

Most of the boxes held little interest for Sarah, but one grabbed her attention. In a small wooden chest with a metal clasp, she found yellowed legal documents dating back to 1838. As she thumbed through them, it was clear they were the original deeds to the property. Sarah could not believe her eyes.

"On this 23rd day of October, in the year of our Lord 1838, this property was purchased by Enid Lewis Washington and Mildred Garret Washington."

Mildred Garret Washington? My father always told me he was named after his great-grandmother's maiden name. Could my family have owned this property and built this house? Has fate brought me back to a place that's more "home" than I could have imagined?

Her cell phone dinged with a text from her mother, asking her if she'd like to join her for lunch. She replied that she'd love to and turned to head down the stairs. Just then, the light of her lantern caught an image on the wall. At first glance, it looked like the scribbling of a child, but there was something different about this drawing. It wasn't a child's work. It was a map.

A map of what?

Her eyes widened as she realized the map detailed the house, the yard, and the gravesite of a small child.

"Here lies our beloved infant, Grace Elizabeth Washington."

Who would draw a map of where their child is buried?

Goosebumps prickled on Sarah's arms. Grabbing the box of porcelain dolls, she made her way out of the attic and to the third floor. The room she'd designated as her office space was just to the left of the attic stairwell. She stepped inside and set the box against the closet door.

I have just enough time to run a few errands before I meet Mom.

She glanced around the room and spied her car keys on top of her desk. Grabbing them, she began to leave, then thought better of it. The morning sun poured in the office window. The heat of the day made the room nearly unbearable in the afternoon, and the last thing Sarah wanted to do was pay more for air conditioning than she had to. She closed the curtains to block the sunlight, picked up her purse, quickly shuffled down the two flights of stairs, and left.

Lunch with her mother extended into a dinner invitation for her and the children. Upon arriving back at their grandparents' house, the kids spilled into the kitchen where Sarah and Katherine sat, chattering about their grand adventure at the lake with Grandpa Garret and "Uncle" Rod. It didn't take much convincing for Sarah and her children to stay until well past dark.

With an hour's drive back to Arrington, it was nearly ten o'clock before Sarah pulled her SUV into the driveway of their home. By now, the children were sleeping, and she had to wake them to get them out of the car. Evan took Elaina by the hand to lead her up the steps while Sarah hoisted Alissa out of the backseat and onto her hip.

Sarah heard the clunk of the front door closing as a giggle escaped Alissa's sleepy lips. Sara stopped for a moment to see what had captured her daughter's attention. Alissa stared up at Sarah's office window, waving.

Waving?

Alissa giggled again, and Sarah saw the partially open curtain flutter.

I thought I closed those, and I was sure I'd shut the lights off when I left.

Tousling Alissa's hair, Sarah said, "Baby girl, who were you waving at?

"The doll lady, Mama." Alissa then snuggled her head into the crook of Sarah's neck and wrapped her arms firmly around Sarah's shoulders.

She must have been dreaming. Mom and I talked tonight about the box of dolls I found in the attic, and that conversation has worked its way into Alissa's subconscious. Even as a psychologist, I'm still amazed by the way dreams thread parts of our days into them.

Grateful that the children had taken baths at their grandparents' house and were already in their pajamas, Sarah tucked each one into bed and quietly shut their bedroom doors. Evan had his own room, but Elaina and Alissa shared one. She'd given them the option of having their own, but both girls were adamant that they share a bedroom.

One day they'll be glad to have their own spaces, but look at those sweet angels sleeping in their matching pink and white canopy beds.

Before going to bed herself, Sarah remembered the light she'd left on in her office. Trudging up the stairs, the activity of the day caught up with her as well. A nice hot bath and a glass of the fruity wine she had chilling in the refrigerator sounded like the perfect end to the day.

Her heart stopped when she reached her office door. *The lights being on could have been sheer forgetfulness on my part, but I know I closed those curtains.*

Sarah quickly walked across the room and jerked the curtains shut, making sure she completely covered the window. As she turned, she stubbed her toe on something. The box of porcelain dolls sat askew from the door of the closet where she'd left it, and to her surprise, an auburn-haired doll sat propped against the wall.

Could it have tumbled out of the box? Yes. But what were the odds that it would land sitting upright, as though it was carefully placed?

I must be more tired than I thought.

Sarah placed the doll back in the box, which she scooted with the toe of her tennis shoe until it once again was wedged against the now-closed closet door.

Her alarm sounded early the next morning. With school starting in a week, Sarah knew she had to invest some time in setting up her office at work, familiarizing herself with the student files, and beginning the online classes she needed to get her Missouri certification. The odd events of the night before were forgotten as she stumbled to the shower.

Mom will be here soon to watch the kids, so at least I don't have to worry about getting them out of bed.

After a quick once-over in the mirror, she decided the dress she'd picked out was a little too formal for a day she'd spend sorting files and arranging office furniture.

Instead, she switched into a pair of slacks, a flowered blouse, and slipped on sandals instead of the heels sitting at the foot of her bed.

Once at school, she was greeted by the school secretary, Tina Mathews, who casually watered plants in the school foyer. Setting down the watering can, Tina extended a hand and a smile to the school's newcomer.

"Hello, Sarah. We haven't gotten to visit much since you arrived in Arrington. I wanted to let you know that I'm here to help you if you need anything."

"That's good to know, Tina. Thank you. Everyone's been helpful so far."

"Well, that's because most of us are related." Tina gave a quick chuckle before adding, "You know we're cousins, don't you?"

Sarah hadn't given much thought to the family connections she had in the area. Arrington was never part of her life before she'd moved back to Missouri.

"I didn't know that."

"Yes, we share the same paternal grandparents. I was Tina Washington before Blake and I married. I thought maybe your parents had told you."

"Mom and Dad don't really talk about the family here."

A flitter of uneasiness crossed Tina's face. "Oh, I'm sorry I brought it up. I'd forgotten about the bad blood between our parents." She turned to go.

"Why is that?" Sarah had a sudden drive to delve into the family she never knew.

"Why is what?"

"Why don't our families get along anymore? Dad never talked about it. Mom never looked like she wanted him to, either."

"It's all a bunch of silliness, really."

"I'd like to hear what caused the hard feelings."

"I don't know the whole story, Sarah, but there was some wild rumor about our great-grandmother that divided the family. You know, just old wives' tales."

"Old wives' tales?"

Tina hushed her voice and leaned into Sarah. "Rumor had it that our great-grandmother, Clida Washington, dabbled in insanity and witchcraft. It all started after her infant daughter died mysteriously. It drove her mad. She talked non-stop about bringing her back from the dead. It made for a great Halloween story, complete with chicken blood and grave dust." Tina gave Sarah a wink.

The map!

"It was just a bunch of superstitious nonsense that upset the older generations, Sarah. I'm sure you and I can become good friends. We will talk more later. Right now, I have a stack of reports I need to send out for the district. Let's catch up again soon. I'm so glad you are back in Arrington."

With that, Tina slipped back into her office, leaving Sarah with new questions--and an uneasiness that dampened her mood for the rest of the morning. A cold breeze of distress blew through Sarah's thoughts as she recalled the odd turn of events at home the night before.

Unsettled, Sarah made her way to her office and kept busy with what seemed like a hundred tasks to complete before school started the next week. The words of her new-found cousin nagged in the back of her mind all day, and when five o'clock rolled around, Sarah still hadn't come to grips with the family history Tina sprang on her that morning.

I can see why Dad's family wouldn't want any part of that nonsense. Now I know why Mom and Dad would never answer my questions. It's creepy to even think about it. But, as Tina said, it was most likely nothing more than a rumor that was blown out of proportions.

Rationalizing the issue, Sarah felt more at ease. She gathered a few items to review at home and headed out the door. She was eager to get home.

Home. Life has changed so quickly, but I do think the kids and I are home.

Evan and Elaina rushed to meet her as she pulled in the drive, and her mother stepped onto the porch with Alissa in tow. Hugs and smiles were exchanged, and the luscious smells coming from the kitchen made Sarah realize just how hungry she was.

"Mom, you're making your famous chicken casserole. You know that's my favorite."

"I figured it was the least I could do while you were off working so hard. Knowing you, you skipped lunch."

Sarah nodded. "Yeah, I did, actually."

"Go change into something more comfortable and meet us down here for dinner. I made pie too."

Over dinner they shared their stories of the day. Evan had caught a frog. Elaina and Alissa picked flowers in their field. Grandma had kept them busy with songs and a nature walk. They looked happy.

"Oh, Sarah, I do have to ask you, though. Last night we were talking about your old porcelain doll that had been your great-grandmother's. I didn't know you'd found it."

"I haven't, though, Mom."

"But it was on Alissa's dresser when I got here this morning."

"I don't know what you're talking about. I didn't put a doll in Alissa's room. And how would you know it was the one from when I was little?"

"Well, it was there, in the same dress it always had with your name embroidered on the tag."

Sarah's heart ran cold. "Can you show me?"

"Alissa, why don't you bring Grandma and your mama the doll?"

Alissa arrived in the dining room carrying the same auburn-haired doll that was out of the box the night before.

I know I put that doll in the box.

"Kids, are you sure none of you put this doll on Alissa's dresser?"

"No, Mama, we didn't." They all shook their heads with sincerity.

"See, Sarah, here is your name embroidered on the tag of the doll's dress. Your dad's mother gave you this doll when you were two."

"I don't see how that's possible. I found that doll in the attic of this house. Which reminds me of something. Did you know Dad's family owned this place? They built this house in 1838."

"I didn't, but I'm not surprised. Your dad has family all over this county."

Once again, Sarah tried to shake the fear rising in her chest. A change of mood was needed. "Hey, kids, let's take our pie into the living room and watch Disney movies."

The three children cheered as they grabbed their plates and raced each other into the other room to claim their spots in front of the television. The night passed with nothing more than happy conversation and goodnight hugs as their grandmother left for Glenwood.

For the rest of the week, Sarah and Katherine repeated the routine. A few days passed before Sarah gave the eerie events a thought. On Thursday night, however, an incident happened that flooded her with dread and fear once again.

Children will have accidents, that's true, but what Sarah witnessed didn't feel like an accident. As she waited at the bottom of the stairs for the children to come down for dinner, Evan fell, landing at her feet.

Evan didn't fall. He was pushed.

"Mama! Mama! Something grabbed my arm and pushed me. You saw, right?" Evan crumpled at the foot of the stairwell in tears, holding his left elbow.

"Now, Evan, are you sure you didn't slip?" Grandma Katherine bent down to console him.

"No, Grandma. I even tried to grab the railing, and it jerked me away from it."

Sarah knelt down and checked Evan for injuries. Thankfully, other than some bumps and scrapes, he seemed fine. She seated the children at the dinner table.

"Mom, can I talk with you for a minute?"

Sarah and Katherine stepped into the kitchen.

"I was standing there watching when Evan fell. He's right. I saw him being jerked down the stairs."

"Could one of the girls have pushed him?"

"No. They were at least five feet away from him when this happened. I'm starting to get horrible feelings about this place. I told you what Tina Mathews said."

"Sarah, honey, don't you put any stock into what Tina says. I knew her mother, and I'm not surprised that they would propagate that sort of thing. To be honest, your father's side of the family has several odd personalities in it, and that's why his parents broke ties with the whole batch of them. After meeting some of them, Garret and I agreed that we'd keep our family distanced from them too. Don't worry yourself. This was a childhood fall and nothing more. You had your fair share when you were his age, too."

"But what about the doll appearing on Alissa's dresser?"

Katherine paused. "I don't have an explanation for that, but maybe the other kids just didn't want to admit they'd messed with something you had stored in your office. They know that kind of thing bothers you."

"Yeah, maybe."

"Let's eat dinner before it gets cold."

The next week work began in earnest, and Evan, Elaina, and Alissa started school in their new town. Sarah met their teachers and was impressed with each of them. The children enjoyed their classes, and they filled the evenings with stories about friends they made, new things they learned, and recess adventures.

Maybe I did overreact to all the hocus-pocus nonsense Tina told me. She seems friendly enough at work and was probably just teasing me.

The odd incidents didn't stop, however.

Lights turned on by themselves in the old house. Footsteps could now be heard in the attic. Evan came to Sarah one night worried because he could hear a woman crying upstairs. Alissa would giggle and wave at empty space.

And that damned doll always seemed to be staring at me. It doesn't stay where I put it, either.

Most disturbing were the cuts and bruises that appeared on the children. Scratches, bite marks, and dried blood afflicted them each morning, and they were now terrified to sleep in their rooms.

For two months, Sarah's life spiraled down a funnel of fear and unease. Bad dreams kept her from sleeping, and she tossed and turned worrying about what it all meant.

Then one night, waking from a vivid nightmare, she could no longer resist the urge to go back to the attic. Somehow she knew her doll waited for her there, and she did.

"There, there, my baby Grace. It's all going to be okay."

Sarah rocked the smiling doll and smoothed her auburn hair.

"Mama isn't going to let anything happen to you now. I got rid of those other children. It's just us now."

Sarah picked up a pencil and began drawing a map on the wall.

A short time later, Katherine, who forgot her purse at the Washington house on Willow Street, arrived in time to find the bodies of her grandchildren laid carefully on the ground in the yard. Her screams alerted neighbors who called the local authorities.

With the blue police lights flashing through the windows, Sarah Washington Crane caressed baby Grace and sang her a lullaby. Her hands smeared the blood of Evan, Elaina, and Alissa on the face of the doll whose eyes glowed with joy.

On the outskirts of town, another song was sung. This one, a chant with a pulsating rhythm, filled the night air. It was a special song. One handed down for generations. Not everyone in the family was chosen to carry on the Old World traditions, but enough had continued in the sprawling family tree to keep it, and the spirit of baby Grace, alive.

As she sang, a smiling Tina Clida Washington Mathews sprinkled chicken blood on the grave of her great-grandmother.

INTO THE NIGHT

The crunching gravel beneath his feet in the pitch blackness of the night unnerved Clarence Schiffler, even as he swore this was a necessary trip. Never a fan of the dark to begin with, the added stress of the evening made his long walk down the deserted dirt road even less appealing.

His day hadn't begun badly. In fact, he awoke that morning from a much-needed sleep with the knowledge that this was his day. Life was finally turning a corner for him, and that brought peace to his weary soul.

Work had been mundane for many years, and he was eager for the opportunity to advance. Not everyone was able to, and the awareness that he'd reached the cusp of that accomplishment gave him satisfaction.

He'd followed in the footsteps of his father and grandfather, as they had their predecessors. It wasn't as though he had any choice. Family expectations and societal demands required that he do his duty. He'd accepted the responsibility of the family business and, while he had regrets, he worked hard to be a success.

What Clarence had really wanted to be was a concert pianist. The joy he felt as his fingers danced across the ivory keys couldn't be found in the drudgery of his career. At times he secretly wished he'd been rebellious enough to break out of the family mold, but Clarence wasn't made of that kind of bravery.

As a child, he begged his parents for a piano and lessons, and they finally caved to his pleading. He was quite good, if he did say so himself. He had to be careful with his prized piano, however. His family lived behind a funeral home, and Clarence needed to be respectful during business hours. He couldn't plink on the piano or break into a thundering rendition of Mozart while mourners gathered to make arrangements or to hold a service. Yes, there were drawbacks to living so close to a mortuary, but his father insisted their locale made getting to his job easier, and who was Clarence to buck adult logic?

Of course, that was years ago, and Clarence had put aside his dreams of playing to a packed auditorium. His father was a workaholic and expected the same from his son. Now, here Clarence was, all grown up with responsibilities and job concerns of his own. Thoughts of those responsibilities brought Clarence back to the present and his lonely walk down this dark and isolated one-track dirt road somewhere between his car and his destination.

Three miles may not sound like much of a walk unless you've been placed in Clarence's shoes. Walking and stumbling through the darkness on a loose gravel road for that distance was no enjoyable stroll. Clarence wasn't the kind to venture off by himself for nature walks during daylight hours, so he felt especially uncomfortable hiking down a dirt road at night. The road meandered through a remote wooded area and was rougher than he was comfortable walking down A recent rain cut ruts into the ground, and more than once Clarence turned his ankle on a rock. Limping only further slowed his progress.

He knew he shouldn't be afraid of the dark, but he was. No grown man should be afraid of a night like this, but Clarence accepted that he was weak, and he lived with the shame of his phobias. He'd spent his life being mocked and ridiculed by family members. They called him "a sissy" and "a scaredy cat." Their comments stung him to this day, so he kept his fears secret now. His face reddened just thinking of the joke he'd become within his family.

Just then, something reached out from the darkness and softly stroked his arm. In another step, it happened again. His heart rate quickened and a sense of panic overtook him.

That was nothing more than the branch of a blackberry bush. I must have walked too close to the edge of the road.

Satisfied with that rationalization, Clarence moved a few steps to the left and continued. He had to make better time if he was to make it to the warehouse to meet his clients. This was a major account, and his bosses made it clear that his future with the firm depended upon his performance tonight. Make the clients happy, and that promotion was his. Screw it up, and his name was out of consideration.

This would all be so simple if my car hadn't broken down just as I turned off the highway. How was I supposed to see that log lying across the road? I've probably wrecked the oil pan or torn some hoses loose. Whatever it was, fluid leaked everywhere. I can't worry about that right now, though. I have to get to the warehouse.

Clarence glanced around him into the pitch blackness. The evening had not gone well and even included a fight with his girlfriend. She didn't think he took her out to eat enough.

"You're in the food business, Clarence, and you never bother to take me anywhere nice. A girl likes to be treated sometimes. My ex-boyfriend, Herb, he always took me out."

Well, that was enough to set Clarence off. He was sick and tired of being compared to Herb, the good-looking, womanizing jerk of her past. The last thing he needed was for Brenda to nag at him or to sing Herb's praises. His self-esteem was tenuous enough.

To make matters worse, thunderheads now lit up with lightning. Storms were another of Clarence's fears. While his family loved a good thunderstorm and would stand in the yard watching them, Clarence stayed inside, usually hugging his pillow and wondering if it was okay for a grown man to suck his thumb. It wasn't, by the way. The one time he tried his little sister walked in and he became the butt of jokes for years.

"Hey, Clarence, it's about to storm. That really *sucks*, doesn't it?"

His family was full of assholes, Clarence decided. He picked up his pace, hoping to be finished with his business transaction before the first raindrop fell. At least his thoughts kept him busy as he made his way closer and closer to the warehouse. That gave him less time to dwell on what touched his arm earlier. It was harder and harder to fool himself into believing it was a blackberry bush. After what seemed like an eternity, he stopped to get his bearings.

Turn right at the intersection. Okay, I think I'm there.

Lightning flashed in the sky, giving him enough of a chance to recognize that he was, indeed, at the intersection. He turned the corner, relieved to see the lights of his client's vehicle turning into the parking lot of the warehouse. His spirits lifted. Heck, he might even pick up a snack for himself while he was there.

A smile broke over his face as he read the wrought-iron sign looming above him. "Eastwood Cemetery." Yes, he'd made it to the warehouse in time to close the deal and get that promotion he'd waited so long for. His walk into the night had paid off.

Being a ghoul wasn't easy, but tonight it felt pretty good.

HERE'S LOOKIN' AT YOU KID

Birds sang in the trees, a bright blue sky lit up the world, and the smell of freshly cut hay permeated the air. It made for a perfect summer day. The kind that six-year-old boys live for. Adventure was out there, and Jonah Pyle rode his bike down the quiet dirt road in search of it. No stranger to adventure, he knew where he was going, and he was prepared.

A bungee cord held his fishing rod and tackle box in place on the rack behind his seat. He headed for the pond on the backside of his grandfather's farm. His family went fishing often, but this spot was his favorite, and he considered it his own. He became lost in his own little world at the pond, and thanks to his independent streak, he rejoiced in the quiet freedom of the place. No whiny little sister. No bossy older brother. Just Jonah and whatever fun he could find.

Sometimes he caught minnows or tadpoles. Other times he skipped rocks or hiked through the pasture with the wind in his hair. Today was a fishing day.

The bluegill should be biting good today.

He turned right at the gate, opened it, and pushed his bike into the field. Hopping back on, he rode the quarter of a mile to the pond. The docile Jersey cows glanced his direction as they chewed their cuds and ate grass.

I'm sure glad Grandpa moved his bull to the other field, or I wouldn't be coming in here.

He slid to a stop at the top of the pond bank and unhooked the fishing pole and tackle box from the rack. A kingfisher chirped and a flock of wild mallards flapped their wings as they skittered to the other side of the pond in a chorus of quacks.

Jonah opened his tackle box and grinned the kind of grin made by those recently visited by the Tooth Fairy. His eyes lit up when he looked over his collection of lures. His birthday was last month, and his mom and dad treated him to a shopping spree at Bass Pro Shops. Of course, he'd headed straight for the fishing section.

Pulling out a lure that caught his eye, he attached it to his line and jumped off the bank, landing right at the water's edge. A water bug scampered away, leaving a ripple in the water's surface. Jonah leaned over to watch the ripples spread into an ever-increasing ring. As the water calmed, he was surprised by his reflection.

Standing next to him was a man who smiled back at him. Jonah jerked upright and looked all around him. No one was there, but when he looked at his reflection, the smiling man remained.

"Whoa…" Jonah didn't know what else to say.

The man then spoke. "Hello, Jonah. My name is Eddie. I'd like to be your new friend."

"Who are you? How did you know my name?"

"Relax. It's okay. I'm just someone who appreciates a good imagination, and you have one."

Jonah looked around him, unsure if running was his best bet.

"You don't need to be afraid of me. Hey, would you like to know where the fish are hiding out today? I can show you."

Jonah hesitated.

"It's okay. Come on. They're going to love that lure you're using."

Jonah stood straight. Eddie was now visible to him, standing alongside him on the bank.

"Come on. I'll show you where they're at. It'll be our secret."

Jonah doubted whether or not he should follow Eddie, but he did. Under a large white oak, Eddie pointed to some tree limbs that were submerged about ten feet out into the pond.

"Cast right out there, right this side of that big limb."

Sure enough, on the first cast, a large bluegill took the bait. Excited, Jonah reeled it in and admired it in the glistening sun.

"That's a pretty one, Jonah."

The little boy smiled and said, "It sure is. I'm going to let him go. I only catch-and-release in Grandpa's pond."

"Oh, I agree. Now let's see how you do on the next cast."

Time after time, the bobber dove under the water as the fish bit better than Jonah had ever seen them bite before. Three hours later, after the two new friends had talked about fishing and growing up in the country, it was time for Jonah to head home.

"Say, have you ever fished in Baker Creek?"

Jonah nodded enthusiastically. "We go there lots."

"Could you join me tomorrow? I'll show you my favorite spot. You'll have as much fun then as you did today."

Jonah thought for a moment. His forehead wrinkled as he squinted into the sun to look up at Eddie.

"Yeah, I can go. Where do you want to meet?"

"How about you meet me at the gate to this pasture? I know a shortcut to get to the creek. Say at noon?"

"I'll be there!" Jonah strapped his pole and tackle box to his bike.

"Just one thing, Jonah. Don't say anything to anyone about me. Folks sometimes get worried about strangers."

"You're not a stranger. We're friends, Eddie."

"Yes, we are. It's just best if you don't say anything. Okay?"

"Okay."

"Alright. Now you get on home. I'll see you tomorrow."

As promised, the next day, and every other day Jonah could get away for an adventure, Eddie met him at the designated spot.

One time, when telling his parents about his day of fishing, Jonah let it slip.

"Who's Eddie?" His mother stopped wiping down the countertop and stared at him.

Jonah froze.

"You've never mentioned him before. Who is he?"

Thinking quickly, Jonah said, "It's kind of embarrassing, Mom. He's my imaginary friend." He dropped his head.

She tousled his hair. "Don't be embarrassed. It's normal to have imaginary friends."

"It is?" Jonah wondered if maybe he'd made Eddie up in his mind.

"Yes, it is. Now go on out and tell your dad to come in for lunch."

After that, if Jonah mentioned anything about Eddie, his family smiled and gave each other knowing looks and nods. Meanwhile, Eddie appeared during all of Jonah's adventures. Over time, he appeared wherever Jonah was, but no one else could see him.

This continued, and the two became virtually inseparable. Eddie accompanied Jonah to school on most days. Eddie turned out to be a mischief maker.

"Hey, watch this," he whispered into Jonah's ear.

Eddie walked over to Kyle Sinclair's desk and jerked his chair out from under him just as he was about to sit down. The whole class laughed, including Jonah and Eddie. On another day, he tripped Paul Hadley as he walked down the aisle. Once again, everyone laughed as the embarrassed boy pulled himself off the floor.

On the playground at recess, Eddie became increasingly rough. He pushed children to the ground, even from the swings when they were in midair. He climbed to the top of the monkey bars and pushed Mike Whitley off. The thud of Mike hitting the ground garnered everyone's attention, but it was the cracking sound of a compound fracture that caused everyone to gasp in horror. Complete silence settled across the playground, except for the agonizing screams of Mike Whitley and the hysterical laughter of Eddie.

Jonah glared at his invisible friend. "What's wrong with you?"

"Lighten up, kid. It's all in good fun."

"Mike's really hurt."

"He'll get over it."

Over time, several children had incidents to "get over." Considering the number of injuries children suffered at recess, the school made an unprecedented decision.

"Boys and girls, I hate to announce this, but for the remainder of the school year recess will be spent inside your classrooms. We don't want any more children having accidents. From now until we get out of school for the summer, we will have art and music enrichment instead." Mr. Halpert, the school principal, made the announcement over the intercom.

The children grumbled, but even they were relieved. Too many had been hurt, and frankly, they were traumatized by the injuries they'd seen. The most traumatized was Jonah who witnessed every fall, cut, and broken bone. The most disappointed person in the room was Eddie.

Months crept by, and finally summer vacation arrived. Daily fishing trips resumed. Occasionally, Eddie tipped canoes over or took part in other acts of minor mayhem. Usually it was nothing serious, but it still bothered Jonah. As the summer ended, Jonah knew he needed to say something to Eddie.

"Uh, hey. I've been thinking."

"What about?"

"When school starts."

Eddie rubbed his hands together and grinned.

"No, Eddie, that's what I'm talking about. You can't just go around hurting the other kids."

"All I was doing was having a little fun."

"I don't think it's fun."

"You laughed when I did things."

"I laughed when you tripped people or pulled chairs out from under them, but it wasn't funny when you broke Mike's arm or cut Tim Collins."

Eddie stared at the pond. "Just what are you saying?"

"I think maybe you should stay home. I'll see you after school."

Eddie's temper flared. He threw a log far out into the water then stood with his back to Jonah, hands on his hips, breathing deeply. Slowly he turned. Through clenched jaws he said, "Fine. Have it your way. I'll stay home."

"Thanks, Eddie. It'll help me pay attention better too. I have a lot of fun with you, but mom's worried I'm not reading as well as I should be. She talked about making me get a tutor."

Eddie ruffled Jonah's hair. "We don't want that to happen. Sure, I'll see you after school. Remember, I'm always here for you. Now let's go catch some fish."

The two walked around the pond to enjoy an afternoon of catch-and-release.

Years went by. Sometimes Eddie was on good behavior. Sometimes he wasn't. His level of aggression seemed to worsen as Jonah reached his teenage years. This became clear one summer day when Jonah was sixteen, and he and Eddie decided to swim in Baker Creek. A popular swimming hole lay directly beneath the McCarver Road bridge. Teenagers for years flaunted their bravery by diving into it. Bravery was needed. To either side of the pool were heavy stones. Dive a few feet off target, and serious injury or death were likely. Someone drew a red line on the side of the bridge alerting young divers to the only safe launching point.

On that day, Andy Callahan, the school's quarterback and all around macho jerk, was also at the bridge. In his normal abrasive way, he pushed other kids around and threatened those he felt he could intimidate.

Jonah wasn't big, and he wasn't athletic. He'd inherited his mother's thin frame. Standing no more than five and a half feet, he made an easy target for the looming Andy. He was used to the constant taunts and jabs. Today, however, Andy set his sights on Tommy Parker. Jonah knew Tommy came from an abusive home, and seeing Andy bully him angered Jonah. Tommy's spirit was already crushed at home. He didn't need to be tormented at a place that was supposed to be fun.

"Hey, Callahan, back off!" Jonah walked to the edge of the bridge. Andy's threat to throw Tommy off the side was the last straw.

"Oh, yeah? Just what are you going to do about it?"

A heated argument broke out, and they shoved each other back and forth. Other teenagers stood in stunned silence. They wondered why any of them never stood up to Andy. Several of the other football players were present, and any of them would have been able to contend with Andy Callahan. Here was Jonah, however, half of Andy's size, defending someone else. None of the teenagers moved as they watched Jonah confront the bully.

As the scuffle continued, Andy shoved Jonah and he fell to the ground. Standing, Jonah hit Andy's chest with both hands, pushing him toward the edge of the bridge, to the right of the red line. At the exact same moment, Eddie ran full force into the much larger boy, knocking his legs out from under him. Down to the edge of the pool Andy fell. A snapping sound crackled through the air, and the lifeless body of Andy Callahan floated to the top of the water. Onlookers screamed.

Jonah turned to the smiling Eddie. "What did you do that for? You killed him!"

"I told you, Jonah. I'm always here for you. I wasn't going to let a jerk like him treat you like that. I just took care of the problem."

Jonah's stomach turned.

Hannah Carlisle, Andy's girlfriend, screamed. "You killed him, Jonah! You pushed him off. We all saw you kill him!"

A crowd gathered around Andy's body as other members of the football team pulled him to shore. Andy's best friend, Gabe, yelled from below. "Call an ambulance!"

The police arrived along with the paramedics, and they told Jonah they needed to take him down to the station for questioning. "You're not under arrest, son. We just need to ask you some questions." Officer Harris walked Jonah to the squad car.

Three hours later, Sheriff McGee walked into the interrogation room. "After talking to the other kids, it's pretty clear this wasn't intentional. We've called your mom and dad, and they're here to take you home, Jonah."

Eddie winked at him.

Word spread across the county of Andy Callahan's death and of Jonah's angry outburst that preceded it. People talked in hushed whispers when Jonah walked by. Once friendly store owners now viewed the Pyle family with sideways glances and greeted them with polite, but cool, exchanges. Andy's father was the president of the local Chamber of Commerce. Accident or no accident, the son of a prominent family was dead at the hands of Jonah Pyle.

If only it had been an isolated incident.

Frequently, Jonah happened to be near someone who was seriously hurt or killed. Victims claimed they saw him step in front of vehicles on curvy highways, causing accidents. At those times, Eddie dragged him into traffic.

"Don't worry, kid. I won't let them hurt you."

Sometimes all it took was for Jonah to walk past someone for them to fly into the path of oncoming cars. Eddie was, once again, to blame. Jonah couldn't take it anymore, and arguments broke out between the two.

"I want you to go away. Leave me alone!"

"That's not the way this works, Jonah. We're friends. I'm not going to leave you."

"Just what are you anyway? You aren't an imaginary friend."

"No, I'm as real as you are."

"But no one else can see you. Are you a demon?"

Eddie laughed an odd chuckle. "No, I'm not a demon. At least not in reality. You humans would mistake me for one, though."

"I don't understand. What are you then?"

"There's a lot you won't understand, Jonah, but I belong here too. I'm an interdimensional traveler. I occupy the same space as humans, just in a different way. I choose to be seen by you."

"You have to stop doing these horrible things to people."

"Why?"

"*Why?* Because you are hurting and killing people."

"That's not my concern."

"You're making people think I'm a monster."

"Yeah, well, isn't everyone a monster in their own sort of way?"

"Eddie, go away."

"No."

No amount of pleading by Jonah made Eddie leave. Day and night, he was by Jonah's side. It wrecked the boy emotionally and physically. He couldn't eat. He couldn't sleep. He was failing all his classes during his senior year. To onlookers, he appeared to be the stereotypical troubled teen. People gossiped.

"It's just too coincidental. I think that boy is evil."

"I think the boy's on drugs. I mean, just look at how he is. Losing weight. Withdrawn. He's nothing like that sweet kid we used to know."

The rumors flew. Local authorities took interest in Jonah, and anytime a tragic accident happened, the first person they thought of was Jonah Pyle. Too often, he was in the area when someone was hurt or killed, and the entire community became fearful of him. Even property loss was blamed on him. If someone's lawn mower went missing, Jonah was sure to have a visit from local police.

The final straw happened six months after Jonah turned eighteen. He'd pulled off the side of the road, getting out of his vehicle to talk to Ike Guthrie. The affable old man was a town favorite, and everyone knew and loved him. That morning he walked out of his woods carrying the wild turkey he'd harvested moments before during the fall hunting season. Ike had long been one of Jonah's grandfather's best friends.

"Hey, Ike. That's a nice looking tom you got there."

Ike grinned. "Jonah, I've been after this ol' boy for years. I finally got him. Look at the size of his beard."

"He'll make a great dinner. I haven't seen you for a while, and I thought I'd say hello."

Eddie rolled his eyes.

Just then, Margaret Fisk came driving along Old Mill Road. She slowed to avoid Jonah's vehicle, and she watched as Jonah and Ike talked on the side of the road. She jumped when a loud boom shook the air.

Ike Guthrie's twelve-gauge shotgun fired, blowing the poor man's head to pieces. Margaret screamed and sped off, fearful that Jonah would turn the gun on her. As soon as she was safely out of sight, she hit the emergency button on her On-Star system.

"What's the emergency?"

"I just saw a man shot to death on Old Mill Road. Please, send help!"

"We're notifying the authorities now, ma'am. Stay on the line with me. Do you feel safe?"

"No. I'm scared."

"Stay on the line with us, Mrs. Fisk. Keep driving until you come to someplace you feel safe, then park. I won't get off the line with you."

The sirens blared as the officers found Jonah crouching on the ground, crying next to the body of Ike Guthrie. The deputies approached with caution.

"He's shouting to someone who isn't even here, calling out to an 'Eddie.' Just who do you think he's talking to, Mitch?"

"I don't know, but call dispatch and let them know we have someone who's either crazy or strung out on drugs."

The trial was speedy, lasting only two days. Jonah had no defense other than to say that it was Eddie's fault. When questioned, the best his mother could come up with on the stand was that Eddie had been Jonah's imaginary childhood friend.

The prosecuting attorney grilled him in court. "Mr. Pyle, did you know it was wrong for Ike Guthrie to be shot dead?"

"I didn't do it."

"That's not what I asked you. I asked if you knew it was wrong for Ike Guthrie to be shot."

"Yes, it was wrong."

"Did you know it was wrong at the time of the shooting?"

"Yes."

"Your Honor and members of the jury, I ask you to disregard any claim of innocence by reason of insanity. The defendant has testified in court that he knew it was wrong. He knew the difference between right and wrong then, and he knows it now. Given this young man's prior behavior in our community, there is no other reasonable assumption to make than that he intentionally killed Ike Guthrie. This was nothing but a cold-blooded murder."

The jury took only an hour to return with a decision. "Your Honor, we the jury find the defendant, Jonah Lee Pyle, guilt of murder in the first degree."

His mother wept, but cheers erupted in the courtroom. At his sentencing hearing, Jonah received a life sentence without the possibility of parole.

***

The door slammed to cell D-321. Jonah Pyle, now known as Inmate 45281, sat on his bunk as the guard in the wing yelled, "Lights out!"

The darkness was complete. A familiar voice spoke. "Jonah, my boy, I've enjoyed our time together. It's a shame you had to take the fall for my actions, but you are a mere human and your life is expendable. I will be leaving now. There's no fun to be found sitting inside a prison cell for the rest of your life."

"I hate you, Eddie!"

"Good. Good. As if that matters to me. Goodbye, Jonah."

***

The next day, Tyler Adams, six years old and full of adventure, tossed rocks into the river. He leaned over to pick up a nice stone for skipping and saw his reflection.

A smiling man stood next to him. "Hello, Tyler. My name is Eddie. I'd like to be your new friend."

A FEW TICKS OF THE CLOCK

"In a galaxy far, far away." Darcy Chilton laughed at the quote he had taped to the top of his dashboard. It came from a movie he'd once seen as a small boy. The film was old even when his father was a child, but modern technology made it possible to not only preserve, but enhance, the quality of obsolete media. How old was he when he saw it? Seven or eight at most. His favorite character was the big hairy beast. He couldn't help but hum the theme song as he adjusted his seat and checked his instruments.

It wasn't accidental that Darcy recalled that movie. The beeping lights and warm buzz of the electronics covering his ship's dash reminded him what his mission was. He and several of his colleagues were on their most vital assignment, and it came at a critical time for mankind. Their commanders, also familiar with the classic cinematic story, dubbed this mission "The Death Star."

Not long ago, the first inkling of trouble arrived. It seemed innocent enough. A faint signal from a distant solar system, nothing more than a few blips on a frequency never utilized on Earth, was detected. Scientists from around the world swarmed to Old New Mexico, the name the state of Libertad used to be known as. A few generations had passed since the United States of his grandfather's youth existed. The search for extraterrestrial life had continued in that area despite changes in political boundaries, and the antennas outside Old Socorro still scanned the skies for proof that life outside our solar system existed. Well, it did.

Less than three months after the first blips were heard, contact was made. A small, seemingly harmless, unmanned ship arrived. Onboard were gifts for any civilization that it came upon. New types of electronics just waiting for the eager hands of engineers to tinker with, mysterious plaques engraved with writing that captivated linguists, and a cryptic music that played constantly from the craft all mesmerized our planet. Strangely, some of the engraved figures resembled ancient Egyptian hieroglyphics, further exciting the masses. Could they be our link to the ancient world?

Then hell broke loose. A month after the unmanned ship arrived, a swarm of battlecraft appeared, and these were definitely manned--if you could call the beings "men." Whatever they were, it didn't take long to realize their intentions weren't friendly. All of the hoopla about connecting with benevolent beings from another planet flew out the window. These creatures were not looking for peaceful cohabitation. Anyone who doubted as much were convinced when multitudes of aggressive crafts began circling Earth. Thankfully, our governments had invested in a space shield, what the renowned historical leader Ronald Reagan called "Star Wars" technology. Our shields and space forces managed to fight off the raiders. Peace wouldn't last long, however, as our satellites detected a large menacing mothership heading our direction. Its dimensions were more massive than our moon, and potentially millions of invaders were at our celestial doorstep.

Far too late, scientists realized that those gifts on the expeditionary craft were used as tracking beacons. Once the gadgets were turned on (which the scientists had prematurely prided themselves over), the home planet forces knew exactly where to set their sights. Sometimes we humans forgot the lessons of the Trojan Horse.

Now, our last chance at survival was in the hands of the elite space squadrons, and this explained the current challenge faced by our hopeful hero, Captain Darcy Chilton. He checked his coordinates, relayed flight information to his squad commander, and drew a bead on the Death Star defenders who streamed from the mothership to attack the incoming rapid-force destroyers.

Firefights, desperate maneuvers, and breakneck efforts went on for what seemed like hours, but it amounted to less than forty-five minutes in real time. At those speeds, seconds dragged, and fear heightened the awareness of every detail experienced by Captain Chilton and his comrades. One by one, Earth's forces were eliminated until only a handful of fighters remained.

Darcy approached the cavernous hull of the Death Star, relying upon instinct and navigational equipment, just as the fictional hero in that long-ago movie had. As the last visible friendly ship blew up in his rearview mirror, Darcy became more determined to find the weak spot of the enemy. Then he recognized his mark. An exhaust duct, larger than ten of Darcy's ships, loomed in front of him. Enemy fighters shot near misses, and he knew he couldn't outrun them for long. With no time left, he had to make a valiant move. Darcy programmed his craft to glide into the entrance and then self-destruct.

***

As we watch the monitors at Mission Control, the thirty-second delay leaves us wondering if his efforts were enough. In a few ticks of the clock, we will know if we live, or if we die.

1472 NORTH SYCAMORE LANE

The winter of 1945 warmed with a jubilance no bitter frost could touch. We had won the war, and our boys returned from the battlefront, eager to regain a normal life. War brides returned with some soldiers, while childhood sweethearts wed in simple ceremonies back home. No one felt the need for folderol. After all, the dark days of the Great Depression were still fresh in the minds of everyone. Instead of postponing nuptials for elaborate public displays, many couples preferred to embrace the simplicity and excitement of a new era. Such was the case for Ellie and Emmett Fields, the newlyweds who moved into 1472 North Sycamore Lane on a brisk December morning. Their short honeymoon to the coastal Carolinas was over, and now Mr. and Mrs. Fields were content to settle into their new life.

Their life together was new, but their surroundings were not. I had known Ellie since she was a newborn. Her parents moved into the family home, built by the Caster side of the clan just after the Civil War. Always a bright and cheerful child, she could be found picking daisies in the backyard or playing hide and seek with her friends in the expansive rooms of her beloved home.

"I'm never leaving this house," she told her mother at breakfast one morning when she was a mere five years old.

"Oh, really, young miss? What happens when Prince Charming arrives on his white horse to take you to his castle?" Her mother, Lois Caster, smiled at her determined little girl.

"I won't go."

"You won't go if Prince Charming wants to marry you?"

"No. He will have to live with me here on Sycamore Lane."

Lois gave her daughter a peck on the cheek and tousled her hair. "You know this house stays in the family, and heaven knows your brother has no interest in living here after he finishes school, so you are welcome to this castle."

Ellie grinned, and her missing front tooth revealed a pink tongue. She was delighted at the idea of making this her castle, and she never let go of that dream.

Ellie spent her childhood days imagining she was a character inside the elaborate tales she spun as she played or sat watching the fire in the living room. She read books by the hour and whiled away sunny afternoons in the woods found just past the boundary of the backyard. Don't get me wrong. She was social, too. Friends were numerous, and Ellie was invited to her fair share of parties as she grew up. That's how she met Emmett.

He was a fine-looking young man, two years older than she was. He attended school in the neighboring town of Alton, which was why they hadn't met sooner. In those days, young people didn't travel any great distance from home. Jake Olsen's eighteenth birthday party brought them together one April evening. It was love at first sight, as the saying goes, and those two were inseparable until the

Japanese bombed Pearl Harbor, and Emmett answered the call to defend our country. Emmett Fields was a good man.

After the war ended, Ellie's parents moved to Chicago to be closer to her brother, Dale, his wife, Laura, and their two young children. The war separated them, too, and now that Dale attended the university under the G.I. Bill, and Laura was already expecting their third child, Ellie's parents, Lois and Henry, decided it was time to be closer to the grandchildren. The elder Casters tired of the same routine and now believed a change of scenery would be good for them. Dale, who was always Henry's favorite, appreciated their help around his place. Ellie didn't take offense to her parents' departure. It meant, after all, that her castle awaited her and her prince.

Years passed as Ellie and Emmett settled into a life of their own. Children came, adding to their happiness. First, little Raymond arrived, followed closely by blonde-haired Lucy. Emmett opened a lumber and hardware business to accommodate the booming housing market, while Ellie maintained the home and raised the children. She volunteered generously at the veterans' hospital, always thankful that Emmett had returned from the war unscathed. Ellie also chartered the town's first Garden Club.

The yard smelled divine throughout most of the year. Jasmine, clematis, honeysuckle, as well as several varieties of flowering trees and shrubs, decorated 1472 North Sycamore Lane. Ellie was known for her exquisite rose bushes, and she grew a vegetable garden that could have fed a dozen families. The extra produce she shared with the wives who lost their providers during the war.

Unfortunately, that number was high in our little town. Platoons were made up of young men from the same community, so when a platoon took a hard hit, say at Iwo Jima or the Battle of the Bulge, a generation of young men was wiped out all at once in a small town. The names of all the boys we lost will forever dwell with me. War is hell.

Ellie and Emmett had normal ups and downs in their life together. Some years were happy ones. Others were sad. They celebrated birthdays, Christmases, and other joyous occasions. On darker days, they lamented the passing of both of Ellie's parents. The children grew, and while they brought much joy, they also brought stress and anxiety to Emmett and Ellie. When Raymond left to go to Vietnam, I thought Ellie's heart was going to break. She stopped eating, and Emmett even took her to see Doc Harris. Those were some tense days as we waited for Raymond's return, but return he did. Life moved forward with time.

Grandchildren arrived. Lucy gave Ellie and Emmett a brood of youngsters to dote over. Her husband, Hal, an electrical engineer, provided an ample living for her and their six children. They lived a few blocks away on Hyacinth Street and the children frequently spent the days with their grandparents. Ellie's home was filled with the children's laughter and play. Raymond added three more to the mix. He lived nearby as well.

Oh, how Ellie enjoyed the sound of little feet running through her expansive three-story home. Her favorite place to spend time with them was the living room with its fireplace. She spent hours reading to her grandchildren. Ellie was a good storyteller herself. She spun yarns of faraway places with castles and dragons. The fire crackled, and the children's eyes widened as Ellie concocted one tale after another.

Sometimes she couldn't believe her good fortune.

"Who would have thought?" she said one night as she nestled into bed next to Emmett.

"Who'd have thought what?"

"All those years ago when we met at Jake's party, who'd have thought that today we'd be where we are."

"I don't know, El. It seems to me you always knew you were going to be *here*." Emmett winked.

Ellie gave him a gentle slap on the shoulder. "You know what I mean. Of course, I always wanted to live in this house. I mean, who would have thought we'd have built such a fine life with a house full of beautiful grandchildren always running in and out? Our children are happy and successful, and sometimes our good fortune just brings tears to my eyes."

"I knew what you meant, dear. Yes, the Lord has truly blessed us. Now let's get some rest. We have that big day of shopping and checkups at the doc's tomorrow."

A quick hug and kiss, and the lovebirds were sound asleep.

Many good memories were made on Sycamore Lane, but not all were happy. Sometimes heartache hits even the most joyful of homes. I loved Emmett as much as I loved Ellie, even though I'd known her since the day she was born. The news Emmett received that next day at the doctor was worse than any of us could have imagined. He passed before the next Christmas came. Ellie was devastated.

Raymond and Lucy both asked her to stay with them.

"Mom, it's not good for you to stay in that drafty old house alone. What if something happens to you?"

"I'm not leaving my home. I miss your father terribly, but that house has been my heart since I was a child. I'm not leaving it. I never feel alone as long as I'm there."

Persistent requests for her to move were ignored.

"What if you fall, or what if the weather turns bad and the power goes out, leaving you without any heat?"

"I'll be fine. There's wood on the back porch, and I have my fireplace. I won't go cold. You don't have to worry about me."

Ellie proved them right. She had frequent company and was never alone. Members of the Garden Club visited, and her kindnesses to the war widows were never forgotten. Someone was always checking on her, making sure she wanted for nothing. The grandchildren continued to visit, and young Elisa was as fond of the old house as Ellie had been as a child.

"Grandma, I want to live here someday."

"I'll tell you what, little one--"

"Grams," she interrupted. "I'm fifteen. I'm not that little."

"Well, you'll always be my little Punkin'." Ellie and Elisa exchanged a hug. "Since none of the other children have any interest in living here, I'll make sure you get it when it's my time to go."

"Let's hope that's not for a long time, Grandma."

"I'll go when the good Lord wants to call me to His home, Elisa. Until then, you focus on your studies and become that nurse you've always said you wanted to be."

Elisa and the other grandchildren beat a steady path to 1472 North Sycamore Lane. Even as they grew up, moved away, and began their own lives, they never stayed away from their grandmother for long. Ellie's home was where everyone went to feel safe and relaxed.

Time passed, and slowly Ellie's health declined.

"Mom, it's time you move in with us or go to a nursing home," Lucy told her.

Stubborn as always, she refused to leave the place she loved on Sycamore Lane. "I'm not going to leave my home. Just stop that nonsense."

During Elisa's last year of nursing school, Ellie passed peacefully in the night.

Now, here I am, alone. Elisa isn't moving in until May, and I sit empty for the first time in decades. Some of you may have heard that expression, "If this old house could talk, what would it say?" Now you know.

CHARCOAL DRAWINGS

The pinks, purples, and golds of an early October sunrise filtered their way through scattered clouds. Autumn was Mylah Kennedy's favorite time of year, and this year was special. After dreaming of becoming an art teacher since junior high, Mylah finally had a position at Highland Hills Elementary. For the area, this was a plum job. How she was hired over teachers with years more experience, she didn't know, but she wasn't going to question her good fortune.

"It's obvious, honey, that your positive attitude and enthusiasm won them over," her mother told her.

"Mom, you've always been my biggest cheerleader. I just hope I'm good enough and don't let the school down."

Her mother took Mylah by the elbows and leaned in, her green eyes on fire with love. "You listen here. You are the best teacher for this job. You've lived for this moment. Everyone loves your spunk. Now go make the world a brighter place for those children."

With her mother's pep talk in mind, Mylah poured herself into the school year. Teaching kindergarten through fifth-grade art kept her on her toes, but she loved every second of her job. Each grade brought its own challenges, but she did her best to instill the fundamentals and to inspire a love for art.

"Children, look at the world around you," she would say. "Everything you see can become art if you view it that way. Did you see something today that you think is art?"

Jimmy Garner raised his hand as twenty other first-graders raised theirs.

"Yes, Jimmy."

"I saw a bird this morning. A bluebird. It sat on an old wooden fence. It was pretty."

"Very good! Who else?"

Liza Gantry spoke next. "My grandmother has a rose bush in her front yard. It's yellow. Yellow is my mom's favorite color."

"I'm sure it's beautiful."

Liza wrigged and smiled a shy little grin, pleased that her answer was correct.

Around the class, Mylah, or Ms. Kennedy as her students knew her, called on each child.

"My brother's new truck."

"The red barn at the Clouse's farm."

"My dog, Pixie."

Each child had a piece of real-world art to talk about.

Every day, Mylah Kennedy asked her students to think of something they could see that they considered art. It could be as simple as the pencil on their desk or as exotic as a peacock. After a month or so, she asked her students to picture art objects in their minds.

"Close your eyes. Imagine what it would look like if you drew it on a piece of sketch paper."

She could tell by the expressions on their faces that her eager students visualized their art. This was what she'd always wanted. Art became a part of her students' daily lives.

One day, Mr. Reynolds, the principal, stopped her in the hallway.

"I'm not sure what magic you're casting in your classes, Ms. Kennedy, but the students love your room. Parents have even told me that when they're driving in the car or taking a walk, their children point out the art they see. Keep it up!"

Mylah blushed. "Thank you, Mr. Reynolds. I'll do my best."

"We're glad to have you here." With that, Reynolds, always a man on the move, strode down the hallway.

His encouraging words fueled Mylah to think of innovative ways to teach her young students the fundamentals of art. They'd begun the year with hands-on clay sculptures. The children loved feeling the medium in their little hands. Now she needed another engaging project. One idea had tickled her brain for a few months, and she decided the time had come to try it.

"Today, class, we are going to put the art we see down on paper. Peter, will you pass out the charcoal pencils for me? Lydia, will you give one sheet of sketch paper to each student?"

Smiling, she patiently stood at the front of the room as the supplies were handed out.

"What I want you to do is close your eyes and imagine something that is in this room that you would like to draw. Imagine it as a piece of art, just like we've been practicing."

She gave the squirming students a moment to focus on what they envisioned drawing.

"Now, open your eyes and draw what you could see."

"But, Ms. Kennedy?"

"Yes, Hannah?"

"We don't have any colors. Just black."

"That's right. I want us to practice the basics first. Later this year, we will add color to our drawings. For now, we are going to work on getting the shapes down. Make sure you give your drawing a title, too. We will be practicing these same drawings every day for the next two weeks, improving on the idea you come up with today."

Her students loved her, so they set to work, doing their best to please her. At the end of class, a few students rushed to put the finishing touches on their creations. As she'd taught them, when the bell rang, they carefully turned their work into their hour's slot in the wooden cabinet next to Mylah's desk. They placed the charcoal pencils back in the supply box. With smiles on their faces, they filed out of the room. It was the end of the day, and the students hurried off to their homeroom.

Eager to see what her students drew, Mylah pulled the papers from the cabinet and flipped through them. She was puzzled.

Hmmm. The children did as I asked. They gave their drawings titles, but these are all of the same thing: people. But these aren't people who were in our room.

One boy's drawing was entitled "Gregor." A little girl's was named "Jano." Another named his "Belzor."

Each child's drawing was a version of either Gregor, Jano, or Belzor.

Perplexed, the next day she addressed her class. "Yesterday, students, we were supposed to draw pictures of something in this room. All of you drew figures of people. You named them all the same three names. I'd asked you to draw something in this room."

"But we did, Ms. Kennedy." Lydia looked at her with wide blue eyes.

"You asked us to close our eyes and draw what we saw." Peter shifted in his chair and looked around the room at his classmates for support. They all nodded in agreement.

"Yes, I did."

"We always have our friends with us, Ms. Kennedy."

"You do, Billy?"

"Yes, ma'am."

She stood in thought for a moment before she realized what her first-graders meant.

"Of course! Are these your imaginary friends?"

Peter looked to his left and whispered something to no one in particular. He paused, then nodded.

"Yes, Ms. Kennedy. Gregor says he's our imaginary friend, and he's right here next to me. He's in this room, so can we still draw him?"

Having imaginary friends was natural for children. Mylah didn't want to dash the creativity of her students. This world would have enough chances to destroy their imaginations, and there was no reason for it to start today in her classroom.

"I did say we'd practice these same drawings for two weeks, and this is what you chose to draw, so yes. You can continue to draw them."

Sighs of relief swept through the classroom. Jimmy said, "Jano says thank you."

Mylah chuckled and said, "Tell Jano he's welcome. Now for our lesson."

On the board, she modeled how to draw a body, legs, arms, and a head. The students went to work. Following her lead, they created new versions of their previous drawings.

Each day a new aspect was practiced. At the end of the week, Mylah was amazed by how much their drawings had improved. They became more detailed and less rudimentary. For being first-graders, they showed a great deal of talent.

She marveled at how the children's depictions of their imaginary friends were so similar. Mylah assumed they'd told each other so many stories about these imaginary figures that they had a common description in mind. She didn't want to brag, but the children were rapidly learning the drawing techniques she modeled for them. She left work on Friday feeling invigorated. Her project was coming along better than she had hoped.

The air was crisp and the sky was clear as she walked to her car. Mylah pulled her coat closed against her chest as the wind whipped past her. The crimson of the maples mixed with the golden cottonwood trees. How could an artist not love autumn? A palette of colors was laid out across the countryside, and Mylah took the long way home so that she could enjoy the sights a little longer.

The next Monday, Mylah picked up her lessons where she left off. Again, the children's work was better than the time before.

"Children, I'm so proud of you! Your artwork is really improving, and I am very impressed."

"Thank you, Ms. Kennedy!" Shouts of joy erupted in the classroom.

"Gregor says he's glad you like what you see." Peter smiled and nodded to the air beside him as he passed out the charcoal pencils to his classmates.

By Wednesday, however, an unusual change in the drawings took Mylah by surprise. A darkness enveloped them. The details had improved yet again, but there was an unsettling look in the eyes of Gregor, Jano, and Belzor. These imaginary friends looked downright, well, evil.

Only two more days to the unit remained, and Mylah looked forward to moving onto a happier project. Next week they would create Halloween decorations for the school hallway.

On Thursday, Mylah's mind played tricks on her. As she looked over her students' work, she could have sworn the eyes of the figures watched her. She heard someone whisper in the back of the room as she reached the end of the stack of drawings. She jumped, and a sound akin to laughter behind her made her turn. Of course, nothing was there.

She gathered her purse and coat, looked back into her classroom, then shut and locked the door. This project was no longer fun.

Friday, of course, brought even more vivid images from the children. Nervously, she paced around the room, checking their work as they furiously drew to finish their masterpieces. Mylah was eager for the week and that project to be over. She was exhausted as she made her rounds.

Was she losing her mind? Surely Jimmy's eyes didn't flicker black for an instant? No, that couldn't be.

Then a deep voice behind her said, "Ms. Kennedy, what do you think? It looks real, doesn't it?"

Startled, she spun around. Peter held her picture up for her to see. She forced a smile and said, "Yes. Yes, it does." And it did.

The bell rang, but the students didn't place their drawings in the cabinet. Instead, they left them sitting on their tables and rushed out the door, laughing.

"Well, I guess on Monday I will have to remind them what our end of class procedures are," she muttered to herself as she reached to pick up the first drawing.

The piercing glare of Gregor made her blood run cold. Before she could pick up the paper, a clawed black hand came out of the drawing and grasped her wrist. Gregor cackled. Mylah struggled to free herself.

A rush of air swept through the room, and the papers swirled into the air, spinning frantically in a blur. Gregor continued his hold on her wrist.

"You cannot escape my hold, Mylah. Can I call you Mylah? Ms. Kennedy seems so formal. After all, we're friends. Not-so-imaginary friends. Isn't that right, my sweet?" His other clawed hand reached out and caressed her face.

"What's happening? This can't be real!"

"Oh, but we are real. We just needed your help."
Two voices spoke in unison. Mylah turned around to see
the incarnations of Jano and Belzor.

"My help? What do you mean by 'my help'? You
can't be real."

"We are real now, Mylah. We've waited for so long
to be given form, and with your help, here we are. The
children and their drawings brought us into this world. Now
our work can be done." Jano's eyes sparkled.

The three beings hissed hideous laughs.

"No! You're nothing more than imaginary friends.
I'm dreaming that I see you."

Gregor's razor-sharp claw slid down Mylah's
forearm, and a thin stream of blood flowed. He placed the
tip of his finger in his mouth. "This is all real, and ah, yes,
you are indeed my sweet."

Mylah shuddered and struggled to free his grasp.
"What are you? You're no childhood imaginary friend."

Belzor took a step forward. "You're a smart one,
Mylah Kennedy. No, we are not imaginary friends."

"What are you then?"

Jano and Belzor grinned and gave a nod toward
Gregor, who pulled her close to him. She smelled the putrid
stench of his breath and the odor of singed hair.

"My sweet, we are demons. We have waited a long
time for a means to cross over. We have hovered in this
school for decades. The children were right. We were in
this room, and you told them to draw what was in this
room. You gave us our avenue to materialize in this
dimension."

"What are you going to do? Why are you here? Let go of me!" My tugged her arm, but Gregor only tightened his grip.

"Do? We are only the first. Others will follow. My sweet, we are going to conquer this world."

In a flash, he entered her body.

On Monday, it was second grade's turn to draw what was in the room.

THE HOPE CHEST

A lone watchman sits, leaning against the stonewall of the mountain tower, as he wearily gazes across the desolate valley below. The once verdant fields are mere dreams now. The rolling thunder in the distance is no promise of replenishing rain, but instead it is the ever-present rumble of artillery. The land and its people are all but ruined.

The world wasn't always like this. I remember my grandfather's stories.

Closing his eyes, he smells the delicate aroma of his mother's cooking as it wafts through the air, mixing with the earthy smell of the wood fire as rain pours down outside their modest home. The magic of the moment is forever etched in his mind and rolls through his thoughts. He feels the warmth of the fire and the soft fur of the bear rug that covers the rough floor of his parents' long-ago home as he takes a passage back in time.

***

Sitting at the foot of his wise and respected grandfather, a man of honor and integrity in their village, young Milo gazed at the old man in complete admiration. His grandfather sat in the well-worn rocking chair, taking puffs from his pipe as he amused the children with tales of faraway places and of a time when their land was full of peace and plenty.

"Tell us again about the ancient war, Grandfather."

"Oh, my child, you have heard that story so many times. Surely you are tired of it by now."

A chorus of young voices, pleading for him to tell the story, won the old man over--as everyone in the house knew they would. Milo's parents shared a wink across the kitchen as they prepared the last of the evening meal. They knew their beloved patriarch would not miss an opportunity to tell one of his favorite tales. That's all it was, they knew. These stories were nothing but lore that passed from generation to generation. There was no more truth to them than the stories of imps and fairies. How could there be? It kept the children occupied, however, and it gave the old man a chance to bask in their attention.

"Well, it was a long time ago, back when we didn't have the modern conveniences that we do now. We were still a prosperous people, though. For centuries, our people farmed this valley. Life was wonderful, and everyone had more food than they could eat. Our cattle and goats were fat and sleek. No one saw the trouble that was coming. Our people were content, and sometimes when we become content we lose our watchfulness. Fat and satisfied, we were blinded to the evil approaching."

The children huddled together. A gentle shudder passed among them. Lex, Milo's older brother, wrapped a blanket around Milo and gave him a reassuring hug.

"It was the end of the harvest season, and oh, what a harvest it had been. The trees hung heavy with fruit that fall, and the silos overflowed with grain. Mounds of vegetables sat in everyone's cellars, and the women were busy preserving as much food as they could from daybreak to sundown. The men labored in the fields to bring in the last of the abundance."

"What did the children do, Grandpa?" Shia, Milo's little sister, was smart for her age. At three, she was as involved as the older children in listening to the tales.

"The children?" Grandfather stopped to shake out his pipe and refill it with tobacco.

Impatiently, his audience nudged each other, eager for the story to continue.

"Yes, Grandpa, the children," Shia said in an effort to prod him.

"The children, like children will do, played and made up games."

"What kind of games?"

"Those with sticks and balls and races--the types of games I'm sure you all enjoy once you are done with your chores and your studies."

"Races are my favorite." Milo beamed. He was known as the fastest boy in the village.

"You are quick, my little one, and Shia is quick in her own way, aren't you, dear?" His wrinkled hand patted her on her head. "Shia's curiosity and Milo's speed remind me of the heroes of this story."

Milo and Shia blushed from the comparison.

"Before we can talk about heroes, however, we must talk of the terrible, terrible things that happened."

The faces of the children fell. They knew this story.

"The marauders swept down from the north in a fury. Their horses were fast, and their hearts were cold. They killed and destroyed our people and our land. We fought back, however, and the war raged for many, many years. Starvation spread across our land, and many of our people died from illness. Fierce battles took a toll on them as well."

Shia and her cousin, Ana, clasped hands and held each other. A tear trickled down Ana's sweet face.

"The war went on for years, and even our wisest and bravest leaders didn't know how to overcome our enemies."

"Were you alive then? Did you see this yourself?" Pater, Ana's older brother, was always a skeptic.

"No, son, I was not alive then. My great-great-great-grandfather wasn't alive when this happened. This story has been handed down for centuries, but it is true."

"What happened? How did our people live?" Milo brought everyone's attention back to the story.

"We had all but given up. Our people were ready to surrender and be massacred. But then, two of the children saved us."

This, of course, caused the children to sit up straighter and to open their eyes wide.

"There was a boy." Grandfather nodded at Milo. "And a girl." He glanced at Shia. "They were clever young children. Always curious, even amid war, they played their favorite games. One was hide-and-seek."

"We play hide-and-seek all the time!" The children wiggled with excitement knowing that they carried on an ancient tradition of their people.

"Yes, you do. Now one day these two children, Oli, the boy, and Ara, the girl, went far beyond the boundaries of the village. They ran deep into the forest where they found a cave. This was no ordinary cave. It was in the base of the Holy Mountain."

Looks of awe swept across the children's faces.

"Down, down, down, they climbed into the cave. They were so amazed that they forgot to hide from one another. The wind gently whistled through the cave, and they were drawn to a glowing room. In the center of a room no bigger than this house," Grandfather motioned his hands in the air, "was a chest. A beautiful wooden chest with sturdy metal hinges."

"And on the top of the chest, there were words, weren't there, Grandpa?" Shia knew. She knew the importance of the words.

"Yes, my child. The words said, 'He who possesses this can never lose. Carry this into any battle you are facing, and you will surely never fail.' Oli and Ara carefully lifted the trunk by the handles and carried it to their village."

The moon had risen by this time, and the light from the fire flickered on Grandfather's face.

"As they approached their village, they saw terrible carnage. Homes were on fire, and the marauders were killing families as darkness began to fall."

A whimper escaped Ana's lips.

"Ara and Oli were afraid, but they were brave. Braver than most grown men who have faced battle many times. They knew how to return to their village unseen. Their hours of playing hide-and-seek had taught them nooks and crannies that most adults walked past unnoticed."

The screech of an owl outside caused everyone in the room to jump. Even Grandfather jerked ever-so-slightly. Mother and Father had stopped their activities in the kitchen and were also listening. The story was so powerful that they couldn't deny it their attention.

"Tell us, Grandpa. What happens to little Ara and Oli?"

"It was dangerous, and they were tired from the weight of the trunk. Several times they dodged flaming arrows, and once Oli was caught in the tangle of a fence. Death surrounded them everywhere. Finally, exhausted, they gently knocked on the back door of their cabin. Their mother ushered them inside, shocked by the trunk they dragged into the house."

"They had to be so tired and scared by then." Little Shia's concerned voice caused everyone's heart to ache.

"The children collapsed onto the floor as their parents read the message on the top of the trunk. Their mother called for the oldest son, Link, to find the king, which was no easy task given the battle raging throughout the valley. Find him, he did, however, and the village leaders gathered around the trunk, eager to find what magic it held. What would allow them to win any battle?"

By now, Milo's mother and father knelt on the floor alongside the children.

"The wise men of the community opened the latches on the trunk and a bright light radiated through the crack in the lid. Carefully, oh so carefully, they lifted the lid off the chest as blinding light rushed out of the trunk and shot in all directions. Inside, still glowing, was a golden plate with one word inscribed upon it. 'Hope' was all it said. Hope was all our people needed."

***

The cold wind across the desolate valley brings Milo out of his reverie. He has volunteered to be the watchman for what is regarded as a foolhardy mission.

"You're stupid to believe the rubbish of fairy tales, Milo. Be realistic and flee with the rest of us," Pater told him as the rest of the village scrambled to escape to the rugged mountains of Ryon.

Milo and Lex would not give up, however. They could not accept surrender, even if their plan was built on no more than a misplaced homage to their grandfather's long-ago stories. Lex rode his horse through dangerous enemy territory to the base of the Holy Mountain. Now Milo waits to see if it had been in vain.

As the ashen sun sets, Milo sees the nearly imperceptible movement of his brother's large bay horse across the valley. A distinct amber hue, one bright enough to be seen even at this distance, radiates around the horse and his rider.

When all seemed lost, they had found hope.

SINCERELY YOURS

For several years I've prided myself in being a collector of the unusual. My idea of unusual doesn't always match what others deem it to be. People bring all sorts of things into my shop, but most items are commonplace. Sure, an antique teapot or Grandpa's WWII sidearm might have great sentimental value to the individual person, but as a category, those are typical artifacts that can be found just about anywhere. I'm not discounting the importance of memorabilia. I simply have more discerning tastes.

Two days ago, I heard the jingling of the bell on my shop door. Medium-height with short brown hair, wearing a thin brown coat, I wouldn't have given the man a second glance on the street.

"Excuse me, are you Stanley Perkins?" He set a chest on my countertop.

"Yes, I am. What can I do for you today?"

"I understand you dabble in the unusual. I may have something that would interest you."

I hear that fifty times a week.

Skeptically, I sized up the chest and saw nothing spectacular about it.

"I don't have any use for an old chest, Mr.--"

"Smith."

Oh boy, another anonymous peddler of the unimpressive.

"Looks can be deceiving. The chest itself isn't of importance. It's the contents that you may find interesting."

I stared at the chest, and I'm afraid I didn't hide my doubts well.

"You don't have to make a decision now. I'll leave this here for you to go through. All I ask is that you keep the contents in the same order as they are now."

"Sounds fair enough. How much do you want for it? That is, if I decide I want it?"

"We can discuss the terms once you've taken a look. I'll come back on Friday. I've only let a few people, those with an interest in the unusual and the unexpected, see what's inside. Remember, go through every item, then we will close the deal."

Apparently, no one else wants to buy it. What the hell, though? Business is slow, and I've got some time to go through it.

"Okay, I'll give it a gander. No promises, though."

"I assure you, we will strike a deal."

I turned to unclasp the latch to the chest, and when I turned around, Mr. Smith was gone. The jingling of the bell on my door was my only indication he had left.

Truthfully, I didn't think there'd be anything worthwhile in it, but I opened the lid to find stacks of papers. The pages were yellowed and brittle. Old papers like that require special handling or the oil on our hands will ruin them. I'd learned that when I worked for a year at the state museum as a sophomore in college. So, remembering my lessons from long ago, I found my box of latex gloves and put a pair on. I had to protect the documents, not only out of respect for the current owner, but because I wanted to get top dollar for them if they turned out to be something special and I chose to strike a deal with Mr. Smith.

I picked up a few stacks and set them on the counter. Then I remembered Smith's request to keep everything in order, so I carefully placed them back together and hoisted the chest to the floor. I pulled up my comfy chair, refilled my coffee cup, and took a look at the first paper in the chest.

A letter. An old one. Dated May 4, 1864. Hmmm. What do we have here?

Dear Jimmy,

I have been by your side since you were a small boy. I've accompanied you on many adventures, and I have so many fond memories of you. Do you remember the time when you and your brother dove off Steeple Rock into the river, but the current had moved the location of the pool? Or the time Old Man Gentry mistook you for a burglar and barely missed you with that gun blast? Those were some close calls, but you made it through.

Tonight you are sleeping on the ground, dreaming of home and of those loved ones you have left behind. Tomorrow is a big day. The enemy has advanced farther, and you are going into dangerous territory.

Know I am standing beside you and will not leave you, my good friend.

Sincerely yours,
G.R.

A second page accompanied the letter. An obituary for Jimmy Thompson from a small town newspaper gave the details of his passing. Age seventeen, son of Edith and Ezra Thompson, he died May 5, 1864 in the Battle of the Wilderness.

Why, he died the day after that letter was written.

Always a softy for Civil War memorabilia, I began to think the chest might have potential.

I carefully set Jimmy's letter and obituary on the counter and read letters, one after the other. So many were written to Civil War soldiers on both sides of the fight. Others were to farmers, doctors, school teachers, and people of all ages and walks of life. Filling up my cup of coffee, I pondered the fact that each letter was written the day before the death listed in the obituary. I picked up the next letter, dated November 18, 1904.

Dear Maude,

You are a remarkable woman, my dear. You have come so far in life from that scrawny little girl who caught frogs and climbed trees with her brother to the fine lady you are now. I smile thinking of the time when you were five and filled Mabel Wilby's lunch bucket with lizards just to hear her squeal at the church picnic. Mabel never could take a joke, and you endured the whipping from your daddy like a champion. Your spunk and determination have taken you far.

You survived the Yankees raiding your home and leaving your family near starvation. You and Harmon Mackey raised six mischievous boys without a moment of outward frustration. You've seen births, deaths, cholera outbreaks, and most recently a World's Fair. You became a grandma and a great-grandma, and your family adores you.

I have enjoyed every moment we spent together. I will be seeing you soon.

Sincerely yours,
G.R.

As with the other letters, an obituary for Maude Mackey accompanied it.

I read through several more, and the dates moved progressively forward. The letters were personal and touching, and I felt as though I peered into a crystal ball and could see these people come to life.

One letter to Conrad Milton gave me pause. It was written the day before he died in the Battle of the Bulge. Why would Conrad's letter hit me emotionally? Because he was my father's best friend. They joined the Army the day after Pearl Harbor was attacked, and like all small towns back then, the hometown recruits were put in the same unit. My father was with him when the mortar shell landed smack dab on Connie. I'd grown up listening to stories about Conrad Milton. The letter included a few I'd never heard, like the time he and his little sister almost died from scarlet fever.

Something bothers me, though. Just who is writing these letters? Who is G.R.? Because of the span of years, there's no way it's the same person. Also, these people lived all across the country. There's no way one person would have known them all. How can this be?

Over the course of the next few days, I continued reading letter after letter and obituary after obituary. They always recalled poignant moments of a person's life. They were always signed by G.R.

If these are fiction, I have no use for them. I'm not sure what Mr. Smith thinks he's trying to sell here.

On Friday morning, I finally reached the bottom of the chest. One final letter remained, but unlike the others, there was no obituary.

That's odd.

I carefully opened the last letter written on bright white paper. I checked the date, which couldn't be right. September 14 of this year. Why, that was yesterday. I shrugged and began reading.

Dear Stanley,

You've been one of my favorites since you were a young boy living on South Primrose Street. Always curious and always drawn to people and things that were different or unique, you've lived quite the life. For your senior trip, you chose to go to exotic New Guinea just so you could see real headhunters. Most people your age went to Paris or Barcelona, but you aren't like other people. By the way, I didn't know for sure if we were going to get off New Guinea with your head still attached, but fate had it that you would survive.

Because I've enjoyed following you for so long, I wanted to give you this one last treat. No one else has been privy to the private collection of letters I've written to those I treasured above all others. This chest was my gift to you.

I'm so glad I was able to meet you in person before we embark on our journey. I will see you soon.

Sincerely yours,
G.R.

Who would know about New Guinea? I went there alone. What kind of trick is this?

Just then the bell on my door jingled. At first, I didn't recognize the person who interrupted my thoughts. Instead of an old brown jacket, Mr. Smith wore a hooded robe and carried a scythe.

"Hello, Stanley. I hope you've enjoyed my gift. Now it's time for us to finalize our deal and leave."

He reached his hand out to me, and at that moment I clearly recognized the Grim Reaper. Tomorrow's paper would hold the obituary he'd add to his collection.

WHEN THE CIRCUS COMES TO TOWN

Little Edie Franklin walked through the carnival runway, mesmerized by the colors, the sounds, and the smells. The screams from the Tilt-A-Whirl caused her to stop for a moment to watch. Cassie Nieman, her enemy during the school year, sat in one of the cars as it spun and rolled. Tyson Parks, Carol Renner, and Ashley Stokes also swirled past Edie amid the blaring music and raucous screams. Edie had longed for the arrival of summer so she could escape her tormentors, and seeing them now brought back the pain of their taunts.

The sweet smell of cotton candy and corn dogs drew her attention to the food stand to her right. Digging out her hard-earned dollar bills, she slipped them to the worker and watched as he spun bright blue heaven onto the cardboard cone. Nothing said summer fun at the carnival like fresh cotton candy.

The wind blew as she took her first bite of the delicious treat. Her long, blonde hair became tangled in the blue cloud, and it stuck to both her nose and her chin. She didn't care. She'd waited all year for this.

At thirteen, her family finally allowed her to meet her friends at the carnival alone. Always before, her older brother or her parents insisted on accompanying her. Edie begged them this year to let her ride the rides and watch the circus performers with her peers, and they relented.

The sad truth, however, was that she had no friends to meet at the carnival or anywhere else. She was too short, too skinny, too nerdy, too ugly--all the descriptions made by her classmates--to have any friends. Edie lived a solitary life. Sometimes her heart ached to belong to the crowd, but she told herself that they weren't worth it. No one who could be as cruel as they were to her deserved to be her friend.

She was right, but that didn't lessen the pain.

So Edie walked the strip of carnival barkers and rigged games by herself. She was, for the most part, comfortable with her solitude. Walking through the crowd, Edie found safety in her sense of invisibility. She blended in with the crowd, much like zebras do in the herd. This insulated her from the mocking jabs made by people like Cassie Nieman.

"Young lady, step right up! Five darts for just $2. You're guaranteed to win a prize!" A tall, thin carnival worker with bright red hair and large ears tried to entice her to play at his stand.

Edie politely nodded her head no and quickened her pace so he would set his sights on someone more gullible than she was.

She wandered with no real direction, but she found herself at the circus big top tent. The sign outside said the next show wouldn't happen for two hours. Edie popped her head inside the tent, hoping to catch a glimpse of the elephants. No one was around, so she quietly slipped inside. It took a moment for her eyes to adjust to the dim light.

The tent seemed bigger on the inside than it did from the outside. She edged her way around, disappointed that she found none of the animals. Where would they be? She heard the chatter of a monkey coming from outside the opposite end of the tent. A lion grumbled, and she heard the trumpet of an elephant. Of course, the animals were kept in their pens and not in the tent itself.

A rustling of wings above drew her attention to the ceiling. Sparrows had flown into the tent where they flitted back and forth, sometimes landing on the trapeze swings. Edie giggled at the idea that the birds pretended to be circus performers.

Still in search of the animals, she decided that she'd come this far, so why not slip out the back of the tent and get a closeup view of them? Animals brought her more joy than most people did, so it was natural for her to gravitate toward them. She believed she should spend her time at the carnival as she chose. No law said she had to stick to the midway.

She pulled back the flap and bright sunlight caused her to squint. After a moment, she saw the animals and their cages, and Edie silently walked toward the monkeys, looking over her shoulder to make sure no one was watching her mischief. Peering into their enclosure, she swore they smiled at her. One even waved. They swayed and leaped, putting on their circus show just for her as she stood watching for several minutes. Edie turned her head to the sound of the elephants, and almost as though the monkeys understood, they stopped their antics and waved goodbye.

To get to the elephants, she had to pass the lions. The male contentedly chewed on a large bone while the female lolled about flicking her tail at the annoying summertime flies.

As she rounded a corner to find the elephants, she heard the laughter of children. Had others snuck back there too? She tentatively peered around the corner. Eight or ten children, whom she guessed ranged in age from four to fourteen, gathered in a circle. None of them looked familiar to her. Before now, she'd never even considered that the carnival workers had children of their own who traveled with them. She'd always viewed carnies as adults with no ties to the world at all as they moved from one town to another. Yes, these must be the performers' children.

Undetected, she watched as the children played, amusing themselves by climbing a ladder to the top of a stack of pallets. A stack, equal in height with another ladder, towered about fifteen feet away.

"Now introducing the Elegant Ella. Ladies and gentlemen, please turn your attention to the center ring. You will see an amazing demonstration of grace and death-defying acrobatics." A boy of about seven pretended to hold a microphone as he motioned his arm in a grand swing to point at a little girl who bowed and waved atop the pallets.

The other children clapped and cheered as they played their roles as audience members. Edie smiled while the little girl pretended to perform in the flying trapeze. Her delight turned to horror as Ella jumped high, springing from the pallets into thin air.

Edie gasped. The girl was going to hurt herself, and none of the other children seemed the least bit concerned. Then Edie saw why.

Ella did not fall. She somersaulted and pretended to swing from a trapeze, but she clung to nothing but thin air. After sailing back and forth five or six times, Ella flipped and landed onto the other pallet stack, turning to bow and wave to the audience once more. The other children cheered and another girl clamored to be next.

Bewildered by what she saw, Edie stepped backward, her foot catching on one of the concrete blocks used to keep an animal trailer in place. She landed with a thud and struck her head on rock. When she awoke, the children surrounded her. Before she could open her eyes, she heard them speaking.

"Do you think she saw us?"

"Mom and Dad are going to kill us if she did."

"Maybe she won't remember when she wakes up."

When Edie gained consciousness, the first face she saw was Ella's, and it must have been evident by the look on her face that she *had* seen, and she *did* remember.

"Just what do we do now?" A boy rubbed his forehead in worry.

A brown-haired girl of about Edie's age spoke up. "Well, the first thing we do, Josiah, is help her up. Come on, you guys."

The girl and Josiah extended their hands to Edie and helped her sit upright.

"Hi there. I'm Calinda. They call me Callie." She sat next to Edie.

"I.. I'm Edie. Edie Franklin. I think I should be going. Sorry to have bothered you."

"Not so fast." A tall boy with dark brown eyes stared down at her. "First, tell us what you saw."

Edie, frightened and confused, stammered. "Really nothing. I just need to go."

The boy moved closer to her.

"Stop it, Ryland!" Ella ran to Edie. "Did you see me fly? I think I did an extra twist this time. Did you like it?"

Ryland jerked his little sister by the arm. "Shut up, Ella! We aren't supposed to talk about these things with… others."

Callie held up her hand to stop the comments of the other children. "At this point, I think it's too late to worry about what should or shouldn't have happened. She saw. Didn't you. You saw, right?"

Edie slowly nodded her head and looked up at the crowd of worried faces around her.

Callie stood and faced the others. "Listen, we can't change any of that now."

One little girl began to cry.

"Oh, please don't cry," Edie pleaded. "I promise I won't tell. I won't tell anyone."

Ryland sneered. "I don't believe you. You'll run and tell all your friends. That's what girls do."

That comment drew ugly looks from half of the children in the group, and the other boys tried to act like they weren't part of it.

"I won't tell. I don't have any friends to tell."

"What do you mean you have no friends?" Ella frowned and placed her hands on her hips.

"I mean, I don't have any friends. I have no one to tell."

Ryland was about to say something else when Callie silenced him.

"Listen, you guys, think about it. If we didn't have each other, none of us would have friends either." Callie looked at the other children who shrugged their shoulders and nodded in agreement.

Callie extended her hand to Edie. "Do you think you can stand?"

"I think so." Callie and Josiah steadied her as she rose.

"Someone get her something cold to drink." Callie nodded her head at a little boy who ran off and returned a moment later with a grape soda.

One by one, they introduced themselves to Edie. Thomas, Timothy, Lydia, Abigail, and Jack shook her hand after Ryland and Josiah formally introduced themselves. Timothy was the pretend announcer. Abigail, the girl next in line to play trapeze, was no more than six.

Once the introductions were over, Edie asked Ella the question she needed answered.

"How did you do that?"

"Fly?"

"Yes."

Ella gave a nervous look to her brother and Callie, who nodded reassurance to her.

"I've always been able to fly. We can all fly, Edie."

"What?"

Callie led Edie to a chair. "We need to talk. This has to stay secret. Our lives are at stake."

"I won't tell anyone. I swear."

Callie took a deep breath and paused. "We aren't from here, Edie."

"I know. You travel from place to place around the country."

Callie reached to the ground and picked up a handful of dirt. She pointed at it. "No, we aren't from here. We aren't from Earth."

Edie laughed. "That's not possible!"

"Is it possible that I can fly?" Ella sounded indignant.

"Well, no."

"But I did, and I can. We come from out there." Her little hand pointed toward the sky.

"Are you hungry? Would you like us to get you something to eat? It's not time for the show, but we can get you in for free. Would you like that?" Timothy's eager eyes tried to put Edie at ease. Not entirely comfortable with anything she'd seen or heard, she thought she should try to be agreeable.

"Yeah, I could eat something."

"Come with us, then. Our family is having lunch. You can join us."

Edie followed them to a row of RVs where the carnival families lived as they traveled.

"We're all related. Timothy is my brother. The others are my cousins. I have a little sister named Carissa who is just a baby. My Aunt Nella watches her on performance days." Callie squeezed her hand. "Let me do the introductions."

Callie pulled the RV door open, and Timothy bounded up the steps. "Mom and Dad, we've made a new friend! Her name is Edie."

Callie rolled her eyes at Edie and muttered, "So much for me making the introductions." The two girls giggled and climbed into the RV.

The adults, already in their trapeze outfits, stood from the table, a little shocked and dismayed, but still polite. "Edie, it's nice to meet you. I'm Irene. This is my husband, Art. Please have a seat and join us for lunch."

Edie slid into the bench seat between Timothy and Callie. "Thank you. Everything looks delicious." They piled food onto her plate, and everyone looked nervously around the table.

"Mom and Dad, Edie knows. She knows about us."

Art set his fork down and began to speak, then stopped. Irene's calming touch to his wrist quelled his outburst.

"Hold on, dear. Let's hear what our daughter has to say." Irene gazed at the girls while squeezing her husband's hand. "Before you continue, Callie, I do want to remind you that you knew what the rules were."

"I know, Mom, but it was an accident. We were playing trapeze, and she saw Ella flying. We're sorry, aren't we?"

Both Edie and Timothy joined in with their apologies. "I promise I won't say anything." Edie's heart raced as she waited for the adults to respond.

Art sat silently for a moment. "What's done is done. We can't change it now. We are going to have to trust you, Edie. Our lives depend upon you keeping quiet."

"I understand, and I promise."

"Let's finish up lunch. It's almost time for our show. Would your parents mind if you watched our performance and then came back here so we could talk some more? Now that you know our secret, we may as well get to know each other better." Irene smiled a tentative smile.

"I'd like that. I'm here by myself. My parents won't mind. I'd love to see your show."

They placed the dishes on the counter to wash later and made their way to the big top. Inside the tent, music blared and jugglers entertained the crowd. An elephant walked slowly around the ring performing tricks that brought cheers. Edie and the other children sat on the floor and waited for Art and Irene to begin their act along with Ryland and Ella's parents, Rita and Benny.

"Ladies and gentlemen. Children and the young at heart. Please turn your attention high above you. You are about to witness the death-defying acrobatics of the Flying Estrellas."

Edie remembered from her Spanish class last semester that Estrella meant "star." As though she knew what her companion was thinking, Callie said, "It's a fitting name, isn't it? But we should be known as the 'Falling Estrellas' if we wanted to be accurate."

"They aren't going to fall, are they?" Edie's heart pounded and she almost ran out of the tent.

Chuckling, Callie clarified. "No, they aren't going to fall. They can't, remember? I'll explain my joke later."

The girls passed a bag of popcorn between them as the show began.

"Mom is the most beautiful woman ever," Callie whispered.

Irene was a beauty, and bedazzled in sequins, she was eye-catching. The audience held their breath as the other-worldly performers mesmerized them with their acrobatics. Twisting, turning, flipping through the air, they made it seem effortless. For added suspense, they performed with no net. The only member of the hometown crowd who knew their secret was Edie. They were so daring and graceful, however, that even their children were caught up in the moment.

After what seemed like an eternity, yet not long enough at the same time, their act ended.

"Let's give a big round of applause to the Flying Estrellas!"

The crowd erupted, and they received a standing ovation.

The children met their parents outside the back flap of the tent.

"Did you enjoy yourself, Edie?"

"Oh, Irene, you were marvelous! All of you were!" The four adults beamed.

"Thank you, young lady. Irene says you know our secret and that you're joining us for dinner and a night on the midway. Isn't that right? Our daughter, Ella, promised us that you were wonderful, and I can see she was right."

Benny scooped his daughter into his arms as Ella squeaked, "I did! I did! Edie's my new best friend."

As they walked to the RV, Edie fell silent beside Callie.

"What's wrong? Did someone upset you?"

Tears brimmed Edie's eyes. "No Callie. I guess when Ella said I was her best friend, it just really hit me. I've never had friends before."

Callie gave her hand a squeeze. "Well, you do now."

After dinner, the evening was spent riding all the rides and playing any game she wanted, only this time, Edie won. The Estrellas introduced her to all the carnival workers they encountered. Before she knew it, it was getting late and she had to call her parents to meet her at the front gate.

"Please come back tomorrow, Edie. I can't remember the last time I had so much fun." Callie hugged her, and so did Ella, Timothy, and Abigail.

"Here you go, Edie. It's a free pass for as long as we are in town." Art pulled a card from his shirt pocket. "I'll be glad to talk with your parents, so they know it's legit. Anyone who can keep up with our Callie is welcome with us." He tousled Callie's hair.

"Oh, Daddy." She wrapped her arms around him, grinning.

Once arrangements were made with Edie's parents, she practically lived at the carnival. The children told her stories from their home planet, and they even helped her fly with them. She had to hold their hands like she was Wendy and they were Peter Pans, but she flew.

One afternoon, Callie and Edie took a walk to the park near the fairgrounds. A little creek gurgled through the trees, and the two girls soaked their feet in the cool water under the shade of a large white oak.

"Do you remember the day I met you, how I had tears in my eyes?

"Yeah, I remember."

"I was crying because, in that one afternoon, I felt closer to you and your family, more accepted, than I ever have here." She motioned to the world around her.

"You are always welcome with us."

"But you are leaving the day after tomorrow, and I will be alone again." Edie turned her head away.

"We'll be back. I promise. This is one of our regular stops." She looked dreamily up at the sky. "And someday, if you want, we will take you with us."

"Up there?"

"Yep. Up there. Which reminds me. I never did tell you why we should be called the Falling Estrellas."

"That's right. You didn't. What does that mean?"

"Well, we weren't supposed to land here. We sort of crashed."

"Then how are you going to get back home?"

"We've run the carnival so we could make enough money to repair our ship. We also needed to travel around to get all the materials we need. Zeke, the guy who runs the dart stand, he's our chief engineer. He knew what we needed and where to go."

"Crazy Zeke is an engineer?"

Callie threw her head back and laughed. "Yep! He doesn't look like much, but he's brilliant. It was his idea to use the disguise of being a traveling circus. He said no one would pay much attention to us or keep track of where we were going."

"That is pretty smart."

Edie thought about how looks could be deceiving. She never would have guessed Zeke was so knowledgeable. She remembered her first day on the midway when Zeke tried to sell her darts for his game, and she'd viewed him as nothing more than a huckster. *I'd have been friendlier if I'd known he was an important part of Callie's safety and survival here on Earth.*

"I've already talked to Mom and Dad about it. They are happy to bring you with us, if you'd want to, at least for a visit sometime to our planet."

"Really? I'd love that! I wish I could go now."

"But you can't leave your parents. Not yet, anyway. Once we are older you can, though."

"Promise?"

"I promise."

"Hey, Callie?"

"Yeah."

"How will you get back to your ship?"

"We have it with us now."

"What?"

"Yeah, we've kept it with us and made repairs as we could."

"No way! Where do you hide it?"

"We don't hide it, silly. In fact, you've been on it. Lots of people have. They're on it right now. They just don't know it."

"How?"

"It's the Tilt-A-Whirl. Zeke turned it upside down and mounted seats on top of the thrusters. Of course, he had to make some adjustments so people aren't blown off."

They laughed at the thought, and Edie imagined Cassie Nieman jettisoning out into the atmosphere.

"I want you to have this." Callie handed her a small jewelry box. "Open it."

"Oh, Callie, it's a necklace just like yours." She held it next to Callie's, and the stones glowed.

"This is how we will keep in touch until we see each other. We are friends forever."

The two girls hugged as tears ran down their faces.

"I'll always be your friend, Callie."

Holding her hand, Callie rose and helped Edie to her feet. "We'd better get back."

Two nights later, as the carnival workers tore down their tent, Edie watched, unable to hide her grief. The Estrellas gathered around her and assured her they would meet again soon.

"Edie, I have to admit that I wasn't sure about you when Timothy first burst into the RV with you, but I already love you like a daughter. Keep this to remind yourself you have us as friends. It's not much, but I hope it makes you feel better." Art handed her an envelope.

"Honey, your parents are here to pick you up. One more round of hugs, and then you need to go." Irene wiped a tear from her eye.

Sitting in the back of her father's car, Edie opened the envelope she clutched. Inside was a card that read "Free Admittance When the Circus Comes to Town."

A LONELY NIGHT

The subtle breeze blew the fragrance of honeysuckle across the open field. In the distance, the soft hooting of an owl floated on the wind. Farther away, a pair of whippoorwills called, one mate to the other. The warmth of summer faded into the velvet blackness of the night, and nothing compared to this time and place. The still of the world soothed even the most tortured soul, and the perfect combination of darkness and earthy fragrance made it easy to believe that all was right with the world.

After this long, with so many memories, Sid smiled to himself. Who would have believed that, given his boisterous youth, he would be content in a field during the peaceful midnight hour? He knew, however, that this was where he needed to be. A quiet field in the middle of nowhere provided the solitude he needed to connect with what mattered most.

Mary would have understood. She always understood, even when he didn't know what motivated his own impetuous behavior. Her soothing touch and the sound of her voice whispering his name saved him from recklessness. Where would he have ended up without her? He shuddered to even think about it. Mary was the only destination his heart could have ever known.

The honeysuckle wafting in the air reminded him so much of her. The sweetness. The persistence. Like his Mary, honeysuckle took root in difficult conditions and thrived, sharing beauty in a harsh world. She was the strength of their relationship. Subtle yet unyielding, she was the force behind everything good in Sid's life. His once fierce physique hid a fragile ego that she more than once had put back together. Mary was also bold in her convictions. Her adventurous spirit and pure heart took them far in life. No one could meet Mary without recognizing the power in her laughter or the strength of her confidence.

It was her idea to come here in the first place. Red crept across his flushed cheeks as Sid remembered his indecisiveness, cowardice, really, when she first suggested that they pull up stakes, leave their families behind, and move off on their own. Pioneers. That's how Mary described them. It fit. Sid hesitated at first in the beginning, but the fire in Mary's eyes emboldened him to the point that he, too, felt the wanderlust.

How many others throughout history loaded their most essential items, indulging in only a few keepsakes, to set off on quests to parts unknown? Some pioneers sought adventure. Some sought independence. Others sought wealth, while some merely fled that which they could no longer face in hopes of a better life. Mary wanted the first two. Sid sought the latter.

Time has a funny way of changing our perceptions. Looking back, those problems he thought he had to run from weren't that bad after all. Had he been made of stronger stuff, he would have found a way to make amends with his family. He could have healed the broken bonds and apologized for his foolishness.

But maybe that was not his destiny. Maybe he was meant to find his way without the ties that bound him to his humble beginnings. Sid wasn't sure, however. Sid was only certain that he would have followed Mary anywhere, for any reason or no reason at all. He'd simply wanted to be wherever she was. Worrying about the past did him no good because remaining beside Mary was all that mattered. He had been beside her, too, until her light faded and he found himself alone in the world.

How long had it been? Sid had to add up the years to come to a final answer. It seemed like an eternity, but he knew better. Eternity would be spent with his beloved wife. He longed to join her; to rejoice in the completeness he only found when near her. All that stood in his way was the inevitable: death.

That brought him to tonight, in this place, as he stared up at the stars on this perfect summer night. He focused on a pinpoint of light. Most people in rural America wouldn't even notice it in the cluster of stars to the right of Orion. Sid knew it was there. His Mary had returned home to that brilliant speck in the night sky when her light faded from this world. Eternity awaited him on his home planet now, too.

Excitement coursed through him. He'd been lonely for so long. Once Mary was gone, no one and nothing filled the void. They'd been the only ectoplasmic nymphs on Earth. He'd wandered for centuries awaiting this night. This place. This time. His release from earthly bonds would only happen when death freed him.

A warm surge pulsed over his body as the pinpoint of light twinkled and beckoned to him. Mary's voice whispered in his mind. Her sweet, soothing chords reminding him of all that he missed and longed for. The promise of renewed acceptance by his long lost relatives gently murmured in her voice. He heard it clearly now. In one bright spark, he felt the joy of flight as he shot towards his forever home.

***

Meanwhile, this place and time beckoned another weary traveler in this world. A passing motorist blinked his eyes as he halted in the middle of the lane. He shook his head in disbelief.

"I've seen shooting stars before, but never one that traveled from the earth to the sky. No one would believe me. Was it a sign from God?" He looked up at the heavens in awe.

The man pulled out his phone and pressed a series of buttons in the cab of his truck. His estranged wife's number lit up the screen as he waited for her answer. The glow filled the interior of his truck. She'd always been his light in the darkness.

A groggy voice on the other end said, "What is it? Are you okay?"

She'd answered. After all this time and everything he'd done, she still answered.

"Mary, I miss you. I want to come home. I felt so lonely tonight that I drove into the country, to that field where we used to picnic. The one where we swore we'd always love each other. This is where we started."

His sobs filled the night air.

"Mary, I was going to kill myself, but something told me to try one more time. It was a sign from God. I know it was. I promise, I'll stop all of my stupid ways. Please take me back."

A tear rolled down her cheek as she sat in the darkness of her bedroom. He'd called. After all this time and after all the prayers she'd feared were unanswered, he'd called. Her heart beat so loudly that she almost couldn't hear anything else. A lifetime of loving this flawed man may have been worth it after all.

She wiped her face and found her voice. "I'll put some coffee on. Come home, Sid."

Sometimes fate, and true love, are undeniable. Tonight, in some quiet field, star-crossed lovers, in parallel dimensions, found that no distance is too great to stop the power and redemption of love.

THE GARDEN

The gentle hum of the landing gear soothed Seth Langley's frayed nerves. Usually, he enjoyed his excursions. This time, he craved one. Grateful for a job that allowed him the opportunity to travel, he'd always enjoyed the excitement of an adventure and couldn't imagine life stuck inside an office or a laboratory. Lately, though, he'd become a homebody. Recent stresses made a getaway more of a necessity than a luxury, and he'd jumped at this opportunity when his boss approached him with it.

I never imagined I'd be so happy to get away from home.

Seth winced at the thought. He loved Lisa. He did. Her laughter and sweet smile captured his heart years ago, and life wouldn't be nearly as satisfying without her. However, tensions between them had grown in recent months, and the pressures came from all sides. They'd fought more in the past six months than they had in the twelve years he'd known her. Home used to be his refuge from the world, and now here he was, thankful to have a break from it.

It wasn't all Lisa's fault, either. His job occupied more time these days. His promotion three months earlier forced him to work long hours. A lot was riding on his current project, and while he welcomed the extra income, he wondered just how much of his soul he now traded away for success. Was he happy? Could he sustain the pace he was at? There wasn't much left of him at the end of the day, and Lisa, rightfully so, wanted and needed his attention.

Then there were her parents, Lewis and Lorraine. Ever since they retired, they practically demanded that he and Lisa pick up and move closer to them. They refused to understand why quitting their jobs and moving hours away wasn't reasonable for them. Lorraine constantly asked when grandchildren would arrive, and Lewis made not-so-subtle hints that if Seth would only quit his high-pressure job to focus on the family that their lifelong dreams of becoming Nana and Papa would be fulfilled. Seth knew their intentions were good, but he and Lisa worried that Lewis and Lorraine's expectations were added pressure they didn't need.

Children were a touchy subject and the cause of too many arguments already. Infertility is an ugly word. The doctors had yet to come up with a reason for their struggles, and every month that crept by without a positive test result caused a deeper rift between Seth and Lisa. Neither of them told their parents of their struggles, so Lewis and Lorraine had no idea how badly their words stung the young couple.

Both had their reasons for keeping their infertility a secret from their families. Lorraine's parents would want to be in the middle of the problem. Lorraine, no doubt, would send daily articles on how eating vegetables full of beta carotene would improve ovulation. Seth couldn't deal with that, and Lisa didn't need the added pressure either.

Sadly, Seth knew confiding in his parents would have equal, although opposite, effects. His parents didn't want to hear the word "grandchildren" because their frail vanities couldn't face the reality of aging. No, it was better to keep their personal problems their own without family drama adding to their stress.

While Seth always assumed he'd one day have children, Lisa wanted a baby more than anything. Even before they were officially engaged, they decided on names for their future children. It was no secret that babies were a must for Lisa. The pressure to produce those dreams became too great, however, and their relationship suffered because of the strain.

We're trying too hard. Making love to Lisa used to be so easy. So meaningful. Now it's mechanical. We're going through the motions to try to get pregnant. I don't even want to touch her some nights, and that just hurts her more. I don't know what to do.

This field study came at a good time for Seth. He needed a chance to catch his breath. He loved Lisa, his job, and even Lewis and Lorraine, but he needed the chance to run away from his cares, even if he still had the responsibility of a research team to lead. When his director asked if he would come on this assignment, he jumped at the chance. He'd been stuck in the city for too long. The beauty of the deep forest would rejuvenate his senses. The Cascade Mountains brought him a sense of well-being he found nowhere else. Now that he neared his destination, his nerves began to settle and he relaxed.

During the smooth flight Seth allowed himself the guilty pleasure of a nap during the trip. As one of the leading scientific researchers in his field, the heart of his profession was located in the mountains. While most people never thought twice about where pharmaceutical discoveries came from, it was Seth's life. He specialized in the use of natural elements in medications. Pharmaceuticals for decades carried a stigma due to the overuse of chemicals. Public backlash gave rise to the "Back to Nature" movement that became his passion. Natural cures were for the taking if we looked for them. Seth made a career out of looking for them.

Seth's passion and drive brought him to the dense forests of the Cascade Range at least twice a year, sometimes more, before he'd taken the promotion. He lovingly referred to this area as "The Garden." Seth was certain the flora of the old forest held the cures to many diseases, and his research was proving that to be true. Three new medications neared completion in the testing and approval stages, and all came from plants he'd discovered in The Garden. As often as he could, he stole away to this botanical paradise.

Simply being here healed Seth on so many levels.

His company, BioPharamaceuticals, Inc., was ahead of its time. While maintaining easy access to the field sites, the company still wanted to be environmentally friendly. For these expeditions, they developed a landing pad and a small research lab that blended into the area so well it was nearly undetectable to the casual observer. The shuttle, now ready for its passengers and crew to disembark, slid into the well-disguised hangar. The doors closed behind the vehicle, and the team quickly made its way to the lab.

Safely past the airlock, Seth slipped out of his travel clothes and into the required biosuit. His skin condition required extra protection from the increased UV rays of the high elevation.

He grumbled as he put on the cumbersome suit. *Wouldn't it be nice if I could go without it? Feel the breeze and touch the ground like the other team members?*

He knew he wasn't the only one who had to take special measures, but that didn't stop him from wanting to ditch the suit each time he used one. That thought didn't last long, however. Seth grimaced as he remembered the time he hadn't worn the biosuit. Blistering skin and weeks spent going to a specialist pushed any fanciful thoughts of going without the suit from his mind.

He was fortunate, really. His company spared no cost to protect its rising star researcher. He was too valuable an employee to be sidelined by a hospitalization. The suit was clumsy, but once in the woods Seth always forgot his discomfort. While some team members worked near the lab, Seth was the only one allowed to venture far into the forest. The rest stayed behind to analyze his samples and to record data. His walks in the woods, while not without risks, were his own, and Seth relished them.

With the biosuit safely on, Seth motioned to the staff member in the control unit. The door slid open, the engineer at the controls gave a thumbs up, and Seth plodded out the front of the building into the bright sunlight.

It was a glorious day. Birds sang, and small animals scampered through the undergrowth. The beauty of the area nearly took his breath away. He wanted to run down the path out of glee, but he needed to be cautious as he ventured far from the lab. The raccoons, deer, and other small creatures he encountered were no threat. In fact, he paused, smiling, as he watched their antics. The chatter of a bird above him drew his gaze to the treetops. No, these creatures were nothing to be concerned about, but he knew he couldn't let his guard down.

Large animals were a threat, and because of that Seth knew from past experience that he needed to be careful. Company policy didn't allow anyone other than security to be armed, so he never carried a weapon. Seth doubted the policy's wisdom, but he realized it boiled down to insurance and liability. Sure, there were some trigger happy employees out there, but those could be identified easily enough with a simple psychological exam. Walking through the woods unarmed made Seth vulnerable. More than once he'd been chased by mountain lions and bears. Just thinking of those close calls caused beads of sweat to break out on his forehead. The biosuit, because of its bulk, slowed his movements, was also hot to wear. The risk and discomfort were the price he paid for doing what he loved, however.

Wandering in the Cascade Range involved risk. His suit, covered in material resembling fur, protected him from UV rays. Still, it masked his resemblance as a person enough that some predators mistook him for either prey or competition. Running into a predator could be fatal. This was his job, his passion, though, and he couldn't back out of his research simply because he might be killed. After all, the drugs his company developed had the potential of saving thousands, if not millions, of people over time. The risk to himself was worth it.

He pushed lingering fears from his mind and forged deeper into the forest. His heart swelled with joy the farther he walked.

This. This is what I've needed.

His pace quickened down the trail down to the first cultivation plot. A strain of sword ferns held promise to help the blind. The potential success for this project was both professionally and personally important to Seth. His college roommate, Lonnie, was blind. The two were more like brothers than friends, and the possibility that he could rescue Lonnie from a life spent in total darkness excited Seth. Lonnie was his inspiration to pursue a career in pharmaceuticals in the first place, and The Garden may hold the key to a cure for him.

Seth carefully measured and recorded the plants, collected samples, and put them in velcroed pockets covering the biosuit. He smiled as he checked the plants. They were healthy and thriving. If the trials continued to show promise, a drug might be ready for distribution in less than three years. He stuffed one more bag into a pocket and patted it shut. Yes, they made the suit bulky, but the pockets freed Seth's hands. He could collect pounds of samples and still have the agility to climb steep inclines and the finesse to check leaves for signs of distress. It was a worthwhile trade-off to lumber through the woods with a suit packed with specimens.

Satisfied with the condition of the ferns, he hiked to a grove of deciduous larch. Seth believed it contained an ingredient capable of reversing a rare, but devastating, degenerative nerve disease. As he climbed higher, he stopped along the way, measuring, documenting, and collecting flora. Packing his suit with samples, he then wandered off the trail to explore an area to his right. Untested plants grew wild, and as long as he was in The

Garden he wanted to collect as many varieties as possible to take back to the lab. If they proved beneficial, he'd return later to create plots for them as well.

He hiked and collected as he ventured farther into the forest. The thin air of the high elevation made breathing a struggle, so he found a rock outcropping and sat down. A stunning vista spread out before him and he leaned back to enjoy the view.

Then he heard it: the sound of breaking twigs and footsteps approached from the south. It wasn't a bear, although those did prowl these mountains. It wasn't a cougar either. The footsteps were too clumsy for a predator that relied on the element of surprise to kill its prey. Then he knew, and his heart raced. He was stalked by a more dangerous predator than a bear or a cougar. Adrenaline raced through his bloodstream. Scanning the trees behind him, he rose and began his escape.

Quickly returning to the trail, he took long strides down the mountain, bounding for the safety of the laboratory. He tripped and stumbled, nearly sliding down an embankment. The racing footsteps of his enemy crashed through the underbrush, and Seth knew he must hurry. Pain shot through him as he regained his footing. The fall injured his knee and aggravated an old back injury, causing him to stoop and hobble as he ran. His friends would have laughed at the sight he made, but this was no laughing matter. Life and death were at stake.

He ran, unsure for how long or how far, but he ran until his lungs burned and a dizzying blur filled his head. He had to stop to catch his breath, but fear raged through him, pushing him onward. He was at the mercy of the thin air, forcing him to deploy the emergency oxygen packs built into the biosuit. Would they last long enough to get him back to the lab? He wasn't sure. He knelt to the ground, his legs burning, but soon his lungs recovered and his mind cleared as the oxygen coursed through his suit. He surveyed the woods around him, hoping to find them peaceful once again.

Have I lost them?

No sooner did the thought cross his mind than Seth had his answer. No, he had not lost his pursuers. Instead, his short rest allowed the predators to gain ground on him. He ran, abandoning thoughts of hiding in hopes that the danger would pass. These predators were too dangerous to risk lingering in the area. His only chance of survival was to reach the lab. Fear, always a powerful motivator, pushed Seth beyond his normal physical limits.

Stumbling and struggling for air as the oxygen packs depleted, he searched for the entrance he desperately sought. Then he saw it. No more than two hundred yards separated him from the safety of the concealed lab opening. Could he make it?

I have to keep my head together. I can't afford another fall. God, how I wish I could tell Lisa I love her. That more than anything I want a baby with her, too. I've been an idiot hiding behind work. I made excuses, but I've been afraid of fatherhood. I want children, but the thought has terrified me. Now I'll do whatever it takes for us to have a family. I'll make it up to her when I get home. Right now, I have to make sure I get home.

Mentally plotting his course through the forest, Seth dodged stumps and leaped over ravines. His pursuers yipped behind him. Their high-pitched yells and howls seared Seth's eardrums.

Then the unmistakable crack of a rifle rang out. A bullet whizzed past the back of Seth's head, panicking the exhausted man. He'd had close calls in the forest before, but he'd never been shot at. He'd been chased in past encounters. Now he was hunted.

Fifty yards. Twenty-five yards. Seth's lungs felt as if they would burst, but another volley of bullets pushed him harder.

At the cave-like opening of the lab, Seth slammed his hand on the emergency button. The door slid open, and he flung himself onto the cold concrete floor as a bullet ricocheted off the door as it closed.

That was close. Maybe I need to carry a weapon after all. Policies be damned.

Teammates rushed to his side and peeled him out of the biosuit, whisking him away to the on-site doctor.

Seth's mind raced. *I want to finish this project, get off this planet, and go home to Lisa.*

Outside, his pursuers scrambled to the mouth of the lab.

"He's got to be somewhere. He couldn't have gone far," one yelled.

His companion leaned over, breathless with his hands on his knees and nodded. "Dave, can you believe that? We almost bagged ourselves a Bigfoot!"

Kicking the ground, Dave took his frustrations out on a bracken fern. "We sure enough did. Let's look around for a blood trail. There's no way he disappeared into thin air."

Inside the clinic, Dr. Salk examined Seth. "Are you okay? Do we need to abort this mission?"

"No, sir. I'm just shaken. We can stay here. That was close, though."

"It was far closer than we are willing to risk right now. Commander Vinn has ordered the team to return home. Let things calm down a little bit here on Earth before we come back."

"But--"

"I know your research is important to you, but we can't have our leading scientist killed by wild men with weapons. Besides, Lisa would be devastated, and we don't want that."

"No, we don't. I owe it to her to come home."

Commander Vinn leaned against the doorsill. "Technician, put his samples in the containment pod. We can analyze them as easily back home as we can here. These plants may save our people one day, but this planet is trying to kill us."

"Yes, sir."

"Seth, thank you for all your hard work. Get into your travel clothes and take a seat if you feel up to it."

"I will. Thank you, sir."

Seth dressed, carefully hanging the biosuit up to be used another time. Making his way into the craft, he sat in the cushioned seat, buckling the safety harness before takeoff. The engines hummed as the craft swiftly flew into the night sky. The stars twinkled as Seth stared out the window, focused on the bright light in the distance that was home.

A CHIP OFF THE OLD BLOCK

Martin Van Kirk never intended to be remarkable. Growing up in the small suburban town of Warrenville, Illinois, not much set him apart from his classmates or anyone else residing in his sleepy little Midwestern world. Nothing except his uncanny resemblance to his deceased father.

Grandpa always called him "a chip off the old block." He'd shake his head and say, "I swear, when your father was young, you two could have been twins."

This made Marty smile. Marty loved to hear stories about his father, and he envisioned them as imaginary playmates at times.

The two of us would have been best friends. I'm sure of it.

"Scrawny" was how his fifth-grade teacher, Mrs. Hamilton, referred to him, but she was in her twenties and had never met Marty's father. Marty was tall and thin with a shock of brown hair he constantly had to flip out of his eyes. He was a normal little boy. He played baseball, climbed monkey bars, swam in the local creek, and agreed with his friends that girls were gross, especially that Annalee Phillips who seemed too perfect with her long blonde hair and bright blue eyes.

Marty, along with his band of friends, took part in neighborhood mischief. Nothing serious. They'd rake leaves onto the porch of grumpy Old Man Newport and placed glitter inside the mailbox of the stern town librarian,

Miss Winston. In truth, they did nothing worse than is depicted in Norman Rockwell's paintings.

Childhood days passed as Marty lived a rather normal life. Few in Warrenville dreamt of leaving the quiet bounds of their fine community. However, Martin made up his mind when he was ten that he would go to college to study genetics and molecular biology. This was not the average dream of the average little boy on Millsap Lane.

"Those Nova shows on PBS have filled your head with all sorts of wild ideas," his grandfather told him.

"Now, Grandpa, you let him be. It's good for youngsters to have dreams," his grandmother interjected.

Marty had lived with his grandparents, Ethel and Audie Van Kirk since he was six years old. His parents, Pritchard and Melba, suffered a series of catastrophic illnesses, culminating in the loss of his father on Marty's fifth birthday and the death of his mother three days shy of the anniversary of his father's passing. Compounding matters, his grandparents weren't exactly spry and constant trips to the doctor heightened Marty's interest in science and the world of cells and genomes.

There must be something I can do to help people live longer, the young boy mused. More than anything, he wished he could have helped his parents have long, productive lives. They died in their early thirties, and the thought that nothing could be done for them haunted Marty.

The older he became, the more often he heard from older residents, "You look just like your daddy. If I didn't know better, I'd swear I was talking to Pritchard Van Kirk himself. You even sound like him." He'd smile, and they'd walk away shaking their heads in wonderment.

Once he'd made up his mind to study genetics, life became all business for the young Van Kirk. Given his family's limited financial worth, Marty spent junior high and high school focused on earning grades high enough to land him college scholarships.

"Come on, Van Kirk. Let's cruise the strip," his friends would plead. But, determined to keep his grade point average up, Marty usually said no and went back to his studies. Even when his best friend Andy prodded him to ask Annalee Phillips, whose beauty had only grown over the years, to the prom, Marty opted to stay in and do one more review before Saturday's ACT exam he'd take in the high school library with ten or fifteen of his classmates the following week.

"Annalee has no interest in going anywhere with me," Marty said matter-of-factly, and he dismissed Andy and his other friends, wishing them a good time at the dance.

His hard work paid off. At the end of his senior year, he was accepted to one of the most prestigious genetics programs in the country. Attending Stanford University was a dream come true for the young man who, so far in life, was only known for his uncanny resemblance to his father. Moving to California and leaving the only life he'd known behind was daunting, but it was a challenge that excited Marty.

"Don't worry, Gram and Grandpa. I'll be home for Thanksgiving and Christmas breaks, and we can call each other often."

"I can't even begin to tell you how proud your father and mother would be of you," his grandmother told him, tears brimming her eyes.

"Really? Are you sure they wouldn't think I'm hairbrained for being obsessed with genetics? It's not something most people around here even think about."

"Martin," Gram said with a sudden fierceness as she stared into his brown eyes, "I know you were cheated out of time to get to really know your parents, but I promise you they would be proud. Now isn't the time to talk about this in-depth, but know that they would approve. This is important for me, too."

Marty's heart warmed at his grandmother's encouragement, and something about what she said fueled his determination to excel in his studies.

Excel, he did.

By the end of his first year in the program, he'd made a name for himself. By the end of his second year, professors asked him to work on small research projects and to write reports for scientific publications. All of his professors encouraged him to apply for early admission into the post-graduate program. Marty's academic success sped rapidly forward. His hard work didn't come without a sense of guilt, however.

I promised Gram and Grandpa that I'd come home on breaks, and I haven't gone to Warrenville even once since arriving at Stanford. I've let my work swallow me whole.

The elder Van Kirks' health had deteriorated since Marty's high school graduation. Dementia forced Grandpa into assisted living, and a broken hip and other health issues sent Gram to the same facility. The thought of them dying stung Marty. They were old and frail, and any medical crisis could spell the end of them both. Still, he had responsibilities that he couldn't abandon in California. The more successful he was, the more demands on his time were made, and the months passed without a trip home.

I'm doing this to help people. I want to find a way to let everyone live longer. I lost my parents when they were young, and nothing is going to stop me from making breakthroughs. For now, phone calls with Gram and Grandpa will have to do.

At the end of his third year, Dr. Kellar, the professor leading an elite and confidential genetics study, called him to his office one afternoon.

"Mr. Van Kirk, please have a seat. Is it okay if I call you Martin?"

"Yes, Dr. Kellar, you can. Call me Marty if you'd like."

A warm smile crossed the professor's face. "Yes, I'd like to, Marty. There's something I'd like to discuss with you. It's something I think you may already be aware of."

Puzzled, Marty said, "I'm not sure what that might be, but I'm all ears."

Dr. Kellar double-checked his office door to make sure it was shut tightly then returned to his seat. "Your father was an important person in my life, Marty. I hope you know how deeply saddened I was at his passing. The loss of your mother so soon after Pritchard's death was a profound blow to myself and many others here at Stanford."

The room spun. *Did he just say he knew my father?* Martin Van Kirk sat speechless. Confusion clouded his face, and he rubbed his forehead with his right hand, trying to make sense of what he just heard.

"Pritchard used to do the exact same thing when he tried to figure something out. But I suppose you have heard your entire life how much you resemble him."

"Dr. Kellar, I have to admit, I have no idea where any of this is coming from. I'm from a small town in Illinois. My father worked at the local factory, and my mother was a housewife. No one even knows that Warrenville exists outside the Chicago area. How could you possibly know my parents?"

A deep exhale escaped Dr. Kellar as he leaned back in his lushly upholstered office chair.

"I didn't know I was surprising you, and I'm sorry if this is a shock. Before we move forward, I want to invite you to join my team. You've shown incredible ability in your classes, and you are just who we need for our research and development project."

"I'm honored and accept."

"Good. Before I get into the specifics, I think it's best that you have a conversation with your grandmother. She knows the particulars. I'm glad to have you on my team. Classes end on Wednesday. I'm going to contact your professors and let them know you need two weeks off to return home. You have some business to take care of there."

Marty didn't like the idea of dumping his responsibilities. He had two reports to write and a lab to run.

"I've got some things to do here. How about if I go in July?

"I need you to start the program before then, Marty, and if you are going to be a part of the project, you need to go now." Dr. Kellar's stern look was convincing.

"I'll do that. Sir, is there anything I need to do in the meantime?"

"No. I'll meet with you after you return in a few weeks. Be prepared to hit the ground running." Dr. Kellar rose to his feet and shook Marty's hand. "It will be a pleasure to work with you."

The next few days passed in a blur as Marty grappled with Dr. Kellar's cryptic words. *How does he know my parents? Why does he want me to speak to my grandmother?*

Uncertain of what he would learn, Marty arranged a flight to Chicago and for a driver to pick him up at the airport for the thirty-minute drive to Warrenville.

Arriving in Chicago at 10:45 Thursday morning, Marty was eager to see his grandparents. The Holy Oak Retirement Home sat on a bluff overlooking the still sleepy town of Warrenville. Riding through the streets of his childhood brought back memories.

Those days of riding bikes with Andy and Mike sure were fun--and sometimes painful. That corner is where I flipped over my handlebars and broke my arm. There's the ice cream shop where we dared Mike to eat ten ice cream cones. I thought his mother was going to kill us. He turned green and was sick for two days. And there's Old Man Newport's house. Gram said his children sold the place and now a young couple who works in the city lives there. I've missed being home.

Marty soaked in the sights, sounds, and smells of a familiar world he had forgotten about. Then he saw Holy Oak towering above him with its ornate white column and brick facade.

I'll meet with Grandpa later. Gram already warned me that he might not recognize me. Besides, Dr. Kellar said Gram was the one I should talk to.'

Room 306 was on the top floor of the retirement home, and as Marty entered his grandmother's room, he was relieved to see bright sun shining through the window and a fresh bouquet on her dresser.

At least they aren't living in a miserable place.

Gram struggled to stand at her bedside, but Marty rushed to her. "Gram, you stay right where you are. It's taken me this long to come to see you, and I'm the one who needs to make you comfortable."

She winked back tears and smiled. "You have always been such a thoughtful boy."

For about half an hour, they chatted about local gossip, Grandpa's condition, and whether or not Marty had gotten enough to eat at school.

"Don't worry, Gram. I eat well enough. I put in so many hours in the lab that I keep food in the fridge at work. You don't need to worry about me."

"A good home-cooked meal is what you need. But you didn't travel all the way to Warrenville to talk with me about food. What's really on your mind? You haven't answered me on the phone when I've asked what brings you here."

Marty smiled a sheepish grin and flipped his hair out of his eyes. *I could never hide anything from Gram.*

"What I'm going to say to you might not make any sense. I know it doesn't make sense to me."

"Spit it out, boy."

"One of my professors, Dr. Kellar, has asked me to join his project at Stanford."

Gram stopped in mid-sip of her coffee. "Kellar? Anson Kellar?"

Now Marty was genuinely perplexed. How would his grandmother know the first name of the leading geneticist at Stanford?

"Yes, Gram, but how--"

"It's time we have a talk, Martin. How much did Anson tell you?"

"Not much. He said he knew my mother and father. Then he told me before he said any more that I needed to talk with you."

"Oh, Marty, he's right. It's something we should have talked about long ago. I just couldn't bring myself to get into it. Did he tell you how he knew them, or what it is exactly that he works on?"

"No."

"Anson Kellar is good at what he does. He and your father were classmates at Harvard."

"Wait, Dad went to Harvard? I thought he worked at the local plant."

"That's just what we told the neighbors, son. What Pritchard and Melba were involved in was way too top secret for us to go blabbing to the Cunninghams across the street. And we wanted life to stay as normal for you as possible, so we told everyone Pritchard worked at Dell Chemicals."

"What did he really do?"

"Government work. Top secret government research. He and Anson accepted positions at Stanford to work on their projects."

"Research into what?"

"It's no mystery, Martin, why you were drawn to genetics. Your father and Anson were some of the first scientists to study cloning. But it went farther than that."

"Farther?"

"Look, Marty, I want you to know first and foremost that you are very loved, and you have always been very welcome in our lives. Your grandfather and I always wanted Pritchard and Melba to have a family, and when you came along we were thrilled. I don't want what I'm about to tell you to change that in any way in your mind."

Marty sat motionless as Gram began, as all things should, at the beginning. She detailed the first signs that Pritchard was different from other people. How Anson was the first to notice his body's special abilities.

"So Dad researched cloning because of some physical ailment that he had?"

"Not exactly. He was already on the research team. Each member volunteered tissue to be used in the experiments. Only Pritchard's sample was different from everyone else's."

"How so?"

"Most of the tissue samples weren't viable. They failed to duplicate, regardless of how many ways the researchers attempted to clone their cells."

"And Dad's?"

"His never failed. Something about Pritchard's cells made them replicate, perfectly, every single time. And that explains you."

"Wait... What do you mean it *explains* me?"

"Well, you and the others..."

For a moment, the room froze and Marty's world came to a halt.

"Others?"

"Yes, there are others. At least thirty. All are older than you. They were quickly scooped up by other research centers and the government. It bothered Pritchard and Melba to know his genetic offspring were snatched away, but it was part of the territory for the work he was involved in."

"So I have siblings?"

"Not siblings in the normal sense. You have duplicates."

"I was created in a petri dish?"

"In the most basic way, yes."

"And my mother wasn't really my mother?"

Gram's anger flared. "Now let's get one thing straight, Martin Van Kirk. Melba Dawson Van Kirk was and always will be your mother. It's because of her that we were able to keep you in the first place."

Martin reeled.

"Have a seat, Marty. It's time you understood it all."

"First of all, your grandfather knows nothing about any of it. Pritchard always had a distant relationship with his father, and he didn't want to risk state secrets escaping. Your grandfather loves to tell stories, and the temptation may have been too great for him to keep his mouth shut. Just Pritchard, Melba, myself, and Anson and the research team, of course, knew the truth."

"Just what is the truth. Why was I raised by you? What happened to my parents?"

"Pritchard became the subject of many studies. The government lacked the finesse it has now in studying such things, and they subjected your father to high doses of radiation, hormones, and other chemicals, attempting to find the key to his ability to replicate. It took a terrible toll on his body, and even Melba suffered secondhand effects of the radiation. That's what killed them."

"Why did I stay in the family when the others were taken away to be studied?"

"It was your mother's idea. She knew Pritchard was becoming weaker with every test, and she didn't know how long he would last. She begged him to create you--to have a part of him that would live on. Melba had always wanted children, but the scientists warned that your father's reproductive system was compromised by the experimentation. Having children, in the normal sense, was out of the question. Instead, they had you. And you were the apple of their eye, as the saying goes. No little boy was ever loved more."

Marty's entire existence shifted on its axis.

"Dr. Kellar has known all this?"

"Anson has known the entire time. He helped make the arrangements for Pritchard and Melba to have, and keep, you. He had to pull all the strings he had to do it, too."

A realization struck Marty. "I didn't get accepted to Stanford because of my ACT scores, did I?"

"No, Martin, you didn't. Anson has tracked you throughout your entire life. He and I have talked often about exactly how you would cross paths with him."

"When I was little and you took me to the doctors, those trips weren't always for you or Grandpa, were they?"

"They weren't. We took you in for monthly routine observations. Those suckers they gave you to taste, then took away, were for testing purposes. They used your saliva and DNA to study how your cells reacted to duplication. Anson wanted to know if you had inherited Pritchard's ability to replicate."

"And?"

"You did. You are a perfect replicator."

"Are there other versions of me out there?"

"No, they never crossed that line. You were a child. Now, however, you are an adult, and a scientist, and you and Anson Kellar have some conversations in your future. You are special, Marty, in so many ways. We waited until the time was right to tell you. We felt you deserved a carefree childhood. Now you have some decisions to make."

How do I continue to walk around like normal knowing my very existence isn't what I thought it was?

"Gram, I love you, and I know you never intended to hurt me. I am hurt, though. I can't even wrap my head around this. I'll be back to see you tomorrow. For now, I'm going to see Grandpa. I need some time to clear my head."

"I understand. I really do. I've known for decades, and it's still too much for me to take in. Just remember you are loved."

He was relieved when his grandfather momentarily remembered who Marty was as he flooded him with tears and questions about college. Grandpa only knew him as his grandson and not as a test subject in an experiment. After their short visit, Marty walked out of the Holy Oak Retirement Home.

The sun was shining and birds sang as he walked towards the only home he could remember: 1625 East Millsap Lane. Passing Monroe Park, the ice cream shop, and a thousand other points of memory, Marty wondered if his life had been too focused. The friends he'd made as a boy truly cared about him. What would life have been like if he'd stayed behind and never went to California? How different would his life be? Andy always teased him that he and Annalee Phillips would make pretty babies.

I wonder if Annalee would ever believe that I can make my own kids without anyone else's help? How would anyone understand that? How I wish I had my innocence back. Warrenville seems like a perfect world. Now I don't even know where I fit. Am I going back to Stanford to become a laboratory rat?

Marty's thoughts were distracted by a honking horn.

There, at the intersection of Honeysuckle Road and Kramer Avenue, sat a stunning blonde in a baby blue convertible. "Martin Van Kirk! You're just as handsome as ever. Are you going my way? I'll give you a ride."

Annalee Phillips, glowing in the bright May sunshine, sat before him, smiling that dimpled grin that turned the head of every boy in Warrenville.

I've spent every waking moment of my life thinking of nothing but science. Now I question what my life even means. I've never had any fun like other kids my age. It was always study, study, study. Maybe it's time for a change. Maybe, just maybe, there's more to my future than labs and tests.

Martin Van Kirk flipped his hair and opened the passenger door. "Annalee, I'd love to be going your way."

The next two weeks were a rush of emotions Martin had never felt before. His grandmother's confession, on the one hand, left him feeling betrayed.

How could they let me spend my entire life in the dark? All those times people said I looked just like my father, Gram knew. She knew, and she didn't tell me.

Betrayal wasn't the only emotion stirring in Martin. From the moment he sat in Annalee's car, he was swept away by everything about her.

One night they sat under the stars in Monroe Park, and he cradled her in his arms as they talked about the constellations. Annalee looked up at him as she ran her fingers through his brown hair.

"Marty, I have something to tell you."

Please don't let this be another wrecking ball.

"Remember when we used to play 'It' on the playground when we were little?"

"Of course, I do."

"I always let you catch me. You had to notice."

"No, I hadn't realized that."

"I did, Marty. I've spent my whole life waiting for you to catch me."

A look of disbelief crossed Marty's face. "There's no way you were interested in me. I was always the science geek. And you... You were the girl every boy in town wanted to date."

Turning to face him, Annalee gazed at him, then smiled her dimpled grin. "You really were oblivious, weren't you? I tried getting Andy to set us up on a date for years. Didn't he ever say anything to you?"

"He did. I always thought he was trying to make me look stupid. You know, have me ask you out so you would shoot me down. He was such a prankster that I never thought he meant it."

"This time he was serious, Marty." A long, sensuous kiss convinced him that she was telling the truth.

Night after night, Marty and Annalee fell more deeply in love.

On a walk through the town park, Marty stopped and turned to Annalee. "What would you think of coming with me to Stanford?" he hesitantly asked her.

"You'd want me there?"

"I want you wherever I am. I've even thought about throwing the whole Stanford thing aside and just staying here with you."

"Martin Van Kirk, you can't give up everything for me."

"Ever since I came back, I haven't been sure where I belong, but I know I want you with me."

"Count me in, honey. I'll go anywhere with you." She held him tight, and they spent the night making plans.

Marty's days were filled with frequent trips to Holy Oak to visit his grandparents. Grandpa could barely communicate, but the heart-to-heart conversations he had with Gram soothed his aching soul.

"That Annalee Phillips sure is one sweet girl, Martin."

"Yeah, she is…"

"That dreamy look you get in your eyes whenever she's mentioned tells me that you've been hit hard by Cupid's arrow."

"I do love her, Gram. What surprises me is that she says she loves me too."

"Nothing to be surprised by. You are a wonderful young man. I'm pretty sure she's had her sights set on you for years. I *might* have had a few conversations with that young lady from time to time."

"Gram, you are just full of surprises on this visit."

"Well, now that you mention it…"

The nurse interrupted their conversation, and Marty stepped out of the room. "I'll see you again, Gram."

"Tomorrow's your last day in town, so I certainly hope you do," she said with a wink.

Just outside her door, Dr. Finley gently tapped Marty's elbow and led him to a quiet area. "Has your grandmother said anything to you about the test results from yesterday?"

"No, she didn't. Is she okay?"

"I'm afraid not. Her heart is giving out, Marty."

"How long does she have?"

"Days. Maybe a few weeks. I'm glad you were able to come home when you did,"

Something inside Marty crumbled.

"We're running more tests this afternoon, and then she will need to rest. I suggest you wait until the morning to come back.

As angry as he'd been with Gram, he couldn't imagine life without her.

That evening, he and Annalee made their final plans for their trip to California. In the morning, he'd make one final stop to see his grandparents before heading to the airport.

He awoke to a dark sky and a misty rain falling as he made his way to Holy Oak. Thoughts of regret filled him.

I'd forgotten how much family and this town means to me. Grandpa is lost in his own world, and Gram's time is running out. My family is steadily slipping away from me. If it wasn't for Annalee, I'd be all alone.

Gram sat in her bed, reading a gardening magazine as he entered her room. At the sound of the door, she waved him in and smiled.

She looks so tired and frail.

"On your way to the airport soon?"

"Yes, Gram. I can change my flight and stay longer if you need me to."

"That's very sweet of you, but you *can't* do that. You *have* to return to Stanford, and I have a favor to ask of you while you're there."

Puzzled, he sat at the edge of her bed and took her hand in his.

Why is she so insistent that I leave?

"Gram, what favor would you need at Stanford?"

She paused. A tear trickled down the side of her face as she looked out the window with a faraway gaze.

"Gram…"

"Marty, I know I hurt you when I hid our family secret from you."

"Gram, don't feel bad about that. I'm sorting it out. I'll be fine. *We* are fine."

Her wrinkled hand patted his.

"It's just, son, that secrets tend to keep company with other secrets."

"Gram?"

"There's another family secret you must know about before you return to work on Anson Kellar's project. Please understand how important this is to me, and please promise me you will help."

"Gram, you're worrying me."

Quiet sobs choked her and she fell silent. After a moment, Gram found her voice and began again.

"You know that Pritchard was special because he could replicate. Anson wondered how that was possible, and in his quest to unlock the mystery, he collected a sample of cells from me. Martin, your father inherited his abilities from me."

"So there are others of you out there?"

"No, at least not yet."

"Not yet?"

"This is the real reason why Anson wanted you to come home, to talk to me, before he told you any more about his research."

Gram took a drink of water and dabbed her eyes with the tissue she clutched in her hand.

"Gram, what is it that you want me to do?"

"Anson saved my sample. He promised me he wouldn't do anything with it until you could take part."

"Take part? Gram, I don't understand."

"I was heartbroken when the replicates of your father were cast into research and secret government tests. No child should go through that. It's tortured my soul to think my duplicate would face the same fate. You must promise to help." Jagged sobs escaped her.

"Oh, Gram, I promise. What do you want me to do?"

"Anson promised that only one clone will be made from my sample. Marty, I want her to have a home. I want her to have a family that loves her. I can't stand the thought of her ending up as nothing but a test subject. She will be the only thing left of me in this world."

"What do you want me to do?"

"I want you and Annalee to raise her. She can be your daughter. She needs you, and I need you." Gram's breathing became heavy and she squirmed in discomfort.

"Gram, I promise. We will give her a family."

"Oh, Marty," she sighed, 'you've given me the peace I need. However much time I have left, I know she will be okay. Now go find your future."

Marty flipped his hair out of his eyes, kissed Gram's forehead, and walked away to find his destiny.

SCARCITY

The sharpness of the wind caused the feeble old man to tighten his grip around the collar of his tattered coat. Occasional bits of sleet from scattered clouds added to the misery of the impending evening. Alone and hungry, this weary soul found himself once more reduced to begging.

I remember a day when life was easy. I didn't suffer like this. The world has become a miserable place.

Arnie Hammond then chided himself for his grumbling.

At least part of this is my fault. I put myself in this position, and I can't blame anyone else for that. I've become too dependent on others, and that's why I'm where I'm at. I knew better.

Still, the biting cold was hard on a man of his age. Street lights turned on as the amber sun sank, peeking through a stormy horizon. The trees lost their leaves weeks ago, and they were now reduced to mere shells of what they once were, much like Arnie himself. He stopped walking to take in the scene before him. The trees stood like skeletons silhouetted against the darkening sky, and their branches reached up as though in a fervent prayer toward the heavens.

"God grant us mercy," Arnie muttered.

He blew on his cracked hands and his breath filled the air.

"It's going to be a rough one tonight. I'm not asking for much. Just a little comfort for my weary bones."

Shuffling along the asphalt of the city, Arnie approached an intersection frequented by panhandlers. He was in luck, it appeared, because none of the regulars worked the spot tonight.

I guess it's too cold out here even for the young ones.

A short line of cars waited for the light to change. Arnie carefully approached the first, a white sedan, driven by a man yelling into his cell phone. He gently rapped on the passenger window.

Glaring, the man rolled down the window. "What in the hell do you want, old man? Do I look like I care about your problems? I've got problems of my own. Go somewhere else!" With that, he pushed the button to raise the window, shutting Arnie out of his small, angry world.

Arnie shrugged his shoulders and stepped to the next car in line. His heart leapt as the window lowered before he even reached the vehicle. His joy was short-lived.

"Listen, buddy, go get a job. Stop freeloading off honest Americans. You should be ashamed of yourself."

"There was a time when--"

"Save it! Leave me and my wife alone."

It's 'my wife and me' Arnie thought as he shuffled along to the next vehicle, a large diesel truck. His luck was no better there. No one screamed at him, but no one looked at him either. It was as though, if they ignored him, he would disappear into thin air. For the next hour, he faced one rejection after another.

A bustling parking lot to the west of the intersection offered some promise. His knees creaked as he climbed the embankment. The exertion wore on his battered body, but the shortcut saved him an added quarter mile of walking to reach the entrance of the big box store. Busy holiday shoppers rushed about, eager to finish the last of their errands. The wind whipped, and the sleet intensified. Christmas carols rang out over the store's speakers, wishing peace and good will toward men. "It's the season of giving," the soothing voice announced between songs. The jingling bell of the Salvation Army volunteer mingled with the wind.

Arnie thought about peace and joy a lot. He yearned for the time when his world was filled with peace and joy. Wiping his dirty hand over his face, he remembered what it was like to be loved. He fought back the tears welling in his eyes. A combination of emotion and stinging wind made his efforts useless.

He tottered toward the exit of the store and leaned against a post for a moment to catch his breath. *This may be my last chance to find any relief tonight.*

He mustered his strength and slowed his breathing as he approached a woman briskly stepping toward her Mercedes. He didn't want to appear desperate, although, as a beggar on the street, that was exactly what he was at this moment.

"Please, ma'am, I'm not asking for much, I was wondering if…"

His words faded away as she clutched her purse and gave him a baleful stare. "Mister, you can just back away. I'll call the police on you."

"I'm sorry to bother you."

"Well, you did. Go away."

Arnie turned to see a gentleman pushing a cart loaded with bags. "Excuse me, sir."

"Listen, you can take your panhandling someplace else. I don't have time for thieves like you. Take one step closer and I'll beat the hell out of you. You nasty thing, you. Stop trying to sponge off others. Get a job. Make yourself useful."

The comments crushed Arnie's spirit. His bearded chin slumped against his dirty shirt. As ashamed as he was by his current appearance, nothing hurt worse than the accusation that he wouldn't work for his own living. He was willing to do any job, but his failing health made work nearly impossible. The past year was a vicious circle. The longer he went without adequate food and shelter, the less capable he was to work. The less capable he was to work, the worse his living conditions became.

"God Rest Ye Merry Gentlemen" floated through the air as the angry man turned once more and raised his fist toward Arnie.

"No need to become violent, sir. I won't bother you again."

"You won't bother anyone ever again if you provoke me one more time. If I don't see you walking out of this parking lot, I'm going to take you around the corner and make you wish you'd never met me. I'm going to stand here and watch you go. Now get!"

"But--"

"I don't want to hear it, creep. Go!"

The man's eyes flashed, and Arnie knew he had no choice. If he lingered, the man would make good on his threats. There were a lot of ways to die, but beaten on a cold winter's night was not how Arnie wanted to face his end.

He turned to walk away, looking over his shoulder one more time at the man whose fist remained raised. With shoulders drooping, Arnie made his way back to the main road, accepting that no sustenance would come on this night. He slowly made his way across town.

All alone in the dark corner of an industrial building, Arnie Hammond leaned against the cold brick wall. The freezing wind seared his face and swept the breath from his lungs. Pellets of sleet fell in earnest now, and Arnie slumped onto the icy concrete. There would be no Christmas cheer for him.

Peaceful thoughts washed over Arnie as he dreamed of better days. He'd come so far from home and had asked for so little. He knew he'd been foolish. Even in his reverie, he knew he'd expected far too much from the cosmos. His dream was so vivid it felt real. Memories of home came to life. The love he felt during childhood flooded over him.

He heard his mother's voice and felt her hand caress his hair. "Arnie, my boy, I'd have saved you if I could."

"I know, Mama."

"Tell me, son, what have you learned?"

"I learned that the cosmos is unkind to a lonely traveler. A man like me had no business coming to a foreign planet thinking I could survive on what, I now know, is a scarce commodity: human kindness. Please forgive me, Mama." He fell into a deep sleep, wrapped in dreams of her love and home.

Hypothermia and hunger took their toll on our weary visitor. Two, maybe three, days later, someone would stumble upon what remained of a hobo, frozen and alone in an icy, barren alley.

THE JOYRIDE

Teenagers have a habit of pushing the envelope of their parents' patience. Sometimes they push the boundaries of what society and the law allow, too. Such was the case with young Yurgen. He had never been an unruly child, but as he moved farther into his teenage years, he developed a rebellious streak that caused his parents and community leaders alike to shake their heads and whisper words of concern for his future.

Tonight Yurgen crossed the threshold of what was acceptable, and what was not.

The evening began with a double date between Yurgen, his best friend, and two pretty girls, who happened to be twins. They went to the movies, and because the girls had a father no one wanted to anger, the boys dropped them off at home a half-hour earlier than their curfew. The father was a known tough guy with a shady past, and actual hell would have been paid had those girls not arrived home on time. Yurgen was stupid, but not that stupid.

At midnight, Yurgen parted ways with his pal, who dropped him off at the end of his street. Yurgen wanted to enjoy the beautiful night by walking the rest of the way home. The stars were out, and a warm breeze blew through the trees. In the moment, Yurgen reveled in being alive. Young and adventurous, he wasn't ready to call it a night, however. A big world stretched before him, and surely there was something he could do to quench his thirst for fun. He weighed his options. By this hour, most of the hangout spots were empty. The diners were closed. None of his friends were anywhere to be seen.

This town is dead.

He nearly gave up, but something caught his eye in the moonlight. A shiny new model just sat there for the taking. He knew he didn't have his license. He didn't even have his permit, for that matter. Yurgen knew he shouldn't, but when would he get a chance like this again? He'd have bragging rights amongst his friends, and they'd be jealous of his brave adventure. Recklessness was an admired trait in the hearts and minds of rowdy boys, and he'd be the hero of his peers.

The keys sat there nearly begging him to take it for a spin. He'd seen models like this in magazines, and dreamed of one day being behind the wheel of such a fine vehicle. He'd longed for the opportunity to try one out, and here it was. How could he turn down this opportunity? He'd never forgive himself if he did. His friends would be so jealous.

It's just a little joyride. What could it hurt?

Isn't that the question all rebellious teens ask when they do something they shouldn't do? Even adults use it as an excuse, after all.

Yurgen nervously looked around, but the street was empty. Not totally without a conscience, thoughts of what could happen flashed through his mind. He knew his mother would cry if he were caught breaking the law, and his father would… Well, he didn't want to think about what his father would do.

For a second, he considered walking away. That would be easy and safe. But who had fun playing it easy and safe? Certainly not a young firebrand like Yurgen. The world was at his fingertips, and come hell or high water, he was going to make the most of his youthful energies. Tonight would be a memory maker.

Checking one more time for onlookers or security cameras, Yurgen grabbed the keys and slid into his shiny little number he'd discovered. He turned the ignition and revved the motor. The exhilaration of being in control was unlike any feeling he'd had before. His body melded into his new ride, and they became one. His heart raced, and he felt giddy.

He put it in gear and headed for open stretches of road to test the power of the engine. Tearing across town, he squealed its tires, spun donuts, and rejoiced in creating mayhem. He reached speeds he'd only dreamed of, and a few times he nearly lost control. For two hours, he wallowed in unrestrained abandon.

Then it happened.

The crashing cascade of glass as he flipped end-0ver-end, went through the front window of the local department store, and then landed in a ditch, brought his night of frivolity to an abrupt end. The flashing lights of the police cruiser let him know, without a doubt, that his joyride was over.

Down at the station, his parents thanked the officer for contacting them first without filing formal charges.

"Do you have any idea how worried your mother was, young man?"

His father towered above him while his mother dabbed her eyes with a soggy tissue.

"I--"

"Save the excuses, Yurgen. You know what you did was foolish and wrong. Someone could have been killed."

"Yes, Dad."

"I'm grounding you for a month, and I'm calling your Uncle Jack tomorrow about the Newbury Demon Reform School."

"But, Dad--"

"Your father is right. You knew better than to take possession of a human before you were legal to drive. It's a wonder you didn't kill her. Then we'd have really had a lot of explaining to do to the higher ups. For now, we are going home."

His father's tail flicked toward the open door leading to the parking lot. "I hope you've learned your lesson."

Yurgen's tail dropped to the ground as he lowered his head and slunk out the door behind his parents.

ESSENTIAL ELEMENTS

The windswept auburn plains were a vibrant backdrop to a dismal day. No sooner had hope reared its fickle head than the engine failed for a second time on the rover.

Major Amelia Foster was frustrated. *Remind me to never depend on a first-year production model, especially when my life is on the line. My old rover never let me down.*

The Air Force Space Exploration and Development Fleet sometimes embraced the use of new technology before the bugs were worked out of the system.

After rapping her knuckles on the engine to the point that they bled, again, Amelia threw the wrench she grasped in her left hand. Two engine failures tested her patience. A trip that held so much potential hours earlier had taken another ugly twist.

Clenching the radio, Amelia called base camp. "This is Foster. Rover 14. Is anyone there?" Static was the only reply.

Damn. No help would be coming, and she could hardly blame them.

We are at war. There are bigger concerns for those left at base camp than my dilemma. Thousands--millions--could die if we don't win this war.

"You are one pebble in the path to victory." She smirked at the line used in the latest recruitment ads the Air Force circulated back on Earth.

Three days earlier, the directive from District Command spurred the entire camp into action. The once distant war was at their doorstep. An immediate evacuation order was given, and all but "essential staff" were loaded onto transport ships, cargo planes, and even refueling vehicles until the camp was a ghost town.

Amelia Foster was essential staff, and her last bit of business included disabling the power stations across the sector. Five of the six were now out of commission, but time was ticking. She understood the demands of her position. In fact, she thrived on the adrenaline rush that came with high-stress situations. Seeking a thrill had landed her in many sticky situations throughout her life.

"You're never going to find a husband when you insist on taking part in these shenanigans," her mother had scolded her when she was a little girl.

"Mom, you found a husband, and a lot of good that did you."

Amelia's memory brought with it the sting from her mother's backhand. She could still feel the trickle of blood that ran down her face, and she heard the sound of her mother's sobs as she slammed her bedroom door. Those sobs echoed throughout the house and throughout Amelia's childhood.

Well, Mom, all your worrying about my marital status doesn't help now. Husband or no husband, if I don't make it back to the base in time for the last ship, you didn't have to wonder whether or not you'd ever have grandchildren.

Amelia Foster's glib outlook quickly shifted to a moment of panic. What *was* she going to do? Death, at this point, was no laughing matter.

Searching through her supply pack, she pulled out a nutrient bar and a drink that passed for orange juice. With twelve miles ahead of her, on foot, she needed all the energy she could muster. Stuffing bags of peanuts mixed with cereal and chocolate chips into the pockets spread across her uniform and grabbing both canteens of water she'd brought along in her rover, she began the arduous trek across the seemingly endless plains. This was no recreational hike. Her life, and countless others, depended upon her success.

If I don't get to the last power station to disable it, not only will I die, but I'll go down as a failure to my base and the entire Air Force. I can see my tombstone's epitaph: Major Amelia Foster: Essentially Useless. God, please don't leave me stranded here. All I ask is that someone left a working vehicle behind so that when (or is it if?) I get there I have a chance of making it off this planet in time.

Getting there was the trick. Daylight wasn't a problem. It was summer, so a day lasted for what would have been days back on Earth, with short periods of nightfall in between. The real obstacles were the meandering series of small, narrow canyons she must travel through with little more than her own sense of direction to guide her. She gazed across the horizon. The seemingly placed plains, filled mainly by the ten-foot-high red shafts of ripening grain, were anything but smooth and serene.

The canyons criss-crossed one another, creating a maze even the ancient Greeks would have been inspired by.

The waves of grain slowly swaying in the breeze under the gorgeous amber sun belied the dangers of the uneven and unpredictable paths she must follow to reach the last critical stop on her mission. Without her vehicle's guidance system, she must navigate on instinct and situational awareness. More than once officers, smart ones traveling in groups, had been lost to the endless labyrinth beneath the stunning, yet deceptively unsafe, vista.

One small step for me, one giant leap... Her mind tumbled back to her childhood once again.

"Amelia, why don't you play with your dolls or read some stories? That television is getting on my nerves. What are you watching anyway?"

"It's the moon landing, Mom."

"That happened before your grandfather was born. What interest could you have in something that old and boring?"

"One day, I'm going to be like Neil Armstrong and go into space. After all, I'm named after a famous pilot."

"Naming you after Amelia Earhart was your no-account father's idea."

"I'm glad he named me, and I'm going to be an astronaut."

"Over my dead body, Amelia Jo Foster! You're just like your useless father. Always dreaming big and wishing your life away. You'll end up a nothing. You'll be lost if you don't keep your head in this world. Lost, I say."

She felt her blood pressure spike. *Lost.* Her biggest fear in life was becoming what her mother harangued her the most about. She didn't want to be lost or a failure. Now she found herself in terrain that killed and becoming lost had never been more imminent a threat than it was at that moment.

I may not have been the first to set foot on a planet, but I'm still making my mark in life. I'm not going to be the failure Mom always said I would be. Sometimes I hate my father for burdening me with her vitriol. Sometimes I envy him for escaping it. Maybe he wasn't as lost as Mom thought. He'd just found himself and knew he had to go. I'm not going to be lost, either.

Finding a point of reference as she descended into the first valley was futile. Everything looked the same. Looking east or west or north or south meant nothing.

Nothing except my survival.

A covey of birds, disturbed from their hiding place, throttled into the sky, jolting her from her thoughts. The burst of color against the clear blue heavens reminded her of flamenco dancers swirling across a dance floor. Still, the sudden frenzy of activity caused Amelia's heart to miss a beat.

I need to regain my military bearing. This childish fear is unbecoming of an officer.

As the chief energy engineer on the mission, she'd been too busy to enjoy much of the scenery of her temporary home. In the ten months since she arrived, she made, at most, five outings. Those were usually in the company of three or more coworkers. Orders were clear that service members not leave the compound in groups of fewer than three. Unknown dangers made solo treks foolhardy.

As a relatively new outpost, war cut short the amount of exploration typically preceding the installation of a base. The abundant solar power and natural gas supplies made the planet, jokingly referred to as "Exxon," a natural outpost for energy production. Those same elements now made it a prized target for the enemies of Earth.

With little known about the planet, officially known as Xenia Minor, rumors spread late at night in whispers and quiet confidences about wild beasts that roamed the countryside during the scanty hours of darkness found on the planet. The maze of canyons, however, was viewed as the greatest threat to the planet's human inhabitants.

The rushed evacuation and Amelia Foster's orders to disable the power stations negated the safety of numbers rule. Hers was a solitary mission today. The ample fuel sources on Xenia Minor made it a modern day Midway Island in the First Universal War. Earth had to retain control of this part of the galaxy.

Within fifteen minutes, she found herself in the first canyon, darkened by its walls which blocked out much of the sunlight. She squinted her eyes as she tried to adjust to the lowered light.

Grandpa used to say that moss grows on the north side of a tree. If I'm going to make it out of here, I need to use every resource and bit of trivia I can think of.

Sure enough, the small lichens clinging to the right-hand side of the canyon walls proved that she was, in fact, heading in the direction of the power station. After several hundred yards, an intersection of canyons stopped her in her tracks.

Which way do I go? I don't see any moss, but my gut tells me I need to veer left to stay on course.

Another flock of birds, these an electric blue with canary yellow wingtips, flew over, drawing her attention to the world above her. There she saw the grain, crimson and towering, leaning forward under the force of the breeze that had blown all day.

This morning's weather report said winds would be coming from the south, blowing towards the northeast. Another sign that I am on the right path.

Stopping for a drink of water, Amelia listened intently to the silence. *Nature is my compass today.* The normal buzz of patrol craft was missing. The evacuation and the total absence of humanity around her drew her to thoughts of isolation. She hated being alone, but it was a feeling she knew well. Thanks to the frenzied activity of life on a military outpost, she hadn't thought about it for a while. Loneliness was her constant companion during childhood, but as long as she buried herself in work it stayed in the shadows of her mind. Now those dark thoughts crept to the surface in the form of more memories.

"Mom, can I have a party for my birthday?"

"Name me five people who would come to it, Amelia Jo."

"Well, there are the girls in my class at school."

"Really? You think I want those nasty creatures in my house? I can't trust them."

"Why not, Mom?"

"They will steal us blind, and I don't want them to talk you into misbehaving. Besides, we are moving on Tuesday. This town has nothing to offer us."

Tears rolled down twelve-year-old Amelia's face. "Again?"

As a child, moving was an accepted fact of life. Her mother constantly changed jobs while seeking a "better" life for her and her daughter.

Ironically, the one thing I wanted in life was a stable home and friends. Here I am, working in a career that sends me across the universe fifteen times in the past five years. Maybe I was born to be alone.

A shrieking cry from Xenia Minor's version of a hawk brought her back to reality. She once again began her trek through the puzzling canyons. Using clues from her surroundings, she made good time even though the sandy ground created tough walking conditions. Her feet sank into the silt and the grains penetrated through her boots into her socks.

She stopped frequently for water breaks and took a few bites of peanut mixture.

I'm drinking my water supply away. Get with it, Foster. You have miles to go.

After hours of wrong turns, backtracking, breaks for dwindling water, and an unending determination for success, she finally reached the plateau overlooking the last of the power stations. The sun still hovered above the horizon and would for a while longer.

I made it, and I have time.

Approaching the compound, which consisted of three small buildings and an office, she swung her backpack off her shoulder. Setting it on the ground outside the building that contained the "brains" of the station, Amelia unlatched and lifted the lid to the control box. Punching in her security access code, she seized the door handle. It remained frozen. Her eyes darted to the control panel.

"Access Denied."

What in the hell?

Amelia punched the numbers one more time.

"Access Denied."

Shaking the door handle to no avail, she kicked her right foot into the solid metal door. Pain shot through her toes, and she realized she'd made a foolish blunder out of anger. She slumped to the ground to collect her thoughts.

Wait a minute. The power station manager sent me a memo last week. There was a failure in the control box and the technician had to retool the security system. What's the new code?

She wiped sweat from her brow and practiced the breathing exercises her high school coach taught her to relieve anxiety. Breathe in. Exhale slowly. Breathe in. Exhale slowly.

It worked. Her mind, cleared of panic, remembered the new code was the last four digits of the mission number. She leapt to her feet, entered the code, and stepped inside the humming interior of the building. She quickly went to work. Disabling the system was a relatively simple procedure, and within ten minutes the humming stopped. The natural gas well auto-filled with concrete to seal it and the solar panels crumbled to dust.

Now, is there a vehicle?

Running to the garage, she found the last of the small cargo trucks, keys on the dash, sitting there as if it was waiting for her.

Finally, something is going my way.

She had time, if she hurried, to get to the base camp before the last ship left. Staring in the direction of the base, she scanned the skies when she heard the purr of engines in the air. Three small crafts, not from Earth, flew a reconnaissance mission moving southwest from where Amelia stood.

Those aren't friendly, and I need to hurry!

She drove the long way to avoid detection as she kept one eye on the sky. She made the bumpy drive toward camp as quickly as possible. The sun was setting, and the faintest of stars appeared in the sky.

Only they aren't stars.

The pinpoints of light moved in formation.

Holy hell. Those are enemy patrols. The invasion has begun.

She'd hoped that panic was something she could leave behind in childhood. Life with her mother was filled with anxiety and instability. Amelia joined the military for two reasons. First, her adventurous spirit drew her to the thrill of high-stakes missions. Secondly, she believed it would help her overcome her insecurities. Military structure and routine gave her the stability she'd craved as a child. After she became an officer, leading other service members gave her the confidence to move past most of her self-doubts. Still, the cobwebs of her mother's words resounded in her mind.

"Mom, I've decided I'm joining the Air Force."

"Over my dead body!"

"Mom, you've said that about everything I've ever wanted to do. So far, you're still alive."

Amelia winced at that last memory. Her mother died ten years ago, just four months after Amelia left for the training academy. The pain of that loss never went away. She wasn't close, in the traditional sense, to her mother, but that made the loss more troubling for Amelia. The dreadful feeling that nothing could ever improve for them haunted her. The hope of reconciliation died with her mother in that house fire.

The droning of engines pulled her out of her painful recollections. The invasion was in full force, and those left at the base were powerless to stem the tide of alien hordes now encircling the encampment. That last ship to safety was never going to fly.

Explosions forced her to dive for cover. The largest of the detonations came from the booster rockets intended for the escape vessel. Incoming mortar rounds ignited a huge fire. All hope was lost. It was only a matter of time.

Moments after she hid behind the guard station on the edge of the base, Amelia heard the unmistakable sound of voices. They were not human. She shuddered

They're inside my head! They're in my thoughts!

"We know you are here. We have come for you. Do not bother hiding anymore."

Resolute to not die cowering in the face of the enemy, Amelia stepped forward onto the pavement and faced her executioners.

"I am Major Amelia Foster of the United States Air Force Space Exploration and Development Fleet."

"We know who you are. We have read your thoughts."

A tremor passed through her at the knowledge that she was so completely violated. Even her thoughts were not private.

"It appears you have been busy today. Isn't that right, Major Foster?"

"I will tell you nothing more than my name and rank."

"You realize the comedy of what you are saying, don't you? Your thoughts have already told us everything we need to know."

"What do you want with me?"

"I think you know we need Xenia Minor as a fueling station."

"I guess as much, and you must be aware that I permanently disabled the power stations."

"Yes, we know you did, and you were extremely heroic in your efforts, Major Foster. You just made one mistake."

Amelia cringed. She hated making mistakes. "What would that mistake be?"

"You and your strategists completely misread our intentions. We want Xenia Minor as a refueling station, but it has nothing to do with solar power or petroleum."

"Then what? What could you possibly use as fuel for your aircraft?"

"Ah, there is your mistake. It isn't fuel for our machinery. It is fuel for us we seek. You, and your kind, Major Foster, are perfect for our nutritional needs. You were considered essential here, and you are. You will provide us with our essential elements."

The horror struck Amelia and her knees buckled.

"I'm just one person, and there can't be more than twenty people left on this planet. How can we feed you for long?"

"You are merely decoys, Major. After we have consumed you, we will send out a call to your fleet commanders. We are excellent at mimicking. We will tell them that fears of an invasion were mistaken and for the thousands of evacuees to return."

"But if they are tricked into returning they will spot your aircraft and know to go into full battle alert.'

"They won't see us. Those confusing canyons and fissures running through this planet make excellent cover to keep our whereabouts hidden until we need to show ourselves."

The monstrous reality that she and the fleet faced were beyond what Amelia could stand. She wretched and fell to her knees.

"We will make it quick. It will take only a matter of minutes, but I can't promise you it will be painless." A terrible cackle rattled the inside of Amelia's mind.

Fight though she may, she was incapable of putting up more than an inconsequential struggle. Forced aboard a kitchen, of sorts, Amelia was stripped of her clothing, and injected with a liquifying agent much like those used by spiders on their prey. The aliens hooked her up to tubes and slowly drained her of her life.

In her last moments, Amelia felt an uncanny closeness to her mother. Instead of the fighting and the ugly barbs, she reminisced about the good times. Tea parties for two. Shopping trips. Sunday drives in the country when her mother felt genial.

Mom, I'm sorry. I wish things had been better between us.

A tear escaped her clenched eyelids. A warm embrace took her by surprise, and she caught a whiff of the rosewater perfume that was her mother's favorite.

"It's okay, Amelia Jo. It's me. I'm here. Over your dead body."

THE CARDINAL

The hot summer sun beat down on the Little League field. Parents sat on metal bleachers, cheering for six-year-olds donning Ava Lumber jerseys and ball caps. Out in leftfield, a blond kid kicked at an anthill. The shortstop hiked up his pants and wiped dripping sweat from his eyes. They only needed two more outs to stop the ten-run surge of their opponents.

"Look alive, boys!" An anxious father paced back and forth outside the chain-link fence. "Billy, throw those strikes like I taught you."

Given his physical appearance, a few parents doubted the athletic abilities of the man demanding excellence from a first-grader. Those vicarious expectations were as much a part of the summer baseball experience, however, as the grimaces made when foul balls bounced off the hoods of vehicles unfortunate enough to be parked in range.

A hot breeze blew, and younger children begged their parents for another snow cone. Mercifully, the inning came to an end, and so did the final three quick outs that added to the defeat.

"It's okay, boys. You win some, and you lose some. Practice is Tuesday at three." The coach gave high fives to his little warriors.

Parents collected their sons, and pep talks filled the night air as their footsteps kicked up dust in the parking lot.

Young Luke wanted nothing more than to be an outfielder, or a pitcher, or a third baseman for the St. Louis Cardinals. He really didn't care which position he played. He just knew his heart would never be content until he held a bat under the mighty arches encircling Busch Stadium.

Every day, from morning until dark, he either played baseball, thought about baseball, or watched baseball. At night, he dreamed about baseball. The Cardinals were the only team that occupied his nightly slumbers. As the years went by, his teammate heroes in those dreams changed, whether it was Bob Gibson, Lou Brock, or Curt Flood. He imagined sitting in the dugout joking with his buddies while the cameras caught their antics. Or he stood on deck, waiting for his chance at bat. In the really good dreams, he felt the crack of the bat and heard the roar of the crowd as he rounded the bases. A grand slam.

As he grew up, the voices of Jack Buck and Mike Shannon reverberated in his head. Some days he spent hours tossing the ball up, over and over and over, perfecting his prowess at snagging pop flies. He squinted as the sun blinded him, but it was just preparation for when stadium lights battled him for his focus and the ball arched then descended while fans inside Busch Stadium held their breaths.

Baseball was loved by everyone he knew, but Luke was certain no one had the burning in his heart for it like he did. Still, it helped that everyone else was enthusiastic. He couldn't get to the majors throwing his own pop flies forever.

The neighborhood children gathered to play Wiffle ball. Some were even pretty good at it. Luke appreciated the opportunity to hone his skills against adept players. Others, well, they were place keepers he tolerated so he could field enough for a game.

Luke's sisters played catch and 500 with him day after day and year after year. Brothers would have been better, but the girls usually filled in well enough for him to perfect his curveball, or to throw endless pop flies on the side lawn. He liked teaching them how to slide. Though neither of them was keen on trying Pete Rose's face-first belly flops, his little sister mastered the art of tucking one leg under the other as she slid into base, avoiding the tag. He also made her learn how to switch hit so he could practice pitching against lefties.

Playing for the Cardinals was all he ever wanted. If he just tried hard enough, practiced long enough, and dreamed big enough, he could do it. He had faith.

Dreams are tough things to see dashed in a little boy. Mononucleosis struck in sixth grade. Everyone on his school's basketball team came down with it, but Luke's case was severe. The high fever that raged for days leveled the boy. He lost all coordination, and he struggled to tie his own shoes.

"He won't be able to play sports." Those grim words came from the neurologist at the University of Missouri Medical Center in Columbia. "If you let him play, he will just hurt himself."

That possibility was too devastating; simply too much to take away from a little boy, so his mother allowed him to play.

"He will never get better if he doesn't have something to fight for. I can't take his only chance away from him."

He fell running the bases. He misjudged those pop flies. But he played. Practice was more than a love of baseball. It was the only hope he had to regain a normal life.

Slowly, his coordination returned. The dream continued.

Little League became a memory as he entered high school. Those hours of using his little sister as a batter's box guinea pig paid off, and he became a starting pitcher for the hometown team.

Harsh realities set in when he knew he'd never be good enough to catch the eye of a big-league scout, so he changed direction. He could still be on the field at Busch Stadium, but this time in a different uniform: that of a professional umpire. A new passion caught fire as he studied those figures crouched in blue leaning over the catcher's shoulder or running the baselines to call fouls and outs. The big leagues awaited him yet.

Hot summers were spent umping Babe Ruth League ball at the city fields. Hard work, determination, and ferocity to make it happen fueled him day and night.

But it wasn't to be. Instead of leaving for umpire training school, harsher realities drove him to the military. Years passed, and he found himself at Scott Air Force Base, as close to his beloved Cardinals as he could get. He even splurged on one of those personalized license plates to go on his red Chevy truck. "9Cdnls" (the exact number it took to make a team) made it clear to all fellow travelers where his heart resided.

A few decades of ball games, scorecard in hand, kept the bittersweet fire alive. The pain never entirely left his eyes. The thought of not stepping foot in the stadium as more than a fan broke his heart.

Then cancer destroyed all dreams. On a cold October night, he lost the biggest game he'd played.

On opening day of the next season, light crept into the hallowed arches of Busch Stadium. Crowds hadn't entered the stands, and groundskeepers scurried across the infield, raking the dirt into pre-game perfection.

The voices of Jack Buck and Mike Shannon whispered through the empty field if one listened carefully. Glenn Brummer stealing home, Lou Brock stealing second, and the scowling grunts of the Mad Hungarian could be found as the memories of a storied team blew through the arches and past the scoreboard.

A lone red bird softly fluttered to a landing on the dugout railing. His eyes burned bright, and his chest puffed ever so slightly. He then flew to the grassy area just past second base. The Cardinal had finally taken the field.

A TIME OF PEACE

Sweat trickled down his back as the sweltering equatorial sun blazed in the clear blue sky. So much destruction. So much bloodshed. A smile crept across Sharo's face.

From his vantage point, he pictured it all. Memories flowed through his mind, breathing in and out of his consciousness as easily as the heated air came and went through his nostrils. Sharo closed his eyes and drifted back to the beginning. He could nearly taste the anticipation of those early, carefree times. The sound of laughter and the excited chatter of the village tinkled like a bell in his mind. He was made for this day. His whole life existed for no other reason.

Had the cost been high? Yes, it always was, but oh… victory was sweet. Looking at his hands, he carefully studied the blood smears of his enemies and friends alike. Loss of life is nothing compared to the joy of winning.

***

"My son, you understand the dangers ahead. Are you sure you want to lead? As the chief's son, you have the right and ability to cast this burden onto another."

Sharo stood to face his father. "Because I am your son, I am the only one suited for this battle. Do not try to dissuade me from my birthright."

Sharo knew the dangers. His father expected nothing less, but the questions still must be asked for the ritualized preparations to be complete.

He'd heard the stories of his people as they passed from generation to generation. As a child, he and his playmates pretended to play Haru. Dividing into eight teams, they strategized their moves in the dense forest undergrowth as they launched their attacks from the rainforest canopy. Even in child's play, Haru was dangerous.

Sharo's best friend, Manu, nearly died playing an intense version of the game one sweltering day. The jungle, always full of hazards, reminded the village children to never mistake youth for safety. Sharo would always remember the accident.

While attempting to outdo one another, Manu climbed to the top of the highest Mandolou tree he could find. Lean and stealthy, Manu clutched his knife in his teeth as he climbed the mighty tree. Sharo watched as his friend slid across the branches, planning an ambush on a rival tribe member. All boys trained for the right to represent their tribe one day, and they took turns roleplaying as warriors from different tribes. Mardi, Sharo's cousin, crept below as Manu prepared to drop a net on his foe.

The cracking sound the limb made as it fell was horrifying. Manu screamed as he tumbled down, down to the forest floor. His fall was so great that he bounced when he hit the packed dirt below. The crunching sound of bones upon the forest floor brought all play to an end for that afternoon.

Manu would never be right again. His once-strapping legs were reduced to shriveled sticks. Manu, a prime candidate to be a warrior, now made his living stringing beads in the village, a job normally reserved for women. His family lived in shame from that point on. True, he was injured during play, but Haru was serious business and no room was allowed for error. Loss came with a heavy toll, and a mangled Manu would never bring pride and power to his people.

Manu's injuries did not stop the pretend Haru games. In fact, they drove the children to try harder. All young men in the village knew their generation carried the burden and the honor of participating in the real Haru. For nearly four hundred years, their people reaped the benefits of winning the past two Harus.

Day in and day out, the villagers worked with the children, coaching, nourishing, and pushing those who bore the responsibility of keeping their people free. Yes, the children laughed and enjoyed their childhood games, but all of them knew they prepared for the challenge of their lives.

Haru, the real one, not the childish game played by Sharo and his friends, was a life and death competition. Occurring every two hundred years, the stakes were all or nothing. The winner laid claim to all the lands. The losers died, and the victor's tribe enslaved their people for the next two hundred years.

The young men of the other seven tribes in the competition practiced from the time they could walk to overthrow Sharo's tribe during the next Haru. Enslavement is a bitter state, and men are not content to endure it. Little drives a man to succeed more than the need to cast off the shackles of oppression for the tantalizing right to oppress another.

Years passed, and Sharo's tribesmen and adversaries arrived at the anticipated moment when bloodshed determined the victor. After decades of waiting, Haru was about to begin.

Each tribe's warriors traveled through the sacred blackened tunnels where time itself melded into nothingness, arriving in the arena specially chosen for this year's Haru. Excitement rippled through each group as they planted their feet for the first time on the lush green equatorial battleground.

The next two weeks brought not only vicious combat but a mind game of strategy. Tribes aligned with one another to take advantage of a weaker foe. Each time an alliance formed, rival teams worked together in the hot sun to reach the next round. Some alliances were better than others, and those who made poor choices paid the ultimate price. The players knew alliances were temporary, and no one lost sight of the end game: total domination or total destruction. Even as they worked together, teams sized each other up, constantly watching for weaknesses in their enemies. Even members of the same team evaluated who was an asset and who was expendable. All that mattered in the end was winning for the sake of their people, regardless of the cost.

Sharo was young but ruthless. In another time and place, he would have been a consummate politician or business executive. In his universe, however, he was a calculating killer. It suited him best.

He'd spent his young life carefully assessing the strengths and weaknesses of the warriors he'd known since childhood. He knew how to use his influence and power to have others do his bidding. Many times during Haru, he placed fellow tribesmen in harm's way to save himself. Numbers didn't matter. As long as the winner was from his tribe, his people were victorious. Sharu was intent on making sure he was the winner.

His cunning accounted for Sharo remaining atop the once verdant hilltop now laid waste in the scorching heat. No method of destruction was left unused as he sacrificed his own tribesmen to secure the bloody win against his rivals. Sharo felt no remorse. Why should he? He'd won. His tribe could produce more young men. Individuals could be replaced. They had two hundred more years to build another winning team.

Sitting in the blazing sun on the pinnacle of the coveted hill of victory, he heard the whirring motor of the transport pod arriving to pick him up. He would return to his planet the victor.

Safely inside the vessel, he stared out the window of the accelerating ship. The decimated blue orb the tribal leaders chose for this satisfying bloodbath faded into the distance. Yes, Earth had been a wise choice for this Haru.

ROCKET MAN

Last June the world was supposed to come to an end when an asteroid hurtled through space on a collision course with our planet. Mankind had never faced a graver threat. Riots erupted, governments collapsed, and anarchy reigned in the streets. Things were so simple then. We faced unstoppable annihilation, and that truth couldn't be changed. Until it was.

We had two months of warning as the asteroid approached. Two months was plenty of time for us to tear ourselves to shreds. At a time when altruisms like peace and brotherhood would have made our deaths seem somehow noble, old wounds, barely covered hatreds, and primal fears wreaked havoc on civilization. Hatred, race against race, country against country, and religion against religion tore nations and allegiances apart. Neighbors and family members killed one another over bunkers and bread. Utter mayhem ruled the land for two months until we were surprised by what initially was good news.

Two days before impact the asteroid slowed to a stop. No, an asteroid can't come to a halt. Nor is it possible for it to break up into smaller parts which then began separate orbits around Earth. Baffled, scientists scrambled to find answers. The mystery was solved when one of those pieces crashed into a remote part of New Mexico in Rio Arriba County not far from Farmington. Teams of researchers raced to the area. There they found a severely disabled alien craft, no bigger than a Volkswagen in size. The asteroid was no asteroid at all. It was an alien spaceship sent as an expeditionary force to our planet.

Inside the damaged craft, scientists found the remains of five aliens, mutilated by the crash. Top researchers whisked the bodies off to government labs for study. While hideous from our perspective, the aliens were not so different than humans when it came to the basics. They breathed oxygen. Their bodies were 70% water. They had a well-developed brain and nervous system. Perhaps they were curious about their earthly cousins.

Two days after the crash, however, their intentions proved less than peaceful. The alien force blew up the International Space Station then methodically took out one satellite after another. The United States, Russia, and China quickly pooled their abilities and scrambled a space force to neutralize our hostile visitors. Mankind set aside its petty differences in the face of possible annihilation by a foreign species.

A battle blazed across the sky, and losses were heavy for the international forces. They did prevail, however. Every alien craft, save for one, was destroyed. The lone craft made its way, damaged but still functioning, out of our solar system.

We breathed a sigh of relief, and our leaders vowed to spare no expense to take the fight to the aliens. In a joint statement, world leaders announced a plan:

"We will work tirelessly to use our latest technology in order to destroy our enemy. With the use of our space telescopes, we have located the alien planet. We have a plan in place to end the threat."

A top-secret project was launched that spanned the globe. For decades, robotics engineers had perfected nanotechnology. The joint military effort of Earth's developed nations created an army of nano soldiers. Millions of tiny robots, the size of grains of sand, would be placed on a deep-space rocket. Once landed, the micro force would spill out across the enemy land, destroying everything it encountered.

Due to the delicate nature of the mission, backup scenarios were in place. In the event of a crash or the destruction of the rocket, the tiny soldiers would jettison their way to the alien planet. If the project had to abort, the nano troops would self-destruct and become inoperable. This fail-safe method insured security while handling the dangerous force and allowed for contingencies in case things didn't go as planned.

Researchers who studied the dead aliens in New Mexico provided vital information that allowed the nanotechnology to target the life forms. The discovery that the beings utilized oxygen was a critical breakthrough in programming the nanobots. Armed with that information, scientists went to work ensuring that no oxygen-breathing organism would escape alive once the kill command was activated during the mission. The leaders of the world praised the efforts of the scientists and technicians who built our miniature saviors that would soon sail across the universe to protect us once and for all.

The entire operation was top secret, however, as the project reached the end phase before launch, the public was informed of the plans. After so much grief, leaders believed that the citizens of Earth needed to know what mankind was doing to save itself.

"It is our honor to inform the men, women, and children of our planet that we have devised a plan to end the alien threat forever."

The world breathed a sigh of relief as the message from world leaders was translated and broadcast. Shouts of joy erupted from every corner of the planet. No New Year's Eve celebration rivaled the exhilaration of our people.

For months, top scientists from around the world worked day and night on Operation Hourglass. A Cal-Tech graduate, Edward Filmore, was the perfect fit to work as a senior technician on this vital project. Edward was a genius. He had a mad scientist look about him and, fortunately for him, his wife was attracted to his brilliance. It certainly wasn't his looks or athletic ability that caught her eye. Edward had been known to trip over his own shoelaces, and handsome was never a word used to describe him. Truly, Edward was a klutz, but he was a good man. He had no common sense or social skills, but get him started talking about science and mathematics and the man came to life. At a moment when brilliance was more important than the ability to chat at a cocktail party, Ed Filmore was a highly valued man.

Edward's job wasn't to develop the nanotechnology itself. No, his team was tasked with guiding the rocket carrying the precious weaponized cargo into space. Many worked on his team, but he as an individual played a vital role in the success of the mission. While much of the flight would be controlled by computers, Edward's job was to operate the control panel, adjusting on the fly, so to speak, as necessary. It was the type of intellectual task he was geared for.

Two weeks prior to the launch, Edward and his team were invited into the containment facility where the nano force was stored awaiting its mission. The tiny grains of sand designed to prevail in Operation Hourglass were part of a Show-and-Tell presentation given by the lab.

"Rest assured, ladies and gentlemen, these robots are inert at the moment. Dip your fingers into this Petri dish to feel the tiny granules that will save our planet from any future alien attacks." The head of the lab, Michael Fitzgerald, held a dish out for each of the technicians to take a close look at the tiny warriors.

Each technician pinched a portion between their thumbs and index fingers and examined the tiny mechanical heroes. Inert was a good way to describe them, thought Edward. It was hard to believe that mankind's future depended upon this metallic dust. Edward nearly dropped his pinch of nanotechnology, but he managed to catch himself just in time. A few of his coworkers snickered at his clumsiness.

The project leaders gave short speeches, refreshments were served, and dignitaries thanked every member of the operation for the dedication and diligence.

"No time in our history has relied so heavily on the know-how of our brilliant scientists. Thank you for coming on today's tour. Now, back to work! The clock for Operation Hourglass, and mankind, is ticking."

Edward and his team returned to their stations. With only two weeks to go before the mission, rest came in short breaks. Naps replaced full-fledged sleep.

Unlike the time of chaos during the asteroid crisis, the world had a plan to end the alien threat and peace blossomed on Earth. In our communities and in our streets, marches of solidarity were held. People linked arms with one another, helped their neighbors, and began to act… humanely.

There was hope. Maybe, just maybe, mankind had learned a lesson.

On the day of the launch, the world tuned in and held its collective breath. Bands played. Speeches were broadcast. Mainly, however, everyone watched the countdown clock. Breathlessly, the whole world watched the numbers dropping second by second down to the magic number of T minus zero.

As the final seconds ticked away, the rocket's engines flared to life. Millions, more like billions, of people roared with the thrust of the engines. Jubilation burst from every person as though the breath the world had held suddenly erupted in a dynamic cacophony of joy.

Edward Filmore and his team pored over the controls. All systems were "go."

Until they weren't.

The rocket, ignoring all commands, toppled to its side, spilling its precious cargo of heroic warriors. Frantic, the scientists scrambled to regain control.

In the nano lab command center, panic ran wild. Instead of self-destructing, the tiny robots weaponized and spread out across the grounds, intent on destroying all oxygen-dependent life in its path.

There was no stopping them.

Machines have no emotions. Or do they?

The tiny robot that had fallen onto Edward Filmore's shirt sleeve two weeks ago when he nearly dropped his sample during Show-and-Tell had successfully landed in the keyboard of his computer. It now celebrated a job well-done. That tiny piece of metallic dust, as Edward called it, had worked hard in recent days reprogramming the rocket circuitry and overriding the self-destruct command.

A new day had dawned, and the world lay before his comrades.

AT DAY'S END

Daylight peeked through the looming storm clouds as Anderson Whitley finished his last shift as a train conductor. Thirty-three years had flown by. It hardly seemed possible that in a flash, a brief moment in the scheme of things, he had married, raised a family, and had a career that was mainly a good one. Not everyone could say that, and Anderson took pride in knowing he'd completed a job well done.

His thoughts drifted back through the years. The scene played out before him as he remembered the nervous sweat trickling down the back of his neck when he interviewed with the railroad for his first job. Old man Zeb Haskins had arranged the interview for him. He had always taken a liking to young Anderson. Partly out of respect for Anderson's father, Isaiah, who died in the war, and partly because Zeb raised five lovely daughters, but no sons, Anderson held a special place in the life of Zeb Haskins.

"Andy, I see my job at the railroad as a heritage. My father worked for them, and now I'm nearing retirement age. I have no son to pass my heirloom onto, but I have you. I'd be honored if you'd consider it."

Anderson smiled a reminiscent smile. Zeb never did call him by his full name. To him, he was always Andy.

"Zeb, I'm more than happy to interview for the job, but there must be two hundred people vying for that spot.

You know, times are tough. Don't be too disappointed in me if I don't get it."

The old man blinked a few times and shifted his weight from side-to-side as he stared off into the distance before fixing his gaze back on the young man. "Andy, don't you worry about that. You could never disappoint me. Just promise me you'll do your best. And I mean do your best as an employee because I firmly believe the job is yours for the taking."

That nervous kid in the sweat-drenched shirt sitting in front of Wilford Corning, the head of the railroad division in that region, wasn't convinced he had earned the spot on the crew. His voice shook. He stumbled over the basic questions asked of him. Two days later he received the call, however.

Of course, Zeb was the first person he told. "I can't believe it. I got the job!"

Zeb seemed almost too confident when he replied, "I knew you would."

Anderson had no doubt at that moment that Zeb had pulled strings. The job was his before the old man even asked him to apply. He didn't care, however. It made Zeb happy, and it was a professional windfall a boy from a dirt poor family only dreamed of having. A career with the railroad would open many doors for Anderson.

Within six months of starting his job, Anderson saved enough money for the down payment on a place he'd eyed for quite some time. The house had potential, and the land provided one of the prettiest views in the county. He dreamed of one day sitting on that front porch swing, holding the hand of a beautiful girl, and watching the sun go down.

Anderson smiled. He always smiled when he thought of his Maryann. They had those sunset evenings, and after a whirlwind courtship he brought her home as his wife.

He vowed to do anything to make her happy. Maryann was all he could have ever asked for in a wife, mother, and companion. She was a marvel, and oh, how she loved to cook. One of the first renovations Anderson made to the house was a custom kitchen for his aspiring gourmet chef. Maryann flipped through catalogs and scoured the aisles of home improvement stores until she found exactly what she wanted. Anderson's hefty paycheck with the railroad allowed him the ability to pamper her. Any chance he had to dote on her, he did.

On this last trip as a conductor, Anderson wondered what the future held for his darling wife and him. His family as a whole, really.

Yes, his family. He had so many warm memories of the kids. His job kept him away from home more than he would have liked, but Anderson made every moment with his family count. He was driven to make sure they had wonderful experiences and a solid foundation to build their lives upon. The loss of his own father when he was a toddler compelled Anderson to be the best father he possibly could be. All six of his children assured him he had succeeded, and now he had grandchildren to help raise. Because of his position, and with tonight being his last trip down the tracks, Anderson hoped for many more days with his growing family.

"Hey, Mr. Whitley. Excuse me, sir, but how much longer before we get there?" A young employee interrupted his thoughts.

"Gates, you know as well as I do that it's another thirty minutes before we reach the station."

"I know. I guess I'm just nervous."

"Yes, I understand. It's alright. This is a big night."

"Thank you. Sorry for bothering you, sir."

"It's okay, Gates. Now go back to your position."

Tonight was an unusual night. That was for sure. The sun had been all but lost in the gathering storm clouds. Lightning flashed ahead of the train, and the rays through the clouds cast an odd yellow hue to everything around the train as it barreled to its final destination. This was not an ordinary trip, and not simply because of his upcoming retirement. Anderson tried to soak in every sight along the way. He wanted these images burned into his memory forever.

He recalled the first time he'd heard the news. It wasn't broadcast on the television or radio. No, he learned of it when he'd been called into a corporate meeting in Chicago. Over the years, his personable disposition and flawless work ethic earned him friends in high places in the company. It paid off for Anderson. His connections led to him having the privilege of this night. They allowed him to have hope for tomorrow as well. Not everyone, in fact, not most, were as lucky.

Guilt swept over the conductor. He tried not to think of what tomorrow would bring for those less fortunate than his family. It wasn't their fault they were on the losing end of this hand, nor was it Anderson's fault for being dealt better cards. It was fate and luck. Nothing more.

Anderson shook his head in silence. He wasn't sure how lucky any of them were. Not anymore.

Deep in thought, he'd lost track of time. He was surprised to see the lights of the station entrance tucked into the side of the mountain. The Rockies had been one of his most scenic routes. Their grandeur captivated him for years. He'd taken Maryann and the kids on vacations there many times. His family, and soon the other passengers on this last train, would see the mountains from a new perspective. They'd see them from the inside.

A few months ago, Anderson was given a tour of the facility, or at least part of it. The gargantuan structure buried deep inside the range was too large for one man to walk in a day. Then again, there were portions of the facility that regular citizens, like himself, would never have access to. Those were reserved for government employees and the military.

As they approached the entrance, a sophisticated gate slid open, allowing the train to be swallowed by the mountain. The tracks were empty, and the station was desolate, as Anderson guided the last train into the stop. Everyone else sheltered a few stories below, awaiting what tomorrow would bring.

As the gate slide closed behind the train, the last vestiges of daylight fell behind the clouds and rain pelted the ground outside.

Anderson watched the passengers disembark, eagerly awaiting Maryann, his children, and his grandchildren to join him. He was thankful they were with him for his final day as a conductor.

He stood looking at the train that carried them on their last cross-country journey. Nicknamed "The Ark" by many, it carried the last of mankind to be saved from the cataclysmic asteroid impact that would happen at 5:17 the next morning.

A WORLD OF POSSIBILITIES

A sliver of sky cut through the bustling cityscape ahead of me. No matter where someone came from, blue skies, thinly veiled with clouds that wrapped us in their embrace, brought a universal sense of peace and well-being. After the long trip I'd had, I was grateful for anything that made me feel less alone. The blue skies reminded me of home, and right now I needed reassurance. A new city stretched before me, and at times I felt overwhelmed as I tried to acquaint myself with my surroundings. Anyone who grew up in the countryside and then found themselves dropped into the hustle and clamor of a large city knows the loneliness I'm talking about.

In the middle of unfamiliar sights and sounds, my mind reeled. It didn't seem that long ago that I was safely at home, in the quiet of my rural community, focused on my studies at the institute. Graduation day meant celebrations with friends and family, many of whom I hadn't seen in years. My grandmother flew in, and my cousins who had been living abroad made the trip home to be there for my big day. Even my hard-to-please father admitted I'd made him proud. I'd waited my entire life to hear him say that.

Graduation also meant I was no longer a child. I now had adult responsibilities, and those included becoming a productive part of my community. Everyone needed a job, and after I was recruited by one of the biggest headhunters in the country, I didn't think twice about taking a job far from home. I was flattered that the company wanted me to be the lead man in their new venture. Excitement overrode my fears, at least for the most part. The fears still invaded my mind and caused my heart to seize at times. I battled those inner demons of self-doubt. More than anything, I didn't want to screw this up.

As nervous as I was about the size of the city and the enormity of the task, I knew fitting in wouldn't be difficult. Not on the surface, anyway. I'd always had a knack for slipping seamlessly into whichever group I found myself. That ability was part of the repertoire I brought to the company.

Where to start was the question at hand. This project was important, and my inexperience caused me to doubt whether I had what it took to even recognize the correct starting point. As lead man, I'd already jumped ahead of seasoned employees to have this position. The resentment in their eyes was clear. After two days at the jobsite, a nagging fear that I wouldn't perform up to snuff paralyzed me.

Looking around, the sheer number of possibilities in this place caused much of my anxiety.

Did I become an executive in one of these high rises? The excitement of infiltrating a corporate ladder intrigued me. The capitalist system revolved around making money, and the ability to wheel and deal would open a lot of doors for me.

I looked at the stores lining the avenue. I could become a shop owner. I'd hear all the local gossip and have keen insight into what made the people in this city tick.

What motivated them? What did they fear? Who did they trust and distrust? This was valuable information my bosses could use.

A honking horn brought another option to mind. What about a taxi cab driver? They met customers from all over, and most customers didn't show discretion in their backseat conversations with others. Many loose lips sailed on those yellow ships carrying people back and forth from airports, hotels, and backroom meetings. I'd be privy to conversations meant to remain confidential, especially if they viewed me as no more than some foreigner who drove a dingy cab for a living.

Just where to start? I could be flexible, but I didn't want to waste time on fruitless efforts. If I didn't make a good impression on the company execs, I'd find myself on the bottom of the heap sorting mail while my former classmates climbed ahead of me in the corporate hierarchy. No, this was my chance to prove I could do something big. I had to do it right.

Just then, my phone rang.

"Michaelis, a lot is riding on this project."

"I realize that, sir. I arrived two days ago and was familiarizing myself with the area."

"Well, we aren't paying you to sightsee. We need you to act quickly and decisively."

"I understand that, and I apologize."

"As venture capitalists, it's our job to move in, use what we can, sell the rest for scrap, and move on. We can't waste time with this. Other projects are on the burner, too."

"I'll start on it immediately."

We hung up the phone as the light turned green.

Looking in the rearview mirror of my car, I watched as my face and body completely transformed. Gone were my long green dreadlocks. My golden eyes turned into a putrid brown common to the citizens of this area. My clothing switched from the shaala wool sweater and pants I'd been wearing to a neatly tailored Armani suit. The closely cropped black hair and a smug expression completed the look I was shooting for.

A corporate insider it was.

Once this job was complete and I'd stripped Earth of all useful resources, I'd return home for my next assignment.

DISTANT RELATIVES

A Thursday evening was as good a time as any to have her entire world change. It was a beautiful night. The kind photographers love to capture. The sunset cast an array of subtle hues, and the surf created a lulling backdrop for the spectacular view. Cassandra Robbins sat in her study enjoying the sight through the French doors leading to the balcony. She relished her life and her condo tucked away in Paradise Cove.

With a glass of chilled white wine in one hand, she studied the computer screen before her.

Should I do it or not?

The $129 price tag was no issue, but pangs of guilt caused her to hesitate. She'd scrolled through this site time after time, but each time she backed out. Guilt had a stronger pull than curiosity, and before tonight it always won. An offhand comment by a stranger that afternoon brought Cassandra to the website once again.

She winced at the memory. A random voice had ruined the lovely scene at McGyver Park.

"You must come from good genes. I wish I could eat ice cream and stay as skinny as you are."

Cassandra sat on a park bench, thoroughly enjoying a large frozen custard cone, when a woman nearby made the uninvited remark. She'd heard similar comments before, but this time it struck a nerve. It stabbed at her heart tonight, and she couldn't push it out of her mind. She spent her whole life as an outsider in her own family. She didn't look like them, act like them, or think like them. They told her they loved her and that she was one of them, but she wasn't. The woman's mindless comment reaffirmed that fact.

Cassandra always knew she was adopted. It was no secret. Her adoptive parents couldn't have kept it secret if they had tried. Her blonde hair and blue eyes were in stark contrast to their brown hair and eyes. She was taller than they were, too. At six feet, she towered over even her father and brothers. There was no denying she was different.

Yet they were the only family she'd ever known. *I love them, and I know they love me.* Her parents had desperately wanted a girl, and the Robbins family doted on her since they brought her home as a newborn. *I've wanted for nothing, and I should feel nothing but gratitude, but I don't.*

Growing up, people told her how lucky she was to be adopted. She was chosen. She was special. She was lucky. She was wanted. She watched her mother's eyes light up each time an affirmative comment arrived for her existence as a Robbins. She also watched her mother's eyes fill with tears each time someone asked Cassandra if she was ever curious about her "real" family.

We *are* her real family," Madeline Robbins told them as she hugged Cassandra closer to her.

Still, Cassandra wondered who she was. A craving grew in her as years passed to know who she *really* was. She'd entertained the idea of searching for her birth family a thousand times, but the guilt of hurting her adoptive mother in the process stopped her.

Until tonight. The comment she'd received that afternoon drove Cassandra to the genealogy testing website run by a company called Be Yourself.

I'd like to know who I am. I need to feel comfortable in my own skin. No one needs to even know I had the test done. I'm twenty-five, and I shouldn't still worry what Mama thinks while I sit in my own home a thousand miles away from her.

The website made it so appealing. "Find out how to Be Yourself. Our database spans the globe. One simple test is all it takes to find out who you really are. Learn family history. Meet new relatives. Build deeper connections with the world around you. Safe, confidential, and fun. Our money-back guarantee makes this the easiest test you'll ever take. Go ahead--Be Yourself!"

It seemed safe enough. Cassandra could find her relatives, and her adoptive family wouldn't even need to know. She filled out the registration form, plugged in her credit card information, and clicked the purchase button.

That was simple. Shipping takes three days. By next Wednesday, I'll have my DNA on its way back to the company.

For the next three days, Cassandra tracked the shipment progress on her phone. Excited and apprehensive, she refreshed the tracking information at least once an hour until she finally set up text alerts to save her the stress of constantly looking.

On Tuesday, she received the message she'd waited for. Her package was delivered. *I'll skip lunch so I can leave work early. I'll tell my boss I have to be at an appointment.*

When the clock struck four o'clock, she gathered her purse and a file to work on later that night and headed to the parking lot. Fighting the urge to speed, her heart raced as she pulled into the condo complex. Sure enough, sitting outside her door was a nondescript box. She picked it up and fumbled with her keys as she clumsily unlocked her door.

My past, and my future, will be determined by what's in this box.

Pulling a knife from the utensil drawer, she carefully sliced the tape open. Moving to the living room, she emptied the box into her lap as she sat on her couch. She carefully removed every item. Included was a swab stick for taking a mouth sample, a sealable sample container, instructions, and a return shipping label.

Cassandra read the instructions three times, fearful she might make a mistake. She followed them word for word, first rinsing her mouth then swabbing the inside of each cheek with the long, wooden sample stick. Cotton swirled around each end. Each cheek used a different end of the swab. Gingerly opening the sample container, she slid the stick inside, sealing it as directed. She filled out the prepaid return label, taped the box shut, and set it on the kitchen counter.

I'll drop that off at the shipping center on my way to work in the morning.

Then it hit her.

Oh my God, I've really done this. For the rest of the evening, her emotions swung from excitement to pure anxiety.

Sleep came in fits as she dreamed of being a little girl on the farm outside Des Moine. Summers at the ballpark watching her brothers play little league. Family vacations to the beach or Yellowstone. Awkward comments from people who asked how hard it was for her parents to "get" her and all the other thoughtless words strangers said when they realized she was adopted. A hundred scenes played out in her restless dreams that night.

The jagged sounds of her alarm stirred her from the only deep sleep she'd managed.

Isn't that the way insomnia works? I don't sleep until it's time to get up? Ugh. Today's going to be a hard one to get through at work.

A mixture of dread and anticipation filled her as she scooped up the box and was on her way. The shipping center was only three blocks from her office, and she said a prayer for strength as she slid it into the large metal container used for prepaid outgoing packages.

Now I wait. The instructions said it could take six weeks to get my results in the mail.

Cassandra spent the next month and a half trying to push her nerves to the side. It wasn't easy. Every time she checked the mail, her heart beat wildly. Then, one day, it arrived. A large white envelope awaited her in her mailbox, and she knew it had to be her results. For a moment, Cassandra forgot to breathe, clutching the envelope tightly.

The answers are in here.

She rushed into her condo, slit the package open, and sat on her bed. Her hands shook as she pulled the contents from the envelope. Confusion overrode excitement.

Instead of results, the company president, Elliott Roseman, invited her to meet with him personally in New York City. All expenses would be paid, including a three-night reservation at one of the most expensive hotels in the city. According to the letter, "Your DNA results make you a prime candidate for one of our upcoming marketing campaigns. Please consider this exciting opportunity."

Disappointment poured over Cassandra until she realized her results awaited her in New York City. *I'll appear in future ads for the company. Those years spent in high school drama club might pay off!*

The catchy tune used in the commercials played in her head, and she thought about past ads. One featured a grandmother who found out she descended from Vikings. She wore a horned helmet and swigged from an enormous beer mug. In another, a fellow adoptee reunited with his birth family. They all looked so happy.

Could I be that happy?

It never once crossed her mind that her adoptive family might see those same ads she was now so eager to do. She dialed the number listed in the letter, gave the representative at their corporate office her confirmation number, and booked her reservations with them for the following Monday.

Our office manager did tell me if I didn't use some of my vacation time soon I'd lose it. I'll let her know tomorrow that I'm going out of town on vacation next week. I'll tell her it's a family matter.

Excitement returned. After a restless night of a thousand possibilities running through her mind, she arose and left for work without even eating breakfast. She was too nervous to think of food, and the few sips of coffee she'd taken only upset her stomach. *I hope work doesn't give me any grief. My next vacation days aren't supposed to be until September, but I don't want to back out of my trip.*

Marsha, the office manager, was actually relieved when Cassandra asked for the time off. "This comes at a good time, Cass."

She always shortens everyone's name. I guess she thinks it makes her sound like a friend. I hate to tell her, but that's not making anyone like her more.

"Why's that?" Cassandra resisted the urge to call her "Marsh."

"Well, we're kind of in between projects right now. Before the next one starts would be a perfect time for you to go on vacation. I hope you have fun with your family."

"Thanks. I do too."

The next two days of work felt like forever. That weekend, Cassandra obsessed over what to pack. Practically her entire closet full of clothes was spread across her bedroom before she finally settled on the eight outfits she packed for a four-day trip.

Before she knew it, Monday afternoon arrived. The flight into La Guardia was short, and a limousine service met her as she exited the secured gate area.

"Hello, Ms. Robbins, Mr. Roseman is eager to see you." The clean-cut young man sent to pick her up at the airport took her luggage from her. "Follow me. If you're hungry or thirsty, the limousine is equipped with food and beverages. The hotel where you will be staying has excellent restaurants as well."

"I'm going to meet the president of the company today?"

"Yes, you will meet him, but that won't happen until tomorrow."

"Does he meet all of the people who do ads for him?"

"No. Only the special ones. I'm parked over there." He nodded his head toward a shiny black limo across the street."

The only time I've been to New York was when Mom took my cousins and me here to see a Broadway play when I was sixteen. I'd forgotten how crowded this place was.

She settled into the limo, and the driver closed her door. Bustling streets and high rise buildings whirred past. When the limo driver stopped in front of the luxury hotel, even the facade took her breath away. The driver carried her bags and made certain she checked in before he left.

"I'll be here at eight o'clock tomorrow morning to take you to our headquarters. Have a lovely evening."

A lovely evening.

How could she not have one? Cassandra gawked at the opulence around her. The hotel attendant escorted her to her room and dropped her bags off at the threshold. "Let us know if you need anything, Ms. Robbins. We want you to enjoy your stay."\

"Thank you. I will." She tipped him and stepped inside her room.

It was exquisite. Real art, not cheap prints, hung on the wall. A balcony looked out at the sparkling skyline as darkness fell. Cassandra decided she liked how the wealthy lived.

The refrigerator held her favorite snacks, and the bar came fully equipped. She made herself an amaretto sour, tossed in extra cherries, and sat on the balcony while she took in the view. Room service brought her dinner.

Lost in the moment, time escaped her. When she checked her phone, she was surprised to see it was past midnight. She hated to miss a single second of this experience, but her eyes struggled to stay open. She slid under the silk sheets and lolled in the comfort of the king-sized bed.

The next thing she knew, her alarm rang, and she awoke to early morning rays of sunshine streaming into the room from the balcony. She couldn't remember having a sounder sleep, and exhilaration over the upcoming events of today swept over her as she threw back the comforter. *By this evening, I'll star in an ad shown nationwide on nearly every channel. This is a big deal!*

Lost in the reverie, the ringing of her phone jarred her back to reality. *It's Mom.* A pang of guilt shot through her. Suddenly, she felt as though she commited a mortal sin by searching for her biological family. Like a cheating spouse who'd just been caught, she froze, uncertain of what to say, worried that her infidelity would be evident in her voice. Fear and pain washed over her, and she almost didn't answer in time.

"Uh, hi, Mama."

"Good morning, Cassie! I hope I'm not calling too close to when you have to be at work."

I never told Mom about my trip. It's my secret, my business, but I don't want to lie to Mom. She decided to split the difference.

"Oh, no, you're okay."

I've spent my whole life making sure Mama is okay. She never knew the turmoil I've gone through wondering who I am. I'm not picking today to upset her.

"Oh, good. I know you need to be in the office soon."

"Actually, I've taken a few days off." Her free hand played with her hair, a habit she'd had since childhood whenever she was nervous.

"Oh?" She heard the hurt tone in her mother's voice. "I didn't know. Are you doing something special?"

"I'm sorry I didn't tell you. It's nothing important. Marsha told me this would be a good time to use a few vacation days since we're between projects. I decided to come to New York City and just see the sights for a few days."

Her mother paused. "New York? Why New York? You usually don't do anything unless there's a reason. Is there a man?"

Cassandra blushed. Ever since high school, her mother had been too interested in her love life.

"No, Mom. I'm here alone. I just decided to do something spontaneous. That's all. It's only for a few days. I couldn't take enough time off to fly home. I'll do that in September like we'd already planned."

She knew Madeline Robbins well enough to know her mother felt slighted.

"Oh, good. Well, be safe, will you? I've heard on the news about the crime rate spiking there."

"Mom, I'm fine. I'm in a safe place. But I really need to get ready."

"For what?"

Cassandra's mind reeled. *I've boxed myself into a corner. Think of something quick!*

"Oh, there's a tour at a museum I want to take this morning. The hotel clerk told me it's best to do the early one or I might get caught in traffic and rack up extra charges in my taxi."

Madeline seemed satisfied with that explanation. "Give me a call later on, Cassie, and tell me all about your adventures."

"I will, Mama. Love you."

She hung up and sat on the bed as she regained her composure. While she'd lived her whole life as a lie, she hated the feeling that she'd only delayed Madeline's heartbreak. Time was ticking, however, and she had to focus on the day ahead.

She ordered room service, showered, and put on her favorite dress with just enough time to meet the driver in the lobby below.

"Good morning, Ms. Robbins. I hope you had a pleasant evening and that the accommodations suited you."

"Good morning. Yes, this place is amazing."

"I'm glad to hear that. Mr. Roseman always likes his guests to enjoy their stay. We need to be on our way. He's expecting you shortly."

"Do you mind me asking what your name is?"

"My name?"

"Yeah. Right now, you're the only person I know in New York City, and I don't even know your name."

The man hesitated for a moment.

"Is there a reason you can't tell me?"

"No. Most people never ask. Your question just surprised me. My name is Thomas. Thank you for asking."

Cassandra extended her hand and shook his. "It's nice to meet you, Thomas. Where I come from it's rude to not get to know other people. Please call me Cassandra."

"That's refreshing. It's the same where I grew up. I guess I'm just used to the anonymity of the big city now. Thank you, Cassandra."

The ride to Be Yourself headquarters took roughly forty-five minutes given the morning traffic. Thomas mentioned all the points of interest along the route. Now that they were on a first name basis, conversation flowed easily. She told him about growing up on a farm in Iowa. He told her about growing up in small-town Illinois.

"I came here to escape what I viewed as a prison growing up. I didn't want to spend my life trapped working at the local factory like my dad and brothers did. I thought there was something more." Thomas almost sounded wistful.

"I hear ya. That's why I left Iowa as soon as I could and moved to Paradise Cove."

"Do you like it there?"

"For the most part, yes. It gets lonely sometimes, but it's a beautiful area."

"I can't imagine you being lonely. You've got to have a boyfriend."

Thomas glanced in the rearview mirror at her. She met his gaze.

"No, I don't. The last guy I dated turned out to have three other women on a string. I cut the rope and have stayed away from dating ever since."

Thomas tried to suppress a relieved smile.

"Men can be jerks. I'm sorry about that."

"I know not every guy is a jerk. Thank you for talking with me, Thomas. I'm really nervous about today. I guess I've always felt alone and out of place, and now I'm about to find out if there's anyone else out there like me."

"What do you mean?"

Cassandra poured out her entire story. The struggles of being adopted. The constant worry of hurting her adoptive mother.

"I can't even fill out medical history information when I go to a doctor. I don't know if there's heart disease, breast cancer, mental illness, or anything else in my background. I don't know if I'm some sort of genetic time bomb about to blow up. What if there's something I could pass on to my future kids? There's so much stress and so many unknowns."

"I'm sorry you've had that weight on you all this time. I guess I've taken all those things for granted."

"You're one of the few people I've ever said any of this to. I have a few friends at work who know, and my college roommate knows, but I never felt safe talking to anyone about it when I was growing up."

"Today you get a lot of those questions answered. That will make you feel better."

"Yes and no."

"Why no?"

"I'll have to decide whether or not I let my adoptive family know. I'll break their hearts if I tell them. If I don't tell them, I'll still be living a life of lies. There's no way out of my problems."

"I know we just met, but I want you to know you can always talk to me."

Cassandra wiped a tear away. "That means more than you know. I've felt alone and guilty for feeling this way my whole life. It's nice to have someone who wants to listen."

"Soon you'll at least have some answers to go off of. The rest will sort itself out."

Hating to see her forlorn, he tried to change the subject by pointing at a well-known restaurant. "That place has a waiting list to get in a mile long. I've been told the food isn't even all that good, but everyone who is anybody has to be seen there."

"I'm not really into status symbols. I'd rather have a quiet dinner someplace where I don't have to worry about which fork to use."

"You and me both." He paused. "If this is out of line, let me know, but would you want to have dinner sometime?"

Cassandra's blue eyes lit up. "Yeah, I'd like that a lot."

"Please don't say anything to anyone at Be Yourself. The boss doesn't want me fraternizing with his clients. I'm nothing but a blond guy in a suit with a set of car keys as far as he's concerned."

"Not a word. Are you going to pick me up after my meeting?"

"Yes. We're almost there. I'll be waiting." He pulled the limo into its reserved parking spot in the garage below the headquarters. "Have fun."

"I'm a little nervous."

"You'll be fine."

It's been a while since I've felt butterflies about a man. A date will be a bonus to an already exciting trip." A smile crept across her face.

Exiting the limo, she followed the instructions in the letter she'd received, checked in with the front desk clerk in the main lobby, and was given directions to the corporate office of Elliott Roseman.

"Enjoy your meeting, Ms. Robbins. Mr. Roseman has been expecting you."

"Butterflies of another kind swarmed through her nervous system as she pushed the elevator button for the 32nd floor of the high rise.

This is really happening. I'm about to find out all the answers to the questions I've asked myself since I first realized I was different from the rest of my family.

It was true. She not only looked different, but her whole being seemed different than theirs. She gravitated toward music and art. They were athletic. She had a keen sense of humor, and her laugh was boisterous. Madeline Robbins seldom cracked a smile. Cassandra was on the verge of finding out who she really was. She teetered between euphoria and nausea as she approached Elliott Roseman's office.

The receptionist, a slim brunette in a smart designer suit, greeted her. "Hello, Cassandra. Mr. Roseman is this way." Her voice was pleasant but cool.

The woman rapped gently on Elliott Roseman's door. He opened it with flair, gave the receptionist a knowing nod, and ushered Cassandra into his office.

If the hotel the night before seemed luxurious, it was eclipsed by the opulence of the office where she now stood.

"My, how nice to meet you, Cassandra. I've been looking forward to this."

A little stunned by his interest in her, Cassandra could only reply, "Yes, I'm excited about being in a commercial."

Elliott Roseman chuckled as he reached under his desk. His long, tanned fingers met the button he sought, and Cassandra heard the clunking sound of the office door locking shut. Startled, she began to speak.

"Not now, Cassandra. Please save your comments until later. You did, after all, come to my office for answers, correct?"

She nodded yes.

"Right then. It's my turn to speak. You're wondering why I personally invited you here. Why, out of the thousands of clients who send us their DNA, would I choose you to pamper and bring to my office?"

She sat in stunned silence, her eyes widening as he walked from behind his desk to her. He then took her hand in his, caressing the inside, gently tracing around her fingers. She stiffened and tried to pull away.

"Now, my dear, have you noticed that your fingerprints are unusual?"

Cassandra had wondered why her fingerprints contained a double loop. Her father explained it away by telling her that everyone's fingerprints were unique. She learned the same in science class and from watching true crime television shows. She'd pushed that mystery to the side, chalking it up to one of the many ways she was not the same as her brothers or parents. She couldn't bring herself to speak.

Turning his own hand over in hers, Elliott Roseman pointed at his own fingerprints. To her surprise, he, too, had double loops in his.

"Do you know what this means?"

Cassandra's head slowly turned no.

"It means we are the same." He clasped her hand and pulled her from her seat. "Come with me."

He led her across the room to a painting. It stood in stark contrast to the other art in the room. The detailed starscape clashed with the Monet and Degas artwork covering the other walls of the office.

"Do you know what this is?" A small dot, found in the center of the painting's swirling mass of dots, was directly under his index finger. "That's home."

"Listen, I don't know what you're into, but I'm leaving." Cassandra turned to go.

"Good luck with that. The doors are locked. You aren't leaving. You wanted answers. I'm giving them to you. Now sit back down." He lifted the chair she'd sat in ever so slightly and slammed it back into place on the carpet.

Cassandra slowly returned to it, grasping the arm of the chair to steady herself. The room spun. *What's happening?* She wanted to run, but instead sat frozen in place.

"Now, for a little history lesson. This is nothing you would have learned at Holbrook High School in Iowa." A chuckle escaped his wet lips as he licked them again.

"How did you--"

"I know all about you, my dear. Now just listen. This is important."

He pointed at the painting across the room.

"Ten thousand years ago, our ancestors came here looking for a better life, much the same as settlers have throughout the millennia. We thrived for a time, but then war within ourselves weakened our strength, and our people intermingled with others. The Greeks, the Romans, the Germanic hordes. Our civilization was lost. Swallowed whole by the diluting effect of migrations and conquests."

He rose to get a glass of ice water from the pitcher sitting on the table behind his mahogany desk. He stared at the painting then turned his attention back to Cassandra.

"My family preserved the oral history of our people. Generation to generation learned about the great battles and losses. We learned how our people scattered across this globe. I decided to end the destruction of our people. Do you know how?"

Cassandra nodded no.

He set the glass down and motioned around the room. "By creating *this*."

Cassandra began to rise, but he deftly moved across the room, placed his hands on her shoulders, and forced her back into the chair.

"You see, Cassandra Robbins, I knew that mankind was an egotistical lot. Always asking questions. Always fixated on their own being and self-worth. What better way to gather the genetic data needed to track down our scattered people than to appeal to the vanity of humans?"

He lifted a stack of papers from his desk. "These are my prizes. These are the lost descendants of my people who will be used to rebuild our civilization. We will rule this world in time."

"What does this have to do with me? I really should be going?"

Elliott Roseman laughed. "This has everything to do with you, and you have no way of leaving."

"The driver is waiting for me."

Shaking his head, Elliott Roseman said, "Poor Thomas. He should have known better than to become too friendly with you. Sharing all those heartfelt stories of your rural American upbringings. Oh, that was entertaining to listen to as I awaited your arrival here. He had one job to do, and that was to get you here. Nothing more. He's an unfortunate casualty now."

She cried out, "Why would you do something to him?"

"He was a useless human boy, Cassandra." He stepped behind her and played with her hair. "His DNA was, unlike yours, useless to us. There was no place for him in our breeding program. Oh, but you…"

FLY, FLY AWAY

The time has come. I never pictured myself as an Edward Snowden type. You know, the guy who leaked government information, becoming either a hero or a traitor in the eyes of Americans. I, Joe Beeker, have lived an average life, and I thought nothing interesting would ever happen to me. I was wrong.

Sure, I'd played on my high school's football team when we won state, but the truth is I was a third-string bench sitter. I didn't do anything to add to the glory of the win. My dad let me know it, too. Still, it worked to get a few dates, and that was good enough for me.

Since high school, I've worked one bland bureaucratic job after another, slowly making my way up the Civil Service ranks. The pay hasn't been bad, but it's hard to impress anyone with tales of paper cuts from file folders or stories about the eye strain I've had from staring at my computer screen. In the world of bureaucrats, there are no scars from ACL tears or other war wounds to brag about. I had nothing exciting to impress women with, and I didn't even impress myself to be honest, so I can't blame the girls. Let's just say my dating scene's been a game of solitaire my entire adult life. Geeky clerks in the Department of Defense aren't exactly hot items on dating sites.

But none of that means anything. Not after what I discovered. I have to talk about it with somebody. I have to warn you.

On October 23rd, as I did a routine inventory of files in the backroom, I stumbled across something that changed the way I view the world. All the signs have been here for generations, but none of us caught on. The government has kept us in the dark, even while the enemy has lived among us for centuries.

"They" will claim that they did it to avoid mass hysteria. That sounds like a nice gesture, but I don't believe it. I think they've kept us ignorant so we wouldn't question why they've taken away our rights and made decisions for us. It also explains why they and their cronies made money while the rest of us were considered ignorant peons. Big secrets mean big money. The bigger the secret, the bigger the money.

Forgive me if I ramble. There's just so much to tell.

Have you ever wondered why mega-chemical companies, the ones whose products were proven to cause cancer, have thrived? The makers of all the big insecticides knew their products killed us, but the government never did anything to protect us. Why is that?

Now I know why. I always thought lobbyists had too much power, but it goes beyond pure greed. It has to do with power, control, and fear. It has to do with leaders who want to keep us ignorant so we can't question if they're making good decisions for us. A blindfolded populace can't see what's really going on.

Have you ever wondered why we were raised to loathe certain things in our world? "Don't touch that. It might be dirty," our mothers and grandmothers warned us. We were groomed to hate insects, especially flies, because they were "dirty." No one moved faster than my grandmother after a fly in her kitchen.

My dog eats God knows what, and he rolls around in all sorts of nasty things he finds, but I was never told to hate my dog. I never really thought about it before, but now it makes sense.

I used to be ignorant. I was blinded by the kind of innocence the powers-that-be hope we maintain. I wasn't supposed to know any of this, and now that I do, my life is in danger. Before I die or am exiled like Snowden, I have to tell the truth. The public has the right to know. Please listen to me, even if part of you wants to blow me off as some sort of lunatic. I never wanted to be a whistleblower, but here I am. I'm speaking up because someone has to warn you.

I found it by accident when I was cleaning out those files at work. My world view shifted that October day. I was afraid of what I found, but I ferreted the information out under my jacket. It seemed like such a simple way to get secrets out of a government building. I guess I'd watched too many spy movies where suspenseful music played in the background cueing a high-stakes game of cat-and-mouse. In comparison, my experience was humdrum. I stuck the folders under my coat, waved to the receptionist as I left, and that was that.

Don't think I wasn't stressed. I shook so badly that I thought someone would notice. How could they not see the fear on my face? The sweat beading on my brow? The squeaky tone of my voice as I squeezed my way onto the elevator and asked to be excused when I bumped into others.

Then I thought about it and realized no one *ever* noticed me. Why should that day be any different? I could have worn a t-shirt that said, "Hey, Look At Me Stealing These Files," and I don't think it would have caught anyone's attention. Maybe I was born to be a spy. I've proven I can do the unthinkable and draw zero attention doing it.

I sat up that entire night, staring at the stack of secrets, about to have a nervous breakdown. I went to work the next day wondering if I'd be arrested by the FBI, but no men in dark suits arrived. Day after day, I went to work and no one noticed that I'd stolen top-secret materials.

It's taken a few weeks to wrap my head around what I need to do. I considered burning the papers and remaining just another office clerk lost in the stacks of government files. Our lives are at stake, however, so I've decided I can't keep quiet.

It's too late now anyway, but you should know. I'm not giving this information to today's version of Julian Assange, a man I personally despise. No, I'm posting this on social media so it can be read and shared by everyday Joes, just like me, Joe Beeker.

I'm leaving this manifesto in case I disappear. Time may run out for me. I don't know if it's paranoia or if they really are trailing me. It's become hard to tell. I may die, but too many of you will now know for them to silence everyone.

But just what do I have to tell you? The rocket is taking off right about now. The die is cast. I need to warn you.

You see, those flies that our parents, and their parents before them, going back through the generations, taught us to hate aren't some common pest that mankind has lived with forever. They arrived on our planet a few centuries ago, aliens from another world. Our leaders haven't wanted us to know there's life outside our blue sphere. They worried we'd panic if we knew alien invaders lived among us. They've waged a battle against them without our knowledge, and so far, it's been an even fight.

The flies adapted to our planet easily, and even though they reproduce rapidly, we've kept them at bay. Whether it was grandma's fly swatter or the cancer-causing chemicals we spray with abandon, humans kept the alien menace in check.

Do you doubt me? I'm attaching copies of the files I stole with this manifesto. In them, the human casualties from chemical exposure are called "unfortunate collateral damage." You can read their words yourself. My brother, a patriot who retired from the Air Force, was exposed to who knows what. He died of cancer. I don't find any comfort in those bureaucratic euphemisms. They knew they were poisoning their own people.

We should have known what was happening, but we didn't. We should have known before the alien threat became what it has. In the last few months, our government's known about is a mass movement of flies, trillions of them, headed our direction. Their goal, according to our intelligence, is to take over Earth once and for all.

The rocket launch, reported by the media as just another mission to send a weather satellite into space, is far from mundane. Advancements in science and engineering have allowed our government to build a mass army of billions of nano-soldiers. Those troops will fight the war on fly territory before they reach our planet.

Some will call me a traitor. I broke my government's trust by revealing what I uncovered. I know that. As an American, I find shame in disappointing Uncle Sam. However, as a human being, I couldn't let us face annihilation, should this rocket's mission fail, without people knowing why this happened.

If you never hear from me again, good luck and godspeed.

TRIAL AND ERROR

The light in his office served as the only bright spot in what felt like a void of darkness. It was late, and like most days, he'd worked long past regular business hours. When a scientist and inventor is cursed with a perfectionist bent, it leads to one series of scrapped projects after another. His family had grown used to this.

A soft knocking at his door drew his attention away from his workbench. He knew who it was and didn't even bother turning to look.

"Son, what are you doing up so late? You know your mother won't be happy if she catches you out of bed. That will be bad for both of us."

"I know, Daddy. I just like to watch you work. You're the best inventor ever."

"Come here." He opened his arms wide as his little boy climbed into his lap. These were precious moments that he treasured as a father. "I don't know about all that, son. I will keep tinkering here in my office until I finally get it right. Thank you for having so much confidence in me."

"I'll always believe in you. What are you working on tonight?"

"Well, this is a new prototype. I'm trying to get the chemistry just right on it." He pointed at the trash can to his left. "Those just went wrong. Some didn't have enough water. Some had too much gas. I don't know if I'll ever get it right."

His son gazed wide-eyed at the one sitting on his father's workbench. "Daddy, I really like this one. It's pretty."

"You like the blue, huh? Yeah, so do I."

"Do you think this one is the one?"

"It could be."

"Will you make things to go on it if it works out?"

"I suppose I will. I didn't have any luck when I tried that with these others." He looked at the trashed projects and shook his head. "A lot of wasted effort here."

"Well, I think this one has real potential. Look at the way it kind of glows here in the light."

"It is a pretty one. You're right. This is just the basic model, though. I have my doubts about how successfully this will grow a garden or support a good kind of life. It might be too harsh, and the only living things I can put on a model like this have been kind of volatile in the lab."

"I think you need to give it a shot. You won't know until you try it."

"Maybe you're right. I've got a better idea in the back of my mind, though, so I'm going to toss all these out tonight and try again tomorrow."

"Can you go ahead and try some of the lab organisms on this one before you do, though, Daddy? I'd like to watch over them. You know, kind of like a terrarium."

The father hesitated.

"Please, Daddy."

"Well, okay. Then it's off to bed for you, understand?"

The little boy nodded, and the man walked into the lab that adjoined the office. His son thought having a scientist as a dad was the best thing ever.

The man returned with a few Petri dishes and smiled as he sprinkled the contents onto the blue globe. His son clapped in delight.

"Okay, here we go." He opened the back door, and into the night he threw the contents of the trash can, blue globe and all, into the void. Earth and all the other moons and planets spun into the universe.

"Now, off to bed."

The little boy gave his father a sleepy hug and tottered back to his room. He watched his son leave, rubbed his aching neck, and decided it was time to go to bed himself.

Standing to leave, God flipped off his office light.

A BOX OF MATCHES

Tuesdays were Henry Slidell's favorite days. His love for them began when he was a boy, and his grandmother gave him a stamp collecting set for his tenth birthday. His celebration fell on a Tuesday that year, and every week at the same time, he and Grandma Pat added to his collection. They spent hours poring over his new acquisitions, and his grandmother would show him her own displays. Those were special times, and Henry would forever equate Tuesdays with happiness and warm memories.

Grandma Pat lived in one of those old, carefully preserved homes that made Henry feel like he stepped back in time when he stayed there, and he stayed there a lot. His parents weren't involved in his upbringing, so he practically lived at Grandma Pat's. That was just fine with Henry. He developed a special bond with her that shaped who he was and who he became. Even after her death, he felt that she had never entirely left him. On some days, he was certain he felt her gentle guidance in decisions large and small.

Henry's grandmother was well-cultured and had exquisite taste. Having grown up as the daughter of a librarian and a museum curator, she was well-versed in fine literature and art. Beautiful carpets covered the hardwood floors, and expensive paintings adorned the walls. Years of travel deeply influenced her eclectic style. If a piece caught her eye, she made it fit her decor. Primitive mingled with modern museum-quality pieces. Somehow, his stately grandmother made every new addition to her home blend with her other pieces. She had a real eye for placement.

Grandma Pat was also quite the collector, and of more than just stamps. Of course, she acquired fine art and exoctic home furnishings. However, one of her favorite pastimes was simpler in nature. She loved gathering an assortment of teapots. It was an interest that lasted from her childhood until she passed. When she was ten, she was given a unique teapot that she loved to show off. This sentimental favorite held center stage above all others. It was unique, whimsical, and shaped in the form of a little girl's head with a purple butterfly on the lid. That teapot began her foray into picking up the beautiful and the unusual. She never worried about an item's current worth or if they were antiques when she purchased them. She bought from the heart and used her artistic eye to judge if a new find was worthy or not.

As she told Henry, "Everything gets old, so someday, as long as it's cared for, any item will become an antique. That includes you and me. If it appeals to you, get it, and you won't have any regrets later."

She'd then hug Henry and take him to the kitchen for cookies or some other treat. Grandma Pat was an excellent baker, and Henry was her biggest fan. He never turned down one of her creations.

Henry fondly remembered her sunny yellow kitchen highlighted by a wall of windows across one side. The oven, range, and countertop covered the opposite wall. Ornate wooden cabinets filled with figurines and, of course, teapots, adorned the area under the windows. The sunlight streaming in made the figurines almost come to life in the mind of a little boy already jubilant from cookies.

A long wooden table filled the center of the kitchen, acting as both a cooking island and social gathering place. Henry spent hours at that table, visiting with Grandma and staring out the windows into her lovely yard. In the spring and summer, the luscious smells of flowering trees and vines wafted through the open windows, causing Henry to believe there was no better place in the world. Henry, even today, believed no better place could be found, and if it weren't for the tragic fire shortly after his grandmother's death, he would have lived the rest of his days in her house. Henry missed those times with her.

Grandma Pat was an enigma. As fine of a woman as she was, she was not a snobby elitist, and Henry was quick to remind himself of that. Sometimes his own lavish tastes blinded him to the world around him, and he was keenly aware that Grandma would disapprove of his disdain for the common person. At times, Henry's face flushed knowing that his grandmother watched him from the other side and chastised him for his haughty ways.

His grandmother never lost touch of her place in the cosmos. Her life of wealth did not mean she was above anyone else, and she approached all aspects of life with the same humility. While she had fine furniture and household adornments, Grandma Pat also collected strange, ordinary items such as doorknobs, buttons, and beautiful rocks. Grandpa Jamison left her a hefty fortune to live on after he passed, so monetary value meant nothing to Grandma when it came to her collections.

She told Henry many times, "Collect what makes you happy, regardless of what anyone else thinks."

Henry took her advice to heart. Grandma's enthusiasm for acquiring and categorizing odd things helped Henry not only with his own hobbies but in his career, too. Insects fascinated him as a child, and his grandmother encouraged him to collect those. It turned into a profession. As the chief entomologist at the university, he displayed insects from everywhere imaginable. Some were common. Others were exotic. Henry loved them all, but the stranger, the better, was his motto. He traveled far and wide and never failed to bring specimens back with him.

One unusual quirk of Henry's was that he insisted on finding pairs. He wouldn't place a single specimen in his cases until he knew he had its mate. Both male and female of a species must be together, or the display was worthless in Henry's mind. Who knew where his compulsion came from? Even Grandma Pat wasn't so rigid, but Henry was a stickler. Fellow professors marveled at his ability to so thoroughly display specimens they only dreamed of acquiring.

Henry spent Tuesdays at home. In honor of his grandmother, he used that time to go through his collections, making sure all was well with each one and adding to them when appropriate. One perk of being the top professor in his field at the university was that he could call some shots. One reason he'd been drawn to academia was the flexibility in his work schedule. As long as he gave his lectures, held consistent office hours for students, and continued his research (thereby bringing grant money and prestige to the institution), he could pretty much do as he pleased. Spending Tuesdays at home to dote over his collections pleased Henry.

Henry became lost in his memories of his grandmother. He could see her pruning rose bushes, wearing that silly bonnet of hers. Henry sighed.

She was such an instrumental part of his life, right up until her death. After all these years, he could smell her perfume and hear her sweet voice. She taught him all that was important in life including the need to travel and the need to have a healthy curiosity. With the money necessary to support his every whim, she had indulged Henry. He always had whatever toy he wanted as a child, and he had the fastest sports car money could buy as a young man. She also provided him books to read about faraway places, and as he became older she gave him the ability to travel to those far off destinations. Her one requirement was that he bring back souvenirs for his collections.

Oh, Grandma Pat, how I miss you. I feel so alone without you.

A tear welled in his eye. It was true. Henry was alone. Both of his parents died in a crash ten years before. Not that they'd ever been close to him, but they were all the family he'd had. One child was all they chose to bear, so he had no siblings to grow old with. As an adult, he'd yet to find friends who shared his sense of adventure and enthusiasm for finding the oddities you encounter when traveling out of your comfort zone. Once he thought he had a girlfriend, but it turned out she had dust in her eye and hadn't been winking at him at all. Such a lonely life Henry led.

I can't dwell on that right now. Grandma wouldn't want me to be sad. It's time to do my rounds.

When looking over his collections, he always began with the stamps because that's where the passion they shared had started. Yes, those stamps were his prized possessions because they represented a bond that neither time nor his grandmother's death could diminish.

Henry moved to the next room where he checked his collection of traps and weapons. It's funny that he had a fascination with such devices. For all his love of travel, Henry wasn't what you'd call an "outdoorsman." Not even the pith helmet hanging on the nail over his trap collection allowed him to pretend he'd ever be mistaken for a man's man. No, he'd always been weak and scrawny. The closest he came to a big game hunt was watching with binoculars from the vehicle. Still, his love of traps and weaponry held his attention, and it even came in quite handy at times, for work and play.

The chime of the clock in the living room reminded him it was almost time to eat. Henry considered himself a connoisseur of fine food and drink and kept a well-stocked refrigerator, pantry, and wine cellar. His stomach rumbled at the thought of the fine lunch awaiting him in the kitchen. He'd brought it home as take-out last night, knowing he'd be too preoccupied today to go anywhere to eat or to cook for himself. His mouth watered in anticipation.

Before lunch, however, he had a few tasks to attend to. The next display was a sentimental favorite of his. He perused the collection of fine books, some left to him by his grandmother, and others acquired on his own. He always loved an excellent piece of writing. Some poignant memories washed over him as he relived trips he'd made to find these literary beauties. Life as a collector and traveler was full of so many joys that common citizens just wouldn't understand. Wealth was a means of achieving a life well-lived.

With that thought, Henry reached his most intriguing collection of all. The sheer size of it nearly filled an entire room, but it was worth it, especially now that he'd found the missing mate to his crown piece.

A collection is never complete until each piece has its match.

Joy filled Henry as he carefully lifted the lid on the glass box. Using tweezers specially designed for this purpose, he lifted the wriggling female so he could place her in the display case next to the fine male counterpart he'd already secured with pins.

My, you're a feisty one! This will only take a moment or two. I need to mount you just right. You're more beautiful than any butterfly back at the office. Don't struggle, my sweet.

With that, he applied a dab of glue and raised the first pin to put her in place. His most recent trip to Earth had been worth it to find a specimen such as this. He finally had his matched set of Homo sapiens.

TRIDENT

The buzz of last night's drinking binge fogged Harris Murphy's mind as he tried to shake himself awake. Sharp pain dug into his temples, and nausea swept over him from the slightest of movements. Even the dim light from the overcast sky streaming through his bedroom window made his skin crawl.

"Damn. I really need to quit drinking."

A nine o'clock deadline for his story on the school funding bill was the only thing driving him out of the stillness of his bed. The state House of Representatives voted it down yesterday evening, and the station expected him to give a report during the noon broadcast. He knew when he ran into Sean Kennedy and the boys down at The Shady Star last night that he should head to his cubicle at Trident Media and slam out the story. He didn't listen to his better judgment, and now here he was, sick and under the gun.

The failure of the bill bothered Harris. His mother and sister were teachers, and his uncle was the principal of a small school in the northern part of the state. While reporters were supposed to be unbiased, Harris always caught himself cheering for good education bills. He was usually disappointed.

"You'd swear those politicians had a thing against teachers. Did they get sent to the office in fourth grade or something?" Harris muttered as he pulled himself upright and staggered gingerly to the bathroom.

Maybe a warm shower will bring me to life.

As the political beat reporter, Harris frequently questioned both the wisdom and the motivation of politicians at the capital. Last night's debacle was just one in a string of worrisome votes he'd witnessed this session.

The warm water cascading out of the showerhead stung his eyes as the alcohol fought the water for control of Harris's senses. His head ached, and his mind was weary. Still, he pondered the seeming vindictiveness he saw from the state legislature towards education.

Some of the bills they do pass, well, they cut schools off at the knees when it comes to testing, curriculum, and funding.

Harris knew he'd have to sound objective once he was in front of the camera. The report would last a mere sixty seconds on air, and he could pull off professional coolness for that long, no matter how personally frustrated he felt. First things first, though. His head had to clear, and he had to look respectable enough that no one watching the clip would mistake him for a drunk on the street.

Becoming the political reporter for Trident was a promotion Harris fought hard to earn. He'd been the Boy Friday reporter for traffic accidents, weather conditions, and human interest stories. He now had his professional legs under him and held a position with some clout.

I'm finally able to uncover important news. I can tell the public about their elected officials and the bills they support. And the ones they let die. It's time voters know that they aren't being represented by the politicians.

People need to know their elected officials really work for, and it's not them.

Last year's legislative session was his first as a political reporter. He'd spent most of it getting to know who the state representatives and senators were. With nearly three hundred members in the assembly, that was a time-consuming task his rookie year. He also had to familiarize himself with the heads of all government agencies in addition to the throngs of lobbyists who skulked through the halls using their pocketbooks to garner favor with politicians.

Who works for $32,000 a year as a state representative when they could be earning big bucks with their law degrees or working in private business? Something has to be the draw. It sure isn't doing good for the people of this state. If I've learned anything from this job so far, it's that politicians listen to who has the money. It's the lobbyists, and not to their constituents who have their ear.

He was so busy that first year getting to know the players that he hadn't dug as deeply behind closed doors as he intended to. A new legislative session had arrived, however.

This is my chance to open the public's eyes to what happens in our government. It isn't just our politicians, either. What the bureaucrats are doing should trouble us all, too. Department heads are into some pretty shady stuff. Now I just have to figure out what it is.

Harris finished his shower and dressed. He kept the light off and hoped his clothes matched.

I feel too bad to care.

The pain stabbed anytime he leaned over and that made putting his shoes on torture. He couldn't face food yet, but a strong shot of caffeine sounded like a good idea. A pot of coffee later, Harris left on his way to Trident Media.

Pulling into his assigned parking space, Harris grabbed his briefcase off the passenger side floorboard. He hit the lock button on his key fob twice by accident and winced at the honk his car emitted. It echoed through the parking garage and reverberated in his aching head. The brisk winter wind hit his face and made his red eyes water as he walked toward the entrance of the outwardly nondescript building. Only the station's name in large letters on the wall gave any indication to passersby that a broadcast company owned that address.

Passing through the automatic door, Helen Gooding, the meteorologist, stopped him. "Damn, Murphy. You look like you've been run over by a train. Were the politicians that rough on you yesterday?"

Harris laughed. "No, I'll be fine. Just feeling a little under the weather today."

Above him the Trident motto was displayed: Truth. Integrity. Diligence. Those three words were emblazoned onto the marketing department's version of Poseidon's mythological trident. Harris wasn't any Walter Cronkite, but his journalist's heart embraced those virtues. The public deserved truth and integrity in the news, and that was made possible by the diligence of reporters who exposed corruption. Reporters had to get to the heart of issues because no one else would. Our communities and country deserved the truth.

Taking the elevator to the third floor, he avoided eye contact with coworkers as he walked through the maze of cubicles to arrive at his. Certain that Helen had already told several people about his "condition," he wanted to steer clear of as much attention as possible. He had a story to write, and he wasn't in the mood for spectators.

Finally, in the temporary shelter of his office space, Harris pulled his notes from his briefcase and typed up a news-ready rendition of the bill and its failure in the hands of politicians. Void of emotion on the page, Harris was satisfied with his achievement.

Next, he checked his voicemail. Nothing of interest came until the fifth call. A hushed voice came on the other end of the phone. Harris had to press the receiver to his ear to make out what the man said.

"Mr. Murphy, I've got some information you'd like to have. Meet me at Parkview Plaza in that little coffee shop at two. I can't say anything more now."

Harris received calls like this a couple of times a week. The information ranged from the absurd to the even more absurd. Once he had an irate husband call who wanted a private meeting. He was convinced that Harris had an ongoing affair with his wife. Why? Because his wife always "shushed" him when Harris came on the screen.

A few other times, people came forward with the "truth" behind the Kennedy assassination. A few alien abductions, cries for help finding missing pets, and the average pothole complaints were thrown in for good measure. Occasionally, however, he was given a good lead. This kept Harris open to biting when he received a mysterious meet-up message.

Besides, by then I'll need some good quality caffeine in me. I haven't been to that place in quite a while. The food was good, and the coffee was top-notch. Oh, man, I should have never thought of food.

Beads of sweat welled on his forehead, and he had to swallow hard to keep his head in control of his stomach. For now, his focus had to be on work.

Now I just have to bide my time until my segment airs. Afterwards I'll tell the boss I'm off to pursue a lead.

Time crept by, and the fluorescent lights did nothing to lessen his hangover.

One thing I love about journalism is the ability to find interesting stories, even if most of the time these meetings never amount to anything worthwhile.

Since childhood, Harris had an insatiable curiosity. It helped in this line of work. The world was never boring if you kept a sense of wonder about you. He'd always been fascinated by people and what motivated them, and journalism gave him an open door into the lives of others. Furthermore, it gave him the opportunity to do good. Keeping politicians and bureaucrats in line was good, in Harris's opinion.

He filled a small paper cup with water from the cooler next to the staff room and tossed down three over-the-counter pain medications. Sitting at his desk with his head in his hands, he readied himself to film the segment. Finally, it was time to go on air.

Once the camera's red light turned off, Harris made his way, a little unsteadily, towards his desk. Hoping he pulled off his piece without looking hungover, a voice behind him grabbed his attention as he walked out of the recording studio and back to his cubicle.

"Good job, Murphy. You know of any other hot bills coming up for debate? Get me a good news story by tomorrow morning." Larry Levins, the station manager at Trident, followed him down the hallway.

"Well, there's a gun control bill coming up for debate, and I'm heading out to follow up a lead on a potential story."

"Good. Glad to hear it."

Harris put his sports jacket on the back of his office chair and picked up his briefcase before riding the elevator back down to the ground floor.

He squinted as he stepped out of Trident's building. The clouds were clearing and a sharp blue broke through the grey. On West Larkspur Avenue, traffic sped past, and a honking horn caused him to reel. Pain stabbed behind his left eye, and Harris placed his hand over his forehead as he made his way to his car. His sunglasses, old and slightly scratched, sat where he left them, carelessly tossed on the seldom-used passenger seat next to an empty fast food wrapper and a half-eaten bag of chips.

Between the drinking and the junk I eat, I'll be lucky to see thirty-five.

Parkview Plaza was only a twenty-minute drive from the studio. The afternoon traffic was light, so Harris anticipated smooth sailing on his way to meet with the mystery caller. The air was crisp, and Harris rolled down his window an inch or two, hoping the frosty wind would eliminate the last remnants of the hangover. By the time he parked in front of the coffee shop, he felt well enough that the first pangs of hunger rumbled.

The storefront sign read, "Perk Up!"

I'm trying! Harris chuckled as he dug through his briefcase for the recorder he used to take notes.

The restaurant wasn't busy, which suited him just fine. He couldn't take the din of customers or the sound of plates clacking together. Not today. Harris took a booth seat in the back corner and waited. Looking at his phone, it was two o'clock on the dot. Just then, the bell jingled on the door. A blond man of average height dressed in blue jeans, a plaid shirt, and a tan winter coat crossed the threshold. They made eye contact, and there was no doubt this was the man from the phone call.

You can always by tell the look of recognition in their eyes. This guy knows who I am, and he knows why I'm here.

In a hushed voice, the newcomer said, "My name's Jake." He extended his hand and Harris shook it as he offered to order the man a coffee.

"Yes, thank you. Black, please. I walked here so no one would recognize my car. It got a little cold with that wind. Coffee sounds great." Jake rubbed his hands together to warm them.

Well, he seems friendly enough, so it's not a jealous husband. He does act a bit spooked, though.

The waitress took their orders, and Harris cut to the chase.

"So, you said you had some information for me."

"What I'm hoping for is a working relationship."

"Oh, boy, if you're looking for a job at Trident, I can't do anything for you."

Jake rolled his eyes. "Seriously, Murphy? I took you to be smarter than that. Not *that* kind of working. I mean I think we could help each other out."

The men paused as the waitress brought them their coffee and the slices of pie they'd ordered. Harris doused his coffee with cream. The spoon clanked along the inside of the cup as he stirred. He winced. The sound seemed deafening in his head, and with no other customers in the place it drew the attention of the waitress who smiled at him.

"How so?"

Jake looked around to make sure no one else was nearby. He took a glance out the window and hunched his shoulders as he leaned in toward Harris.

"I give you leads to the biggest story of your career, and you get the truth out there. That's all I want. Just the truth out there."

"Okay, that sounds good. Just what is the truth?"

"These people are evil. I'm certain they'd be willing to kill over this. You're going to have to be gutsy, Murphy. Can you do that?"

Not wanting to have his male ego threatened, he straightened a bit in his seat and said, "Of course, I can. What's this about?"

"Good, because I've been trying to get someone to look into this for months, and none of the other reporters will touch it. I think they're too afraid to go against something this big."

Both men sipped their coffees for a moment, and Harris took a few tentative bites of his apple pie.

Jake broke the silence. "To be honest, I've become skeptical of the press. If you don't do this story, I'll have to figure out some other way to get the truth out to the public. Publish a manifesto online or something. You should know, however, that it's not without some risks. These people are cutthroat."

Harris was intrigued. That insatiable curiosity of his was emboldened by the sincerity in Jake's voice. Eyeing his new companion, Harris, while still skeptical, was impressed.

This guy doesn't seem like the average crackpot.

"What if I told you there's something really wrong at our state Capitol? The budget numbers don't add up. Not if you dig deep enough. What if I told you that our prisons are producing hundreds of millions of dollars in profit while taking hundreds of millions in tax money from us at the same time?"

"Do you have proof? I agree that the Corrections budget seems to grow by tens of millions every year, but just how do you know they are producing that much money each year? I've always been told the prison system costs us money. It doesn't make it for us."

The waitress stopped and refilled their coffee. "Would you gentlemen like anything else? You've been here for a while, and you devoured that pie, so I'm guessing you're hungry. Phil, our cook, makes a fine chicken sandwich with fries."

The two men nodded. "Yes, that sounds great. Bring one for me and one for my friend here. Oh, and bring me some more cream for my coffee."

She winked at Harris and said, "You've got it, sugar. By the way, you're my favorite reporter at Trident. I keep the noon news turned on every day just so I can watch your reports, Mr. Murphy."

"Call me Harris."

"Thank you, Harris. I'll get those sandwiches right up." Her cheeks flushed slightly.

Harris watched her walk away.

"She is a sight to behold, Murphy. You probably have women all over you."

Harris blushed and stammered. "Uh, no. No, not at all. Um, let's get back to what you were saying."

"Proof? If you want proof, I've got it in here." Jake tapped a large manila envelope he pulled out of his jacket and placed on the table. "I'm going to let you take a look at it yourself. You're right that the government, including the Department of Corrections, is costing taxpayers. It's making big money for some of the politicians and their cronies, though."

Harris reached across and picked up the envelope. "I won't open this here, and I can't make any promises, but I'll take a look at it. If I find something I can use for a story, I'll let you know."

"Oh, you will, if you are smart enough to connect the dots. I've got more where that came from if it looks like you'll put it to good use."

"How did you come by these documents?"

"I'm not going to reveal my sources, but you'll see that most of them are either on letterhead, are time-stamped, or they have signatures. I'm not throwing anyone under the bus on this, but these are all legit."

Conversation stopped as their sandwiches arrived at the table.

"Will that be all for you guys?"

"Yeah, this is all. It looks great, thanks."

"I'll leave you your ticket then." Setting it on the table, she winked and tapped the bottom of the pale green check. "Trina" with a phone number was jotted in red ink.

Harris blushed again.

"Looks like you have a date in your future, Murphy."

Uncomfortable with his embarrassment, Harris got back to business. "If I have any questions, how can I get ahold of you? You didn't leave me a call back number, and all I know is your first name."

Grabbing the green ticket, Jake flipped it over and scribbled a number. "This is a throw-away phone I got. Don't confuse the two numbers." Laughing out loud, he rose to leave. "I hope to hear from you, Murphy, and I hope to see some results."

"Can I get your last name?"

"Not right now. Let's see how this plays out. It's better for both of us to leave things as they are right now."

Just like that, Jake put on his coat and walked out of the coffee shop. A cold breeze swept into the diner through the open door. Harris dabbed a few more french fries into the ketchup on his plate and made his way to the cash register. Pulling out his wallet, he slipped the diner ticket into it after he paid with a twenty-dollar bill and left an additional ten-dollar tip for Trina. She winked and gave a shy grin as she pocketed the tip.

"You have a nice day, Mr. Murphy. I hope to see you again."

Harris felt his face redden. "Yeah, that would be nice."

No longer feeling the effects of the hangover, the day looked better. A hot shower and some quiet time to look through the stash of documents Jake left for him was all Harris had in mind for the night.

No more trips to The Shady Star for me for a while. Maybe I'll even call Trina sometime. I can't remember the last time I went on a date, and she was a looker. Sweet too.

Finally, at home in the peace and quiet of his apartment, Harris changed into what he always wore around home: sweatpants and an old t-shirt. With no girlfriend to impress, he had slipped into the habit of never worrying about appearances unless he was on set at work. Settling into one end of his leather sofa, he undid the metal clasp and opened Jake's envelope.

I'm going to sleep early tonight, but I want to take a look at what this guy gave me.

Jake was organized. Harris had to give him that. Each set of related information was strapped together by separate rubber bands. The first set puzzled him. It appeared to be nothing more than sales and expense reports from the prison canteen. Flipping through the receipts, Harris saw the name "Legent Enterprises" at the top of many of them. The next stack included a detailed budget report released from the capital. Another was a series of purchase orders made out to the state's Rehabilitative Manufacturing Division of the Corrections Department.

Man, I never realized the inmates made so many different things. Furniture. Print jobs. Small engines. Even toilet paper, along with a score of other products. They also provide services like laundries and recycling. And all these P.O.s come from at least a dozen different states.

Looking at the totals and the dates, it was clear that millions of dollars' worth of materials and services flowed in and out of the prisons.

Where is that money going?

The last stack of papers in the envelope was a list of legislators. Some had single stars next to their names. Others had plus marks and minuses in various colors of ink.

Lastly, he found a handwritten note.

Mr. Murphy,

Here is your first piece of the puzzle. Let's see if you're as smart as I hope you are. If you are, I have more where this came from. This is the tip of the iceberg.

Jake

Harris studied the documents, referring to the checklist of legislator names, and each time a bell went off in his head as glimpses of what Jake was after flashed in his mind.

Something isn't right here, but I can't put my finger on it.

Three hours later, Harris looked at the time. He gathered up the documents and carefully put them back into the envelope. His curiosity had a fire under it now.

Over the course of the next several days, he called multiple state agencies, including the state auditor's office. Something tickled his mind about the Rehabilitative Manufacturing Division. Surely Pamela Rhodes, the state auditor, could shed some light on where those millions of dollars went. After a few calls, he finally scheduled a meeting with her.

It wasn't the first time he'd sat in the office of a high ranking state official, but it was his first visit with Ms. Rhodes who won her office in the last election with a firebrand approach to tracking down waste and corruption. If anyone gave him the goods on the Department of Corrections budget, it would be her.

After a brief wait, he was ushered behind the dark oak doors and was face-to-face with her.

"Good afternoon, Mr. Murphy. My secretary said you wanted to take a look at the Corrections budget after my audit this past fall. Is there something in particular you are looking for?"

"Yes, there is. I was wondering if you could give me the numbers for the Rehabilitative Manufacturing Division. I have reason to believe it's producing millions of dollars for the department, but when looking at the numbers from the legislative report I don't see where that money is going."

"You won't find it in that report or in my audit."

Cocking his head to one side, Harris stared in disbelief. "Why not?"

"The Rehabilitative Manufacturing Division isn't a part of the Department of Corrections, so it isn't a state entity."

"But it uses state-provided facilities and inmate labor at pennies on the dollar. Their factories are inside the prisons. How can they not be part of the department?"

"I was surprised by what I found myself, Mr. Murphy. That division is a private for-profit contracted business."

"What about all the money it makes?"

"That's not under my jurisdiction. It doesn't go back to either the state or the Department of Corrections. It's privately owned, and all the money generated is earned by the owners of the company."

"Who owns it?"

"That I'm not sure about. Perhaps the Department of Revenue could assist you, but I've heard rumors that no one really wants to talk about RMD. Here is a copy of the Corrections Department audit that you requested, however I wish I could give you more information, but this is all I have."

Harris rose from the velvet-covered chair and reached for the binder she handed him. "Thank you very much for your time, Ms. Rhodes."

"It was my pleasure, Mr. Murphy. I appreciate your reports. I watch them every day during my lunch. Keep them on their toes."

A brief handshake later, he was on his way back out into the hallway of the state capitol building.

I need to call Jake.

Once in the privacy of his car, Harris dialed the number Jake had given him at Perk Up!

"Murphy?"

"Yeah, Jake, I need to talk with you."

"It's about time. I was beginning to think you'd blown me off."

"No, not at all. I've been doing some digging into what you gave me the other week. I just had an interesting conversation with the state auditor. RMD is a private company!"

"I could have told you that. I wanted to see if you were willing to poke around enough in the sleazy corners to come up with it yourself."

"Well, I did. Jake, just how much money are we talking about?"

"Last year the laundry service alone made $118 million. Now think about the dozen other enterprises they have going on. It adds up to a lot of dough."

"And none of this gets turned into the state?"

"Not a penny. At least not directly."

"What do you mean?"

"Oh, there are some people in the government who get plenty of this cash. You saw the list of politicians with marks next to their names, right?"

The gravity of what he heard silenced Harris.

"Murphy, are you there?"

"Yeah, I'm here. Those dirty bastards are pocketing the money off basically free inmate labor. What else are they into?"

"For that information, you need to meet me again. I've got more documents for you. See you at the coffee shop tomorrow at four. Okay?"

"I'll see you then. Thanks for putting me onto this, Jake."

"There's more. See you tomorrow."

The next day Harris gave his report on the most recent political movement on the gas tax bill. Democrats and Republicans were duking it out in committee. The producers ordered him to stay on top of that story. It was, they said, the most important thing going on in the capitol building.

Oh, I think I'm onto something much bigger than the gas tax.

At four o'clock, Harris sat in the same booth with Jake who had another large manila envelope lying on the table for him.

Trina brought coffee to the table. "I have extra cream for you, Mr. Murphy. I remembered you liked it that way."

Harris blushed. In the intensity of following Jake's leads, he'd forgotten to call Trina.

"Call me Harris. When we're done here, I'd like to talk with you for a moment if you're free."

Trina's eyes sparkled. "Sure, Harris, that would be nice."

The men ordered and got down to business. Jake fidgeted with the ring on his left hand. He caught Harris staring at his hands as they talked.

"Sorry, I guess I'm a little nervous. The stress is getting to me lately."

"That's an interesting ring you have there. What are those symbols?"

"My wife and I met when I was stationed in Guam. It was such a special place to us that we had these made for our wedding bands. The symbols each represent something from there. Like this one…" He pointed at a squiggly line. "It represents the waves in the ocean."

Jake suddenly stopped talking.

"I hope I didn't say anything to upset you, Jake."

"No, It's just that Liz died two years ago. It's still tough to think about. And lately, I've been certain someone is tailing me, so my emotions are a little raw."

"Because of what's going on in the prisons?"

"Yeah, they don't like whistleblowers, and there are a lot of powerful people you and I are about to expose. This goes even beyond the governor's office and those piss ant legislators who are pocketing money."

"How high up?"

"I don't know. Honestly, I think the media is in on it too. You need to be careful who you talk to about this at work."

Harris hadn't considered his bosses a threat. After all, Trident Media prided itself on truth, integrity, and diligence.

"I don't think that's an issue at Trident."

"Really? Have you mentioned any of this at work?"

"Not yet. I wanted to have the big picture before I brought it up to the team."

"I think you should bring up just a piece of this to them first. You can see what their reaction is before you play your hand. I'm telling you, Murphy, this is big, and it's widespread. I don't know just how big, but it's big."

After a two-hour conversation, Jake left with assurances that he would be in touch with Harris soon.

Trina stood nervously behind the counter, glancing Harris's direction. He wiped the sweat off his palms onto his pants, picked up the envelope, and made his way to the cash register.

"Was everything fine, Mr. Murphy? I mean, Harris?"

"It was delicious as always. Say, Trina, I don't want you to think I was ignoring you."

"Oh, well…"

"No, really. I haven't been. I got caught up in a project for work, but I'd like to see you. How about Friday night we go to dinner?"

"I'd like that, Harris. You have my number, right?"

"It's in my phone already. I'm just an idiot and haven't called you. I'll call you soon to make the final plans."

Harris left Perk Up! with a lightness he hadn't felt in, well, he couldn't remember how long.

I've got a huge story to work on, the biggest of my career, and I have a date for Friday night with a pretty girl. Maybe life is looking up for me!

The next day, Harris brought up investigating the Rehabilitative Manufacturing Division during the team meeting at work.

"Why would anyone be interested in that, Murphy?"

"I think there's a story to be found. I have it on good authority--the state auditor--that RMD isn't even part of the Corrections Department. It's raking in millions a year with all the overhead being paid by taxpayers. They pay inmates next to nothing, and the profits are huge."

Stern looks shot around the table.

"I think we need to direct our energies to more relevant topics than what happens to inmate workers, Murphy. No, you need to focus on the gas tax and that other bill. You know, the one about ending punitive damages against the state in the event of a frivolous lawsuit." Stan Carlisle, executive producer at Trident, sat stoically at the table, shooting a stern look at the other producers. Harris knew their decision was final, at least for now.

I'm not done with the RMD story. Once I have the big picture, they'll have to run it. We'll have the exclusive on a blockbuster expose.

Harris did as his bosses told him and reported on the gas tax, the punitive damages bill, and the boat safety week bill that was proposed by a former highway patrolman turned legislator.

He didn't feel comfortable with the punitive damages bill. It rankled him to think the state could walk away with no responsibility for injuries or wrongful deaths. However, the farther he delved into the RMD story, the more he began to think the state could do whatever it wanted to.

As weeks of investigating passed, a nagging fear crept into Harris's subconsciousness. The more he found out, the more doors slammed in his face whenever he asked about RMD, the more he felt as though he was walking in deadly quicksand. He thought about Jake's nervousness.

The slight eye twitch. His constant looking over his shoulder. The fiddling with his ring on his finger. Harris now found himself jumping at the slightest out-of-place sounds.

Then the break-in occurred. At least, Harris was pretty sure his apartment was broken into. Nothing was missing, but his lamp was tipped over, and drawers in his desk were left slightly ajar one night when he returned to his apartment. His neighbors claimed they saw nothing out of the ordinary, but they also didn't want to talk about it. Dread stalked him day and night. A black car showed up everywhere he went. At first, he thought it was his imagination, but it was everywhere he was: the grocery store, the gym, and he even saw it following him when he was on his date with Trina.

What a date it was, too. That girl...

The rush of emotions he had when thinking about Trina was quickly replaced by the undeniable truth that he was being watched.

Someone doesn't want that story coming out, which only means I need to work twice as hard because I'm onto something.

Two weeks later, he tested the waters and brought the RMD topic up at the team meeting again. He was surprised by their sudden change of heart.

"You know, Murphy. We think you may have something here. In fact, the people at the Department of Corrections need to meet with you about this. Set up a meeting with them. Go in there with guns blazing. Ask them some of those tough questions you're so good at."

"Really? You support this story?"

"Oh, absolutely." Stan's words were supportive, but his eyes betrayed a hardened glint.

It's a start. At least I have the go ahead. Once I blow the lid off this story, they'll be glad they gave me their blessing. This will make national news.

After only one phone call, a meeting was set at DOC headquarters.

That was way easier than I thought it would be.

The upcoming meeting only fueled Harris's desire to find the truth. With the help of Jake and some late-night meetings with bureaucrats who had access to tax filings and supply chain logistics for RMD, Harris finally connected the dots.

Those dirty bastards. They love using the cover of being "tough on crime" to skim millions into their own pocketbooks. Dozens of high ranking legislators are in on this. The governor has to be too. He was a member of the House for years until he reached his term limit and ran for higher office.

The night before the meeting at DOC headquarters, Harris gave Jake a call. There were a few loose ends he wanted to tie up before hitting them full-force.

No answer. Harris tried again and again. Still no answer. While disturbing, Harris chalked it up to Jake using throw away phones.

He must have a new one. He's got my number. He'll be in touch.

On the warmest day in weeks, Harris arrived at the office of the DOC director. The elegant walnut furniture in the waiting room was one of the products made by RMD. Through his research, Harris discovered that every state office was required to buy any product made by RMD through them, even if the cost was higher than other retailers. Not only that, but RMD had similar contracts with dozens of states across the country.

What a racket.

Harris waited patiently, then the secretary said, "Director Ramsberry is ready for you."

Confident he had caught them in their web of corruption, Harris grinned as he walked through the door. His expression rapidly changed, however once he entered the room.

Sitting in the spacious office, he recognized not only Amanda Ramsberry but also several legislators, the lieutenant governor, the head of RMD, and Larry Levins, the station manager of Trident Media.

What in the hell is Larry doing here?

"Hello, Mr. Murphy. Please have a seat." Amanda Ramsberry motioned to the only empty chair left in her office. Several of the legislators stood in a semi-circle around Harris and Director Ramsberry's desk.

Suddenly, Harris felt less like a fearless reporter and more like a child called into the principal's office. The momentum shifted to the side of the powerbrokers surrounding him.

"We understand you've been looking into some matters on your own, without your station's permission." Ramsberry sat behind her desk, fiddling with her pen. The legislators took an obvious half-step toward Harris.

"Well, I…"

"You don't need to explain, Harris. We know."
Larry Levins stared impassively at him. "It's not as though
you were hard to keep track of."

"What? You're involved in following me?"

"I'm sure you can understand the gravity of what
you have planned, Mr. Murphy. It just can't happen."
Kendall Crockett, chairman of the House Corrections
Committee, leaned forward with a piercing glare.

"We've worked too long to protect ourselves to
have you try to unravel all we've accomplished. You know
we can't let that happen." Amanda Ramsberry tapped her
pen on the stack of papers before her, making an object
sitting on her desk rattle every time her pen struck. She
smiled as Harris's gaze settled on Jake's wedding band. For
good measure, she rapped her pen once more to make the
ring bounce on the mahogany.

Harris stood to leave.

"Not so fast." Larry Levins and five other men
surrounded him in a tight group.

What is it about Larry's eyes?

Harris stared in disbelief as his boss's eyes
flickered. A second eyelid he'd never noticed closed
vertically across Larry's pupils. An uncontrollable shudder
passed through Harris's body.

I must be losing my mind.

Everyone in the room chuckled. The room spun,
and Harris grasped the back of his chair.

"Why are you laughing?"

"You just told yourself you're losing your mind.
You're a perceptive man, Harris Murphy."

"Wait. How did you know that? I didn't say that out loud."

"You don't have to. We can read your thoughts. We've known what you, and the others who have been stupid enough to interfere with us, have been thinking." Amanda Ramsberry smirked as she looked at Jake's wedding band.

"You and your friend were right to believe you were being followed. We can't let trouble walk around unattended. It's too dangerous for us." Larry Levins blinked his strange eyes again.

"Us?"

"Yes, our kind. We've managed to keep ourselves secret from you lowly creatures for over a century. We're certainly not losing our grip on the masses now."

Christopher Bradford, the Speaker of the House, moved blithely toward Harris. "You see, we have been in control of this planet for a long time. Do you really believe that you are a 'free' press? You tell your ignorant public the news your superiors, like Larry here, tell you to report. We can't have you asking questions and causing unrest amongst our laborers." A lizard-like tongue flicked out of Bradford's mouth.

Harris's knees buckled slightly.

I've got to get out of here.

Another chuckle erupted in the room.

"Oh, you will leave here, Harris, but before you do we have to take care of your first concern." Amanda Ramsberry opened a compartment on her desk and withdrew a long needle attached to a machine similar to a portable heart defibrillator. A thin metal wire connected the needle to the machine. She pushed of a button, and the machine lit up, emitting a gentle hum.

"My first concern?"

"You know, the one about you losing your mind."

Panic gripped Harris Murphy, and he dashed for the door. He made it two steps before the superhuman strength of the beings in the room brought him to the floor.

"This will only hurt for a minute, and we promise you won't remember a thing."

The last sound Harris Murphy heard was cackling laughter as the needle punctured his brain through the base of his skull.

***

The next morning, Harris arrived at Trident Media feeling fuzzy and not quite himself.

I really have to stop drinking. This hangover is terrible. I don't even remember anything before waking up this morning. Sean Kennedy must have talked me into The Shady Star again.

In his noon broadcast, Harris Murphy delivered a bland report regarding new regulations for crossing guards at schools. Tomorrow he would report on the latest partisan infighting that dominated much of every newscast across the country.

The viewing public would never know the real news. After all, the cogs didn't need to know what the engineer had in mind.

BEFORE AND AFTER

On a dreary January morning, Billie Henson sat in his favorite chair, drinking coffee and contemplating the years since his childhood. His life was bound to this place, and he loved looking out the window into his familiar backyard as he daydreamed. Except for a short stint in the military, he'd lived here since he was born. He knew every nook and cranny of the old two-story farmhouse, and he was comfortable.

He hadn't planned on becoming sentimental this morning. Nothing more than a relaxing cup of coffee in his recliner had been his goal. Time weighed heavily on him today, however. Years have a way of dulling some memories and accentuating others, and this morning the sharp ones flooded over him like Blackjack Creek on a rainy day.

Looking out the window, he could picture his brother Pete and their friends sledding with him down the hill. He felt crisp air on his cheeks and the numbness of his hands as his boyhood self steered his sled, slowly gliding to a stop next to the barn. Oh, how those were carefree days. Time went slower, or so it seemed, back then. Hours spent playing with his brother and friends lasted what felt like days. Oh, the innocence of youth.

Sledding was a favorite winter pastime when he was a child. He was given his own sled when he was six, and he remembered how proud he'd been that he was finally "big."

Big was a relative term he'd learn over the years. As a boy, he continuously played catch-up to his brother. Pete, three years older, always got to do things ahead of him, and that was a source of jealousy during much of Billie's youth.

Billie winced at the thought. Pete was also drafted three years before Billie was at a time when the war was going strong. He never made it back from those fields made crimson by the blood of young farm boys like Pete. After that, Billie never looked at the passage of time the same. There was Before Pete's Death and After. No other event so strictly defined his life more than the loss of the only one who knew him that well.

The chiming clock in the background reminded him that time still passed. No matter what joys or sorrows life brought, time passed. He stirred his cup, and the scent of freshly brewed coffee filled the air around him.

Yes, those years with Pete were fun ones. They'd had their share of squabbles, but for the most part they were inseparable. Memories of ball games, double dating the Crawford sisters, and milking cows in the early morning hours held special places in Billie's heart.

The two brothers differed, however. Pete yearned to see the world and had even looked forward to being sent overseas by the Army. He was going to meet interesting people… and be killed by them. Billie never wanted to live anywhere other than the farmstead, and he hadn't. The minute his plane touched ground on American soil, he made a beeline for home. He hated going to war. Nothing separated him from the place he loved.

In the years after his brother's death, Billie cared for the farm and his parents as they aged. There was always something to do, whether it was feeding livestock, mending fence, or patching the roof of the house. Time with his parents, whom he adored, was treasured by Billie. Never once did he resent caring for them, and neither spent a day in a nursing home. When asked if he was ever lonely, the answer was no. He was a shy man and never bothered to marry. He wasn't sure what to say to women and couldn't fathom spending a lifetime trying to figure it out. That whole thing with the Crawford girl had only been to keep Pete happy.

Over the years, the neighborhood changed. When he was a boy, it took a three-mile walk to get to the nearest neighbor's place. Going the other direction, the Stiltmans had a large dairy operation about four miles away. Those were simpler times. On summer evenings, folks in the area sometimes stopped to visit for a while on front porches and, of course, everyone saw each other on Sundays. Except for mean old Lester Parsons. That pinched-up heart of his wouldn't even let the Gospel in. In the old days, people were self-sufficient and didn't need the constant companionship of others. Each family worked hard and handled its own affairs. In Billie's opinion, more people should try that.

In time, the county paved the road going past the farm, and developers bought up farmland to create subdivisions. Multi-storied apartments now covered the Stiltman place. Why people wanted to live smack-dab on top of each other was a mystery to Billie. The influx meant new neighbors who had little respect for personal space. Gone were the days when a simple tip of your hat as you drove past was enough socialization for all involved. Now people even made friends on this thing called "social media."

Carefully, Billie considered all the changes he'd seen in his time. New inventions and medical breakthroughs were almost daily occurrences now. Billie learned it was true that time sped by faster the older we became. Why, it had been eighty years since his parents passed away. True love kept them together, even in death. His father died just three days after his sweet mother. Had it really been eighty years? Yes. Almost eighty-one come March. They both died the week before what would have been Pete's seventieth birthday.

New neighbors became the bane of Billie's existence, and the latest ones were the worst yet. This batch was continually coming in, opening his cupboards, and turning up the volume on that new-fangled flat-screen television they put in his living room. These people really had some nerve. As best he could, he just left them to their own devices. He stayed out of their way and tried to make his presence as unnoticeable as possible.

Just then, the thunder of footsteps pounded down the stairwell. Two teenage boys jostled each other to reach the refrigerator first. Talking loudly and carrying on, they didn't even notice Billie. He slowly set his coffee mug on the windowsill and faded quietly away. After all, he had an eternity to spend in his home, and these newcomers were just passing through.

MEMORY LANE

Evangeline Moore brushed the wisps of brown hair out of her eyes as she sailed down Concord Avenue on her bicycle. This old bike took her wherever she wanted to go, and she smiled as the familiar places of her youth passed her by while she picked up speed.

"Be careful, Evie," her father always cautioned her. "You have the heart of a lion, and I'm afraid you're going to hurt yourself one day on that contraption."

"That's impossible, Daddy. My bicycle is my freedom."

Freedom.

Yes, this old bicycle was her freedom. Whenever she felt down or useless, she hopped on her trusty bike and pedaled. All her cares slipped away as she rode to her heart's content.

She remembered her first real bicycle. It had training wheels, and she was four that Christmas. More than anything, she'd wanted a bike so she could keep up with her three siblings. Looking back, she wasn't sure how her parents raised four children on her father's paycheck, let alone bought them the very presents they desired most, but they managed. Having grown older and wiser, she now guessed that Grandma Wilson had her hand in the gift getting. It was a testament to Granny's character that she never wanted credit if she had, in fact, bought those presents.

All Evangeline knew for certain was that her family loved her. What she wouldn't give to ride bikes with Sallie, Dot, and Mack again. Their absence was the only drawback to her solitary bike rides. She couldn't bring the people she missed along with her these days.

She could, however, take rides down memory lane where she heard their peals of laughter and the whirring of their wheels as they raced each other to Sutter's Orchard or to the top of Crabapple Hill. On especially daring trips, they took moonlit rides around the perimeter of the cemetery. That, of course, didn't happen until their teenage years. Their parents would have killed them for being out at that hour, so the four had developed a system for leaving their home undetected.

Evangeline laughed out loud at their antics. They were brave and they were daring, that was for sure. Mack bragged that they came from pioneer stock and that's what made them fearless. Not a one of them turned down some wholesome fun when they could find it.

Turning right, she rode past the barber shop, the grocer, and Doc Gower's office. She winced at the thought of the time she'd fallen from the top of their maple tree and Doc Gower had to reset her arm. Glancing down at her tanned, smooth skin, the white scar near her elbow was a reminder of that mishap. She swore she could still feel the pain and hear the sounds as the gentle doctor manhandled her arm back into place. That was one memory she did not care to relive.

Up ahead, a cottontail hopped across the road in front of her then stopped to stare at her while sitting on its hind legs. It was early summer, and she had a suspicion that the bunny came from Mildred McEnany's garden.

"Little one, I won't hurt you, but I can't make any promises about old Mildred. She's got buckshot waiting for you if you're not careful."

Evangeline slowed to watch the rabbit. It cocked its head, almost as if it considered her advice. A neighborhood dog barked, spooking the cottontail just enough that it decided to hop on along.

Evangeline, in turn, quickened her pace. Her hometown hadn't changed a bit, and she wanted to take in all of her favorite spots before her ride was over.

She turned a corner and saw one of her special places. The glorious oak tree stood as it always had. Just as it stood the night Jacob Moore kissed her for the first time. Butterflies took flight in Evangeline's heart as she thought of that warm summer evening.

There is nothing like true love.

If she listened carefully, she could hear the birds sing the same as they had the night Jacob swore he'd love her forever. And he had. At least until his plane was shot down during the war. The diamonds on her wedding ring lit up as brightly as her heart did whenever she thought of that sweet man.

Evangeline wiped a tear, blew a kiss at the tree, and rode past. There was no sense dwelling there. Her memories with Jacob would always be just as vivid.

Next, she rode down Culver Hill and past the schoolyard. Oh, the fun she and her classmates had. The swings. The monkey bars. The teeter-totter. Now those were some good times.

Kids these days just don't know what they're missing with their noses stuck to a screen.

She was half-tempted to hop off her bike and try out the swing herself, but she thought better of it. She needed to stay on her bike. It was enough to catch a look at the recess yard.

The church bell tolled noon, and she knew what that meant. It was time to return home. She didn't dare have Layna arrive at the house while she was gone. Too many questions. Too much unnecessary prying.

My daughter seems to think I can't take care of myself.

Evangeline wasted no time pedaling home, wind whipping past her, as she breathed deeply. The rides did so much for her.

"Exercise is important," her mother always said.

She slowed as she approached her house, relieved that Layna had yet to arrive. Leaning her bicycle against the yellow wall by her garden gate, she slowly made her way up the steps and into her kitchen.

I'd best fix my hair before she gets here.

Evangeline looked into the mirror. The wrinkled old woman staring back at her reminded her of her grandmother. Her wizened hands, knuckles swollen from arthritis, grasped the brush as she untangled her long, grey hair.

Gone were her youthful arms and legs. Gone was the burst of energy she had while riding her special bicycle.

Someday. Yes, someday I will tell Layna about my little secret. She, too, will use my magic bicycle to go down her own memory lane. It's my very own time machine.

Her daughter rapped gently at the front door.

"Mom, are you ready for me to take you shopping?"

"Yes, dear, I'm coming."

For now, though, it's okay for this old girl to keep this secret to herself.

JUST ANOTHER DAY IN DAYTON

A small town morning dawned in picturesque Dayton, Tennessee. Its beauty was hard to beat, and Jenny Russell smiled a sleepy grin as she sipped her coffee and watched the wild birds at her feeder. Cardinals were her favorites, but wrens, chickadees, and occasional woodpeckers were also welcome sights as she watched the morning sunrise from her back deck.

Moments like these, when the quiet of the night met the new day, were magical. Each morning brought a promise of hope as the rush of the workday hadn't fogged the mind with worry or beaten down the body with fatigue. Yes, these still moments caught between night and day were heaven on earth, and ever since she was a little girl, Jenny relished them.

A whiff of lilacs in bloom caused her to lean forward on the railing and breathe deeply. Her grandmother planted a dozen bushes shortly after she and Grandpa Willis moved into this rambling Victorian-style home they built in the 1940s. Their scent was indelibly linked to Jenny's memories of her grandmother, slender and graceful, and her grandfather, wise and mischievous. Willis, who returned safely from the shores of Normandy, swore he and his bride would surround themselves with beauty for the rest of their lives, and the lilacs were among the many beautiful things they enjoyed.

"Margie, my dear, I've seen more death and destruction than anyone should witness. We are going to have nothing but the good things in life from now on."

That desire, and a plum engineering job he landed with the newly-founded Anderson Mechanics plant, took them from the clogged streets of Pittsburgh to small town life in their adopted home of Dayton. Willis, an expert woodcrafter, in addition to being a fine engineer, created a home full of beauty. Door sills weren't simple wood frames. No, Willis hand carved ornate details into the doorways, and he built exquisite furniture for his beloved wife.

"Willie, you've turned our house into a real showplace. A castle."

"My dear, you're my queen, and you deserve a castle. Your king is at your service." With that, Willis bowed to his wife and then swept her into his arms.

Grandma loved telling me that story.

Looking around her, Jenny admired the lovely home her grandparents left her when they passed away two years ago, just six hours apart from each other. So much love could be felt in that grand old home. Memories of boisterous family gatherings and quiet moments alike resounded through those rooms. Jenny always felt at home there, and she was grateful her grandparents gave it to her in their wills.

Dayton had been good to the Russell family. The move her grandparents made there after World War II was an investment in their children and grandchildren. Working at Anderson Mechanics provided a lucrative living for her entire family. Her father and his four brothers followed in their father's footsteps and worked their way up in the company. It was expected that their children would follow suit and also return home after college to work for the company that sustained not only their family but the entire community.

When her college roommate, Nora, asked her what the draw was to returning to such a small town when the world was full of opportunities, Jenny had replied, "It's family tradition, for one thing."

"Well, what exactly do they do at Anderson Mechanics?"

"Do?"

"Yes, do."

Jenny paused.

"They make something, Jen. What is it?"

"To be honest, I'm not quite sure, and if I did know, I couldn't tell you, Nora."

"Why not?"

"Look, all I know is that they have government contracts and aren't allowed to talk about what exactly it is they make. You know, like the factory you told me your cousin works at."

Nora bit her lip. Jenny had a point. "Yeah, the one that makes some kind of coil that they're in competition with LTE for. I get it. Trade secrets and all. Sorry if I seemed pushy."

"Nah, you're just curious. I am too. I guess I'll find out after graduation when I start work there too. Dad did say there's a big new contract coming up, and his boss was asking if I was ready to join the company yet. He told him to let me graduate first."

Nora laughed. "Three more months, girl. But we'd better get back to studying for this chem midterm or neither one of us will be walking onto that stage graduation night."

Jenny stretched and rolled her eyes. "Okay, taskmaster…"

They both passed their tests, and they both graduated. That was nearly a year ago. Nora took a job in Chicago, and Jenny returned to her beloved Dayton.

That brought her to this morning. She finished her cup of coffee just as the sunrise turned into daylight. Stretching once and taking a few more deep breaths of the lilacs, she looked at her phone.

I'd better get a move on. Work won't wait just because it's a beautiful spring day.

Running behind, she rushed through her morning routine. Just as she was leaving home, her phone rang.

"Hey, Daddy, good morning! What's up?"

"Good morning, sunshine. Hey, Jenny, do you have a moment to talk? There's something I'd like to run by you."

"Sure. I'm on my way to work, but we can talk on the way."

"Okay, good. What I wanted to ask you about has to do with work, as a matter of fact."

Jenny tossed her briefcase onto the passenger seat, pausing to give a brief wave to Mrs. Ramsey who lived across the street. She was out walking her Yorkie, a sweet little dog named Poppy. Mrs. Ramsey waved in return and lifted Poppy up, moving her paw up and down to wave back too. Jenny grinned. She'd known the Ramseys since she was a toddler.

Small towns, where everyone is like family, are the place to live. I know I made the right decision coming back here.

"Did you hear me, Jen?"

"What? Oh, Daddy, I'm sorry. I got distracted. I'm here now. What was that?"

"I said, 'This could be a big day for you.' Are you listening now, Tinkerbelle?"

Jenny laughed. No matter how old she was, her dad would forever call her Tinkerbelle. "Yes, I'm listening. A big day? For me?"

"I was talking with George Mathews."

"George Mathews? The president of Anderson Mechanics?"

"The one and only. Anyway, we were talking out on the links. He has a special project in mind. He's heard you're bright and a hell of an engineer. He wanted to know if I thought you'd be up for the position."

"What position are we talking about?"

"He's beginning a new project, and he'd like you to be on the team. I told him I thought my little Tinkerbelle would be interested."

Embarrassment washed over Jenny. "Oh, Daddy, please tell me you did not call me Tinkerbelle to George Mathews."

Silence on the other end of the call gave her her answer.

"Daddy? Really?"

"Before you get mad at me, George and I have known each other for years. He's always known I call you

Tinkerbelle. Secondly, that nickname gave you this shot at a promotion."

Still angry, Jenny wasn't willing to let her dad off the hook that easily. "Dad, I'm a grown woman. A professional. Please don't talk about me like I'm five."

"Jennifer Marie, did you hear what I said? Tinkerbelle got you this chance."

"What do you mean?"

"The new project is called the Peter Pan Project. He got the idea to bring you onboard because I call you Tinkerbelle."

Jen frowned, debating whether or not to stay mad at her father. Since she didn't want to give in just yet, she said nothing.

"George said he hadn't thought of it before, but when I mentioned you he realized you'd be the perfect employee to round out the team. If you want the job. Do you?"

"Well, yeah, I do. I think. What's it involve?"

"That's for George to explain. I can't talk about it. Confidentiality and all."

"Yeah, I get it."

"George will be expecting you when you get to work."

"I'm just about there now. Thanks, Daddy. I love you."

"I love you too. Now go see what this is about."

Well, today is starting out better than I ever imagined. First an incredible sunrise. Now a promotion? I never knew Dad and George Mathews were friends. Then again, he never talks about work very much.

She pulled her blue sedan into the parking lot. Anderson Mechanics was an imposing complex. It seemed out of place, in fact, in a town like Dayton. The rest of the community was quaint, much like a Norman Rockwell painting. Anderson, however, was massive and state of the art.

To passersby from out of town, the complex might be mistaken for a junior college. Large brick buildings spread over several acres of neatly manicured grounds. On second look, however, the highly guarded security fence surrounding Anderson Mechanics would disprove the college campus notion. No school had twenty-foot fences guarded by armed security forces. Instead, the complex more closely resembled a prison than a campus.

No one in Dayton gave the security presence much thought. Over the years, Anderson had expanded building by building. The changes were slow, and the residents in the community took them in stride. A growing complex meant more jobs, and jobs meant a higher standard of living for the people in Dayton. Schools reaped the benefits of the lucrative tax base. Support businesses boomed. Residents didn't question much of anything Anderson Mechanics did since the community wasn't inclined to look a gift horse in the mouth. That was good, considering employees weren't allowed to talk about what they worked on behind the guard posts.

Jenny put her lanyard around her neck. From it hung her ID badge and keys to her locker, desk, and office door. To get into the complex, she had to slide her badge through the reader at the front gate and then place her index finger on a glass screen at the top of the box so her fingerprint could be scanned. The guard on duty nodded to her, gave a slight wave with his hand, and released the locked gate to slide open and allow Jenny entrance.

A warm breeze blew as Jenny briskly stepped down the sidewalk lined with carefully cared for flowers. Anderson spared no expense in providing a beautiful workplace for their employees. Granted, inside it was much like any other assembly line or research facility, but the grounds were worthy of a spot in *Better Homes and Gardens.* That is, if outside cameras were allowed on the property. Still, it certainly made a pleasant sight for its dedicated employees.

I can't stop and enjoy the view right now. I'm almost late, and it sounds like George Mathews is expecting me.

Arriving at the front door of the administrative building, Jenny punched her code into the box mounted to the right of the door. The distinctive clunk of the lock let her know her code was accepted and she had exactly three seconds to get into the building before the door locked again.

All employees had to pass through the administration building, regardless of where they worked on the compound. Staff mailboxes were to be checked upon entering and leaving the facility, so entry through only one building insured that employees routinely checked for messages. More importantly, it streamlined security. In a tightly guarded complex like Anderson, it was important that the movements of all personnel were closely monitored.

Why? Well, all the community knew was that Anderson worked on government contracts. That's all anyone needed to know. In this patriotic, red, white, and blue stronghold of Americana, the community took pride knowing they contributed to the safety and well-being of the country. In a practical sense, the town's financial prosperity rested on the blessings brought by having Anderson Mechanics in their area. Steady paychecks and the chance to pursue the American Dream were not taken lightly by the good people of Dayton.

Jenny walked through the spacious lobby and made for the room where mailboxes P-Z were housed. An envelope with the company logo awaited her. She turned it front to back then opened it.

Jenny Russell,

Please come see me when you arrive at work on Monday. I have something I'd like to discuss with you.

Yours,

George Mathews

A handwritten note from the head honcho. I won't keep him waiting.

With that, Jenny found the elevator and punched the button for the twelfth floor. The executive office lay before her as the doors came open.

Dolores, the smartly dressed receptionist, greeted her. "Good morning, Ms. Russell. Go ahead and have a seat. I'll let Mr. Mathews know you're here."

After a few moments, George Mathews, tall and athletic with salt-and-pepper hair swept out of his office to meet her.

"It's so good to see you! Please, come in. He guided her into his office and shut the door. "Have a seat. Can I get you some coffee?"

"Yes, thank you." Her nerves were already on edge, so caffeine wasn't necessary, but she didn't want to be rude. This was the big boss, after all.

"Cream? Sugar?"

"Black."

"A young woman after my own heart. You certainly have changed since the Jenny I remember at employee picnics. Gerald is very proud of you."

"Dad always enjoyed taking us to those events. He's happy to have all three of us kids working for Anderson. It's family tradition for a lot of people around here."

"Yes, it is. Now, Jenny... Can I call you Jenny?"

"You may." She couldn't suppress a chuckle.

"Did I say something funny?"

"Oh, no, I'm sorry, sir. I was just relieved you didn't call me Tinkerbelle. My father told me that's what he called me when you were golfing the other day."

A smile spread across his face. "Oh, yes, *that*. Don't worry, I have nicknames for my children that embarrass them, too. I think it's a cross most of us have to bear growing up. My father called me 'Spud.' To this day, I don't like potatoes because of it."

A hearty laugh broke the tension Jenny had felt.

"It was actually a good thing Gerald called you by your nickname. It made me realize you may be just who I need for my new project. What has your father told you?"

"Dad didn't say much of anything. He just said you may have a position to discuss with me. Dad has always prided himself in keeping the company's private information private."

"That is true. That's also one reason Gerald Russell has been my trusted friend for years. He understands the delicate nature of our business."

"I'm not sure what the position is, but I'm eager to discuss it."

"I have to say, Jenny, that I took the liberty of looking in your personnel file. Your transcripts from the Georgia Institute of Technology are impressive. Magna Cum laude in aerospace engineering. Excellent letters of recommendation.

"I worked hard to make my family proud."

"You succeeded. Do you enjoy the field?"

"I do."

"I ask because it's important to have a job you find fulfilling. Are you an engineer for your own sake as well as wanting to follow in your father's footsteps?"

"Why, yes. Ever since I was a little girl, I've been fascinated by math and science. Aerospace was my dream career."

The spark in her eyes as she talked about her chosen field convinced George Mathews she was sincere.

"I believe you. Your credentials are notable, and it means a great deal that you chose to come back home to Dayton to work for us. With your qualifications, you could have gone anywhere. I value your loyalty to our company and community."

"I never had a doubt I'd return to work at Anderson. This is home."

"I'd like you to be a part of a new project we are beginning. It's one close to my heart. My grandfather, Edward Anderson, started this company years ago in hopes we would reach this point."

"I'm definitely interested."

"Someone named Tinkerbelle will surely appreciate this particular project." A spark lit his eye. "I've dubbed it the Peter Pan Project."

A grin spread across Jenny's face. "I'd like to hear more."

"Before I tell you more, I need to know if you accept the position. Confidentiality is, of course, vital."

"Yes, I accept the position."

"Very well. Peter Pan is intended to take mankind beyond our current limitations. Our goal is to develop a high speed space vehicle. One faster than any ever built on Earth."

"A spaceship?"

"Yes. Beyond what was attempted by previous companies. More than an orbital craft. A manned deep space transportation means. You see, Peter Pan could fly. We want to give mankind the ability to fly farther and faster. I need your help, Tinkerbelle." He winked.

"I'm flattered. This is the type of project aero scientists dream of being a part of. Thank you, Mr. Mathews."

"Call me George. We are team members now. I'm not just a stuffed suit who sits in the office. I get into the trenches and work on special projects myself. My degree is from MIT. That's why your dad and I are such good friends. We've been team members more than a few times."

"Wow! I had no idea."

"Of course not. As you said, Gerald is conscientious about not discussing work. So are Gavin and Jake."

"Are my brothers on this project?"

"No, they're working on other jobs. This one is especially important to me. I'm glad you're onboard."

"Me too. When do I start?"

"There's no time like the present. Go to your old work station and gather anything of yours that you want. Meet me in an hour in Sector B."

"I'll see you then, Mr. Math--George."

He walked her to the door and opened it to the reception area. Dolores sat at her desk typing a transcription. She smiled as Jenny passed and gave a quick wave.

I don't know if I'll get a raise with this position, but I'm about to work on something transformative. Imagine mankind being able to travel at speeds like they do in science fiction movies. This is big."

In less than an hour, Jenny was in Sector B. She'd had to ask for directions from the security officer at her old station. Officer Brennan made a quick call to dispatch to make sure he was authorized to give Jenny directions. Sector B wasn't the typical engineering lab Jenny was accustomed to. This part of the complex was heavily guarded, and no one could enter without special permission. Located five floors beneath Building 6, Jenny was in awe of the magnitude. She walked through what felt like a mile of corridors, escorted by security, before she reached the location where she was to meet George Mathews and the rest of her new team.

No one would ever know any of this was here. There's no hint of it above ground. I'd expect to find something like this underground at NORAD.

No sooner had she arrived at the designated area than George Mathews stepped from an elevator, precisely one hour after he'd spoken with Jenny in his office.

"What do you think? This is quite the setup, right?"

"Mr. Math--George, yes, it's very impressive. I had no idea this was here."

"Few do. Do you want to know a secret?"

"If you don't mind telling me."

"Sector B is the reason why Anderson Mechanics exists."

Her eyes widened.

"It's true. As a Peter Pan team member, you are about to see why. Before I introduce you to the rest of the team, I want to show you something. Let's step this way."

George Mathews led her to a sealed door and slid a key card through the reader. Then he punched in a code and leaned forward for a retinal scan. The door slid open, and in front of them lay an immense room.

Jenny couldn't believe her eyes. "Is that what I think it is?"

George smiled. "That it is."

A large metallic disk was secured in place by scaffolding.

"How is this possible? UFOs don't exist."

"Oh, but they do, Jenny. We have had this one since the 1940s when my grandfather first began this company."

"This is why Anderson Mechanics began?"

"Yes. My grandfather was a leading engineer in his time and a shrewd businessman. He negotiated a government contract to study and advance American technology. What we have learned from this downed ship has led to many modern breakthroughs."

"The confidential projects my family works on are spin-offs of this ship?"

"They are. For nearly a century we have brought advances to nearly every aspect of life with what we've learned from this craft."

"And no one in quiet little Dayton has a clue that a UFO research center exists beneath their feet."

"Only a handful of us know. My grandfather chose Dayton for the very reason that no one would suspect such an operation in a quaint town such as this. There are good employees here. Honest, hard-working Americans who understand ethics and loyalty. It's the only way to keep a place like this secret."

Jenny couldn't take her eyes off the craft. "True" was all she could utter to George Mathews's explanation.

"Thanks to our community, a lot of good has come from our work." Jenny stood dumbfounded. George tapped her on the shoulder. "Tinkerbelle, would you like to go aboard?"

Hearing her nickname brought her out of her trance. "I'm sorry. What?"

"Would you like to go aboard?" Jenny nodded as George led her up the ramp. "You will see some technology that we have been able to replicate. Some we are still trying to unlock. That's where Peter Pan comes in."

"You want us to figure out how this craft flies at such high speeds? And then build our own flying saucers?"

"That's the plan. It's the last piece of the puzzle my grandfather started out to solve."

"How did your grandfather even know this existed? I'm surprised the government let anyone outside the military know."

"Well, he was in the right place at the right time. He was working on a dam project out west when the alien spacecraft crash landed in front of him and a handful of other engineers. It was an isolated area with few witnesses. Only my grandfather's crew saw it."

"I'm sure the government didn't want word getting out."

"No, it didn't. For once, the government was smart, though. Instead of trying to shut the witnesses up, it made them part of the research team."

"And that was the beginning of Anderson Mechanics."

"Yes. The technology we've given the world through our research has been superficial, though. The goal has always been to build our own fleet of these. This is where we are at today."

"What happened to the people onboard when it crashed?"

"People? I don't think we'd call what came off that craft 'people.' The beings were taken to a military base, and I have no idea what happened to them after that."

"Oh, yeah, I guess they are being studied like we're studying their ship."

"Exactly. Now let's go on a tour." George pointed to the room on their left.

"Feel free to examine anything you'd like to. I want you to learn this ship inside and out. I'm counting on you to help us reach our goal."

"This is a lot to take in. Excuse me if I'm in shock."

"It's quite alright. I have grown up knowing about this." He paused to gesture to the craft. "I'm still in disbelief on some days that all this is real."

"But it is."

"And it's our mission to use this to give mankind the ability to travel through space. Not taking years to send an unmanned craft to Jupiter, but sending people there safely in the blink of an eye."

"I hope I don't let you down."

"You won't. Now let's go to the shop where I can introduce you to the rest of the team."

Jenny's knees wobbled as she descended the ramp. *This is so much to take in. I can't believe this has been going on right beneath my sleepy little town. Most people here would laugh if someone told them aliens are real. Our town is actually ground zero for proof they exist.*

Jenny's thoughts were interrupted as George led her to where the real work was done. Her six team members greeted her as she arrived.

"Jenny, meet your team."

To her surprise, she didn't have to meet them. She already knew them. Mark Hanson "introduced" himself. "Welcome aboard, Jenny! I'm the team leader. It's great to have you join us."

Jenny extended her hand to shake his. "Yeah, Mark, it's always good to see you. I'm just a little surprised to see you *here*."

Mark chuckled. "Usually, it's Sunday mornings at church. I know this is a little bit of a shock."

Mark not only led the Peter Pan Project, but up to this moment Jenny knew him as the youth group leader at church and the oldest son of her third grade teacher.

His wasn't the only familiar face. Scott Filmore, her nephew's soccer coach, stood before her as did Debrah Hastings who made Dayton High School history with the highest number of points scored in a basketball game. Rob Manning, brother of her insurance agent, was there. Linda Mitchell, the pianist at church, and Quinton Ramsey, son of the Ramseys across the street, also welcomed her.

"Fancy meeting us here, right?" Rob nudged her with his elbow.

"Yeah, it's a real surprise. I mean, I knew you worked for Anderson, but I never imagined this."

"Neither had we before we started this project. It's okay. We'll show you the ropes. We've heard nothing but good things about your engineering skills, and you know we already consider you family."

"That's right," Debrah said. "We are doing this for our country and our community. I think it helps that we already know each other. We are a ready-made team."

Mark made a sweeping gesture towards the room. "Let's get started."

This began the next five years of work for the seven engineers. Each day Jenny joined her friends and neighbors as they unlocked the secrets of intergalactic flight. Each day she drove home to her lovely old house on Orchard Road, and each day she thought about the lives of the people in her beloved hometown. They lived ordinary lives, oblivious to what was going on around them.

I used to live in oblivion too.

Each Sunday she sat in her family's regular spot as Mark Hanson and his family sat in theirs. They sang hymns accompanied by Linda Mitchell on the piano. Each Tuesday she watched her nephews play soccer, and every Saturday morning Quinton stopped by his mother's house to care for her lawn. To the outside observer, they were quiet, simple folk without a care in the world.

At work they strained under the enormous pressure to learn all they could from the alien craft as quickly as possible. The government expected them to produce results. Slowly, but surely, the secrets were revealed. Each new advancement the team made led to the next discovery. Once the key to the propulsion system was deciphered, the project moved at, well, warp speed.

"Team, I can't begin to tell you how pleased I am with you and this project." George Mathews addressed the engineers flanked by high ranking Defense Department officials.

"It's been an honor, Mr. Mathews." Mark Hanson turned to his team. "I can honestly say this wouldn't have been possible without the skill and dedication of these people right here."

"We won't forget your service to this country." A man with medals covering his chest spoke to the group. "You will be financially rewarded for your efforts."

George cleared his throat. "There's another perk you will have."

"Really?" The team looked at each other then back at George Mathews.

"Isn't that right, General Hopkins?"

"Yes. Our contractors have completed the prototype of your design. We offer you the opportunity to ride in it on its maiden voyage."

Enthusiastic shouts erupted. "We'd love to accept your invitation!" Mark Hanson shook the general's hand. He looked at George. "Are you going to be with us?"

George's shoulders slumped. "No, I can't. My doctor would never allow me to. I've had two heart attacks already. I want you all to go for me, though."

The team members silently nodded. They knew how much it must hurt George to not share in this experience.

The general cleared his throat, uncomfortable with the sudden emotion filling the room. "Very well. We will begin your in-flight training immediately. No, you will not be a part of the flight crew, but as passengers you will need to be trained to adapt to the rigors of the flight."

"We understand." Mark checked his team members' expressions for agreement.

"Meet us here at 0700. Tell your families you are going to a conference in Baltimore and will be out of touch for two weeks. At the end of the two weeks, you will take flight." George Mathews beamed. "This is what we've worked so hard for."

"Yes, sir."

The next morning, Jenny walked towards her new SUV she bought with last year's bonus. Sweet Mrs. Ramsey and Poppy were out for their morning walk.

"Leaving a little early, aren't you, dear?"

"Yes, I'm going to a conference. Say, don't worry if you don't see me for a few weeks. My dad will be stopping by to get my mail and check on the place. Nothing is wrong."

"Thank you for letting me know. I do worry about you, you know."

"I know. I'll see you when I get home."

The training was rigorous, and eighteen-hour days exhausted Jenny and her team. The adrenaline rush of knowing they'd be the first people to travel at those speeds overrode their need for sleep, however. The days were a blur, and before they knew it, it was the day of the launch.

Climbing aboard the sleek craft emblazoned with the American flag, their hearts raced. Each passenger meticulously strapped themselves into the seats. Reclining, a voice came through their headsets telling them to relax and close their eyes. The countdown began by a control room commander whose soothing voice calmed their frazzled nerves.

Suddenly, the sensation of being sucked down a drain enveloped them.

"Whoa, boy!" Mark Hanson exclaimed. "I thought there'd be a roar of engines first, even though I knew better."

The seats automatically rose to the sitting position as the astronauts looked out the panoramic windows. The stars looked like streaks of light, as though they were in some 1970s science fiction drama.

The craft smoothly glided to a stop.

"Ladies and gentlemen, what you see ahead of you is our solar system. That's something no human being has ever laid eyes on. I've dreamed of this my entire life. Thank you, engineers, for making this possible. Commander Raymond Kipling made the announcement to the crew.

First Officer Merritt spoke next. "Take this all in. It's beautiful."

For the next thirty minutes, they sat in stunned silence. The view was, in fact, beautiful.

Commander Kipling came back on the radio. "I could stay here forever looking at this, but we need to get back to the base. Prepare for reentry."

In a flicker of time, the craft silently arrived back on Earth. The wonder of the moment kept conversation minimal. Awaiting them on the ground were physicians who whisked them off to be monitored.

"We'll keep you under observation for the next twenty-four hours, but your vitals all look excellent." The chief medical officer scribbled down a few notes on his tablet. "I'll be back to check on you myself in the morning."

To everyone's relief, no one suffered any ill effects from the flight. The military flew them back to Anderson Mechanics via helicopters the next day. There they debriefed George Mathews.

Once the meetings ended, the space travelers made their way to the parking lot where their more pedestrian vehicles awaited.

"Let's take the morning off. I'll see you back here at noon."

"See you then, Mark."

Jenny didn't want to rush home. Too much was going through her mind. Instead, she drove through the neighborhoods of Dayton, reminiscing about the childhood memories made in this town. Dayton had given her so much. As night fell, she finally made her way to Orchard Road.

Mrs. Ramsey and Poppy sat on their porch. Happy to see her young neighbor return, she smiled and waved to Jenny. "Oh, it is so good to see you are back home. How was the conference? Did anything interesting happen on your trip?"

Jenny paused then smiled. "The conference was great. No, nothing exciting happened. You know, just a lot of engineering talk."

"Well, you can't always expect these things to be out of this world excitement."

"No, you can't. And how about you? Did anything exciting happen here while I was gone?"

Mrs. Ramsey patted Poppy who had jumped into her lap. "Oh, lands no. It was just another day in Dayton."

With that, Jenny stepped into the home her grandfather built last century during a time when standard air travel was a rarity. As she drifted off to sleep, her mind was a million miles away.

Much closer than a million miles away, a frenzied discussion took place.

"I'm afraid our test subjects have discovered our secrets to space travel. They were more intelligent than we suspected."

"You are correct. If they have discovered the key to our flight technology, it will be no time at all before they can recreate our weaponry."

"They will pose a danger to the rest of civilization.

"We have no other options, do we?"

"It's time to put an end to this experiment. Tomorrow I will order the decontamination squad to sterilize the region."

SURVIVAL

Where there's life, there's the will for survival. Man's curiosity, in its basic form, is a desire to find out if some benefit exists around the corner. That desire is fueled by a need to find a backup plan, to have a chance at an insurance policy, in case life takes a sudden downturn.

My mother says I've been curious since the day I was born. I was the kid who took things apart to find out if I could put them back together. As I grew older, I usually wanted to adapt them to a better purpose. I always pushed envelopes to find out more or to improve what was at hand. Mom said I was destined for a career in space, exploring the vast unknown and improving life for mankind.

I'd like to believe in destiny. To have faith that things turn out the way they are supposed to in the end would be a comforting thought. Not only does that notion take away our personal and collective responsibilities, but destiny is a soothing balm for our souls when we don't like the end result.

Space was, however, a dream of mine since I was a small child. I studied hard and even attended summer camps at NASA. The idea that a vast, unexplored universe spread before me tapped into the curiosity I'd carried with me since the womb. New worlds, new theories, new adventures all played in my head like a dazzling video game I wanted to take to the next level.

After graduating with degrees in aeronautical science and microbiology, my path was set when I accepted my dream job. I joined a team of scientists searching for alien life in the cosmos.

Decades of design and planning led NASA to the threshold of exploring an environment mankind had previously only dreamed of reaching. We'd found evidence that life may exist in the cosmos when we studied asteroids, but our best chance came with an expedition to Ganymede, one of Jupiter's moons that had long held hope of containing liquid water.

The trick to finding that water lay in burrowing through the frozen surface to the presumed ocean below it. My team consisted of the fortunate few chosen to guide the high-tech drill, retrieve the contents of what it collected, and then analyze the results back in our lab. This wasn't without risk. So many steps along the way could fail. Sheer distance, the need for prototypical equipment to function on cue, and the necessity to successfully bring the cache back to Earth meant the possibility of catastrophic failure abounded.

For those of us bent on discovery, the risk was always worth it. Day and night we worked tirelessly to bring our project into operational mode. Ten years of my life was devoted to this project, and nothing else mattered to my team.

When the date was set, August 24, 2089, we were ecstatic. Dr. Kelman, the lead scientist on our mission, threw a lavish party at his home for us, and we even had our fifteen minutes of fame on national television as science correspondents interviewed us about our work.

Amongst the team, we christened our new adventure "Genesis." New life and the ability to study it were within our reach.

What new information could we learn from microbes suspended deep in the frozen ocean of Ganymede? Were there cures for human diseases we could find through our research? Could these microbes be bio-engineered to help our crops become healthier or to produce new methods of feeding people on Earth? What surprise discoveries would we make? Mankind always felt the needed to boost our chances of survival, and this was one more door to open.

The mission went off without a hitch, and scientists around the world clamored for the opportunity to join us in our research. The drilling mechanism exceeded our hopes and brought back canisters of what we deemed liquid gold. There were plenty of samples for a host of scientists to delve into, regardless of their particular field of study.

Initially, we were thrilled to discover that the microbes thrived in Earth's atmosphere. They withstood wide ranges of temperature variance, and they were not much different than the microbes we found in the greatest depths of our own oceans. The scientific world was abuzz with conjecture.

Could Ganymede and Earth have begun in much the same way? Were there other worlds out there that would be compatible for mankind to explore and colonize? Had we found our chance at a safe haven should our own world's systems fail? The threats of global warming and overpopulation were still major themes for us, and it gave us hope that mankind itself may not become extinct simply because Earth one day was no longer tenable.

Then the accident happened. It was simple enough. A vial was dropped, and a careless lab worker did not completely decontaminate his clothing before leaving the facility. At first, the government kept it hush-hush. It was a minor error, and there was no sense making politicians and private donors nervous about supporting our research.

Then the first cases began. The oozing sores and soaring fevers swept across the eastern United States. As with any epidemic in this world of global travel, it spread quickly. A full-fledged pandemic was at hand. While the symptoms mimicked the Black Death, this plague did not come from this world. The microbes, having found their chance at survival, had taken it. No longer confined to the brutal conditions of a moon circling a distant planet, they now had a world to conquer.

So, here I sit as the initial stages of the disease increasingly ravage my body. The sweats and fevers, the appearance of cold sores across my torso and limbs, and the aching throb of my head let me know that I will not last long. There's no sense going to a hospital. Most of the healthcare workers have already succumbed to the plague, and any that are left have no weapons to fight this foreign invader of our bodies. I am doomed. We are all doomed.

Hundreds of years ago, Native Americans suffered from smallpox infections brought by the Europeans when they first stepped foot on this continent. They came to the New World out of curiosity and the need to find what benefits existed beyond their shores. Our own curiosity has brought these microbial adventurers to our world. Nothing can stop what has begun.

We are lost, but the alien microbes have patiently won their bid for their own survival.

WINGS OF GLORY

Enveloped in a sea of blue, the jet hurtled through the bright sky rushing to its destination. Tom Harper gazed out the window. Below him, city skylines and checkerboard farm fields passed by. Cities looked like dots spread out among the vast open spaces. Tom was amazed by just how much farmland was out there. He'd lived in the city for so long that he'd lost track of the agricultural base of the country. Little houses speckled the view, and farm-to-market roads crisscrossed the landscape.

I can't help but wonder about the people down there. Who are they? Are they happy with their lives? Would we be friends if geography didn't separate us? Are they celebrating the birth of a child or the loss of a loved one? People from all different walks of life are going on about their days as we fly overhead. Do they ever think about who I am flying above them? I know I've stood on the street by my office building and stared up at the flights taking off from La Guardia, wondering about the people in those thin metal tubes. Not only that, but flight still amazes me. I may never understand how planes stay aloft. I guess the important thing is that they do. I shouldn't worry about that now.

The clanking of a cart brought Tom's attention back to the flight he was on. The monotonous hum of the plane engines droned in the background as flight attendants made sure passengers were happy with their meals and beverages. The food was incredible, which surprised Tom. It certainly wasn't the standard bag of peanuts he was used to on commercial flights.

With radiant smiles, attendants checked on each guest, doling out pillows and warm blankets. The gentle flutter of movement as the attendants went about serving the needs of passengers was comforting. Real care was given each member of the journey, and Tom had never seen an entire flight receive first-class treatment before.

I knew the perks would be good, but this goes beyond what the company rep told me. Everything from the friendly flight attendants to the food is amazing. New hires usually don't get this kind of treatment, at least not in the jobs I've had in the past. I think this is going to be a good gig, even if it's a long flight. Thank God there's plenty of legroom.

A 6'6" Tom Harper needed the extra room. He stretched his lanky legs and yawned. He gladly accepted one of the pillows and a warmed blanket as the attendant stopped at his seat. He was tired.

While exciting, the unexpected string of events he was experiencing took a toll on him. On the one hand, Tom had an overwhelming sense of well-being. This was the most important job he'd ever taken, and he knew he was in the right place doing the right thing. On the other hand, he mulled over the whirlwind events from the past twenty-four hours and couldn't fight off a sense of guilt.

Just yesterday morning, Tom's biggest concern was dropping his daughters, Lily and Hannah, off at school on time. His oldest had lost her homework from the night before. His youngest had insisted on wearing her Cookie

Monster slippers as shoes. It was chaos getting them fed, dressed, and out the door in one piece.

Thanks to Michelle's new work schedule, Tom was now responsible for getting the girls to school and picking them up in the afternoon. He smiled. He didn't mind the extra time with them. He loved being a dad, in fact. A wistfulness fell over him as he thought about the spring break plans he had with them. He was going to take them fishing at the family cabin in the Adirondacks.

A dinging bell drew Tom's attention to Mrs. Swenson in seat 4C. A sweet woman with a southern drawl, she asked for earphones. The flight offered a variety of movies to break the tedium of the trip, and she'd chosen an old western to occupy her. Tom overheard her tell the blonde stewardess that she'd once met John Wayne. Mrs. Swenson became animated as she retold the memory. She was especially pleased when the attendant told her that she, too, had met John Wayne.

Looking up and down the aisle, Tom noticed the flight was surprisingly full. Not a seat was vacant, and Tom marveled at his fellow passengers.

This wasn't what I expected. I'm impressed by the diversity. I don't know why, but I thought we'd all be a little more... homogenous.

People of all races, ages, previous professions, and political beliefs were aboard. Tom chuckled.

Not that long ago, given today's divided political climate, you'd never see Democrats and Republicans getting along so well.

Two rows ahead of him, proving his point, was a stylishly dressed twenty-something having a charming discussion about fine art. This wouldn't be unusual, except her companion was a man in his sixties who made his fortune as a venture capitalist. It was unlikely, before their addition to the company payroll, that they'd have been so fond of one another.

Across from Tom was another odd pairing, at least from outward appearances. Sharice Davis, a liberal councilwoman from one of the rougher neighborhoods in her city, talked and laughed about grandbabies with the man sitting next to her. Mike Perry, a red-headed police officer with years of experience patrolling Sharice's same neighborhood, told Sharice how sorry he was that he'd arrested so many young people in her area. In reality, they weren't all that different from her beloved grandsons, or his. They'd just made bad choices and hadn't had opportunities. He could see that now. He held her hand as he learned that Sharice still carried wounds from the loss of her brother. His death fueled riots that made national headlines some time ago.

Two days ago, both Sharice and Mike might have seen each other as adversaries. Now common ground and empathy were apparent on their faces. Family meant a great deal to both, and they cared about young people in general. Sharice and Mike both wanted the world to be a better place, and children were their hope for the future. Now that they could talk, without the artificial constraints of race or profession, they saw they had so much in common.

Tom's thoughts returned to Michelle and the girls. He winced.

By taking this assignment, do they think I've turned my back on them? Will they hate me? Will they ever understand that I had to take this opportunity? How afraid were the girls when I got on this flight and left them standing outside their school? Is Michelle angry with me that I accepted this job without talking with her first? She didn't even get to see me before I signed the contract and boarded.

Visions of his girls crying in the rain when he never arrived in the parent pick-up lane at Hunter Grove Elementary stung. Those wouldn't be the only tears they cried.

Yesterday's storm was fierce. Lightning flashed non-stop, and the streets were overcome with floodwaters. Driving conditions were hazardous, and Tom was thankful he'd been the one crossing those treacherous intersections and not Michelle.

Why do people have to drive like idiots when it rains? Don't they know speeding doesn't get them home faster? It just makes it more dangerous for everyone else.

Well, with his new job neither he nor the other members of the company would have to worry about their safety. No, they'd be on security detail for others, and there was plenty of worry involved with the job description.

I still don't understand why I was chosen out of all the other possible candidates out there. I mean, I've always worked hard, and I've tried to be a good man, a good husband and father and friend. I never thought I'd be offered a chance at a job like this, though.

Tom's thoughts were interrupted by the brunette flight attendant who asked if she could get him anything. Another beverage? Perhaps a magazine?

Her name tag said "Christine." That was Tom's mother's name. She'd have liked this Christine. Her warm smile and soothing nature would have appealed to Tom's sweet mother. Beneath Christine's name, Tom saw the company logo: Guardian Angel Express. As she handed him his soda, her right wing brushed his arm.

Christine smiled sweetly and said, "Don't worry, Tom. I know you're nervous. You'll make a great guardian angel. And your wife and daughters? They're in good hands. The Big Guy takes special care of his employee families."

Peace filled Tom, and he relaxed. Important work was ahead, and soon he'd be wearing his own wings of glory.

BABEL

The dimming light of a long day hung over the horizon. A lone workman stared across his birds-eye view and smiled in wonder. For the past fifteen years Lou Wilkins had climbed towers like this one to troubleshoot and repair failing transmissions equipment.

"You're crazy for climbing up something that high." His brother Wes never understood Lou's career choice. "If you fall off one of those towers, there won't be enough of you to scrape off the ground. Hell, we won't have to bury you. You'll already be six feet in the ground."

Lou simply shrugged and smiled in his own quiet way. He'd learned years ago there was no sense trying to argue with Wes. Besides, there *was* an element of danger to his job. Danger, in fact, was one of the things he liked best about it. Lou, the quiet daredevil, began this tantalizing life early by climbing a Forest Service fire tower when he was eight years old. Heights never bothered him. People did. Up here on a tower, no one could intrude upon his thoughts, and Lou Wilkins was a thinker.

Making the last adjustments before he began his descent, Lou took a moment to look up into the skies. Faded hues of pink and purple formed. Soon the blackness of the night sky would fill with blazing stars. A few times Lou stayed on a tower past quitting time just so he could admire the view. At this height, it almost seemed like he could touch the stars.

Few men ever experienced the perfect solitude he sometimes took for granted. It became a part of him, and sometimes he forgot to enjoy it. Tonight he enjoyed it.

Always a philosopher, Lou considered mankind's condition. Why did people act the way they did? What motivated them to strive for something else? Was it boredom? Curiosity? A sense of inadequacy or overcompensation? He'd seen men who, as individuals, did everything they could to appear more important than what they were. Did mankind as a whole fall into the same trap?

Lou swiveled in his harness to look at the twinkling city lights below as streetlights and houses illuminated. Most homes and businesses in the area relied on the communications towers he made a living servicing. Few people these days lived without television, internet, or cell phones.

Lou wasn't that old, but he remembered a time when people weren't so obsessed with listening to, and being heard by, so many others.

Is this the hubris that I read about in my Greek studies class? Are we so full of ourselves that we are have set ourselves up to fail? Lou looked at the equipment on the tower. *Signals sent from it reach how far? Really, couldn't radio waves travel infinitely farther that we can imagine?*

The faintest twinkling stars appeared in the night sky.

Lou thought about science fiction movies in which humans sent signals toward distant planets in hopes of making contact with alien races.

Do we want them to know we are here? Would we learn from them? Be equals to them? Be subjugated by them? Be eaten by them?

A breeze swept past Lou and he shivered. It was silly, really, to get himself so worked up that his ideas unsettled him so. Still not ready to climb down, he pondered other stories he'd heard.

The Bible tells of people who built a tower to reach heaven. They wanted to make themselves equal to God. He struck them down and scattered them across the globe as punishment. Could they have reached heaven? Could they have become gods? Is that why God knew he had to destroy that tower and their society? Would he no longer be alone as the supreme ruler of all things?

The wind picked up and reverberated the metal. The sensation flowed through Lou's body and mind. He felt at one with the tower.

Why, could the messages sent by this tower reach as far as heaven? I guess it's possible, depending on what your idea of heaven is. Are we modern-day gods? Do we know more than anyone has ever known before? Would lesser beings view us as gods if we stumbled across them on some distant planet? Are we becoming equal to God? Is technology our way of becoming gods like the people of Babel wanted so badly to be?

He envisioned alien workers worshipping him and chuckled at what a sight that would be. As a nobody here on Earth, plain, simple Lou Wilkins, the thought was appealing.

As darkness fell, Lou decided he'd been left to his own daydreams long enough He had a two-hour drive to his next service call in the morning, and he needed to get home, eat dinner, and sleep.

We mortals don't have the luxury of having others wait on us. I sure wouldn't mind finding out what that was like, but tomorrow it's back to the grind again.

***

Far away, beyond the clouds and stars, the Entity watched with concern. Known as God, revered by some, mocked by others, He and His Counsel gathered.

"We must act soon. No longer can we wait to deal with the menace."

"I agree. We know what we must do."

It wasn't radio waves or satellite beams that drew the final wrath of God upon mankind. It was the thoughts of one man, Lou Wilkins, who dared to sit upon a tower and imagine himself a god.

A TINY SUM

Nothing says "the American Dream" like home ownership. Aaron and Alisha Wells had waited their entire lives to have a place they could call their own. Today that dream finally came true. 1082 Winchester Drive was theirs.

Before the first stars twinkled in the night sky, they carried the last of the boxes into their new home. The furniture was in place, and the helpers had left. In the quiet found at the end of an exhausting day, the tired, but happy, couple finally relaxed.

It hadn't been easy to get to this point. They'd sacrificed. They'd worked second and third jobs. Years of planning and dedication were devoted to this goal. In fact, Aaron and Alisha scrimped and saved for a home before they even met.

Five years ago, on their first date, they shared their visions of what a perfect life would look like. Their dreams were similar: Find the right house in the right neighborhood and raise a family. They wanted to be grounded and to have a place to belong. That common need drew them even closer together as they dated and finally became engaged and married.

"Don't worry, honey. We won't live in an apartment forever. We're on the verge of making our dreams come true." Aaron hugged her close to him on their wedding night, promising they would have that life filled with children, a home, and stability.

Both had their reasons for craving security.

Aaron's mother, God rest her soul, had tried. She really had, but constant emotional stumbling blocks got in her way. One failed relationship after another, too many upheavals chasing each new man's dreams, and her despair over relationship failures stopped her from reaching her goals. Combined, they created a continuous cycle of moving from one rental to another. She always hoped for a better life, and she wanted her children to have stability, but she never found the key to having it. Her methods relied on hitching her wagon to whichever man's star was convenient, and it left its mark on all five of her children. Aaron wanted nothing more than the peace he was convinced came with home ownership. He also knew he had to choose a wife wisely, and he had.

Alisha's parents, on the other hand, had a long and happy marriage, but they still lacked stability. Her father's career in the military meant their family moved often, and sometimes those moves took them across the globe.

"It never fails, Mom. Just when I finally make friends, Dad's transferred again. I just want a home."

"I know it's hard, Alisha, but we always have a home when we're together, regardless of where that is on a map."

That was great for her mom and dad, but it hadn't been enough for Alisha. She dreamed of rooting herself in one spot. She longed to raise a family as part of a community. She'd been denied the opportunity to have lifelong childhood friends, but she was determined her children would have that and more.

Now the young couple made their dreams a reality. Why now was the right time to act on those dreams was evident by looking at Alisha. She rested her cup of herbal tea on her increasingly large stomach while she sat to relax for a moment.

As Aaron walked past, he watched in wonderment, and the couple laughed.

"Did she just move your tea cup?

"You saw that? Yes!"

Aaron walked over and gently placed his hand on her stomach. He grinned as a knee or elbow moved like a wave beneath his hand. He knelt down and kissed Alisha's stomach. "Baby Polly, you're going to be here soon enough. It's a good thing Mama and Daddy are getting settled into our home before you arrive."

Alisha ran her hand through his hair. "We've done it, haven't we? All of our planning and saving, and here we are in our perfect home. Our forever home."

"Yes, honey, we are home."

It was a perfect home, too. A grand three-story house with spacious rooms, carved banisters, and beautiful hardwood floors that was built by one of the founding families of Owensville. Neither Aaron nor Alisha could believe their luck when the house became available. They'd driven past it dozens of times, and they often commented on how it would be the ideal place to raise a family. The yard was huge with towering oaks, and the house was close to the elementary school and shopping. Winchester Drive was quiet in spite of its proximity to all the amenities. The wraparound porch conjured visions of peaceful summer nights spent on the swing watching fireflies light up the night. When it came up for sale, they jumped at the opportunity. It was almost as though the house had been waiting for them. They prequalified for the loan, and within thirty days the house was theirs.

Exhaling slowly, Alisha smiled as she rose from the couch. "It's been a long day, and I'm already sore. Let's leave the boxes until tomorrow and get some sleep."

"I already made the bed."

"Aaron, you're the most thoughtful man ever."

"I knew you'd be exhausted. Polly wears you out these days."

"In less than a month she'll be here. It can't come soon enough for me. Pregnancy has been fun, but holding her and looking into her eyes will be more fun. Plus, it will be wonderful to not feel like a beached whale all the time."

Aaron laughed and rubbed her stomach. "Agreed about seeing her, but you're beautiful no matter what. Okay, it's time for the three of us to go to bed."

The peace of being in their own home and the sheer exhaustion of the day caused them to sleep soundly. The sun was up for a few hours the next morning before they awoke. At first, they blinked and looked around the room and then at each other in surprise.

"We're really here. I didn't dream this last night. Here we are, waking up in our own home."

Aaron kissed her. "It's real."

The next week they spent unpacking and setting up the nursery. The walls had to be painted and there was last minute shopping to do before Polly arrived.

"Any day now, baby girl." Alisha rubbed her stomach.

"What do you think of our new home?" Aaron patted her stomach, and they both jumped when Polly kicked--flailed--in response.

"I think she's as excited as we are." Alisha beamed. "Come on, let's eat and then pick up the last few things we didn't get at the shower."

During the days, Aaron worked at the accounting firm while Alisha put the final touches on the nursery and continued unpacking boxes. Her days were her own to turn the house into a home. She'd quit her job at the bank when she reached her eighth month of pregnancy so she could prepare for Polly's birth. The decision was easy. When the baby arrived, she wanted to devote herself to full-time motherhood. Their sizeable down payment made the mortgage manageable so they could afford to live on a single income. With this unexpected blessing, they took it as a sign that she should stay home.

Standing in the nursery, Alisha smiled as she folded each tiny outfit and put it in the cheery pink dresser. Her parents had it specially made for Polly. Every little sock, hair bow, and sleeper made Alisha's heart swoon.

A baby! We're about to meet our baby!

A knocking downstairs drew her attention. She gingerly made her way down the stairs and reached the front door just as the rapping stopped. She opened it only to find no one there.

Maybe a delivery man left a package.

There was no parcel on the porch or even in the driveway, however. She shrugged her shoulders and went back inside.

Halfway up the stairs, the knocking began again. Polly kicked, almost in response to the knocks at the door. Sighing, Alisha made her way back down to the first floor.

Once again, no one was there.

Hmm. I guess the screen door came loose and was flapping.

Alisha pulled the door tight and went back upstairs. She soon forgot about the knocking.

That night, Aaron came home ill.

"Another one of your migraines?"

"I'm afraid so. I took my prescription, but it's not even touching it."

"Just relax and lie on the couch for a while. I'll fix some chicken noodle soup and get you some soda and aspirin. That usually helps."

Aaron rolled over, and Alisha flipped the switch on the wall as she walked into the kitchen. A moment later, Aaron called out to her.

"Honey, I hate to ask, but can you turn off that light?"

Puzzled, Alisha walked back into the living room. The light glared brightly. "Yeah, sorry about that. I thought I had."

Aaron mumbled, and she went back to stir the soup. When she returned with a bowl of soup in one hand and a can of cola in the other, Aaron was face down on the couch. The light was on again.

"Baby, I don't know what's going on, but I know I know I turned that light off."

"I know you did. There must be an electrical problem. It's an old house. I'll call Ben at All State Electrical tomorrow."

"Well, for now, try to eat a little something then off to bed for you."

Aaron ate half the bowl of soup, took the aspirin with a few sips of soda, and then the two stood to go upstairs for the evening. Alisha flipped the switch as she walked out of the room, and it flickered behind her.

Aaron must be right. There's something wrong with the wiring.

The next day, Ben Rader arrived in his truck. Alisha explained what happened the night before.

"No worries. I'll figure out what your problem is."

An hour later, Ben knocked gently at the nursery door. Alisha busily lined up the stuffed circus animals she'd collected for Polly. "Hey, I just wanted to let you know I checked out the wiring. I went over the breaker box with a fine-tooth comb. I looked at the switch, too."

"How bad is it? We knew we could be looking at some repairs in a house this old."

"That's just it. There's nothing wrong with the wiring. Everything's updated and meets code. I'm not sure why you had any problems with it."

"That's really weird."

"Well, let's hope it was a one-time deal. Maybe there were power surges or something. I'm glad I could give you some peace of mind that the electrical system is safe here, though."

"Thanks so much, Ben. Let me go get my checkbook."

Five minutes later, Ben pulled away and Alisha made her way up the stairs to the nursery. Her back hurt, her feet were swollen, and she was out of breath. Patting her stomach, she said, "Baby girl, you can't get here soon enough." As if on cue, she felt a twinge. "Maybe I should take a break from working on your room and just relax. I haven't eaten all day. Maybe your mama needs to eat and take a nap."

She had no sooner reached the bottom of the stairs when her water broke. Another sharp pain caused her to take a deep breath. She pulled out her phone. "Aaron, come home. My water just broke."

"Looks like your dad wins the pool. He said it would be today. I'm on my way!"

"Drive safe. But hurry. I think my contractions are coming faster than I thought they would."

"Don't do anything. Just sit down. When I get home, I'll run upstairs and get your bag."

Ten minutes later Aaron pulled into the drive. In a whirlwind of activity, he ushered her to the car as another round of strong contractions hit.

Four hours later, Polly Elaina Wells was born.

"She's perfect. Absolutely perfect." Tears streamed down Alisha's face as she cradled her newborn daughter.

Aaron leaned over and kissed each of them. "Polly, we've waited our whole lives for you."

A day later, they were back home on Winchester Drive. Everything was as they'd left it. That is, until they walked into the nursery. The circus animals were scattered on the floor.

"That's weird. I lined them up on her dresser."

"I'm sure there's nothing to it. Let's put Polly down in her crib, and I'll pick these up. Go get some rest, and I'll be there in a minute."

In the coming days, rest was something they'd need.

"She's such a good baby, but I'm still so tired. Aaron, I'm glad you were able to take paternity leave so you can be with me these first few weeks. I'd be overwhelmed."

Putting his arm around her, he pulled her to him. He kissed the top of her head and said, "No need to be overwhelmed. You're an amazing mom, and just look at our beautiful little girl."

"We've really done it, haven't we? We have what we always wanted. A home. A family. Life is good."

Life was good, but that didn't stop odd nuisances from happening around the house. Even though Ben Rader checked the wiring a second time, lights still turned off and on at random times. Occasionally, drawers opened that were closed moments before. A chilly draft blew through rooms in the heat of summer. Aaron and Alisha were so focused on being happy, however, that they paid little attention to these nuisances. They chalked the strange happenings up to floors settling or power surges.

They had a lot to be happy about. Polly was pure perfection. Even strangers commented that they'd never seen a more beautiful or happier baby.

"We're the luckiest parents ever," they'd tell each other.

Weeks and months went by, and as Polly crawled and became more active, so did the unusual events in the house. The doorbell rang by itself. Plates fell to the floor from the cupboard. Alone in the house during the day, Alisha sometimes felt spooked.

"Aaron, I don't want to complain. After all, we have everything we've always wanted, but sometimes I'm scared here at home. Weird things happen, and I feel like something is watching me."

Aaron held her to him. "I can't explain what's happening either. Do you think we should consider moving?" Aaron doubted it was possible, but he worried about the strange occurrences.

The thought of closing the door on what they'd worked so hard to have broke her heart. "No, I'm sure there's a good explanation for all of this. We can't give up on this place now. It's been our dream."

Still, the occurrences continued--and intensified. Instead of harmless knocking or the loss of a plate or cup, more sinister events began to happen.

"Hey, honey," Aaron called to Alisha one morning.
"Yes?"

"Can you come here?"

She dragged herself out of bed, wishing she could have slept for a few more hours. She knew that wasn't likely. Polly seldom slept past seven o'clock.

"I'm coming. Where are you?"

"The kitchen."

She made her way down the stairs. "What's wrong?"

"Look."

A bloodstained knife sat on the kitchen counter next to one of Polly's circus animals. Terror overtook them as they raced to the nursery. Baby Polly lay fast asleep.

Nothing was disturbed in her room except for the now mutilated toy.

"I want us to leave, Aaron. Let's get out of here."

"We're too strapped financially. I've gone over the numbers time after time. We can't afford another place to live as long as we have this mortgage. I'll contact Susan Atkins who sold us the house. I'll tell her we want it sold quickly."

Alisha scooped Polly into her arms, more to comfort herself than the little girl, who was oblivious to the invasion of her nursery by, well, whatever "it" was. Silent tears trickled down Alisha's face as she shook uncontrollably.

Weeks passed, and there were no prospects for selling the house. The haunting became more vicious over time. Knives appeared in Polly's room. Her toys were decapitated. Then, one night. Aaron awoke to see his wife levitating above their bed. She was sound asleep, but her body floated across the room towards the door.

Aaron rushed to her and grabbed her by one arm, but her body continued out the door. Something powerful had her, and he struggled to wrench her from its grasp. Alisha awoke during the tussle and her screams pierced the night.

As suddenly as it began, it was over.

Alisha begged Aaron to flee, but he refused. "I'm not going to walk away from everything we've worked so hard for to be financially ruined. You and I both know we're stuck here until the house sells.

A coldness came over Aaron, and he began treating the attacks as if they'd never happened or were commonplace. Was he numb from the stress, or was it something else?

"Aaron, we can't stay here," she pleaded.

"Not until we sell the house."

More weeks passed and encounters became more frightening. Alisha lived in a constant state of terror and, at times, she questioned her own sanity.

"Maybe I should talk to a doctor."

"Don't say anything to anyone. If word gets out, we will never be rid of this house." Aaron would not relent.

Hushed whispers like the breeze over dry leaves could be heard. A voice spoke, and they knew what the whispers said: "This is mine. You are mine. You cannot leave." The message replayed day and night, always in the background of their lives.

Alisha caught glimpses of something out of the corner of her eye. A figure? A form? It was fleeting, but she was certain she saw it.

A few days later, Aaron saw it too. The whispers grew louder, and at times they heard a voice, still low, but clearer than a whisper.

One night they awoke to Polly giggling in the nursery. Rushing to her, they found her levitating in her crib. Her circus animals circled around her like a mobile. A bloody knife sat in her crib next to her pillow.

"Whatever you are, leave us alone!"

"Who are you to tell me what to do? You are mine now, and you do not tell me to do anything!"

A gust of wind whipped around the room, slamming the door open and shut.

"Go to your room and leave me be!" the voice commanded.

In the coming days, a definite form was visible. No longer a wispy flash on the periphery, distinct features could now be seen. Glowing red eyes surrounded by an unfathomable blackness stared at Alisha and Aaron, and it took a keen interest in watching Polly.

Sheer terror overtook them. Sleep was impossible when strange sounds, wind, and even rain happened inside the house on Winchester Drive. Aaron struggled to work. Alisha was a shell of her former self. Every moment the couple spent trying to appease the entity in their home.

Finally, at one in the morning on a warm spring night, a year after they'd moved into 1082 Winchester drive, they'd had enough.

"Grab the baby and let's get in the car," Aaron whispered to Alisha.

They grabbed a few belongings and fled into the night. The lights flashed on and off in the house as they pulled out of the driveway. They heard a howl escape into the darkness.

Aaron squeezed her hand. "I'm sorry I waited so long. I never should have been so stubborn. If we have to live under a bridge, it will be better than this nightmare."

"It's okay. We're free now. That's all that matters."

They drove half an hour and finally began to breathe easier. Polly slept in her car seat in the back of the car. Rain fell gently on the windshield, and the rhythm of the wipers lulled their senses.

Suddenly, the car spun out of control. The engine roared as the car whiplashed between drive and reverse. As though a giant hand grasped it from above, the car rose into the air, and the radio turned on. A familiar voice mocked them through the speakers.

"Did you really think you could just drive away? I've told you for months you are mine." The demonic voice hissed through the speakers.

The vehicle shook like dice about to be rolled. Alisha screamed uncontrollably.

"What do you want from us?"

Want? Now you are talking, Aaron. I've been waiting for you to ask."

"Please, please, whatever it is, please just leave us alone."

"I could ask for so much."

Alisha sobbed. Aaron pleaded with the demon. "Tell us what you want."

"I'm merely asking for a tiny sum. Not so much, really."

"What? What is it?"

"I will tell you the price for your freedom. If you refuse, I will own you and your wife for all eternity. You will be my slaves. Forever. But it's so simple to end that possibility. If you doubt me…"

The window rolled down, and Alisha began to be pulled from the vehicle. Screams filled the car.

In tears, Aaron begged, "Please, don't hurt my wife. I will pay your price. Please don't hurt her."

"Very well, but once our deal is reached, it is final. You will be free of me and your home will be yours. Agreed?"

"Yes. We agree."

The demon laughed. "I accept your offer and will collect my tiny sum."

A force froze Aaron and Alisha in place, paralyzed, as they heard the unmistakable sound of Polly's car seat unbuckling.

THE LIGHTHOUSE

It seems barbaric to exile someone to a desolate land. Granted, traditional prison bars don't surround penal colonies, but the exiled are trapped nonetheless. Stripped of their identities, no longer members of society, they lose more than their freedom. Many who are exiled lose their will to live and commit suicide rather than exist as a solitary person. Others lose all that is good in them. With no one to be good for, they spiral downward until all that's left is pure evil. That happens too often.

That did not, however, happen to inmate 7652590, previously known as Percy Lansdown. He was one of those rare individuals who maintained his sense of self. He knew he deserved punishment. His crimes were many, and he didn't expect society to simply wipe his slate clean. When sentenced, Percy winced in pain, however, as he heard the words "You will hereby be sentenced to life imprisonment on Penal Colony 524."

Percy was a sociable man, and he knew 524 was solitary confinement. He would never again see another soul. The loneliness he'd endure was worse than if he'd been sent to a standard prison. At least there he'd have someone to talk to. Hell, maybe even someone to be friends with. He'd never again hear another person's laughter nor see the twinkle in another's eye. He'd never again wipe away someone else's tears--or have someone do the same for him.

For the first two years, the isolation nearly drove him insane. The days and nights filled with his lamenting screams. He begged God to allow him to die in his sleep, but the morning sun always rose again.

One day, while looking at his reflection in the pool of water near the cabin he was provided, a realization struck him. *This. This is all I have. All I will ever have.*

He looked around him. Deep forest surrounded him on three sides. On the remaining side, a vast ocean, foaming and crashing upon the rocks, reminded him daily of the folly in attempted escapes. Sure death would befall anyone who ventured onto those rocks and into the crashing waves. He looked back at his reflection. *If this is all I have, I need to make the most of it. I need to do what I can to give my life meaning. But what?*

What indeed? The next several days he spent organizing his living space. He'd let the place pile up with debris of all sorts back when he thought it didn't matter. Now it mattered. It *had* to matter or Percy was admitting that *he* no longer mattered. Within a month, he expanded his efforts. The cabin and surrounding area were immaculate. Pristine and picturesque, it would have made a lovely park. Standing in the yard, he admired his handiwork.

In another time and circumstance, tourists would pay top price to stay in accommodations as fine as these with a view like this. An emotion he'd lacked for far longer than he'd been imprisoned came over his heart: satisfaction. *I can't remember the last time I felt satisfied. Isn't that why I committed my crimes in the first place? I looked for something to fill the void, to leave me satisfied?*

The irony of losing everything in order to finally be satisfied did not escape Percy. However, as time passed, he lost the sense that he'd completed something worthwhile. He was no longer content simply maintaining the improvements he'd made to his living area. *There has to be more.*

On a particularly stormy night, the crashing waves kept him awake and left him with nothing but his thoughts. *Those rocks would rip someone to shreds. A ship wouldn't have a chance on a night like this. Except for my little cabin, there are no lights to warn travelers of the danger. In the pitch black, it would be certain death to come near this shore.*

At first, he dismissed the idea. *That's a moot point. Seldom, if ever, would a ship come near this place. The court sent me here because it's so isolated.*

However, it wasn't impossible for a ship to come this way. It *could* happen.

What if... What if I could do something to help someone besides myself? What if I did something that could help others, even if no one ever actually came by here? If there's even the slimmest of chances I could be of service to others, that would truly make my existence here meaningful.

Percy knew what he needed to do. It wouldn't be easy, and it would take years, but he knew he must build a lighthouse. *All I have is time. I can be patient.*

He began by gathering stones. When the low tide occurred, he rushed to collect as many as he could before the waters raced back to the shore. He chopped down trees and slowly cut planks from the wood. Years passed as he gradually built his labor of love.

Up, up, up his lighthouse grew from the rocky shore. It took a while, but he conceived of a way to bring light to its cabin. By combining fire and minerals he dug from the clay in the forest floor, he happened upon the perfect formula.

On the night of its completion, Percy struck a match and lit the lantern containing a wick and the precious minerals. He smiled in wonderment as bright greens, yellows, and reds lit up the beacon. Every night Percy manned his lighthouse, warning fellow celestial travelers of the dangers along the rocky shore.

For those of us who long ago were left in other areas of Penal Colony 524, we and our descendants, on nights when the air is crisp and clear, we can also marvel at the glory of Percy's lighthouse.

We call them the Northern Lights.

THE FOCUS OF MARBURY HILL

The soft breezes of spring were a welcome relief to the bitter grip winter had held in Amish country. Rolling hills gave just a hint of green hue--a promise that the land was coming back to life. Cassidy Fisher needed a change as badly as the countryside around Lancaster needed spring.

The deaths of both her parents in an automobile accident last fall and the subsequent emotional breakdown she suffered caused her to drop out of her studies at Penn State. The harsh winter was a metaphor for her depression, and the greening of the fields, she hoped, meant an awakening in her own life.

The Amish farms dotted the countryside, and modest buggies driven by men in drab clothes made their ways down the wide shoulder of the state highway.

Life seems so simple here.

Cassidy loved the beauty that stretched out before her along this quiet road, and her thoughts drifted to the journey that brought her to this place where time seemed to have jumped back two hundred years.

She pictured herself as a young girl when her dreams of becoming a photojournalist began. For her ninth birthday, Grandma Beatrice ordered her a subscription to *National Geographic*. Mesmerized by the photos she saw, she imagined being among the people and places caught in the stunning images. She wanted to be there, and she knew photography was her ticket to travel. At the age of ten, she begged her parents for a Canon Sureshot and, seeing no harm in her new passion, they bought her one. To their surprise, Cassidy was quite good.

"Cass, you have a real eye for this. Nearly every photo you take captures the moment perfectly," Grandma Beatrice told her one day.

"You're the one who made me want to take them, Grandma," she said as she hugged her.

If I'd known Grandma would die before I was twelve, I would have taken more photos of her. Tears welled in Cassidy's eyes. At twenty, she'd had more loss than many, and she felt fragile and vulnerable in this world.

By the time she was in high school, a few of her photos were published in nature magazines. As a sophomore, she became the lead photographer for the school newspaper and yearbook. The local newspaper even hired her to shoot photos at events they didn't want to send their regular staff to. No event was too large or too small in Cassidy's mind. She loved capturing moments in time. Catching the essence of people and places was at the heart of her love for the field. The passion she had as a child flamed into a wildfire, and her senior year Cassidy was accepted into the journalism school at Penn State.

"Grandma would be so proud of you. Of course, your father and I are, too. We have a gift for you." Her mother smiled brightly on graduation day as she handed Cassidy the most advanced professional-grade camera within their means. "We know you'll make good use of this."

Her memories were clear. She saw her mother wearing her favorite blue dress. Her brown hair was swept behind her ears with the classic beauty of Grace Kelly. Her father, tall and handsome, never a man of many words, let her mother do all the talking. The two balanced each other perfectly.

During her freshman and sophomore years of college, Cassidy learned the technical aspects of the field while she networked with professionals. Before her parents' deaths at the beginning of her junior year, she applied for an internship which would have taken her to the Costa Rican rainforest the next summer. She was an excellent candidate. Then her world fell apart. The internship was only offered to full-time students, and when she dropped out, that dream also died.

For a time, all Cassidy could feel was the touch of death. Days were dark, and nights were darker still. She'd had no choice but to dis-enroll from school before her credits were recorded as Fs. If she had any chance of returning to school, she couldn't have one devastating semester ruin her GPA.

A bitterly cold February day, ironically, brought the first spark of hope to her world. It came in the form of an unexpected phone call. The man on the other end of the call had an interesting proposition.

"Hello, is this Cassidy Fisher?"

"Yes."

"This is Dr. Burton from the Penn State journalism department. How are you?"

Cassidy paused.

"I apologize. That was not a thoughtful thing for me to say. Dr. Rankin told me of your family's tragedy and that you'd taken a break from your studies. I hope I didn't upset you."

"No. No, you're fine. Honestly, I've been better, but thank you for asking."

"I'm calling because I have an offer for you. If you aren't up to it, I completely understand. I wanted to give you the first chance at the position, however. I've never had you in class, but my colleagues have told me nothing but good things about you. I've seen your work. It's quite good."

"Thank you, Dr. Burton. That's very flattering coming from you. What exactly do you want me to do?"

"Well, I have a project in mind. It involves traveling for a few months to an Amish community, and that's why it's not really something someone could do while attending classes. It will be a full-time position while it lasts."

Travel? The thought intrigued Cassidy who had hardly left her apartment for the past five months.

"Okay. Tell me more."

"It's a paid internship for a special project I'm working on. You'd earn college credit, a paycheck, and I'd also provide you a daily stipend for expenses."

"That actually sounds like a great offer. What would I be doing?"

"I've been given a grant to photograph the Amish community. It's part of a sociological study conducted by another university, but I'm partnered with them to give a photographic record to accompany their oral interviews. Those will be done separately. You would travel to the chosen community and photograph individuals."

"How many credits would I earn, and how long would this project last?"

"It lasts from the beginning of March until the end of the school term. I've arranged for you to earn an entire semester's credit if you are interested. You are, by far, the most talented student for the position, according to both Dr. Rankin and Dr. Stowell. Are you interested?"

An entire semester's worth of credit for two months of photography work?

Cassidy was excited about the prospect of salvaging at least part of her junior year, but she wondered if she was up to it. She thought about what her parents and grandmother would have wanted her to do. She knew the answer.

"Yes, Dr. Burton, I'll accept the position. Let me know what you need me to do."

"How about you meet me at my office on campus three weeks from today? Say about two o'clock? I'll have everything ready for you, and you can get started the following week. How does that sound?"

"It sounds perfect. I'll see you then."

Exactly three weeks later, she sat in Dr. Burton's office. The ornate mahogany desk sat on one side of the room, backdropped by a large picture window that faced a courtyard. Around the room photographs hung from exotic locations. Pygmies, New Guinea headhunters, bushmen from Africa, Amazon tribesmen, and others stared out at her from stunning photos reminiscent of those she'd grown up admiring *in National Geographics*. The haunting images captured their expressions so perfectly that Cassidy felt they were in the room with her. Her grandmother's words softly called to her.

"Honey, I don't know how you do it, but I feel like I know the people in your photographs. You do such a great job of catching their personalities. Just look at that little girl holding the balloon at last week's parade in this one. I can feel her happiness."

Cassidy blushed at the thought that her work compared to that of Dr. Burton. Grandma was right, however. A good photographer, one who actually had a passion for the art, could suspend a moment in time with their work. Obviously, Dr. Burton had that ability.

"You like the photographs?"

"Oh, yes!"

"I fully expect some of yours from this project will join these on my office walls."

Cassidy blushed again. "Well, sir, let's hope I can live up to your high expectations."

"I have every confidence in you, Cassidy."

"So, you said I'd be documenting the Amish community. I've thought about this over the past few weeks, and I am wondering how we can do that. I thought they didn't believe in getting their photographs taken."

Dr. Burton chuckled. "Oh, they are a superstitious bunch, that's for sure. They do not want their photographs taken. They believe some idiocy about their souls being captured. It's rubbish. I know it, and you know it."

"That's what I'd heard, too. So how do I go about doing this project? They aren't going to give me permission."

Burton cleared his throat. "No, they won't. You will have to be crafty about it. Think of yourself as an Amish paparazzi for the next two months. Hide out if you have to to get the shots. What they don't know won't hurt them, and you can make a name for yourself with this."

Cassidy had never deceived people before, but she did have experience with candid shots. Besides, when taking nature photographs, she often had to position herself without the wildlife knowing she was there.

"Do you think you can do that?"

"I do."

"My only condition is that you use the camera and equipment that I provide. Don't use your own camera, although I'm certain you have a wonderful one. Under the terms of the grant, all work must be done using the equipment I purchased with those funds."

"I can do that. Let's get started!"

That brought Cassidy Fisher to the peaceful stretch of road outside the quiet Amish enclave located in an area the non-Amish called Marbury Hill. Named after a local Revolutionary War hero, people refused to call it anything else. The incorporated name remained despite the disgruntled feelings of the Amish, who referred to it as Beiler Crossing.

There's no time like the present to start taking photos.

The community gathering place looked to be just ahead on the left. Several buggies were parked in front. Women and children came and went through the doors as the men stood around outside discussing… What? The weather? A new barn to be built? Their crops? Who knew?

They certainly wouldn't share that information with an outsider like Cassidy, and she hoped the interns involved in the oral interviews had better luck than she would have. The sign in front of the store said Zook's Farm and Home.

A neatly kept park sat across the road and would provide Cassidy a perfect vantage point to clandestinely snap some shots. She swung her car into the park, found a suitable space beside a tree, and turned the engine off.

Using her zoom, she captured the tender moment of a mother lifting her young son from the buggy. She caught an older brother's mischievous expression when he teased his little sister. The solemn look on a man's face as he scanned the skies while talking to the other men, most likely about farming concerns, made a great shot. All might be the kind of photograph Dr. Burton and the project wanted. After several shots, the bulk of the customers left, and Cassidy set the camera aside.

I need to get a sense of who these people are. I'm going to take a look inside the feed store. After all, it looks to be an important part of the community.

Pulling into the now vacant parking lot, she looked through the windows. Rustic, but tidy, was the best way to describe what she saw. She pulled the door open and was surprised by the pleasant scents that greeted her. Earthy leather mingled with the sweet smells of grain and hay. She walked the aisles, stopping to touch the bridles and other tack. Two rows over, bolts of fabric stood upright along the shelves. No bright calicos were in sight. In keeping with the culture, only modest colors were for sale.

Her heart jumped when she heard a deep male voice behind her.

"Good morning, ma'am. Can I help you find something?"

"No, thank you. I'm just looking."

"If you're here for the big quilt festival, that doesn't happen until this weekend. You're a little early."

Cassidy made a mental note that the festival might make for some good photographs.

Looking up at him, Cassidy saw the most amazing blue eyes she'd ever seen. Transfixed, they stood motionless, staring into each other's eyes. A lightning bolt sensation glued Cassidy to the spot.

His face reddened. "I'm sorry. I didn't mean to pry." He turned to go back to the counter.

Cassidy wasn't ready to stop talking to the tall blond man. "No, you didn't. My name is Cassidy Fisher." She extended her hand to him.

Embarrassed, he ducked his head, faced her, then caught her gaze once more. "I'm Samuel Zook. This is my family's store. Fisher? Are you related to the Fishers who live here?"

"I'm not. I'm here for a work project."

"We don't get many visitors here except for the festivals. Keeps it kind of quiet."

"It's beautiful countryside, and I needed to get away for a while."

Their eyes met once again. The same lightning bolt coursed through Cassidy.

Does he feel the same thing?

Cassidy lingered for a while longer, then turned to leave. "It was wonderful to meet you, Sam."

"Same here, Ms. Fisher."

"Call me Cassidy."

For the first time in months, her heart felt light.

Cassidy began her work in earnest during the next few weeks. Sometimes she waited outside homes or fields to secretly catch candid photos of the Amish. Every day she found a reason to stop by Zook's Farm and Home. Each time she and Sam were drawn to each other.

"I haven't felt this at ease since my parents' deaths. You're so easy to talk with, Sam."

"I enjoy your company, too. Would you want to have a picnic lunch tomorrow?"

"Let's plan on it."

Those lunches became daily occurrences, and they turned into late afternoon drives through the country in Sam Zook's buggy. A genuine friendship grew between them, and if soul mates were real, Cassidy felt she'd found hers. They shared hopes and dreams and talked about their families. Sam's grandfather had died recently, and they talked about grief. They understood each other without having to say much at all, and sometimes it was during those quiet moments that Cassidy felt the closest to Sam.

She dreaded the end of her project at Marbury Hill. Sam's twinkling eyes and easygoing laugh brought her out of the depression she'd languished in for so long. Was there a chance they could make a relationship work when she stepped back into the modern world?

On the next to the last day of her project, Cassidy brought her camera with her on their afternoon ride. She'd brought it in the past, snapping photos of the picturesque farms. Cows grazed in lovely pastoral scenes. Horses galloped in the fields. She wanted to remember the breathtaking beauty. She was careful never to mention to Sam that she had been taking photographs of his people.

She couldn't shake the temptation to take a photograph of Sam. Yes, he was etched into her memory, but she wanted something tangible of him to keep with her. Knowing the cultural taboo, she hesitated.

This is my last chance to take one.

As Sam came around the corner of the buggy to help her down, he looked up at her with his bright blue eyes. A broad grin covered his face.

She snapped a photo.

The twinkle left his eye and he became sullen. "Why would you do that, Cassidy?" Anger replaced all the good nature in him.

Shaken by the ferocity in his voice, Cassidy stammered. "I'm... I'm sorry, Sam. I just wanted to have something to remember you by."

Saying nothing more, Sam helped her down and pointed to her car. He turned his back on her.

She was shunned.

"Sam, please, don't be angry with me over some ridiculous superstition."

He walked away and never answered her.

The next day, heartbroken, Cassidy drove through the community one more time. Stopping at Zook's store, she saw Sam standing outside and hoped to make amends. The deadness of his eyes when he saw her told her it was pointless.

She packed the last of her belongings at the bed and breakfast and left, looking back one last time in the rearview mirror before heading to the modern world.

The next day she met with Dr. Burton.

"Cassidy, the work you've sent has been incredible. You're going to make a name for yourself with this project."

"I'm glad you're happy with my work. It was life-changing for me."

"Sometimes, all we need is a change to find our place in the world again."

"Yes, I'm back where I belong. Thank you for the opportunity."

"The pleasure is all mine."

Burton shut the door behind her and placed the camera she'd used on his desk. He paced the room, smiling. Speaking to the thin air he said, "Now, where to put you? Perhaps here where you'll have a view of the courtyard?"

The next week a large frame hung on the western wall of the professor's office. The bright blue eyes of Samuel Zook stared out at the doctor as he admired the piece. If someone didn't know better, they'd swear the eyes followed the doctor as he walked across the room.

ABOUT THE AUTHOR

Caroline Giammanco is an author and high school English teacher. She grew up in Douglas County, Missouri and moved to Arizona for college to attend the University of Arizona where she earned a Bachelor of Arts degree in Political Science with an English minor. She lives on her sixty-acre farm in southern Missouri. Caroline is married to the love of her life, Keith Giammanco.

Caroline's previous published works are nonfiction and deal with the criminal justice system: *Bank Notes: The True Story of the Boonie Hat Bandit; Guilty Hearts: The World of Prison Romances;* and *Inside the Death Fences: Memoir of a Whistleblower.*

FROM THE PUBLISHER

In the five plus years Tuscany Bay has been partnered with Black Dog Publishing we have been fortunate enough to work with some outstanding writers of, well, pretty much all genres. From Sci-Fi, westerns, children and in some cases, Paranormal.

In no instance have we had the opportunity to work with an author trying her first attempt at fiction, much less suspense, paranormal and the unexpected. This is such a book.

Not only did we enjoy working on this book but enjoyed the author's acceptance of our suggestions and criticisms along with the occasional lauds launched in her direction, but the stories themselves grabbed our attention from the start and kept it there for the duration.

It isn't often we comment publicly on a book we have published, but this book is a treat. Not only as a volume we completed, but for the senses as well. We dare you to start reading this book without being drawn into the world of forty-three separate lives and scenarios guaranteed to make you shiver in the dark.

Congratulations to Caroline Giammanco for penning a first-time fiction tome that was a delight to work on and even a larger delight to read.

Tuscany Bay Books